CW00322144

Prue

SERIAL DAMAGE

Thanks for all your help

Liz Cadms

Dund lm.

SERIAL DAMAGE

LIZ COWLEY
&
DONOUGH O'BRIEN

urbanepublications.com

First published in Great Britain in 2016 by Urbane Publications Ltd
Suite 3, Brown Europe House, 33/34 Gleaming Wood Drive, Chatham, Kent ME5 8RZ

A CIP catalogue record for this book is available from the British Library.

ISBN 978-1-911129-45-5
EPUB 978-1-911129-46-2
MOBI 978-1-911129-47-9

Design and Typeset by Julie Martin
Cover by Julie Martin

Printed and bound by
CPI Group (UK) Ltd, Croydon, CR0 4YY

urbanepublications.com

The publisher supports the Forest Stewardship Council® (FSC®), the leading international forest-certification organisation. This
book is made from acid-free paper from an FSC®-certified provider. FSC is the only forest-certification scheme supported by
the leading environmental organisations, including Greenpeace.

ACKNOWLEDGEMENTS

We would like to thank several people for their invaluable help and advice:

Detective Chief Superintendent Alan Mitchell, Metropolitan Police, Scotland Yard.

Detective Sergeant Andy Warne, Devon & Cornwall Police, Bodmin.

Lt Colonel (Retired) Brian O'Gorman, Regimental Adjutant, Irish Guards.

Justice Sir William Gage, High Court Judge.

Sir Tim Cassell, Defence Barrister.

Neil Hudson, psychologist.

Richard Evans, formerly Chief Executive of The Watch Security Company.

Tony Grider, Mayor of Skykomish.

Timothy ffytche, surgeon.

Peter Paice, formerly Managing Director of Reliance Security Group.

Sophie Hayes, former Hong Kong resident.

Sally-Jane Coode, MBE, DL, Cornwall.

Nicola Morrison, Operating Theatre Sister.

CHAPTER ONE

CORNWALL

Helen Mitchell felt content, as content as one could be approaching ninety with a social life made up of too many funerals, and with those few friends left getting ever frailer or being moved into homes.

It was gardening that kept her sane and connected to life, despite the irritating memory lapses recalling the names of plants. It reminded her that life itself goes on. And though not religious, the garden sometimes made her believe in a God, some kind of divine presence – at least far more than any church service ever had.

She paused to take a sip of tea from the mug she had left in the grass, before taking her secateurs to the *Rosa banksiae,* a white rose from China brought back by the great botanist Joseph Banks when he was creating Kew Gardens. Helen knew that he had rather sweetly named it after his wife, Lady Banks. This was a plant she was particularly proud of. Mind you, roses needed a considerable amount of work in Cornwall's damp climate, and at eighty-four and with her arthritis, Helen was finding that the garden sometimes really taxed her strength. And the large house was as rambling as her roses.

She had long ago retired from her children's teaching job and now that her husband, Admiral Sir John Mitchell, had passed on, the garden had become her life. It had been the source of many friends, though she had rather firmly discouraged children from playing with balls and ruining the plants.

It was barely nine and the sun was already warm. The green

fields that stretched away from the village were still rather hazy from the early morning mist. The small white-haired old lady was just finishing off the last of the 'deadheads', when she heard a motorcycle come slowly down the lane and stop. A few moments later, a tall figure in black leather with helmet and goggles came crunching up the gravel path towards her house.

This was quite a surprise. Often big motorcycles roared along the Cornwall lanes in summer, but the riders rarely slowed, let alone stopped to ask the way.

'Can I help you?' Helen asked, shielding her eyes from the early morning sun.

The man smiled, lifted a big black revolver and shot Helen straight in the chest.

* * *

It was her friend and neighbour, Jessica Coade, who found Helen an hour later. She often nipped round the hedge and up the path for a cup of tea and a chat at about eleven. When she saw Helen crumpled into the white roses, a surge of shock coursed through her. Had Helen fainted? Fallen and become unconscious? Or had her heart finally given up its long battle?

Jessica reached over. Helen was lying sideways, still and cold to the touch. She couldn't be sure, but immediately feared the worst. Hurrying to the house, she pushed open the door and went over to the phone in the hall to dial 999 on the oversized numbers that Helen had only put in last week. She begged the operator for the ambulance to come as quickly as possible. Maybe it did, but for Jessica the wait seemed interminable, as she went back to sit beside her old friend, her own heart pounding in her chest.

Perhaps the crew were lost in the narrow, high-banked lanes? Perhaps there were too many little old ladies keeling over in this part of sleepy Cornwall?

Why couldn't they come faster and what could she do while waiting? Find a blanket to put over Helen? Jessica half knew it might be too late for that, but she went to the airing cupboard all the same and brought down an eiderdown to put over her friend's tiny frame.

At last there was the sound of a siren in the distance. And when the ambulance did finally arrive, there was another agonising wait while the paramedics attended to Helen, having politely but firmly ushered Jessica away to a garden bench. She was not to hear their muttered words as they lifted her from the rose bushes and saw the blood.

'Christ! The poor woman's been shot. Call the police!'

* * *

The communications operator took the call in Plymouth's big control room at Crownhill. She noted the message, quickly entered it into the Operational Intelligence System, created a log and gave it a number. She then informed the Duty Sergeant.

'I've just had a 999 call about an old lady being killed, in fact murdered, in Tredinnick.'

'Murdered? How do they know? The public's always jumping to conclusions.'

'No, it wasn't a public call. It came from the ambulance crew. They say she's definitely been killed by someone, shot in her own garden.'

The Sergeant frowned. 'Okay, it could still be an accident. But let's assume it isn't. Jill, send response from Bodmin and tell the CIM. They'll have to organise additional uniform resources. And call the duty Force SIO and the Major Crime Investigation Team to take this on.'

The Sergeant was referring to the Devon and Cornwall

Police Strategic Hub for the A30 corridor, housed on a hill in a brand-new complex just outside Bodmin, once the County Town until it lost that position to bigger Truro. But Bodmin had the advantage of being in the centre of the large sprawling county and therefore ideally situated for the new type of police hub. The ultra-modern building had even been graced with a commemorative visit by Prince Charles, in his role of Duke of Cornwall.

The Critical Incident Manager was Detective Inspector Mike Hemmings and he called in DS Pat Johnson, who quickly chose DC Larkin to go to the scene.

'Jim, there's been a shooting, very strange. An old lady in Tredinnick. Get out there as soon as you can, with some uniform. Go straight for flash house to house. CMI and I will deal with the media or anything else.'

Soon after they got the call, an Armed Response Vehicle, a BMW 5, lights flashing and siren blaring, hurried south towards the crime scene.

* * *

He rode the old bike slowly down the narrow country lanes – a Triumph 500 Tiger Twin built in 1969, beautifully restored with his own hands. *'We're not afraid of the Japanese. They'll just expand the market for British motorcycles'*, he remembered the boast of the Triumph Marketing Director.

Wrong. Those damn Japs, Honda and the others – clean, efficient and reliable – had quickly buried them all: Triumph, Vincent, BSA, Royal Enfield, the lot.

Now he slowed down, clunking through the gears and turned to bump along a long, winding track overgrown with weeds and grass. At the end, a battered Land Rover and mud-spattered horsebox were parked under some low willow trees.

He opened up the back, lowered the ramp, wheeled the Triumph up into the horsebox, carefully strapped it in, covering it with sacking, put his helmet, gloves and black leather jacket in the feedbox and finally closed the fading doors and put on a rather dirty old tweed cap. *Done.*

Just another farmer going to collect a horse.

He had always preferred old things, not just motorbikes and cars, but guns. And if they were old enough, nobody would have a record of them.

Anyway, he wouldn't be using the revolver again.

It might have been more satisfying to have revealed to her who he was. But after all these years, he would have had to spell it out to the old cow. *Never mind. A nice clean kill.*

Near Bodmin , he trundled up on to the busy A30 towards Exeter and London. A police car, lights flashing, rushed past in the other direction.

Perhaps they'd found her.

* * *

Once the first uniformed officer had reported in, the narrow lane outside Helen's house was cordoned off, with both ends blocked by vehicles with crackling radios.

Contrary to what the public might have imagined about 'sleepy' Cornwall, the detectives from Bodmin had several murders on their hands. But it didn't take them long to work out that this one was unusual. Her front door had apparently been closed, and from its thick soft wood, forensics had dug out a bullet. This had gone right through her small body, which lay on the grass covered by a white Trell tent. Even before it was sent off for ballistics testing, it was obvious to the naked, if professional, eye that it was a bit unusual; a big .45 inch slug, of the type fired from an old Colt automatic or a service revolver.

Detective Constable 'Big Jim' Larkin had immediately instituted the 'flash house to house' procedure and was carefully questioning anyone who might shed some light on the strange aspects of Helen's death. 'Big Jim' was actually rather small, but years ago had been given his nickname by an annoying Irish colleague who had vaguely remembered the famous trade union leader of the same name, and had decided 'to take the mick'. Irritatingly for Jim, the name had stuck.

The nearest neighbour was Jessica Coade, a white-haired widow of about seventy-five, who had found the body. 'I'm afraid I'm not sure I can help', Jessica told him tearfully. 'I'm really quite deaf now, and I didn't hear anything.'

Larkin nodded and noted down her words. He was trained to take nothing at face value, and a surprising number of witnesses turned out to have strange private lives. However, he was inclined to believe this apparently harmless old lady.

The postman, who had been at the top end of the little village when he noticed the commotion, seemed more useful.

'At about 9:30 this morning I was coming up the lane, and my van only just squeezed past a motorbike, leaning on its side-stand. It wasn't one of those flashy, big streamlined jobs that howl past you in summer – you know, with young men and girls in fancy, matching gear. No, it was upright, dark-coloured, maybe an old British twin, with, I think, old-fashioned side panniers.'

Jim Larkin noted this meagre information down and radioed Pat Johnson back in Bodmin to ask if it was worth blocking roads or watching the A30 and other major routes. After discussions with DI Hemmings, he concluded that it was now too late. If the killer was the motorcyclist, he would have been able to use minor roads and would be long gone by now.

The motorcycle seemed to be the only obvious line of

enquiry. The coarse gravel path revealed no footprints. The front door had been closed and the forensic team had found no evidence that the killer had entered the house. Everything looked perfectly tidy and nothing seemed to have been disturbed or stolen. Indeed, Helen's handbag was sitting on the kitchen table with twenty-five pounds there in cash, so any theories about a botched robbery could probably be discounted.

Nobody seemed to have heard the sound of a shot. Even if they had, they could be forgiven for not taking any notice. Larkin himself had noted the regular and loud bangs of bird-scarers on the nearby fields.

Someone had tipped off the media and it did not take long for them to arrive. Larkin had asked Pat Johnson to order a no-fly zone, knowing that *Sky News* could get a helicopter to anywhere in the United Kingdom within twenty minutes of hearing about something. He knew all too well that helicopters had a nasty habit of blowing precious evidence all over the place with their downdraft.

The team would work out a selective 'media strategy' as they did on each case, trying to engage the public enough to enlist their help but being careful not to reveal key evidence which might affect their questioning process.

Soon there would be a crowd of journalists from press, TV and radio all focussing on the peculiar aspects of this bizarre case, and asking the same obvious questions as the police. Who on earth would do such a thing, and why?

A gun nut?

A case of mistaken identity?

Something from her past?

But *what* past? For the media, as a senior naval officer's wife, Lady Helen Mitchell did not exactly fit the bill as a drug czar or a 'gangster's moll'. It was not just the *Western Morning*

News, *BBC Cornwall* in Truro, *Atlantic* and *Pirate* radios or the other locals that would run the story. The national media would almost certainly give Helen a mention as yet another example of guns being increasingly used in crime, even in the countryside.

'We can find out ourselves of course, Mrs Coade, but would you happen to know who her next of kin would be – her family?'

'Well, there are no children, but she does have a niece called Alice, who's also her god-daughter. She lives up in London, but she often comes down here.

And there's a nephew, Oliver, somewhere in America, though I don't know where. But Alice will. She's the one to call.'

She looked at Larkin.

'Shall I do that? It would be better if she heard it from someone she knows. She adored Helen.'

'Fine, Mrs Coade. But we'll also ask her local police to send a Family Liaison Officer. Can you give me her address? You can tell her they'll be in touch.'

He paused, 'And when you've broken the news, I need to talk to her.'

CHAPTER TWO

ST BEDE'S PRIMARY SCHOOL, 1973

The art teacher was having difficulty. Hours after trying to write a letter to the boy's foster-parents, the words were still eluding her. How could she put it tactfully? Impossible. The evidence was too shocking.

She'd thought of asking the English teacher for help, but she was busy, recently engaged and with her mind on her forthcoming wedding. The Head would have been obvious; indeed, she had consulted her, only to be advised to try and write a letter first – which wasn't working. She chucked her fourth draft into the wastepaper basket. What could she say?

She looked at the drawings again, wondering if anyone would ever believe her unless she sent them as evidence of what was so plainly wrong. Dangerous even. And then she thought of the child.

Barely seven. Quiet. Uncommunicative, but undoubtedly good at art. In fact, astonishingly good, and that was why her evidence was so unsettling. There was no mistaking the messages and shapes in his paintings, they were frighteningly clear. All his work was good enough to win the term's art prize, but could never be displayed on Open Day for all the staff and parents to see, let alone his own parents.

They weren't his *real* parents, of course. She was well aware that his real mother had been killed in a car smash, and that his father had cracked up and committed suicide shortly after. That was all on his school records. And she also knew that he'd been fostered by a couple who were paying the fees for this school –

hardly cheap, so they must have cared something about him, at least in terms of a good education. Certainly enough to get him the best possible start.

And the whole process of fostering and adoption meant they must have longed for a child, so it was highly unlikely they were mistreating him. The Council would have checked all that out, and long before any order had been granted. But perhaps such a child should never have been a boarder? Having said that, his home life looked pretty disastrous, at least from what she could see.

She poured herself a stiff gin and tonic, and looked again at the pictures, wishing the school had a resident psychiatrist, or at least more easy access to one. She was not qualified to write such a letter, and felt horribly alone. How many art teachers had seen anything like this?

Pinned on the wall were four of his paintings.

The first was for the brief she'd set for the class at the beginning of term, MY PARENTS, expecting the classic big heads and hands drawn by a child of that age. Big heads always, big hands inevitably, and often with stick bodies underneath them. Usually with over-sized smiles and eyes. And lots of colour. She studied the picture. Brilliant for a child of seven, but horribly disturbing. And it was clear that he didn't see his foster parents as his Mum and Dad.

MY PARENTS. A big title above it, copied correctly from the blackboard. Underneath, and quite clearly, a big picture of a church. Beautifully drawn, with a spire. How often could he have seen one well enough to draw like that? And in the foreground, a picture of two large and lopsided graves. Almost all of it painted in black and grey with a splash of colour where orange flowers – dandelions? – sprouted around the gravestones.

She turned to the second one, MY BIRTHDAY. He was

instantly recognizable, standing in front of a cake, topped with seven candles. The same dark hair and blue eyes – again, beautifully painted. But there were no parents, no friends, no-one else around the table. Simply the child, with a knife, not about to cut the cake but held aloft by its handle, as if the boy was about to stab someone.

The third one was worse. A DAY AT THE SEA. A small figure sitting on the beach, with two figures way out in the sea, both with a speech-bubble above their heads, with the words 'HELP!' 'HELP!' as if they were drowning.

She looked again at the little figure, studying it more closely. Not just sitting on the beach, but with his hands to his ears. The message was obvious: deaf to their cries. She took another sip of her drink.

And the fourth? For her, the most heart-wrenching and shocking of all. MY MUM. There on the buff art paper was a huge black question mark, forming the back of a woman's head, with a faint and beautiful profile painted to the left of it. As supremely clever as it was disturbing; someone who simply didn't know his mother, with a large question mark hanging over her. A hugely graphic depiction, when most of the children would have done a front-on interpretation, with a big smile, and of course, big hair and big hands.

How could she send his foster-parents stuff like this? But without doing that, how could she prove that something was terribly wrong? Downing the last of her gin and tonic, she decided to keep the letter short and get it to the Headmistress as soon as possible.

'I am very sorry to have to tell you that your foster-son may not be happy at this school. We have done our best for him, but certain things have come to our attention that have disturbed

*us – not bad behaviour, but certain paintings that may suggest
he is profoundly troubled.*

*Whilst being totally confident that your decision to send him
to boarding school was made with the best possible thoughts
for his future, we feel we must alert you to the fact that he may
be in need of professional psychiatric help, based on evidence
that is, at the least, unsettling.*

*We must beg you to arrange a meeting here at the school at
the earliest opportunity so we can talk things over.*

*I am sorry to concern you with this matter, and would thank
you for your reply at the earliest opportunity.*

Yours faithfully.'

She suddenly felt exhausted. The letter still wasn't right. But it
would have to do, or at least act as a draft for the Head. And
the school had to act soon. Every time she'd seen the child come
into the art class, she'd dreaded the drawing at the end of the
lesson. Always a quiet worker, never asking questions. Always
using what chalks and crayons he was given to create something
quickly. And then producing something highly alarming.

Despair.

Damage.

Destruction.

Drawings with an obvious and desperate message.

She finished the drink and decided to turn in for the night,
wondering whether the child slept at night, and whether she
herself could in the lonely hours ahead. She dreaded tomorrow.
She would have to tell this hugely gifted child that his paintings
couldn't be exhibited at the End of Term Exhibition. She
pictured his face. He would be furiously angry. But what else
could she possibly do? He was far too young to understand.

One month later, she was surprised to hear that his foster-parents had decided to take the boy away, and truly shocked to find out that he was to be returned to the foster home. Apparently he was much more badly behaved at home than he ever was at school. She wondered whether she should have spoken out at all. But what else could she have done?

She assembled the drawings in a roll, somehow loath to throw them, smoothing an elastic band over them and placing them in her art chest.

CHAPTER THREE

PUTNEY, LONDON

Alice Diamond had just turned thirty, happy and fulfilled with her work in psychiatry, although annoyingly less so with her private life, having just broken up with the latest man. So many years learning to be a good judge of character, yet too often failing when it came to her own relationships. It didn't make sense. It was high time to sort herself out.

It was her own fault, she thought to herself as she looked in the bathroom mirror. The face that looked back at her made it easy enough to attract a man, with eyes that had often been described as violet, dark cropped hair that suited her small frame perfectly and skin that barely needed more than a touch of blusher.

Maybe she was using the wrong men, if subconsciously, to find out who the right ones were, and by a slow process of elimination. If so, the process had to stop. People weren't experiments. She had made too many mistakes with men, and often remembered the phrase 'physician, heal thyself' with some irritation, as she did right now.

Sex was quite important for Alice, but she had never enjoyed it as much as the thrill of first attraction and the novelty of something different and had, over the years, taken some risks in her search for fulfilment.

And at times, and disconcertingly, she felt a fraud. Capable of advising her patients certainly, and fully believing in her advice, but rarely able to apply it successfully to her own life, and secretly fascinated how any couple could remain fulfilled partners for decades, even wondering if they claimed that, they were really telling the truth.

Too many mistakes she could so easily have foreseen. How could she have got involved with the local carpenter who had done up her kitchen, just because he was impossibly sexy? And even taken him to a lawyers' party at Lincoln's Inn which he plainly thought was a pub, turning up like that in ripped and faded jeans. Of course, she should have explained the venue and dress code. Did she think she was conducting some kind of social experiment?

And what on earth was she doing with that awful banker afterwards who only ever talked about himself? Perhaps fascinated in people obsessed with themselves? Wondering if she could get them to switch to an outward focus? That too would have to go. Partners weren't patients, learning curves. And nor were they the basis for passing a future exam. If there was any examining to be done, it needed to be on herself.

And she could do that in comfort and in her own time, lucky to be living and working in a delightful tree-lined street in Putney in a house that she could never have afforded if it weren't for her parents: her mother who had died too early and her father who had gone to live in France, unable to live there without her, and deciding to hand over the place to Alice. Space enough to have her own surgery at home as well as a garden now beautifully mature with the help of Aunt Helen who had given her a passion for plants and flowers.

She was financially secure and professionally respected. Only a decent man was missing, and her best friend Liz had just volunteered to fill the latest gap next week by introducing her to an advertising chap in his thirties, apparently very good-looking, intelligent and funny, and surprisingly, still single. So things might be looking up again.

And meanwhile, there was a great deal to do. Thankfully, she had earned a good professional reputation not only in the private sector, but also in criminal psychology, and was used by the Metropolitan Police for about a quarter of her time in complex cases.

This involved providing social and psychological assessments of suspects, evaluation of their backgrounds and behavioural patterns, and at times even their belongings, and studying the psyche of criminals, especially suspected killers.

She also specialised in clinical forensic psychology, occasionally visiting highly dangerous and disturbed patients and prisoners in secure hospitals and high security prisons. This life of secret 'profiling' she kept from even her closest relatives and friends, finding herself working alongside some unlikely characters including former felons and even psychics, whom the Met sometimes used to locate people who had gone missing.

For her private patients, she had opted to work from her house and to create a relaxed, homely atmosphere rather than a clinical environment, preferring to offer her clients a comfortable armchair rather than the type of sofa on which the great Sigmund Freud had laid out his Viennese matrons while listening to their troubles and smoking endless fat cigars.

Alice had just returned from a session at Scotland Yard, and her assistant Maggie told her that someone called Jessica had called twice. Just then the phone rang again. When Jessica came on the line with the news, a shocked Alice at once assumed that old age had finally caught up with Helen.

'I suppose she *was* in her eighties', she said sadly, her tears welling up, picturing her aunt having a heart attack in her garden.

'No, that's not it, I'm afraid.' Jessica paused, not knowing how to get the words out. 'I'm really sorry, but there's a policeman here who wants to talk to you.'

A policeman? Why?

'Miss Diamond? I'm Detective Constable Larkin of Devon and Cornwall Police. I'm very sorry about your godmother.'

He paused. 'I'm afraid it wasn't natural causes.'

'What?' Alice was stunned.

'It's my sad duty to tell you your godmother was shot.'

'Shot? You can't be serious. What do you mean, a shooting accident?'

'No, I'm afraid we think it was murder.'

His words hit her like a thunderbolt.

'Murder? Jesus! But, who on earth would want to murder her? She wouldn't hurt a fly.'

'I know it seems very unlikely. And at this early stage we know very little.

I believe that, apart from her nephew in America, you'd be the closest to her.'

'Yes, I think so.'

Larkin paused.

'Then it would be very helpful if you could come down and tell us everything you can. And as soon as possible. Can you do that?'

Alice knew it might be difficult, but she would have to re-arrange things. There was no choice.

'Yes, I think I can manage that. And probably today.'

'Thank you. We'd like you to come to her house. And you should hear from Wandsworth Police in the next few minutes. If possible, please stay in your house until they come. They'll want to see you for any urgent information, anything that might help us quickly.'

'OK, I'll wait for them and then come down right away. I'll

be there late afternoon.'

Alice would never normally cancel or postpone an appointment. But, glancing at the list, she was relieved to see that the last two scheduled on that Wednesday were, in fact, among her least vulnerable patients, and that postponement would do little harm. So she asked Maggie to rearrange their sessions and unscramble the rest of the week, quoting a sudden bout of flu.

Five minute later the doorbell rang and a policewoman in uniform was ushered in. After a number of questions about Alice, her work and her relationship with Helen Mitchell, she looked at her notebook.

'Miss Diamond, there's another relative, I believe. Oliver Mitchell in America. Mrs Coade, the neighbour, didn't know how to contact him, but said you probably would.'

'Well, I haven't got his home number, but I do have his number at work, and it's on his business Facebook. But we won't be able to try him for a while because he's on the West Coast, Portland, and that's eight hours behind us. I'll call him later from Cornwall if you like, and break the news. Then they can call him with any questions.'

After the Family Liaison Officer had left, Alice hurriedly put together an overnight bag, got in her car and set off.

In normal circumstances, she loved her trips to Cornwall, with its winding lanes and pretty fishing villages clustered on cliffs going down to the sea. She knew the county had once been rich, producing nearly all the tin in the world and even a quarter of its copper. She had been amazed by how the countryside was still dotted with so many of the ancient stone buildings which had housed James Watt's then revolutionary steam engines, installed to pump out water from the deep mines, some of which even extended out under the sea.

Helen's well-stocked bookshelves had been fascinating on local history, so she knew the story of how most of the mines were eventually played out or ruined by the vast new mines in Bolivia, with the result that the famous rugged Cornish miners, the highly valued 'Cousin Jacks', had emigrated all over the world, with communities from Pennsylvania to Australia marked by curious Cornish names. It was sad, she thought, that, except for tourism, the county was just too far away from London and the rest of Britain to be prosperous.

And every time she went there, Alice was reminded of that remoteness. She had always been irritated by the way her Cornwall friends had insisted that it was 'only two or three hours from London', when Alice thought that unless you broke the law in spectacular fashion, it always took much longer.

Her pride and joy was the perfect 'Q car', the 30th Anniversary version of the very first 'hot hatch', the Volkswagen Golf GTI. It may have been virtually identical to an ordinary Golf, but it was capable of a staggering 153 mph. But, however fast it was, she was not prepared to break the law on this occasion.

So she avoided the dreaded A303 with its jams around Stonehenge, and ploughed her way west down the motorways, the M4 west, and then south down the M5 through traffic swollen with early summer trippers and dawdling caravans. Stressed out, she was sure it would take an agonising age. And it did.

As she drove, her mind raced around the obvious questions. Who would do such a terrible thing to a defenceless old lady? And why? And her questions were not just those of a grieving relative, but because discovering why people did such things happened to be part of her life.

* * *

When Alice at last pulled up, the police barriers forced her to park quite a long way from the old rose-covered house, a place of so many happy memories. She was exhausted after the drive and among the blue black police uniforms and the white forensic overalls, she was relieved to see the plump and comforting figure of Jessica bustling over.

'Darling Alice! Thank God you've come, and as soon as they've finished talking to you, come next door for a coffee, or better still a stiff drink. And you can stay with me as long as you need to.'

'Are you Miss Alice Diamond?'

They were suddenly joined by the figure of DC Larkin, who introduced himself, suggesting that they talk inside Jessica's house. Alice knew that the police would already be combing through her godmother's house, and didn't correct the prefix 'Miss'. She was actually 'Doctor Diamond' and she would tell him that later, but only if it was strictly relevant.

'Thank you for coming down as soon as you could. Wandsworth told me that you were in a pretty important meeting with the police. You're not a policewoman, are you?"

'No, a psychiatrist. I do a certain amount of profiling work for the Met.' She slid a card across the table.

Larkin opened up a bit when he realised he was talking to a professional, and revealed they had little to go on.

'I'm sorry, Doctor, apart from the recovered slug, we've very little evidence to follow except an old motorbike, and even then nobody can be sure of its make or colour – let alone remember its number plate. And it may not be relevant, anyway.'

After a few more questions, Larkin glanced at his notebook.

'Wandsworth told me you may able to help us to locate an Oliver Mitchell. Could we try that now?'

Alice had never really liked Oliver, a pretty charmless

individual and always talking about money. And if his social skills weren't exactly endearing, nor it seemed were his business skills any more successful, because his company always seemed to be in trouble. She had always felt sorry for his wife Sally-Jane, amazed that she had ever married him in the first place.

With Larkin watching, she lifted the phone and dialled the Oregon number. Frustratingly, she immediately became entangled in the company's answering process.

'Hi. This is Portland Avionics. If you know your party's number, please dial it now. If not, for sales, dial one; for service, dial two; for technical enquiries dial three.' At last she heard 'Please stay on the line for an operator.'

Eventually, she got hold of Oliver's assistant.

'Can I speak to Oliver Mitchell, please. It's his cousin calling from England.'

'Oh sorry, honey. He's in Europe on a sales trip.' Pause. 'In fact he's in England right now, in London. He's staying in,' she hesitated over the pronunciation, 'the Glewkester Hotel. Would you like the phone number?'

'Yes, please.'

'The number is 0207 730 4621. And I'll email him, if you like, to say you're looking for him.'

'Yes, if you would.'

Thanking her, Alice immediately dialled the Gloucester Hotel, and surprisingly, got straight through to her cousin.

'Oh, hi Alice, what's up?' Oliver had never liked Alice much either, and hardly ever contacted her.

'I'm afraid I've got bad news. Aunt Helen's dead. I'm down in Cornwall now.'

'Oh dear. Her heart, I suppose.' There was hardly an intake of breath.

Alice knew Oliver wouldn't really be thinking about Helen,

more about her money.

'No. It's much worse than that. She was probably murdered, believe it or not, shot by someone.'

'Shot? Good God!' Even Oliver seemed shocked by that. A pause. 'Do the police have any clues?'

'Not so far. How long are you going to be in the UK?'

'I was going off to Germany, but I can change my appointments if I have to.' He already had every intention of doing so. Aunt Helen's wealth might just save the day.

'The funeral's not likely to be for weeks. They need the body. But it would be good if you can come down. Well, you and I are her only family. And I'm with the local police now, and they'd like your help.'

She pictured Oliver, knowing exactly what would persuade him to make the long journey, even if the police didn't need him. 'And we could also go over to the solicitor and talk about her will. I'm sure she may have left us something.'

Oliver agreed instantly. He had been pestering his aunt for money for months, but with a singular lack of success. 'Good money after bad' had always been the irritating and condemning cliché in Helen's gentle but firm rejection of his pleas.

When she put down the phone, Larkin nodded with satisfaction, thanked Alice and arranged to see her and Oliver the next day.

* * *

Jessica had invited one or two of the neighbours in for a drink before Alice's departure, both to meet Alice and to have a bit of a wake for Helen. The elderly vicar made a little speech, becoming quite tearful when he concluded 'and to think she was going to do the church flowers tomorrow.'

In the middle of the gathering, Alice was suddenly accosted

by a strange figure – tall, dressed in a blazer and with a
moustache that made him look like Terry Thomas, the old
comedy actor. But this chap wasn't funny at all – although he
plainly thought he was.

'So, you're Helen's neesh,' he slurred.

'No, god-daughter.'

He studied Alice over his glass of whisky. 'Sho, you'll
obviously inherit a lot of money.'

Alice was appalled, and hugely embarrassed. She didn't
need this.

'She should have left something to me. Had a lovely old
Austhin sheven sitting in her garage. Promised to give it to me.
And then shomeone at a party told her how much it was worth.
Sho the old girl went and shold it.'

'Angus,' Jessica intervened, 'I don't think Alice wants to
hear about your old car quarrel with Helen,' and she dragged
the unpleasant fellow away.

Alice watched him stumbling off. Could someone kill
someone over an old car? No. At least, not that embarrassing,
shambling figure. She decided to get through the rest of the wake
and then go back to London the next day after the solicitor's
meeting, dreading that the executor would be appalled by
Oliver's evident greed. She knew he would be totally unable to
hide it.

He would have to talk to the police on his own. There was
nothing more she could tell them. At least nothing she could
think of for now.

* * *

Early on Thursday morning in the Bodmin Police building,
Detective Sergeant Pat Johnson swivelled his office chair and
looked at the list of ongoing murder cases, marked on large

white boards beside his desk. Eight of them. And people still thought of the county as 'sleepy' Cornwall! At least, the tourists did. Maybe that was a blessing.

Some progress this week, but never fast enough, he thought. But then, that was the job. And it was one he had never regretted, despite sometimes envying his friends who could see results much sooner. Like his fishing pal Rob, a local journalist, who could see the fruits of his labours every Friday in his 'Fishy Tales' column in *Cornish Weekly*.

He allowed himself a minute to think about the weekend. A boat trip with the kids, and a good weather forecast, and with luck, Lorraine's home-made Scotch eggs for the picnic. But now this strange new case, the murder of the old lady, might screw everything up. And, as if on cue, in walked Jim Larkin to review the case, already called by its codeword 'Operation Rugby' and duly listed on Pat's boards.

'God, Jim, this is a really bizarre one. The odds of an eighty-four-year old woman being shot with a big handgun in her garden must be pretty slight.'

'Infinitesimal. Hardly on the radar.'

Larkin ran through the evidence.

'The ballistics results, even on priority, won't come in for a few hours and forensics on the body will take days. She was shot at quite close range, so we've also sent some GSR on her clothing off for analysis. To cross-check the other unusual aspects, the shooting victim being an old lady, the large calibre bullet, the old bike – I've already fed those details into HOLMES.'

Pat Johnson nodded. The Home Office Large Major Enquiry System could be an invaluable database to ensure that a large enquiry could be cross-referenced with other ones round the country.

'We'd better tip off the nearest counties by phone to see if they've seen anything like this, and when we've got a better handle on it we should send it to NPIA as a formal report.' He was referring to the National Police Improvement Agency and its system of checking with other forces for similar crimes.

'Really, really strange. Is there anyone else we need to interview?'

'Yes; Oliver Mitchell, the nephew. He's the only other person of interest left right now. Lives in the States, but he just happened to be over in the UK, and we've persuaded him to come down here. Or at least his aunt's money has. I must say he seemed much more interested in finding time to see his aunt's solicitors than helping us.'

'Could be a link.'

* * *

That afternoon, the Tactical Aid Group was still in the house, methodically trawling through everything they could find. They had already passed Larkin a bunch of letters that he found more than interesting, showing them to D.S. Pat Johnson as soon as he joined them.

'And here's her address book,' said P.C. Sue Meadows. Jim Larkin looked through it briefly. 'I'll go through it and see if there's anything helpful. Probably worth making a few calls.'

D.S. Johnson intervened. 'I suggest we call people in her bridge club and flower arranging club. They might know something, someone who had a grudge against her.' He smiled, thinking of his wife's words. 'Lorraine says flower clubs are hugely competitive these days. She told me people can get murderous if they don't win first prize.'

Sue Meadows grinned at her colleague, Josie, 'I think Lorraine may have been watching too many *Midsomer Murders*, you know, all those vicars and teachers knocking each other off at the Summer Fete. I think the body count's four hundred to date.'

'Makes life seem pretty quiet down here!'

'Well, it's just gone less quiet.'

'Thanks, ladies,' interrupted Johnson, 'now, please check for anything about money. She was quite rich; could be a motive for someone wanting to see her off early.'

'I've already checked an old trunk, but there was nothing there about money. No legal documents or bank statements or anything like that. Mostly very old photographs and drawings and bundles of ancient letters from the husband of the deceased. That Dr. Diamond asked if she could take it home. Is that alright?' Johnson and Larkin conferred and agreed that Sue could tell Alice that she could take the trunk away, after getting another assurance from Sue that she had checked it thoroughly.

They then paused, listening to a car drawing up outside Jessica's house. Jim Larkin looked out of the window. 'Excuse me a moment.'

'Mr Mitchell? Oliver Mitchell?'

'Yes.'

The detective approached Oliver, assessing him immediately; shiny-faced, about forty-three, plump, balding, self-satisfied and arrogant. He scolded himself for making the last two assumptions.

'I'm sorry to intrude, Sir, but I'm Detective Constable Larkin of the Major Crime Team in Bodmin. We're trying to ascertain some reason, some motive for your aunt's murder. You might be able to help. Would you be kind enough to answer some questions tomorrow, either here or at Bodmin?'

Thinking of the tiny, potentially gossipy community in the village, Oliver agreed, rather reluctantly, to go to Bodmin after their planned visit to the solicitor.

* * *

Unlike the rest of Cornwall, once so renowned for its underground mining with men laboriously digging for tin and copper by hand, St Austell's wealth came from 'China Clay' surface mining. As a result, the surrounding countryside was a bizarre and ugly moonscape scarred with huge grey-white mountains of spoil, and conical, volcano-like slag heaps.

Even today, the rocky hillsides were still being dynamited, and then giant high-pressure water guns called 'monitors' blasted the white clay from out of the loosened rocks, to be collected in creamy settling tanks and finally dried into white slabs. Every year three million tons of clay were trucked down to the docks at Fowey and exported, not just for chinaware, but mostly for high quality paper making for shiny magazines and colour-printed books.

The town of St Austell, sometimes fondly referred to by the locals as 'Snozzle', sat on a hill, and Helen's solicitor's office was quite near the top with a view down to the sea. The conference room was distinctly old-fashioned, lined with shelves of old legal books. Harold Goodwin was quite young, but had just been made up to a Partner.

'Of course, probate will take several weeks, but the gist of Lady Mitchell's will is that you, Alice, as her god-daughter, have been left about £100,000 and certain effects like furniture, books and pictures. Oliver, you – as her only blood relative – will receive the bulk of her estate, the house, some shares, bonds and the residue of a life insurance policy. After tax and costs, we estimate it may come to just over a million pounds.'

Oliver tried to suppress a smile. In a flash, he had mentally converted the windfall into one and a half million dollars. It might take a few months, but with that kind of inheritance definitely in the pipeline, he could hold those bastards at Oregon National at bay, as well as those other wretched creditors.

At least they wouldn't be snatching his home as his creditors had threatened.

Once the meeting was over, Alice paused in the car park to announce that she was going straight back to London and that Oliver would have to visit the police on his own, a decision he accepted with his usual poor grace.

* * *

As Oliver walked from the visitors' car park, he noted the shiny modernity of the Bodmin building of the Devon and Cornwall Police. Not like the dusty old police stations he remembered from his childhood in England.

Jim Larkin seemed all concerned affability. Actually, he was not very concerned about Oliver Mitchell and he did not feel very affable. The evidence in his possession pointed to a greedy creep, or worse. And he didn't much like his rather forced American accent either.

Larkin poured some coffee and started with some routine questions; how long Oliver had lived in America, what his company did, his marital status and how often he came back to England.

'Now, Mr Mitchell, how well did you know your aunt?'

'Not very well, I suppose.'

'Well enough to ask her for money?'

Oliver flinched and looked hard at the detective. 'How do you mean?'

'We've been searching her effects and found some letters from you.'

'They're private.' Oliver was visibly irritated.

'No, they're not. Nothing is private in a murder investigation, and anything relevant can, and must be, examined.'

Larkin was gratified that he did not have to keep up the pretence of being nice to this man. He opened a bulky file.

'And in some of these letters, you are pretty pushy, if you don't mind my saying.'

'Well, I was getting desperate.' Oliver was sweating.

Larkin picked up a typed sheet of paper.

'In this one, you talk about Lady Mitchell's house being far too big for an old woman and suggest she sell it for something smaller. That way, you say, she could spare some cash – for you. I gather from the neighbours, and from Dr Diamond, that she adored that house and garden. It was pretty much all she had left in her life.'

He looked up. 'Don't you think that's pushy, Mr Mitchell?'

Oliver was now unnerved. 'No, I think it's perfectly sensible. It's far too big for one person. She was rattling around in it like a pea in a drum. Anyway, I needed the money and she was my aunt.'

'So you would agree that her death, coming sooner rather than later, has been something of a relief to you?'

'That's an appalling remark!' blurted Oliver, suddenly realizing he might be a suspect.

Larkin stared at him coldly and changed the subject. 'You ride a motorcycle, don't you?'

Oliver was puzzled by the question. 'I have two bikes at home. One's an old Indian 'Scout' – in bits. I'm slowly rebuilding it. The other's a Harley, which I ride to work if the weather's good. The rest of the time I drive a Chevvy.'

'Let me ask you another question, Mr Mitchell. Where were you on the morning of Wednesday 5th June?'

CHAPTER FOUR

PUTNEY, LONDON

Alice pulled the blue Golf GTI into her Putney driveway at about seven at night. Because of the meeting with the solicitor, she had hit the beginning of Bristol's afternoon rush hour on the M5 and then very heavy traffic on the M4. So she was already feeling a bit tired, especially as she was resigned to a sea of problems or 'issues' as soon as she met her secretary Maggie next morning.

However, as Alice saw it, the first problem was Helen's heavy trunk and how to get it off the back seat. Luckily, Alice noticed her neighbour Tom coming back from work and quickly persuaded him to help her manoeuvre it up to her first floor landing. There it would have to stay until she could move it again or go through it carefully and sort everything out.

In the morning, there was a regular patient to see, who duly turned up at nine. Alice escorted her into her study and smiled at her, a perfectly attractive woman of thirty who had been through a string of short or failed relationships and was now suffering from a total lack of confidence, as well as a paralysing depression about ever getting relationships right.

'Carrying on from last week, tell me more about your mother.' Even as the words were out of her mouth, Alice wondered how often had she had asked them before. But there was, of course, a good reason. Her patient's past significant relationships would almost certainly have influenced her present condition.

'She's fine. Or should I say, *was* fine.' She didn't expand.

'Fine? In what way? I wonder if you could tell me a bit more?'

Her patient shrugged.

'Well ... no better or worse than most, I suppose. Did what she could...'

'And what was that?'

Her patient paused.

'Well, put meals on the table. Did the usual things. Came to see me at boarding school...'

'Boarding school?'

'Yes. Packed me off at seven.'

'What was that like for you?'

'Very lonely, especially at the beginning.'

'And how often did she come and see you?'

'Well, you were only allowed three visits a term. Not very much.'

'And what did you do on those visits?'

'Not much. Had a picnic. Talked a bit – before she had to get back. To her bridge parties, I suppose.' Her patient laughed bitterly.

'And she died this year?'

'Yup.' A tellingly brisk response.

'And you miss her?'

Another bitter laugh. 'I never really knew her.'

Alice had heard that before, but there was always a twist that surprised her.

'And you miss her? Or perhaps wish you'd been closer?'

'Not really. I don't think it's anything to do with my mother.'

Alice doubted that.

'But what good times do you remember having with her?'

'Not many.' A long pause. 'A lot of it's a blank. I remember her brushing my hair as a child. Oh, and a holiday somewhere on the Isle of Wight.'

'Tell me about that.'

'It was the first time I'd seen the sea. That was lovely, but then my mother suddenly looked at her watch on the beach. That spoilt it. Probably had to get back to a bridge party at the hotel.'

'Do you remember that being the reason?'

'No.'

Another impasse.

'And your father?'

'Lovely, but I never really got to know him either.'

'And why was that?'

'Because he was hardly ever there. Some oil job abroad. That's why I went to boarding school. His firm paid the fees.' Her patient nibbled at her nails. 'I was a kind of orphan. Weird. Spent most of my time reading books about people whose parents were there all the time, or books about orphans – you know, like *Heidi* or *The Secret Garden* or *Oliver Twist.* '

Alice smiled at the memory of three of her own favourite childhood books. 'And you say you find it hard to get on with people?'

'Yup.' Her patient paused, looking out of the window. 'I know what I'm doing wrong. I make such an effort that I switch them off. I'm always so chatty and jolly that I go over the top. I guess I can't relax. And I suppose I'm not listening. All I'm doing is panicking about what to say next.' Her client tailed off.

Again, a familiar story; endless relationships probably ruined by parents initially, then by the patients themselves. But each of them was unique.

'And, despite the fact that your father was rarely there, you loved him.'

'I guess so. I don't really know.' Her patient shrugged. 'As I said, I never really knew him either.'

Alice persevered for another half hour, probing, as gently as she could, about the cause of her patient's difficulties, almost certainly the result of damaged early experiences.

The fifty minutes were up. 'Come and see me next week.'

'Okay, if I can afford to.'

Alice wondered whether she should offer to drop her hourly rate for this patient. It looked like being a long haul. She decided to think about it. Too many people out there struggling, and too many who couldn't get out of that without money they didn't have.

After she had shown her to the door, she went in to see Maggie who had plainly been having a tough time making the necessary changes to her private patients' schedule. She was just beginning to go through the appointments that she had reorganised when the phone rang.

'Alice Diamond Practice,' announced Maggie, expecting yet another frustrated patient, then relieved to find it wasn't. 'Certainly. She's back now.' Cupping her hand, she whispered 'Alice, it's Inspector Marshal. Sorry, I forgot to tell you he called before.'

'Hi, Robin. How are you?'

'Not bad. I've been calling you, but I couldn't go into details with your secretary.'

'Sure, I understand. And I'm sorry I didn't get back to you. The reason I was out of town was that my lovely old aunt, well really my godmother, died. And much worse, the local police think she was murdered.'

'Good God! An old lady?'

'Eighty-four. And shot in her own garden. Unbelievable. No real clues. Somebody saw a motorbike near her house, that's all.'

'Alice, that's really unbelievable. I'm truly sorry. Are the local police treating you okay? Which are they? Devon and

Cornwall? Do you need any help?'

'No, but thanks for asking. They *are* Devon and Cornwall, as you say, and they're fine. Anyway, what were you calling me about?'

'Well, I need you to give me an opinion on someone. But obviously this isn't a good time.' He paused. 'However, is there *any* chance you could come into Scotland Yard tomorrow, at say ten?'

Alice put him on hold, to find that Maggie had, in fact, luckily left the next day free in case Alice had not made it back on time.

'Yes, that would be OK. It'll be a pleasant change of scene. I'll see you at ten tomorrow.'

* * *

Robin Marshal worked out of quite a small office in the huge Metropolitan Police building called New Scotland Yard. It was lucky he was a tidy type. Indeed, he had to be. So much paperwork coming in every day, it would have been easy, though unprofessional, to descend into total chaos – disaster in a job where time was of the essence. A paperless office? A myth in the police force.

Now as he lowered himself awkwardly into his swivel chair, he realized once again that a diet was long overdue; his waistband was far too tight. And once seated he was forced to lean slightly backwards. He'd always been big like his policeman father, but at forty it was time to get a grip or head for diabetes. And to tell Pam – his wife of seventeen years – that she really must stop cooking two-course meals every evening and puddings he could never resist.

Of course, part of the problem was filling up the two boys, always starving and voracious eaters, though thankfully neither were overweight. Both fast calorie-burners like their mother, and the kind that were always on the go. Only last week he'd told his eldest, Tim, that he was getting too big for his boots, only to hear his son riposte' And you're getting too big for your trousers!'

He looked at the photograph of them on the wall. Would they ever be content to sit in an office like this? It was touching that both of them had shown an interest in entering the police force. But it was too early to know. There was university first, if they were lucky to get in like he had. And from the vast number now going to 'Uni' – a word he hated – it didn't even seem to need that much luck these days.

For him, Sussex University had been a real life-changer, as had the special 'fast-track' graduates' course at Bramshill. Okay, there had been initial problems with his less privileged colleagues – and less well-paid ones – but that was changing now as graduates became the norm. His undoubted intelligence and ability had ensured promotion and success.

He had done particularly well at the senior management course which was also at Bramshill College, a stately home that had been untouched by *Luftwaffe* bombing in the war, allegedly because *Reichsmarshall* Hermann Goering had confidently picked it out as a nice home for himself after Germany's occupation of England.

His phone jolted him out of his reveries. Alice had arrived. Bang on time as always, and as professional as she was pretty. He had always mildly fancied her, but in a theoretical way. One of the reasons their relationship was so amicable was because there were clear boundaries. And they had to remain so.

He lifted himself awkwardly from his chair, annoyingly feeling the waist button pop off. Damn! Where was it? No time to look for it now. And no time to take the stairs to get rid of

a few calories. Minutes counted and the security took time for
anyone entering the building, even though Alice was a familiar
enough face, and moreover, a face that was very hard to forget.
Those violet eyes made that almost impossible.

At last they were seated in the conference room, faced by
a team which seemed none too pleased to see her, as police
teams often weren't when psychologists were asked in, vaguely
resentful and wary of outside advisers.

Predictably enough, Robin noticed one young detective
staring at Alice with more than professional interest, although
Alice appeared oblivious, helping herself to coffee. She was
used enough to the wrong kind of attention.

It turned out to be a pretty distressing case involving a
really strange man in for questioning. On the one hand, he was
married, successful, with grown up children, apparently a fully
functioning contributing adult, even bordering on the dull side.

Yet he was seemingly often in the wrong place at the wrong
time, mixed up with young male prostitutes, and associated
with shady, loose connections with trafficking and violent,
ritualized sex. And now this might involve a murder. If they
could find out what drove him, it might lead to a motive. Alice
wondered if she would ever stop being shocked and surprised
by the workings of the human mind.

After a couple of hours, Robin escorted her from the building
and thanked her. She walked the few yards to St James's Park
underground station and took the tube home, trying to shake
off a feeling of depression.

When she got home after a hot and crowded tube journey,
she saw her answerphone blinking. In among the routine stuff,
there was a call from Oliver. He sounded furious.

'Alice, you've no idea what that little shit of a policemen did.
He kept me there for ages, having almost accused me of being

the murderer, just because I'm due to inherit and I know how to ride a motorbike, for Christ's sake. It was almost evening by the time he let me go, so I had to wait till this morning to track down the chap I'd been meeting in London that Wednesday and for him to convince them I had an alibi. Made me another whole day late to go to Germany, so the trip's been screwed. So I'm off back to Portland right now. Bye.'

The call made her even more depressed. Oliver had not once uttered a word of sadness and regret about the shocking fate of a lovely old woman who had just left him almost all her money. You can choose your friends, she thought, but you can't choose your family.

However, there was a string of calls from Liz, and the last one came as a welcome relief.

'Hi, it's me again. I've been trying to get you for days. Remember I said you might like someone, the man in advertising I told you about? Well, I thought we might all meet up in La Famiglia on Wednesday, if you're free. I'll bring Derek and we can make it a foursome. Anyway, let me know. Byee!'

Alice looked at her watch. Not too late to call back.

'Sounds fun. But can we meet up a bit earlier before the others get there?'

'Sure. Any special reason?'

'Yes. To be honest, I've just had a hell of a shock.'

'What?'

'You know my lovely old aunt, the one in Cornwall?'

'Sure, you're always talking about her.'

'She's been shot, probably murdered.'

A silence. 'You can't be serious. An old lady? Murdered?'

'That's why I've been away. I had to go down there and talk to the police. Anyway, I don't want to talk about it now. But if we can meet up before the others, I wouldn't mind a bit of time alone with you. Say at seven o'clock?'

'Fine. I'll book a table at seven, and see you then. And I'm really sorry about your aunt. Dreadful. I can't believe it.'

'Nor can I.'

CHAPTER FIVE

FULHAM, LONDON

Alice was sitting at a table for four at 'La Famiglia' in London's lively Fulham area, already surprisingly crowded even at seven o'clock, and wondering whether she should have come. She was not in the mood to meet a new man, let alone one in advertising.

He would probably be loud, over-confident and full of himself, although it was unlikely that Liz would introduce her to someone like that at the best of times, and particularly not now after Aunt Helen's death. But it was always a mistake to pre-suppose what people were like and make assumptions. Alice reminded herself that she should know that.

She ordered a glass of wine while waiting, half wishing she was back in her own kitchen, but vaguely curious, and telling herself it was good to get out of the house. It had been hard to concentrate on her patients for the last few days, and she knew she needed a break.

Suddenly Liz was at the table. 'Hi.' She looked around her before sitting down opposite. 'Gosh, it's full in here. Let's see if we can grab a waiter and get a bottle of wine. And then we can have a good talk.'

By halfway through the bottle Alice had told Liz more about Aunt Helen and the extraordinary circumstances of her death, the first time she had talked to anyone about it except the police. It was therapeutic, as was the wine and her best friend's company. She almost wished Liz's boyfriend and her advertising friend weren't going to join them, but just after eight they both arrived.

Alice's picture of the sort of man she was about to meet couldn't have been more wrong. She was looking up at someone with a wonderful open smile and a shock of astonishingly unruly and windswept fair hair. She was suddenly reminded of the Mayor of London, Boris Johnson, with his trademark blond locks, always flying around in the wind on outside television interviews, and not looking much better when he was in a TV studio, despite the best efforts of the make-up people. People loved him for it, and she had to admit, she immediately warmed to this stranger who was now shaking her hand and taking the chair beside her.

She could tell he was a big personality, as Liz herself had told her, and his merry brown eyes also told her he appeared to be a warm one. Probably half Scandinavian she thought, taking in his unusual and striking colouring. And although he was nice-looking, he was certainly not vain. Otherwise he would have gone to the gents' loo to do something about that crazy mop of hair, looking as if it were suffering from a force nine gale.

The meal was as good as it always was in La Famiglia, but Alice barely noticed the food in the company of this hugely entertaining man on her left. He could easily have been a comedian with his hilarious stories about cock-ups in the advertising world, presentations going horribly wrong, disasters on TV commercial shoots and crazy copywriters with their even crazier ideas.

She hadn't laughed so much in ages. And better still, he didn't push himself. He had been forcibly persuaded to tell those stories by Liz, and even then was reticent.

'You surely don't want to hear that one again.'

'I do,' Liz had replied, 'and anyway, Alice hasn't heard it.' And he was off again, and with so much resultant laughter that all of them wondered if the people on the table next door weren't getting mildly irritated, especially as Derek's laugh came out as a deafening boom.

As they finished their coffees and the last of the wine at eleven o'clock, Alice suddenly realized that her mind had been taken off Aunt Helen for hours.

'Perhaps you might be able to take Alice home?' said Liz, turning to John when the bill was paid. 'She's only in Putney, not far from you.' Alice was suddenly embarrassed, but John looked at her delighted.

'No problem. Be glad to. And I've got the car outside.'

John helped her into his two-seater Morgan, not the Porche Alice was expecting from a successful advertising man. Liz had told her he owned his company along with two friends. Again, he had surprised her.

And she surprised herself when finally arriving at her house she asked him in for a nightcap. Not her usual style. Maybe a bit premature.

'Would you like a last drink?'

'Love to, although I shouldn't. Maybe a coffee."

Settled at the kitchen table, Alice felt surprisingly relaxed and contented until she suddenly remembered Aunt Helen again and her mind drifted off.

'Alice, I've lost you.' He touched her hand lightly.

'Sorry, I was just thinking about how life takes unexpected turns sometimes.'

He looked at her, smiling. 'And sometimes rather nice ones.'

Alice smiled back.

'On that note, I'd better be going. Heavy day again tomorrow. We've got a big presentation coming up. And if we get the account, it'll see us through for a bit.' He studied her face. 'And when it's over, it might be fun to meet up again.'

'I'd love to.'

As Alice put the porch light on for him to see his way down the steps, he leaned over and gave her a kiss on both cheeks. She stayed under the porch light until he had climbed into the car, his hair flying about crazily in the wind.

CHAPTER SIX

HOLLINGBOURNE, KENT

As a county, Kent still boasted that it was the 'Garden of England', with its thousands of acres of apple and pear orchards, and its fields of wheat and barley, strawberries and asparagus, lavender and peas. Climate change meant that even sunflowers and lemons had now joined such traditional crops. Above all, Kent had been famous for the annual migration of working-class families from London's East End, who used to pour into Kent every September to pick the hops used for making beer. The distinctive-shaped oast houses, used for drying the hops, still dotted the pretty countryside.

In the middle of the county, in the village of Hollingbourne, there was an old people's home called Willowbrook.

Mark and Clare Campbell had first met in 1965 when they both worked at The Rank Organisation's huge Pinewood Studios. Mark had been an Editor and Clare was a Production Assistant, working on the first James Bond films. So it was not surprising that for a while they had run the Film Club in the care home. When Clare passed away, Mark had carried on alone.

Every day, with cash contributed by the members of the club, one of the staff drove to the Blockbuster Video store in Maidstone and rented two videos – or, more recently, DVDs. One film tended to be an old favourite and the other a new release. There was always a constant battle between the wishes of the old ladies, who favoured musicals and romance, and the fellows, led by the opinionated Mark, who opted for violent crime, warfare and westerns. It often didn't matter too much, because a lot of the old people snoozed off after a few minutes, or else stared, sadly uncomprehending, at the screen.

That afternoon Mark had got his way. He boasted that he judged every film by 'the expenditure of ammunition', so the choice of Sam Peckinpah's *The Wild Bunch* really suited his book. The last few minutes – with William Holden, Ernest Borgnine and their friends taking on hundreds of Mexicans – involved as much 'expenditure of ammunition' as Mark could possibly have asked for, with the rifles, pistols and shotguns of the adversaries augmented by the racket of an early belt-fed Maxim machine-gun. All this mayhem was watched at full volume because the elderly members of the audience were mostly pretty deaf.

At the height of the Wild Bunch's incredibly violent and noisy last battle, a tall figure with a briefcase appeared in the doorway, rather incongruously wearing dark glasses and a black hat. He bent over and said something quietly to old Johnny Dixon manning the door, who pointed out Mark Campbell in the gloom of the front seats.

The man waited until the battle was at its noisy height and then crouched down and walked into the dark room, holding his briefcase in front of him. He went up behind the white-haired figure of Mark and leaned over as if whispering something to him. Then he walked back, nodded pleasantly to Johnny and left the noisy room of engrossed or sleeping pensioners.

Ten minutes later the credits rolled as Robert Ryan sadly surveyed the bloody carnage of the Mexican camp. Johnny turned up the lights. He waited for Mark to stand up as usual to announce tomorrow's films. But he didn't move; he was slumped forward and still.

Then Ida Franklin saw the blood. She began to scream in a feeble, rasping way.

Johnny gathered his wits and hit the big red alarm button on the wall, normally used to summon the nurses to deal with some old dear who had keeled over or needed someone to move a wheelchair.

* * *

The Kent police arrived pretty quickly in the form of a Sergeant in a patrol car diverted off the nearby M20 motorway. Other than ushering them from the room, he could do little more than try to calm them all down, both the hysterical patients and rattled staff. Luckily his calls soon brought detectives from Maidstone, quickly backed by a forensic team. Witnesses were then interviewed in the quiet of the Manager's office.

Most of the old people in the television room were not much help. They had either been asleep or comatose, and only Ida Franklin and Johnny at the door had really noted the intruder. Once she had stopped crying about her dead friends, Ida, after hundreds of film-watching afternoons, was the first to comment on his rather strange appearance.

'With that hat and the dark glasses, he looked like, well, Dan Ackroyd in 'The Blues Brothers.'

Johnny's memory went back even further into film history. 'No, more like Lee Marvin in 'The Killers', he insisted, 'you know, when he hits that poor blind receptionist right across the room and then goes upstairs to kill John Cassavetes.' He then added, with some relish about his film knowledge, 'It was the last film Ronald Reagan acted in before he went into politics – and bloody awful he was too!'

The young detective taking notes could only just remember who Ronald Reagan was.

* * *

Luckily Willowbrook's receptionist, Jane, had apparently merely been confronted by a polite, well-spoken man who showed her his solicitor's card and asked for his client, Mark Campbell. So she had innocently broken the rules and sent him up to the TV room as she had done with other visitors to Mark, who usually rewarded them by making them watch the rest of the film.

Jane was now crying with horror and shame that she had sent up a visitor who had apparently killed the nice old chap.

Even before they packed up and left, the forensics team had offered up the cause of death. The victim had been shot in the back of the neck by a small calibre, low-velocity firearm. The detectives also guessed that the gun may have been silenced or quietened in some way. The dull thud would have easily merged with the film's own loud and prolific 'expenditure of ammunition'.

There seemed to be little obvious evidence to go on; no cartridge case, no fingerprints, no tyre tracks and no more witnesses. And, on the face of it, no motive. Yet the whole affair appeared well-planned, even professional.

Perhaps the security cameras, or the autopsy with the extracted bullet might start to reveal some clues.

* * *

A pity the old woman wasn't there as well, he mused. But then, of course, she had died of old age a couple of years ago.

He couldn't help smiling sardonically as he suddenly remembered the old 1920s Irish tale of the IRA men waiting in the bushes to kill an English landlord. He was late. 'Sure, I hope nuttin's happened to the ol' gentleman.'

If there was one person he would like to kill, it was the man who invented the hatchback. At a stroke, all cars now looked the same, no character, no personality at all. But it did make them anonymous.

So this third-hand silver Peugeot 208 suited him just fine. Nobody would give it a second glance.

There was a bleep from below the windscreen.

He slowed down.

No point getting photographed going too fast.

Anyway he was in no hurry.

CHAPTER SEVEN

MAIDSTONE, KENT

The pages he was reading defied belief.

Detective Inspector Brian Young, of Kent's Major Incident Team, had been appointed Senior Investigation Officer for the Willowbrook case. He looked up from the detectives' report with mounting incredulity.

'Dan Ackroyd, Lee Marvin and Ronald Reagan? Is that really all we've got to go on?'

Detective Sergeant Patrick Cowley, the Case Officer, and the author of the report, shifted in his seat and looked distinctly sheepish.

'Well, they *were* all film enthusiasts,' he said rather lamely.

'Okay. Well, let's try to put this investigation on a more normal footing. Let me review the situation. We have to wait for the autopsy to find out anything from the bullet still lodged in the body, from which we *may* deduce that the round was small calibre, low velocity. There'll be gunshot residue as it was shot point-blank, and the clothing's being tested.

There was no cartridge case found, and no fingerprints. Forensics is checking the carpets in case he brought anything worthwhile in on his shoes.

Were there any pictures?'

'The CCTV camera outside was disabled for some unexplained reason,' replied Pat Cowley. 'We've got some pictures from the reception, but the camera is as old as everything else there, so the pictures are fuzzy. And, of course, he was wearing that hat and dark glasses. You can hardly see anything, but we've got the boys trying to enhance the stuff.'

'And there's nothing from the road?'

'Nope', replied Detective Constable Anne Robinson, who had been sent to 'trawl' for CCTV evidence. 'They don't have cameras out in the road. It's just a leafy lane, no shops or garages.

And there are no buses or anything with other cameras we can find.'

'Okay, then we can all agree that it was like a professional hit. Very calm and calculated. But an old man in his eighties? Any ideas?'

A long silence in the room. The DI was well known for not wanting to hear ill-thought-out theories.

'Right, what do we know about the victim?'

'He and his wife came to the home five years ago. Before that, they'd lived north of London, in Beaconsfield. They used to work nearby in the film business, at Pinewood Studios where they met. The old lady, Clare Campbell, passed away two years ago.'

'Any relatives?'

'No children, as far as we know. At that age, he only had one next-of-kin, his old sister who lives in Rochdale, up north. We talked to the local police and they've agreed to send a Family Liaison Officer to break the news and to try to find out more about both of them.'

'Well, if they haven't done so already, tell them to ask if she can think of any enemies he might have had, or anything else in his past that could be helpful. There has to be something.

And we're going to need it.'

CHAPTER EIGHT

BELFAST, NORTHERN IRELAND

It seems only natural for people from Northern Ireland to want to return eventually. In a survey, even at the height of the 'troubles', they voted themselves the happiest in Europe, while the comfortable, rich Germans placed themselves on the bottom of the same happiness chart.

Joe Corcoran, too, had gone back. The place was not perfect of course, but it was improving fast. Gone were the days of regular bombings and sectarian shootings, check-points and those 'pig' armoured personnel carriers with patrolling troops. The Maze Prison was a distant memory, along with the tragedies of Bobby Sands and the IRA hunger strikers. Shops and restaurants were booming. Pubs were echoing to good-natured *craic*. Grandiose industrial failures like the notorious De Lorean car factory and the Learfan aircraft project had been replaced by solid, practical enterprises, cashing in on the excellent educational standards.

Above all, when you were looking for a job, you no longer faced notices and advertisements marked, brutally, *NCNA* – '*No Catholics Need Apply.*'

So Joe had returned home and settled down to a steady security job, mostly admin and paperwork. But he did not give up on swimming. Twice a week he was back at the pool at the Falls Road Leisure Centre, helping the young kids, making them train, polishing their turns, bringing them along. And they loved him for it.

Joe Corcoran revelled in everything about swimming pools,

even the smell of chlorine. Of course, it had a lot to do with his own swimming career. For a Catholic boy from Belfast, this had been his key to unlock the door out of the ghetto of Northern Ireland. A schoolmate had persuaded him to take it up, and gradually he had begun to win races, his powerful frame proving perfect for 200 metres freestyle events. He trained fanatically, spending hours with weights in the gym and then in the water, completing countless lengths to perfect his powerful stroke and endless repetitions of his long flat racing dives and the tumble turns that could so easily win or lose a race.

He had soon grown out of Belfast's short 33 metre pools and left school early to swim for the leading club in Liverpool. His just rewards included Silver Medals in the European and Commonwealth Games and reaching the final of the Tokyo Olympics.

As with most competitive swimmers, it was all over by about the age of nineteen. But Joe had been determined not to leave the sport that had so changed his life, soon enlisting in the British Army and driving his regiment to successes in a string of swimming competitions. After ten enjoyable years, he had left with the rank of Company Sergeant Major and gone into teaching.

On Tuesday night, after the kids all gone home, he had a last long swim by himself, something he really enjoyed. After that, he'd have a pint or two at Paddy Bourke's before getting home to the news and Sheila's supper.

He could still do it pretty well and loved the feel of the water, the steady economical strokes, the minimum roll of the head, and the tuck and feet slap of the turns.

Suddenly he saw a figure signalling at the deep end. Some busybody from the Leisure Centre? Telling him, of all people, to get out of the water?

He swum over, held the rail and looked up.

Then his world went black.

* * *

Deliberately, he stumbled as he came back from the bar, then left two empty Guinness bottles on the table in front of him.

His dishevelled, smelly clothes and unshaven face would do the rest to keep the other people in the bar away from him as he pretended to slump into sleep.

A drunk on the Belfast ferry? Not an unusual sight.

But he did not sleep. He remembered. Liverpool in 1982. He had been sixteen, fit, and already six feet. And a great swimmer. He knew that, and so did Joe Corcoran, the Swimming Master and Coach. He liked Corcoran; good bloke, and just like him he had excelled at the 200 metres freestyle, and also the freestyle relay. And better still, Joe Corcoran seemed to like him. It was rare enough to find any teacher at school who supported you, but better still, Corcoran made it obvious.

'You're good, but you could be really good. It's up to you. Question of attitude. Just that bit of extra effort and you could do really well. Maybe even think about the Olympics.'

The Olympics? He had never had that kind of encouragement and support, and had worked fiendishly to merit Corcoran's enthusiasm, certainly to the detriment of his A levels – as he heard from other teachers. 'You could do so well if you weren't spending so much time in the pool. You can't swim forever, at least not like that. But you could be working for the next fifty years.'

Working for the next fifty years? For Christ's sake, water was freedom. And Joe Corcoran was amazing, even his smile. Incredible how a smile could make one just that bit faster, and be that bit more keen to succeed. There was nothing like the buzz of coming up at the end of the pool, knowing he'd got there first – and seeing Joe, exulted by his performance.

And it wasn't just the pleasure of seeing Joe so delighted. Always a smile for him in the corridor. An encouraging remark. A vague idea of a father he'd have liked to have had. Until that day of the inter-schools competition, the ghastly day he'd got it all wrong, and Joe had dropped him from the team.

Okay, Joe didn't know about the letter he'd had from his family solicitor, suddenly reminding him of the date and even the circumstances of his mother's death. But he could have listened. All Joe seemed to care about was his dismal performance that day. Slow enough in the 200, with a poor start and some really sloppy turns. But even worse, diving off a fraction early in the relay, and getting the school team disqualified.

Hate came fast. Corcoran was too angry to listen to reason, despite the pleas from the rest of the team. Now dropped not just from the relay, but also from the 200 metres freestyle, it shattered him, more than Corcoran would ever know.

He gave up swimming that day, turning to his A levels with a sudden fury – and sailed through them. Corcoran had asked him back. Too late.

Well, it was too late for Corcoran now.

CHAPTER NINE

BELFAST, NORTHERN IRELAND

The men and women of the Royal Ulster Constabulary, now called the Police Service of Northern Ireland, were as familiar with shootings as any police force in the world and certainly more than any other in the United Kingdom.

And the Royal Victoria Hospital in Belfast was regarded as one of the world's centres of expertise on gunshot wounds.

When Joe Corcoran's body was found, face down in the pool, the P.S.N.I. detectives could be forgiven for making some assumptions based on their normal experience. Joe had been shot in the head. The questioning of his distraught wife, his many friends and the tearful swimming kids had revealed little of interest. He seemed to have no enemies, in contrast lots of friends. There was no hint of crime connections, especially drugs, which had turned the IRA from freedom fighters into a vicious Irish mafia.

On Detective Sergeant Derek Robinson's desk were the newspapers. 'POOL HORROR, CHAMP SHOT' was the headline in *The Belfast Telegraph*, 'SWIMMING HERO MURDER' in the *Irish News*. In the old days, he thought, Corcoran's killing might have been sectarian, with a Protestant faction deciding to kill *any* Catholic – perhaps in revenge for an incident miles away and totally unrelated. But that didn't happen very often nowadays.

Having said that, Derek's brother John, also a detective, had just been investigating the street murder of a Catholic teenager by a gang of Protestant schoolboys. When he questioned them, the kids' amazing and depressing reason for attacking 'Taiges' was that they supported 'Celtic' and the Protestant boys followed 'Rangers' – both soccer teams, but over in Glasgow. A killing for a Scottish team, for God's sake!

Derek Robinson realised, of course, that he had to examine such local possibilities. After all, most Northern Ireland murders were local, and nearly all had to do with the tensions of the last thirty years. In his father's day, the people of Northern Ireland could boast that they were the most law-abiding in the United Kingdom. Few robberies, hardly any rapes – and for three years running in the 1960's, not one single murder.

With the possibility that Corcoran had not been killed by a local, Robinson had alerted the ferries to England and Scotland, the airport and the station for the express to Dublin. But of course they had no real idea who they were looking for – except it was probably an adult male. And with the 'Troubles' over, there were now thousands of tourists and business visitors, many more flights and much more travel generally.

And if the killer had used a car, it was even more difficult. In the past, Robinson had been forced to explain to his amazed UK colleagues that, even at the height of the Troubles, there was no real border – no carefully guarded 'Check Point Charlies'. Leaving aside main roads, it was even easy to cross on the main road to Dublin without realising it. It was only after a while that you began to notice the Gaelic on the road signs.

And it was not just normal travellers who crossed all the time. Much of the traffic was economic. A huge number of Irish drivers came up to shop and to fill up with fuel – much cheaper in the North. It had become impossible to run a viable filling station in the Republic within twenty miles of the border. But John's cousin, Charlie, had done very well, thank you, owning one just in the North, in Newry.

Outside help might reveal something, so Derek Robinson had sent the crime and ballistics report to his colleagues in the Republic's Gardai, with whom they often co-operated nowadays. He'd also entered the details into 'HOLMES', the UK's Home Office Large Major Enquiry System. It had proved useful in the past.

But he had to admit that they really didn't have much to go on so far.

No motive, no sightings of the killer, no fingerprints, no DNA, no cartridge case.

Just one bullet, 6.35mm, or .25 inch ACP.

* * *

'Why can't I go to Bella's party?' Five-year-old Morag's look was defiant, her eyes blazing.

Her mother sighed, trying to pull the child closer.

'Look darling, I've told you a hundred times. It's Grandpa's funeral, the time we all have go and say goodbye to him.

Everyone will be there. Granny and Dad, and the boys. All your aunties and uncles. All your cousins. And all our friends. You can't be the only one not to go.'

'Nobody will know if I don't.' Morag burst into tears, pulling her hand from her mother's grip.

'They will, all of them will know.' Sinead looked at her five-year old daughter with infinite sympathy, remembering how she had really loved her grandfather's company during all those times together in the pool. She was now an excellent swimmer for her age, and a confident diver too. But, of course, all this was too much for her to take in.

Morag stared at her mother, bursting into tears again. She was so young, too young to understand the horror of what had happened to Joe and his whole family.

And her mother could remember so well the excitement of birthday parties at her age, especially your best friend's party. The special status of being a best friend. The dress. The anticipation. The games. The cake. And those wretched going-away presents that had made Morag's last three parties so expensive.

'And Bella will have lots and lots more parties'. As soon as the words were out of her mouth Sinead regretted them. Wrong thing to say. Morag's eyes welled up again. But this time she allowed her mother to cuddle her. A year was an impossibly long time in a child's life. An eternity. Another whole year to wait for a best friend's party was almost unbearable.

Would it really matter if she let her daughter go? Would anybody really mind if she wasn't at the funeral?

Yes, of course they would. And one day, far into the future, Morag would too.

Her mind was spinning as she stroked the child's hair. Perhaps she could ask Bella's mother to postpone for a bit? Maybe. But there were so many other things to organize and think about. People to call and email. Caterers to sort out. Florists to call. Father O'Bannion to visit. Numbers to sort out.

She and her sisters couldn't let her mother do it all, not with the hundreds of people likely to turn up. Over twenty years teaching kids to swim and producing champions had made Joe a legend. The church would be packed. Come to think of it, wouldn't Bella's mother want to be there? Her daughter certainly swam at the pool.

She rolled her wrist to look at her watch. It was time to get lunch together. The boys would soon be back, and whatever the news, they'd be starving. Life had to go on.

'Is Grandpa *really* dead?' Morag asked suddenly in a small voice.

'Yes, darling. I'm afraid he is.'

'The sort of dead when you don't come back?

'Yes, that sort.' An awful pause.

'What made him dead?'

Sinead didn't know what to say.

CHAPTER TEN

PUTNEY, LONDON

Alice was going through her case-work at around seven in the evening when the phone suddenly rang, stopping her concentration in its tracks.

'Hello.' She was aware her voice sounded a bit brusque, as it sometimes did if she was interrupted.

'Oh, I'm sorry. Is this a bad time to call?'

'No, no, not at all.' Alice suddenly realized who it was with a frisson of pleasure.

'It's John, John Tibbs. We met the other night with Liz and Derek.'

'Oh yes. Really good fun!'

A slight pause.

'Well, I wondered if you'd like to meet up again? Maybe for dinner sometime next week?'

'Lovely, that would be great. Especially if I can hear more of those crazy stories!'

'That's a promise! How about Monday then?'

'Sounds good to me. Hang on, I'll just check my diary.' She flipped through it quickly, although she was pretty sure she was free. Monday night usually was. Long term habit of staying in for some unaccountable reason.

'Yup, that's fine.'

'Great. Well, the agency is in the West End, so if it's OK with you we could get together after work. How about meeting up in a bar called Bertorelli's in Charlotte Street at seven, and we can take it from there. Oh, and don't bother about public transport. I have a contract with a minicab company, and they could pick you up at 6.15 if that suits you.'

'Lovely, thanks.'

'One thing though…'

'What?'

'Don't wear high heels or anything too warm.'

Alice chuckled. 'We're not going on a hike, are we?'

'Nope. I'll tell you why when I see you.'

'OK. See you then.'

Alice hung up the phone smiling. That was nice and not entirely unexpected, except for the clothes code. That was certainly a bit mysterious.

* * *

When the cab came, Alice was ready. As they headed towards the West End against the rush of the traffic, her thoughts returned to John's instructions as she wiggled her right foot, shod with a boring flattie. She hadn't even dared to wear her really pretty flat pumps in case there was some ghastly trek ahead. 'No high heels.' That's exactly what she would have worn with such a tall guy, but not worth fussing about.

The bar, north of Oxford Street, was extremely crowded and noisy, but John, with his height, was easy enough to spot. He greeted her with a kiss on the cheek.

'Great, you made it. Lovely to see you. Now, what would you like to drink? I got here a bit early, so I'm already on a Marguerita.'

Alice asked for the same, wondering if it sounded a bit feeble, and suddenly thinking about all those legions of girls in the old days who opted for 'Babycham' because they didn't know what to ask for. She surely couldn't be nervous? She certainly wasn't last time, but then Liz and Derek were there.

The feeling soon vanished as John chatted animatedly as he had before, mostly about work and the amusing things happening, but never, thankfully, in one long monologue. He had an attractive habit of pausing to wait for reaction, and looking at her to gauge her response, another reason he was engaging company.

Alice suddenly wished she could talk about her job as easily, and not for the first time. But at the same time it was a relief that John knew better than to pry into details of her work, obviously understanding that for the most part, that was a no go area.

Three Margueritas later, she was feeling distinctly light-headed, and somewhat relieved she wasn't on wobbly high heels when they set off for the restaurant. This turned out to be Turkish, named after the city of Ephesus, and mostly staffed with courtly, white-haired men with moustaches. They obviously knew John well, with at least two of them shaking his hand effusively before leading him to his table.

Alice had never been to Turkey, but the dishes seemed pretty similar to Greek food, with which she was familiar. Starters and kebab dishes were washed down with delicious Turkish wine, until John at last touched on what he obviously thought might be a difficult subject. She knew Liz had told him about Helen.

'Any more news about your aunt? Have the police come up with anything?'

'No, not yet. Apparently, if a suspect isn't caught quickly – you know, almost running from the scene – it can take months or even years of careful work. If only it was like *CSI Miami*, or *NCIS*, you know, all solved neatly in sixty minutes.' Alice smiled. 'The only good thing is they gave my rather unpleasant cousin Oliver a hard time, which was no bad thing. All he cared about was the money he's going to inherit. However, though he may be an obvious prick – excuse my French – he's not a murderer.'

'So, nothing at all?'

Alice sighed. 'No, we'll just have to wait. Whichever way you look at it, it's really peculiar. Almost like mistaken identity. But you can't really mistake a very old lady in her own garden for anybody else in broad daylight.'

'Wouldn't have thought so. Very strange, and very sad for you.' He touched her hand.

'It might cheer you up,' he said as he paid the bill, 'to tell you where we're going. The Hundred Club, at 100 Oxford Street. Hope you don't know it.'

'No, I don't.'

'It's been famous for jazz for years, starting way back during the war as a dancing place for American servicemen. Then it became the Humphrey Lyttleton Club at the beginning of Britain's traditional jazz revival. And now they've got all kinds of other music. I know I was a bit bossy about the clothing. If you don't feel like it, we can just leave and move on.'

Alice smiled as they walked briskly down into Oxford Street, and came to a red sign with '100' and the symbol of a trumpet. As they went down into the basement, suddenly there was an evocative sound that Alice had not heard since childhood, Glenn Miller's 'In the mood'. John paid and they entered a dark, cavernous room.

Lit up on a stage dominated by a huge white '100' was a big band, all girls, formally dressed, about 30 of them, playing 'swing', something Alice's father adored. The band was surprising enough, but what really amazed her were the hundreds of people in the club, around 400 she estimated, all different ages and all dancing. And not the silly jumping up and down that Alice had been forced to endure in 'house' or 'garage' clubs. This was orchestrated jiving and some of the couples were plainly experts.

'It's the Lindy Hop,' shouted John above the music as he steered her to the bar. 'When Charles Lindbergh flew solo across the Atlantic in the twenties, he became the most popular man in the world, believe it or not. And the Americans wrote 200 songs about their hero and created a dance – because he'd 'hopped' across the Atlantic. That's what this is, the Lindy Hop. Lots of people come here early and take lessons. It's great, isn't it?'

Alice nodded with enthusiasm, at the same time noticing the heat. There were some air-conditioning units on the ceiling, but most of them didn't seem to be working, while the dancers definitely were. She quickly removed her denim top, as she accepted a glass of wine. *First mystery solved, 'Nothing too warm'. And second mystery, 'No high heels'!*

The blonde drummer in the band leaned forward to the mike. 'AND NOW WE'RE GOING TO PLAY YOU FLETCHER HENDERSON'S 'CHINA TOWN'. IN THE STATES, THEY PLAY THIS FOR DANCE CHAMPIONSHIPS CALLED – I KID YOU NOT – COLLEGIATE SHAG!'

Suddenly a young man was at her shoulder, asking Alice to dance. She hesitated, until John nodded his approval amiably, focusing on the music. Alice was literally swept off her feet, and was soon thoroughly enjoying herself. Returning for a drink she felt rather pleased with herself.

'AND NOW, ARTIE SHAW'S DOUBLE MELLOW'. A tap on the shoulder. A grey-haired man stood in front of her in immaculate 1940s clothes and two-tone dancing pumps. Again John grinned and nodded, and once again she was off on the floor. Then out of the corner of her eye, she saw a girl grab John and take him off to dance.

On her kitchen notice-board Alice had pinned a cartoon saying, 'I have seen the enemy. They are tall and blonde and have big boobs', which perfectly described John's dancing partner. What is more, they were dancing brilliantly together. Alice, herself being whirled around, felt a surprising pang of jealousy. But at the end of the number, the blonde just wandered off and Alice realized that everyone was there to dance, not for flirtation.

'Pretty good. Looks as if you've been taking lessons!'

John laughed. 'Some, but they start a bit early and I often work late. But, depending on the band, I like coming here later anyway, so you gradually pick up the dancing and have a good time.'

'NOW WE'RE GOING TO SLOW IT DOWN, AND GIVE YOU OUR RENDITION OF BENNY GOODMAN AND PEGGY LEE WITH 'WHY DON'T YOU DO RIGHT?''

Now John guided Alice out on to the floor, while a singer who really did look and sound like Peggy Lee huskily ground out the lyrics.

'Why don't you do right
Like some other men do?
Get out of here
And get me some money too.'

As they danced slow and close, she felt a wave of affection and the beginnings of arousal for this big man.

When they eventually emerged into the welcome fresh air of Oxford Street, John hailed a black cab and they held hands as they headed west.

'I'll see you home,' said John. Alice didn't object.

'Come in for a drink,' she said when they eventually reached her house. Soon she was opening a bottle of white wine, as if they hadn't had too much already, and then making some coffee.

Still no move.

Probably fuelled by alcohol, Alice suddenly shocked herself.

'I know you're good at advertising, and now I know you're good at dancing. Do you want to show me what else you're good at?'

John didn't leave until seven next morning.

* * *

Alice's thoughts – irritatingly – kept on turning to John the next day. By mid-day she was still surprised, and now thoroughly embarrassed by her forthrightness which she hadn't forgotten, but certainly did not regret – only wondering whether it was all too much too soon. She rubbed her head. Still a nagging headache.

And what a ghastly come-on that was, straight out of 'Sex and the City', or worse. Even Hollywood scriptwriters wouldn't have stooped to that. It wasn't that it was a first date. Searing honesty had never much bothered her, but the words she chose to express it did. And they did now. And the irritation was all mixed in with questioning about whether John would want to see her again and whether she should simply accept him for what he probably was – no more than an extremely pleasant ship in the night. She had her pride.

She went to make herself a sandwich, and annoyingly, thought of him again. Amiable, affable, certainly. Attractive, yes. But a bit too comfortable? Possibly. She had always been strangely attracted to people – at least men – with a slightly edgy quality, people with whom she felt faintly off-guard. With John, it was all so easy and companionable. But what the hell was wrong with that? Maybe it was time, at thirty, to enjoy a bit of comfort, to settle down and think about the future, to advise herself as competently as she strived to do for her patients.

She put the unopened tin of tuna back in the cupboard, suddenly not feeling like the sandwich she had planned en route to the kitchen, and admitting to herself she was cross he hadn't phoned. A courtesy, at the very least.

Still hungry, but now utterly uninterested in food, she went back to her case notes. An eighteen-year old girl, addicted to stealing. Not that unusual in a teenage victim of Down's Syndrome, but hugely difficult for her mother who had come to see Alice, forced to alert the local shops with a photograph of her much-loved daughter and warn them of the problem whenever she could, or if she knew the sources of the theft, return the items with an apology and an explanation. Small items usually: lipsticks, mascaras, skin creams, never used – simply kept in the corner of her daughter's bedroom, and with luck, accompanied by some evidence of where they might have been taken. Was this ever going to end, the harassed mother had wondered.

Two hours later, and with a considerable pile of papers referring to similar cases now beside her computer, the phone rang.

'Hi, it's me.'

'Hi.' Alice was delighted.

'Look, I'm sorry I didn't phone before, but that client I told you about came in today, and the whole thing was a disaster.'

'Oh, I'm sorry.'

'Don't be. We got it wrong. Or rather, *I* got it wrong. Made a complete cock-up.'

Alice smiled.

'Can't get it right all the time.'

'No.' John sounded flat. 'Anyway, are you okay?'

'Fine. And it was a lovely evening, thanks.'

Alice suddenly remembered the tie he'd left on the bedroom

floor, deciding not to mention it. Hopefully he'd be back to pick it up soon.

'Look, I'm a bit knackered now, but I'll call you tomorrow.'

She hoped he would.

CHAPTER ELEVEN

BANGOR, NORTHERN IRELAND

This was the first time she had baked anything since Joe's death thought Sheila Corcoran, as she greased a cake tin on her kitchen table in her house in Bangor outside Belfast. Maybe she was starting to recover at last, at least start the healing process and feel up to doing the things she did before, like baking for the Women's Institute fundraising events, something she had done for years but not for weeks now.

They had completely understood when she had told them she wasn't up to it, and they hadn't pressed her – calling her regularly from time to time, but never once asking when she would be back on the rota. Eventually it was her who had called them to say she would be on again this week.

And the process of cooking was somehow comforting. Mixing the butter with the marmalade syrup, beating in the eggs, and then adding the marmalade to the cake mixture. This was one of Joe's favourites – a marmalade spice cake – and it brought back happy memories – almost for the first time pleasurable ones since that dreadful day.

She pictured him at the kitchen table over the years, always in the same chair and always complimenting her cookery. 'This is amazing Sheila, you ought to cook for a living.' Sheila never had, although she loved cooking for charity events, and was always pleased to be told that her cakes were the first to sell out. Maybe she should become a professional cook now? After all, Joe's life insurance was hardly generous, and neither of them had even half decent pensions. Early days, she thought to herself as she turned the mixture and levelled the surface of the cake.

The phone rang.

'Hi, it's Moira'. A friend of Sheila's from the WI.

'Are you okay?'

'Fine' said Sheila, 'but it's a terrible time to talk. I'm covered in cake mix, and now the phone is too. Can I call you back in ten minutes?'

'Fine. It's just so good to have you on board again.'

'Good for me too,' said Sheila. And it *was* good for her, she knew that. Sheila put the cake tin in the oven and poured herself a small Irish whiskey before she phoned her friend back, pleased that she had found whatever it was in her survival techniques to get herself back on the rota, and knowing that Joe would also be proud of her.

Taking a sip of her favourite early evening tipple, Black Bush whiskey, she looked out of her kitchen window over Belfast Lough, with the city in the distance and the two huge yellow travelling cranes – called Samson and Goliath – still dominating the skyline. Sheila had never known whether she loved or hated these two giants; after all, the owners, Harland & Wolff, had allowed discrimination against employing Catholics to go on for years, and she had debated the point with Joe a thousand times.

But Joe had loved them, similarly the sight of the ships sailing by, now loaded with the new and massive giant wind turbines that set off down the river Lough every few days. He had continually reminded her that such business was a blessing for Belfast, now that demand for great ships like the *Titanic* was ancient history. 'You have to move on'.

And she *was* moving on, although it would never be the same. Who could have done that to her beloved Joe? So kind, so generous, such a good friend and husband. What kind of cruel bastard had come into their family life and wrecked it utterly?

Sheila thought of all those wonderful tributes at the wake following the funeral.

Dozens of people had crammed into their kitchen and sitting room, so many she had been forced to hire at least three dozen chairs, and also a loudspeaker system so the people in one room downstairs could hear all the tributes from the other. And what lovely things they had said – and said from the heart. She was sure of that. Even if the Irish had a way with words, you could always tell who was being honest or not.

She smiled when she thought of Fionn Rafferty's tribute. 'Many people think swimming was the love of Joe's life.' He had peered over his glasses and looked at her. 'But it wasn't. It was Sheila. She was the real champion. And Joe was a lucky, lucky man to have met her. To Sheila.' They had all raised their glasses, and Sheila had found it hard not to shed a tear.

And her children, Sean and Liam, had been brilliant, as had their wives and children, un-stacking and arranging the chairs, doing the cooking, ordering the copious drinks and laying the tables, as well as printing the funeral programme with the smiling photograph of Joe on the front, as he proudly held aloft a huge swimming cup.

Sheila sat at the table thinking back over the years until the oven buzzed and turned off.

She suddenly realized that she had been lost in her memories for over an hour.

CHAPTER TWELVE

SKYKOMISH, WASHINGTON STATE

America's Pacific North-West was becoming more and more popular as people increasingly turned their backs on the sun in California and Florida. In fact, Portland and Seattle were reckoned to be the most sought-after cities in the country. Chris Murphy certainly counted himself as a fervent fan of the area.

After years of being a cop in big, crowded, dangerous cities, with their deafening sirens and shouting and shooting, he now yearned for quiet and solitude. The little town of Skykomish in the state of Washington had caught his eye the year before on a driving holiday with his wife Betty-Anne, just before he was due to retire as Chief of Police down in Burbank, next to Los Angeles.

To look around, the couple had flown up to Seattle, rented a car and set off up along the coast at Puget Sound, before turning up into the Cascade Mountains. The road they drove along, Highway 2, had mostly followed the railroad track eastwards, winding along the valley. When they had reached the high plateau between the Cascades and the Rockies, they turned south towards the heat of Yakima, before descending to reach the Columbia River and drive back west to Portland.

Skykomish, Chris had then decided, was a bit special. He soon discovered that it had always been a railroad town, and in the 1920s had quite a large population when the Great Northern had based its powerful electric locomotives there for their task of hauling steam and diesel trains through the eight mile Cascade Tunnel. When steam had disappeared in the fifties, and ventilation had been installed to suck diesel fumes from the Tunnel, the electrics too had gone – along with the jobs. Then the timber mills that used to feed Seattle started packing it in.

So now the population was tiny, barely two hundred in the actual town. Of course, there were more people in the winter with the skiers and snow boarders, and in the summer with the hikers going up on the trails and kayakers along the Skykomish River, and now mountain bikers. But compared with Los Angeles, the place seemed empty. All this suited him just fine, so he had chosen the little town for his retirement.

He loved the magnificent, rugged scenery, he had his new hobby – fishing for steelhead trout, and he liked to go and drink with the lumberjacks and railroad veterans in the Cascadia Inn. And he could walk out and admire the frequent sight of mile-long freight trains, with double-decked containers, as they grumbled through town hauled by up to seven diesels – westwards to Seattle and eastwards to Minneapolis and Chicago. They made a hell of a lot of noise, but it was sort of comforting – a booming reminder of American prosperity. Each day too, Amtrak's most popular train, the shiny tourist-filled 'Empire Builder', once the Great Northern's flagship, still came through town in both directions, although it no longer stopped.

Sadly, Betty-Anne did not share her husband's enthusiasm for the little mountain town.

First, there was the weather. When they had initially visited, it was warm, with blue skies and the mountains bathed in bright sunshine – as they were when they first moved in. And there seemed to be plenty of people. But as summer slid into fall, and with the tourists gone, the place seemed to her to be empty and bleak. Dank, drifting fog and clouds often blanketed the dark, fir-covered slopes, and in December the temperature dropped below freezing and stayed there until nearly April.

And then there was the snow.

The Cascades had plenty of rain. That's why the trees had been so huge in the old days before the logging took them. But when the rain turned to heavy, drifting snow, it was a real trial to get about – and even dangerous. After all, the Tunnel had been built because of the infamous 1910 disaster, when after two days and nights of mounting fear, a whole hamlet and two passenger trains stalled outside the protective snow-sheds had been swept suddenly to their doom by America's deadliest avalanche.

Anyway, Betty-Anne had to admit that she was basically a big city girl. She missed her friends and the crowded streets and lively shops of her native Chicago or the towns of California, where they had spent the last twenty years. Now, for anything other than essentials which she bought in Gold Bar, she had to go down to Everett on the coast or up the line to Leavenworth, which, to avoid bankruptcy years ago, had become a bizarre 'Bavarian' theme town. It had alpine wooden houses, yodelling and even German slap dancing in the town centre– and shops full of Christmas decorations and cuckoo clocks all year round, served by people dressed in *lederhosen*. But at least it had a million tourists and lots of shops.

But in winter their shopping trips were only about once a month, mostly because, with the snow and ice, Highway 2 was easily the most dangerous road in the state. Cars were always sliding off into the river. You could tell how often because they sounded the old air-raid siren whenever it happened – usually to Seattle folk who didn't know how to drive in snow as they headed up the pass. And the siren sounded worryingly often.

Chris and Betty-Anne soon learned to forgo such risky adventures. Chris was always muttering 'You can certainly tell the difference between those who live in the snow and those who play in the snow!'

As for friends, Betty-Anne now had a handful, but nothing like her former wide circle. But for the support of her loving husband, she would have been horribly lonely. God, what on earth had possessed Chris to bring her up here?

Chris was a big man. His large frame had suited him well enough when he was a quarterback playing for his school and college. But soon he had really started to put on weight sitting in patrol cars and eating too many doughnuts to beat the boredom. And later his desk jobs had not improved things. Nor had his drinking with his Irish pals. Betty-Anne had consistently failed in her attempts to get him to go to Gold's Gym in Wenatchee, and had by now given up nagging him.

Today, Chris was really, really happy, almost ecstatic. It was the last Sunday in January and he had spent four hours watching his beloved football team, the Green Bay Packers, beating the Pittsburgh Steelers to win the Super Bowl. It was always gratifying for him to see his team from tiny Green Bay on Lake Michigan, the last of the 'small town teams' started by 'Curly' Lambeau with just $500 from a packing company, holding its own against those backed by huge cities, and *truly* great when it scooped the ultimate prize.

Normally he would have gone to the Cascadian Inn bar on Railroad Avenue or The Whistling Post to watch the game with his pals, but this year he had a cold and decided to stay in. Betty-Anne had sensibly gone round to Marty Williams next door to escape the football ordeal, but had left Chris with a comforting crate of Coors. She had also sent back Marty's English husband Ben, who had also moved up there as a forestry scientist after years in San Diego, to keep Chris company.

Marty and Ben were certainly lively neighbours. Being a

bit younger, they gave rather noisy parties, which started at noon and often went on to midnight. Benny certainly seemed the very opposite of the staid and stuffy Englishmen that many Americans expected. Indeed, it was Chris and Betty-Anne who sometimes felt staid and stuffy as they went to bed early while the rock music blasted in from next door.

But they'd all become good friends, and at least Ben didn't like soccer, which seemed to be sweeping the States. But he had never really understood American Football, being a rugby man himself. Chris had always tried to explain its complications.

'One of the big differences with your rugby is our forward pass. In the 1905 season, so many hundreds of college kids were badly injured and so many actually died, eighteen I think, that they were going to close the game down. So President Teddy Roosevelt stepped in and they allowed them to pass the ball forward. The quarterback is passed the ball and, protected by a pocket of players, hurls it way ahead to a receiver, who goes for a touchdown. THERE! It's happening now. Just watch him – fantastic! Wasn't that just great?'

This went on for four hours, the actual time it really takes to watch four 15 minute quarters in the massive event seen by 100 million Americans and where each commercial costs $2 million to air.

'Did you see that last touchdown, Hal?' he bellowed into the phone after the game ended and an exhausted Ben had gone home. It was always fun to share his delight with his friends back in the Midwest. Many of them were cops, some of the same seniority after all these years.

Chris had moved out to the Coast nearly 20 years ago, becoming a LAPD traffic cop. His career had certainly been colourful. Full of drunks, drugs, and shoot-outs, with high-speed chases and very fast and powerful police cars which unfortunately didn't stop or go round corners like modern cars. Once he had even chased a guy for fifty miles at ninety miles an hour. He turned out to be foreign – English. He was so abusive when Chris pulled him over that he had thrown him into jail for the night.

Chris certainly felt that he had earned it when he was finally made Chief in Burbank. Up here all the police knew him, or knew of him, not just in Skykomish, but over in Everett where he had been invited to a police ball a few weeks ago. In retirement, he still had respect.

His new home was typical of the area – wooden, but well-insulated. It was up the hill a bit, which had been lucky for the previous owner. Many of the buildings further down had been physically moved and then returned months later, even the big hotel, because thousands of gallons of oil over the years had been found to have leaked into the soil and river. Today's railroad, the huge BNSF, had only just completed the great multi-million- dollar 'Skykomish Clean-Up'. It might have been cheaper to pay everyone to leave, Chris had wryly thought, when he heard all about the vast upheaval.

Chris suddenly realised he should have let the dog out hours ago. It must have got desperate during the match. He'd better let it out before Betty-Anne got back and ticked him off.

The house had quite a large garden at the back that sloped uphill, and its boundary had a great view. Despite the snow on the ground, the cold and the fading light, Chris decided to take the dog out and take in the vista again. He opened the back door and Sean shot out into the darkness.

The valley began to fill with the noise of a long freight train out of Chicago. He could just hear Sean barking at something. Probably a deer.

He pulled on a coat. Clutching his Coors, and basking in

the glow of the Packers' victory, he slowly walked the hill, crunching in the snow, looked out and paused to light the cigar that he would never be allowed to smoke indoors.

Sean seemed to have disappeared. Maybe chasing that deer.

The rumble of another long freight train began to build.

At that moment he heard a sound in the dark.

* * *

It was three in the morning and Sergeant Annie Hayes sat at a computer in the Command Vehicle, which was the size of a small bus. She looked up, vaguely distracted.

She wondered why, during any incident, her Everett police colleagues always seemed to leave their flashing lights on even when they'd parked. Cops did it in the movies too. Perhaps it was a macho thing, she mused. Certainly the narrow road outside the Murphy house appeared completely jammed with 'black and whites' – most with their lights flashing. At least someone had turned off that damn siren!

All in all, it had been a very harrowing night. They had been called in by King County's lone full-time policeman, who had never had to deal with a murder in his whole career. He had taken an hour to arrive and the team from Everett even longer, Everett being the nearest town with the proper resources. It was not often that the police team was as sympathetic to a victim's family. But then this time the victim was a cop.

Even as a seasoned police wife, Betty-Anne was unable to cope. Shattered and stricken since she had gone out with a flashlight and discovered Chris in the snow and made her desperate 911 call, she was now almost unable to speak. She rocked backwards and forwards in her chair, keening and pulling at her hair as if shielding out the world with arms across her eyes, occasionally waving her hand as if telling everything and everybody to go away. It had been bad enough taking in the news herself, but having to tell the children was too much – getting from that routine, upbeat 'Hi Mom! How are you?' to their tearful promise to take the next plane.

Marty and Ben had come round at once, of course, and with a young Everett policewoman, were trying to comfort her. And in the moments she could even begin to think straight, she thought that what made it more horrible – and ironic, was the timing. She had yearned for Chris's retirement – out of danger at last, time to be together and fulfil all their plans; maybe travel a bit, see more of the family, perhaps even buy a small boat. And the family knew that. She had so often told them about their dreams.

Murder was one thing when your husband was in the line of duty, out on the street, but quite another when he had just retired to such a quiet spot; unthinkable, unbearable.

Contacted by Marty, her doctor had come around and eventually been able to calm her down and sedate her, but not enough to sleep that night and only fitfully for many long nights later.

And it was hardly surprising that the effect on the whole police team had been very depressing.

* * *

Annie looked up as Captain John Westbrooke appeared out of the darkness, hauled himself up into the big vehicle and sat down heavily with an angry scowl on his face.

'A cop-killer! Murphy was one of our own. We can't have good people like him being taken out like that. I know he was retired, but I met him when he visited us and he seemed a great guy.' He paused, steadying himself. 'So, what have we got, Annie?'

Annie stared at the check-list on her screen.

'The neighbours heard nothing, but then he was killed a fair way from their house. And they told me that when the trains come through, it's hard to hear much else. We'll get the ballistics report when they've extracted the bullet. There was just one.

Otherwise, no real clues so far. The guy, if it is a guy, probably got in through the side gate. It wasn't locked. They're hardly ever locked here, because of getting jammed by the snow.

No fingerprints there, other than the Murphys, the neighbours and a handyman who was last here on Thursday. No sign of a vehicle – if there was one, it must have been left some distance away. We're searching the area near where the body was found for footprints in the snow or a cartridge case, but we'll probably have to wait till daylight to finish that properly. In the house, nothing missing or disturbed, no sign of robbery or burglary.

There's one other thing. They have a dog, an old Labrador. Murphy may have been taking it out for a walk, or for it to relieve itself. We found a dog whistle round his neck. The dog came back hours later, shivering – maybe from the cold, maybe spooked by something. And it also had a graze or cut on the top of its head. We'll get the vet to look at it and try to tell us what caused it.

I'm afraid his wife is absolutely distraught. The neighbours are looking after her, and her family doctor's there too.'

Captain Westbrooke continued to frown, stroking a chin that now had quite a dark stubble. 'Okay, so it wasn't casual. He may have been killed deliberately – carefully planned. The motive? It may have come from his past police career. It's a long shot, but check his records from where he served before – L.A., Burbank or even further back in Green Bay or Pittsburgh, if I remember.'

'I'll get in touch with them,' said Detective Dan Downey, a young graduate keen to make his mark, sitting opposite his boss. 'But as Captain, you may need to pull rank to nudge them into any kind of useful speed.'

'Okay. I suppose what we may be looking for is a grudge. It could be more recent connections from where he worked – Burbank, Studio City or L.A. Maybe the gangs, drug busts, organized crime. First, check the jails, anywhere on the Coast and inland as far as Las Vegas and Phoenix, and cross-check to see if someone has been released who Murphy might have helped to put away.'

'I'll handle that,' volunteered Annie.

'Next, travel. Check Seattle and Portland airports and the bus and railroad depots up and down the line. Check if anyone got on or off 'the Builder', up or down the tracks.

We don't know what we're looking for, could be a man or a woman. See if there's anything suspicious, or out of place. Anything from the cameras?'

'There's only one, on the gas station. Nothing, I'm afraid', said Annie.

He paused. Nobody else spoke.

'I figure that's all we can do here. Might as well get back and start working the phones and computers.'

* * *

With such a high-profile 'cop-killer' case taking priority, it took only about three hours before the ballistics report came in. The team gathered in a conference room in Everett's police HQ.

'It's a rather curious slug,' revealed Sam Stevens, their ballistics expert.

'It's 6.35 millimetre. Or what we call the point two five inch

ACP. It's really very light, designed for baby pistols. You used to see them occasionally in 'Saturday night specials', but most people would now want more stopping power. You'd have to be real close to your vic to be sure to put him down. That might point to a chance intruder, although *most* people would be a bit careful raiding an ex-cop.

The rounds are small and low-powered, normally fired from so-called vest-pocket or baby guns years ago, but they were used in the war over in Europe for the resistance fighters to knock off the Germans. All sorts of clever little guns were disguised as pipes, pens and belt buckles.

Anyway, there are no ballistic matches, I'm afraid.'

There was a long puzzled silence as this information sunk in.

'Jeez! So this may *not* be a local thing?' asked Captain Westbrooke. 'It could just as well have been a foreigner.'

He paused, thinking.

'Get a report out to other forces, plus the FBI and Interpol, and at the airports concentrate on flights leaving for Europe – London, Paris, and maybe Brussels, Berlin and Amsterdam, I guess. Or even to the Pacific. This may be getting complicated.'

* * *

The early morning sun was rising, making the view of the mountains through the curved glass of the West-bound Empire Builder's 'great dome' car spectacular.

About twenty passengers, including some excited children, were admiring the scenery or taking photographs. The snow beside the track was dazzling, so that a quiet man at the end of the car sipping his coffee did not look inappropriate in his dark glasses. The train was only travelling at about fifty, and it was easy to appreciate the view.

As they rumbled through Skykomish, there was another

view that this particular passenger appreciated. There were all
sorts of police vehicles at one end of the town, many with their
lights still flashing.

He knew that the police would have blocked all routes
leaving the scene, which in this lonely snow-bound mountain
country, pretty much meant Highway 2, checking buses, trucks
and cars. They would, of course, have automatically searched the
'Builder', but that would have been the eastbound one last night.

They could never have imagined that their suspect would
make his way to Leavenworth's little unmanned Icicle Station,
and next morning, as a tourist loaded with shopping bags,
board the westbound Builder, and then actually travel *towards*
the crime scene. And by the time the train reached Everett, they
would have abandoned the search, thinking that after twelve
hours their suspect would be long gone. They would take
months to find the old pick-up deep in the woods.

In the old days, it would have been very difficult to track
down Murphy from across the globe.

But now there was Facebook and people couldn't resist
posting up too much, talking too much, revealing too much. It
had not been difficult becoming a 'friend'. He'd got an Irishman
called Murphy to ask to become one. Americans were suckers
for trying to find their roots, especially the Irish. A few messages
from the 'Old Country' from his distant 'relative' and all the
details he needed were in place.

*They were brave enough when swaggering around in cop
cars and waving their guns. Christ, a bloody speeding ticket!
You have to pay them or you never get back into the States.*

*They don't realize what a damn nuisance they are. Not any
more, boyo! Tracked you down all the way here, and got you.
You'd even made Chief. Probably a career built on speeding
tickets.*

As long as you planned things carefully, they tended to go smoothly. He sipped his coffee, looked out at the snow, and couldn't resist a slight smile.

CHAPTER THIRTEEN

PUTNEY, LONDON

Alice looked in the mirror.

Yes, she looked okay, a bit more than okay if she allowed herself a bit of vanity. Someone had once described her eyes as violet, and while she didn't believe violet eyes existed – except in the case of Liz Taylor whom she'd once seen in a restaurant – she knew her eyes were a rather unusual shade. And that violet eye shadow she'd been given for Christmas might just perpetuate the myth. Yes, it suited her. And it matched the violet sweater. She felt a surge of much-needed confidence.

John was due to arrive in twenty minutes, and she felt a tiny bit apprehensive. Not that there had been any problems; but only one phone call since the last rather flat one, asking her to another dinner in town, at which point she'd suggested supper at her place, rather needing the familiarity of her own surroundings.

She'd made a curry dinner, discovering that he liked Indian food. A bit of a cheat here and there, but at least the cauliflower *bhaji* was made from scratch and the cucumber and beetroot *raithia* were relatively authentic: only a matter of adding yogurt, although she was probably wrong. Still, she had more important things to worry about than producing a simple Wednesday night curry meal, and since John had suggested a takeaway anyway, she was more than pleased with the results.

Alice had always enjoyed the few moments before people arrived – boyfriends, family, indeed anyone – to assess her life and surroundings and have what she called her 'contemplations'.

This was such a time. She poured herself a glass of white wine, reflected on past and present, and wondered again about John.

There was no mistake about fancying him. That was for sure. But how long would that last? Alice knew she was as easily switched off as on, and that a sudden remark could kill any desire she might have had. Was that ridiculous? Christ, she should know as a psychologist, yet she didn't. Tiny things could be a turn-off, from which there was no comeback; remarks, observations, gestures, judgements, differences in habits, sense of humour.

It was frequently easier to advise other people than it was herself. And here she was at 30, several times in love, but always – eventually – finding fault in it, preferring her own company, and finding her greatest solace in work rather than leaning on the shoulders of girlfriends, or indeed ex-boyfriends, although she was happy to keep them as mates after desire had vanished. That's if they could accept that, though most of them couldn't.

She looked at the table, already laid. Pretty. A single silver candle, napkins, a small vase of flowers. Understated, but definitely an effort. But still, too much of an effort? Would it have been easier to go out or have a takeaway? Did the table make some kind of a statement she didn't want to make? For God's sake, she told herself, this is only a second date, and if there's not a third, it's not the end of the world. The doorbell jolted her out of her thoughts.

'Hi.'

'Hi, lovely to see you!' That mad blonde hair, blowing all over the place.

'You too. Come in. And you shouldn't have bought that – I've got plenty of wine.'

'Keep it for later,' smiled John, putting a three bottle pack in the hall. 'Hopefully, I'll be coming again.'

Alice smiled. Yes, she liked him. There was something so easy about him. What you saw, no hidden edge. Yet no dreary solidity either; that much was clearly evident. Unless she was very much mistaken, she guessed he'd had a number of girlfriends, and somehow – like she had – decided to move on. Something missing in past relationships perhaps.

Two hours later, Alice had quite forgotten she wasn't entertaining someone she hardly knew. So easy. So relaxed. And, from time to time giving her a look that reminded her of the other night in bed. Nice, but she wasn't going back there, for now.

And she didn't. At two o'clock, she claimed she had a big day ahead. Indeed, she did, working out what to recommend for the autistic child and her mother, and suggested a taxi, whilst being totally amenable to meeting again. There was no pressure, no embarrassment.

'By the way, keep the tie. I'll pick it up next time.'

'Fabulous evening.'

'For me too.'

* * *

Two weeks later, Alice was lying in bed alone on a Sunday morning, with pleasant anticipation. She was delighted to discover that John was an equally avid reader of the weekend papers, and especially the *Times* and *Telegraph*, though he had rather surprised her twenty minutes earlier, climbing out of bed and throwing on his jacket.

'Mind if I borrow your keys? Sorry, can't survive without the Sundays. And I think I know where the paper shop is.'

'Fine,' she smiled. 'Nor can I. They're over there on my dressing table. Turn right, right again, and the shop's about fifty yards on the left. Oh, and I'm almost out of milk, if you can get a pint of that too.'

'See you in a minute.'

She peeled the sheets up to her chin in anticipation of a good read. Lovely. Her idea of Sunday morning bliss. And when he returned, it wasn't just with the papers. Out of one of the shopping bags she kept in the kitchen he produced a bottle of champagne and two glasses.

'Thought I'd surprise you,' he smiled. 'Hid this in the fridge last night.'

Now, propped in bed with a flute of bubbles, Alice felt content.

For a few moments she didn't even glance at the headlines as she sipped the cold champagne, thinking about John and their lovemaking last night. Gentle, thoughtful, caring, companiable. Perhaps not the kind she was used to so early on in a relationship, but supremely pleasant, and perhaps it was time to relax with someone, truly relax.

'Good God' said John, rumpling the *Times*. 'Did you know that the SAS actually trained lots of Libyan soldiers down in Herefordshire?'

Alice was pleased he read out snippets, again companionable, sure that she would do the same – if there had ever been someone to read them out to.

'No, can't say I did.'

John didn't answer. He was once again immersed in the article.

She smiled at him and tore open the *Telegraph* from its irritating sealed plastic bag, chucking all the free offers and leaflets on to the floor.

'I wish they wouldn't put in all this stuff.'

Again, John didn't answer, at least for a while.

'You've got to read this. It's incredible.' He was off again.

'I will, I've got all weekend.'

He turned to her. 'No you haven't. In a couple of hours time, we're going to a great little pub – about twenty miles from here – the Firth and Firkin in Cobham, that's if you'd like to. Had a great review in the papers last weekend. Apparently, they do an amazing Sunday roast. Scored nine out of ten with AA Gill, usually pretty caustic. And they do a fantastic Gloucester Old Spot roast.'

'Lovely' smiled Alice, snuggling her knees up to her chin. 'But you better go easy on this' she added, holding up her almost finished glass. 'Or I'll do the driving. The Firth and Firkin? Never heard of it, so that would be really nice. Always enjoy going somewhere new.'

'Great,' smiled John. 'I've booked a table at 12.30 hoping you'd like the idea. And that means we can be back before three, so you can still get through all that stuff for tomorrow. I'll leave you in peace, promise.'

'Thanks' said Alice. 'Sorry, I have to kick you out then, but....'

'It's okay. There are things I need to do, too. And to be honest, I don't mind the idea of a really early night.'

Alice laughed, not surprised.

CHAPTER FOURTEEN

KENSINGTON, LONDON

Sarah Shaw gazed at the screen, guiltily and slowly scrolling down and pausing, occasionally jotting something on a pad, and as so often, ruffling her mane of long red hair, a habit she'd had since childhood when in a high level of concentration or feeling unsure of herself.

She knew she shouldn't be looking at this. There were urgent deadlines to meet, and anyway, crime reporting was her job, not crime detection, however much she would have liked a combination of the two. Nevertheless, she was fascinated. The crimes she was looking at were so unusual.

It had taken her three years even to reach this lowly position as a junior reporter on the crime desk; three years of solidly grafting away downstairs in an even more humble position in the newsroom, cobbling pieces together for others to get the by-line. But she still considered the wait worthwhile, or sincerely hoped it would be – if she could get a real break. Would there ever be one? Or at least one soon enough?

But journalism wasn't officially detective work, she reminded herself, although it was certainly getting more like that with all that unofficial hacking and press intrusion. She and her colleagues could only strictly report what was said to them, and even that was little enough. Her job was for the most part boring, as was that of most of her colleagues, not to mention the job of her friend Julie in Forensics – a far cry from *CSI* and what people saw on TV. Mostly number-crunching, much to Julie's boredom and frustration.

It was Sarah's own fault, not going into police work. But without going to university, it had been an even more impossible haul up the ladder. Why hadn't she? These days it seemed easy enough. Going to 'Uni' seemed the norm rather than the exception. What's more, if you hadn't been, people always wondered why, a question she could no longer answer herself, apart from being involved with a boy down the road at the time and not wanting to be separated. Her first real boyfriend. She had been flattered into making a stupid decision, something she could hardly tell employers.

But since early childhood she had fed herself on a constant diet of crime novels. It had all started years ago when she was a little girl, discovering her mother's battered collection of 'Famous Five' books by Enid Blyton and devouring almost all of them during one Summer holiday. It had rapidly moved on to Agatha Christie and then to more modern books, and now she had an almost embarrassing amount of them, adding to them every few weeks or so, especially by women writers: Ruth Rendell, PD James, Martina Cole, Patricia Cornwell and Minette Marrin – she had them all, and many more.

And it wasn't just fiction that fascinated her, but fact. Her shelves were also crammed with real life stories of everyone from 'Son of Sam' to Ted Bundy, Ian Brady and Fred and Rosemary West, to the point she had sometimes wondered if any guests staying would be alarmed about her obvious fascination.

Of course, an awful lot of the victims tended to be young, and there were usually sexual motives – just thinking about Fred West, his depraved wife and what they did made her shudder. Old people did get murdered of course, but usually for money like Dr. Shipman's patients.

But very few old people were ever shot.

She looked at the screen again, fascinated. Two completely

unexplained and unresolved gunshot murders of old people. So rare. And it didn't make any sense, that case of Lady Helen Mitchell, an Admiral's widow, gunned down in Cornwall in her eighties.

And an equally old fellow shot in an old people's home in Kent. An *old people's home*, for God's sake! When had *that* ever happened before? And they were both killed, or so it seemed, by a lone gunman who had disappeared without trace, and with no apparent motive. She knew the police were baffled. Understandably.

There had certainly been a flurry of comment in the local media. In fact, she had written or edited a few short reports herself. But then they had drifted out of the news.

But were they connected? Were there any more like them? Was she the only one to think there might be a real story here? This wasn't the first time she had thought about it; in fact, she had quite a flurry of notes and possible conjectures.

Maybe, just maybe, her boss might be interested. She gathered her papers up and went to his room, immediately realizing that she had chosen the wrong moment.

'Sarah, I know you love crime way beyond the call of duty. And that you're virtually obsessed by serial killers, but may I remind you that you're *not* a detective, you're a crime reporter.'

As if she needed reminding.

'You're *not* here to conjecture on the facts, merely to assemble them in a way that we can tell the public at the right time and in the right amount of space. *And to a strict deadline.* And may I point out we've got a strict deadline right now.'

Sarah bleakly thought of the huge fraud case, with implications for the Government and the Americans. Fascinating for some, but amazingly boring for her.

'The Editor wants something on the front page the day after

tomorrow. So please get out of my office and do what I asked for.'

A chastened Sarah, red-faced, almost slunk back to her desk. She resolved to go back to the boring fraud case, but to go on looking at those other strange cases in her own time, knowing it would be wiser to do that at home.

Hard enough to keep any job down these days, even if it was frustrating.

CHAPTER FIFTEEN

LINCOLNWOOD, CHICAGO

Mary-Lou Murphy was in the kitchen of her house in the Chicago suburb of Lincolnwood. She poured herself a stiff drink, feeling she needed one, although it was barely six o'clock.

How was she going to cope if Patrick's mother came to live here? She took the glass back to the sitting room and looked around her – not a big room, any more than the bedrooms upstairs, and now there would be six of them in the house if she relented to his request. And that old dog.

She pictured the future scenario: she and her husband, three strapping teenage boys – and none of them tidy despite her best efforts to get them to clear up. The detritus of teenagers was enough to cope with, let alone the bills for feeding such vast appetites. And Mary-Lou was dreading – if she had to – telling two of her sons that they'd have to share a bedroom. How could they, with all their clothes and sports gear and electronic stuff? There would be a huge scene.

'Please Mary-Lou,' Patrick had pleaded. 'At least we could try it for a while and then see how it works out.'

The funeral had been overwhelming, with hundreds of police in dress uniforms, the three volley rifle salute, the flag-covered casket, the bagpiper playing 'Amazing Grace', and both the former Mayors – from Los Angeles and Burbank.

Betty-Anne had held it together until the end of the much more private wake, as jolly and Irish as it could be in the circumstances. But then she had collapsed emotionally. She had so wanted to enjoy Chris's retirement – with him out of danger, out of the firing line. Now alone, she was unable to cope.

Mary-Lou liked Patrick's mother and had always got on well with her, in small doses. But she couldn't face the thought of another woman in the house, a matriarchal one at that, and suffering from acute depression after her husband's death. She knew the police were doing what they could after that terrible – and still unexplained murder. But the odd visit to grief counselling was obviously not working, and neither were the efforts of Betty-Anne's friends. At least three of them had phoned her recently, extremely worried, especially the English couple.

'Mary-Lou, it's Marty Williams, Betty-Anne's next-door neighbour. I think we've met a couple of times.'

'Oh, hi, Marty. How's things?'

'Look, I'm afraid she's not doing too well. You know she never liked this little town too much, and apart from us she had very few friends. She was lonely even when Chris was around, so imagine her now.'

A pause.

'I wonder if you and your husband could give her a bit of a break? I hate to ask you; I know you've got a big family – but she really needs to get away for a bit. She spends all her time wandering around the house – and crying. We try and get her out and about, but we're really worried.'

Mary-Lou had half expected this. No. More than half. Patrick's mother had called herself more than a few times, her voice miserable, and suddenly bursting into tears. And Mary-Lou had done her best, talking for what seemed ages while trying to cook supper at the same time, and then, getting nowhere, had said, 'Do you want to talk to Patrick?'

'Please.'

She had handed the phone over, feeling a guilty relief –

and then listened to Patrick talking to her for another twenty minutes. And now, this – the prospect of her mother-in-law coming to stay, and perhaps indefinitely.

But what if she put her foot down and said no? Patrick wouldn't reproach her, at least not verbally, but his eyes would. And so would his silences. He was not the sort to say 'I completely understand. If I were you, I couldn't cope with it either,' and brush the whole matter aside with a hug and a smile. No. He was feeling increasingly guilty about his mother, and feeling more and more intent on her coming to stay.

'Just a fortnight or so. Surely that wouldn't be too much?'

Mary-Lou knew it wouldn't be a fortnight, realizing that in normal circumstances Betty-Anne would never have wanted to impose, but that these were not normal, any more than her state of mind. She wouldn't want to leave in a hurry – if ever. Mary-Lou took a big slug of gin. What the hell to do?

She'd agree to three weeks, and that would be it, with a promise – which she and Patrick would fulfil – of visiting Skykomish a bit more often, and on their own, without the boys. In the same breath, Mary-Lou immediately envisioned the mess they'd come back to after even a weekend away. Nothing cleared up. The kitchen a disaster zone, the bedrooms and bathroom even worse. And her sons on the phone calmly assuring her that everything was fine.

She heard the key turning in the lock. Patrick was home.

Right, it would be three weeks, her mind was resolved. She took another slug of gin. Courage. And in that same sip, she again envisaged her mother-in-law staying on forever. Her heart sank.

As the gin slipped down her throat, she knew she'd weaken in the end, and that Betty-Anne might place an impossible strain on their marriage.

CHAPTER SIXTEEN

HONG KONG

It was as stifling in Hong Kong as it always was at that time of year. James Cameron was dropped off by his wife at the May Road stop for Hong Kong's famous Peak Tram.

'Don't exhaust yourself,' Diana advised as he got out of the car, 'it's still pretty warm and sticky.'

She knew that was a classic understatement. She thought it was unbearable. Although she loved Hong Kong and the high life it offered, she could do without the high temperatures, and worse, the humidity which made her hair so frizzy and involved endless straightening sessions in the hairdresser.

Thank God James could afford them, along with the Pilates classes in the cool, air-conditioned gym and someone to cook and look after the apartment. Life was pretty cool even in the stifling summer weather, literally with a team of helpers to 'take the heat off'. She knew she was lucky.

'Don't worry, darling. I never run that hard and I often stop to look at the view. Anyway, its always cooler up at the Peak than down here.'

But James needed to run. He was becoming a 'fat cat' in more than one sense of the phrase. Too many business lunches. Too many drinks, especially the single malt whiskies his clients liked. Not enough visits to the gym. Not enough exercise without running, even if he was certainly taking a bit of a risk in the sticky summer heat with a paunch like that.

James was already dressed in his running clothes when he

mingled with the tourists on the tram. It was always a pleasure to take this venerable form of transport that for more than a century had lifted passengers from the crowded city and port of Hong Kong up the 2,000 feet to Victoria Peak. *Thank goodness you didn't have to be carried there in a sedan chair with two fokis sweating up the hill. God knows how long that must have taken in the old days.*

As they steadily and silently ascended, more and more of the extraordinary panorama of Hong Kong could be seen from the tram's windows, especially on the right hand side. It was getting dark now and the whole place was a sea of lights.

The Peak was no longer just one hotel and a cluster of very rich men's homes. It now had a futuristic Peak Tower with a Sky Terrace looking out over the incredible view. It had even copied the famous 'I love New York' logo, with its own 'The Peak, I love you' logo with the tram going through a red heart. It rather suited the modern, tacky tourist-trap shopping mall and cafés. No doubt some of the Peak's seven million visitors a year were wearing the T-shirts back home even at this moment.

James Cameron alighted, freed himself from the crowd and jogged off down the Peak Trail, dimly lit by occasional lamps and the orange glow of the lights of the city. He was fifty-seven years old, and with his comfortable lifestyle no longer slim, which is why he indulged in this ritual run every Wednesday evening. He really loved Hong Kong. He earned a great deal of money and paid very little tax. He and Diana were provided with two servants, an *amah* who cooked and cleaned, and a driver – the kind of help they could never have possibly afforded back in London.

Their Mid Level apartment on Tregunter Path was also paid for by the bank. It was not huge, but certainly big enough for the cousins to visit every year. They loved coming out, what with the fashion shops in Central, the shopping in Stanley Market or the fake fashions in the Mong Kok night market which they reached by the Star ferries across to Kowloon. Even the ferries were fun, with their great view of the Hong Kong skyline.

Although James was too blasé these days to really enjoy it, his whole family usually demanded to go off to Aberdeen, on the other side of the island, to eat at the amazing huge floating restaurant called 'Jumbo' with its hundreds of seats and its satellite boats delivering a steady stream of tourists. And one day his daughters would enjoy the nightspots favoured by the 'Gweilos' or foreigners in Lan Kwai Fong – far safer than the clubs in London.

His own life was pretty good. If nobody else was using them, he could commandeer one of the bank's two junks with their own crews, and set off for the weekend to entertain 'clients'. After all, everyone in Hong Kong was a potential client. He also enjoyed a flutter on the racing – Happy Valley on a Wednesday night or Sha Tin in the New Territories on a Saturday.

It had been a few years now since he'd been called in by his London boss. 'You've done very well in Hammersmith, James. Very steady, no risks. But I think you're destined for better things, broader horizons. The parent company has been watching you. How would you like to be posted to Hong Kong?'

He and Diana had argued about it a bit. There were all their friends in London and the children, of course. But what with the salary and perks, let alone the career prospects, it was really a no-brainer in the end. Now, he was a Regional Manager of the bank and it took him to other interesting and vibrant centres like Singapore, and of course, the Chinese mainland, especially new and shiny Shanghai.

Of course, there were the old-timers in the Hong Kong

Club who would label people like James as 'FILTH' – 'Failed In London, Try Hong Kong.' But what did he care? Already a member of the Bankers' Club in Kowloon, he had just been elected to David Tang's China Club, which was certainly the future, not the past.

He slowed down, puffing, and paused at one of the viewing points to stare down in the city. From that height, it was the view you'd normally only have from an aircraft, except that he could now hear, above the noise of the insects in the jungle behind him, the roar of the traffic down below and of the air-conditioning plants on the top of every skyscraper.

He could even pick out his own bank headquarters down in Central. There, he had a big office with thick carpets, expensive paintings on the walls and magnificent vistas of the waterfront, teeming with every type of ship and boat. *God, it was so much better than that drab little cramped office in the Hammersmith branch, where little people came in for little loans, which I usually had to turn down.*

Everything here was bigger and richer. Even the boats at the Royal Hong Kong Yacht Club had outrageous names like 'Zillionaire', 'Second Fortune' and 'Hedge Fund'. Of course, for the Chinese, it reinforced the notion of good luck – but it was not the kind of boastful and ostentatious thing you would dare to do in England.

Hong Kong hadn't changed much since Chris Patten had handed the place over to the Chinese. They knew a 'Golden Goose' when they saw one. And anyway, China itself was really capitalist now, stuffed with millionaires. His client and friend in charge of the Rolls-Royce showroom had said that business was positively booming. Hong Kong itself already had more of those cars per head than anywhere else on earth.

And now the plutocrats of mainland China felt that they

had to catch up – Rolls-Royce had just moved their Shanghai showroom from the Bund to even smarter premises in Xintiandi.

James suddenly shivered.

He'd become chilled standing there, and he stirred from his satisfied reverie. He glanced at his watch and set off down the gentle slope. There were not many people now, one or two walkers and the occasional jogger like him. He thought that he'd better speed up. Diana was waiting for him at the other end.

* * *

Diana was playing the radio in the car. Pleasantly tired from her Pilates class, she had been engrossed in *The Archers'*, the ex-pats' favourite programme. She suddenly realised that James was late – in fact more than half an hour late.

She dialled his mobile.

No reply.

Very odd, he always left it on. Her face betrayed a frown of worry.

* * *

After an hour, Diana Cameron called the apartment, and with a note of real anxiety in her voice, asked the *amah* if her husband had by any chance turned up.

'No missy. Mister Cameron no at home.'

'Has he called?'

'No missy, no call.'

Immediately alarmed, she tapped in the number for the police.

After a frustratingly stilted conversation in pidgin English, she managed to convince the police headquarters that this was serious, and it took only a few minutes for a police car to draw alongside her BMW. A Sergeant got out.

'What's the problem, Madam?'

'Oh, thank goodness. Well, my husband goes running on the Peak Trail every Wednesday. He starts at the Tram and then ends up here where I always pick him up. But he's late, *really* late.'

She glanced at her watch. 'It's now over two hours after he should have been here.'

The Sergeant started writing in a notebook.

'What's his name?'

'James Cameron.'

'How old?'

'Fifty-seven.'

'In good health?'

'Very. He does this run and goes to the gym in Central three times a week.' She knew she was exaggerating his healthiness.

The Sergeant nodded and went to his car and talked rapidly in Cantonese to his station. After a few minutes he returned.

'We're sending some people right along the Trail. They'll take a doctor in case he's ill, collapsed or something.'

Diana flinched, and leant against her car. She suddenly began to fear the worst.

'What shall I do?' she stammered.

'I think it's best you go home. We can contact you there.'

He wrote down her address and landline number and both her mobile number and her husband's.

She drove home, her heart pounding. Suddenly the wonderful life they had in Hong Kong seemed threatened. Like someone drowning, all the happy years flashed in front of her.

She burst into tears.

* * *

It was only in daylight that they managed to find James.

One of the police dogs went about thirty feet off the Trail and started barking. A Nike trainer was sticking out of the thick green undergrowth, still on James's foot.

It was getting quite hot and humid when Detective Sergeant 'Jimmy' Wong arrived on the scene, now cordoned off with police ribbon. He was nearly fifty, grey-haired and rather overweight. Trained by the British, he had even been sent over to England to study at Hendon. But he knew that this experience and training were now beginning to count against him in the eyes of the new people being sent down from Beijing. Some form of early retirement was probably in the offing.

One glance at the people round the body told him that something more serious than a heart attack was being discussed.

'What's up, Doc?'

Over the years, Jimmy's 'Bugs Bunny' cartoon humour had actually worn a bit thin with the forensic team.

'Looks like murder, Jimmy. One bullet hole in the thorax. Quite small calibre. No exit wound, so it's still in there. We won't know more until they've extracted it.'

Jimmy reviewed the scanty evidence carefully, made some decisions and issued instructions. Suddenly, they all looked up.

Another car was slowly coming down the Trail. Jimmy's heart sank. He knew who it was, and sure enough Detective Inspector Chi Wang Ho got out. He was young, slim, smartly dressed, clever – and Jimmy thought – pretty obnoxious. He was typical of a 'new broom', likely to have little respect for any kind of the Old Guard in the Hong Kong police, and also bound to be suspicious of any of their British traditions.

In one way, Wong thought, he was right to feel that the new Chinese-led force was more professional. After all, there had been an awful lot of over-promotion in the old days, with lowly Constables out from Britain being made up to Inspectors as soon as they arrived. But that didn't apply to him, and Wong was resentful.

'What do we know, Wong?' the Inspector asked brusquely, with no attempt at greeting or pleasantry.

'Not very much,' replied Jimmy. 'He seemed to be running along the Peak Trail. We think he was killed on the Trail and dragged off across the grass and left in the bushes, not even hidden very carefully. Forensics tell us that the time of death was sometime between eight and midnight. He had no wallet, but did have an identity card.

He's a banker, resident here, with an apartment on Mid Levels. Married with two kids. It was his wife who first called us. I've sent two people down to break the news. He also had a mobile on him, with several calls unanswered, all from his wife. That narrows down the probable time of death, to say forty-five minutes before her first call when she became worried. So it looks like just before nine o'clock.

As to how he was killed, he was shot with some small-calibre weapon – one shot, in the chest. There's no exit wound, so when we get the body back to the lab, we should get some ballistics clues.'

The Detective Inspector nodded in silence. The mutual dislike and lack of respect between the two policemen was palpable.

'Alright, go on searching the area, but finish up here quickly before the tourists arrive. Call me when you've something from ballistics and we'll meet in my office.'

* * *

In the days before the Hong Kong's handover to the Chinese, the Detective Inspector's office used to have a big Union Jack and a nice picture of the Queen.

DI Jack Higgins had been a great guy to work for. He spoke Cantonese fluently and had been in Hong Kong since the fifties. His staff revered him.

Now the office was coldly bare except for a Chinese Republic flag behind Chi's desk.

When Jimmy entered, his new boss was again abrupt to the point of rudeness.

'What do we have now?'

'Well sir, the bullet was a bit strange.'

'What do you mean, strange?'

'Quite small, 6.35mm, fairly unusual now. And not heavy. Designed to be fired from a very light pistol. Also called the point two five ACP when John Browning designed it over a century ago. Lots of people produced vest-pocket or baby pistols for it – Mauser, Webley, Browning, Colt, Beretta – but they all enlarged them to larger calibres decades ago – for better hitting power.

You may even remember in one of the James Bond films that he was forbidden to use his little Beretta.'

Chi plainly did not remember any such piece of movie trivia, so Jimmy quickly continued.

'Walther produced a few after the war, but very rare. Anyway, there's no match with any other bullet or gun on our records – either here or on the mainland.'

Chi absorbed this news without comment, and changed the subject. 'What about the victim? Do we know anything more?'

'Yes. He's actually quite important. Regional Manager for the bank, covering most of Asia, so it's going to cause quite a stir among the ex-pat community, and of course, the English-language press. *The South China Morning Post* and *The Standard* are already pestering us.'

'Who cares what *they* think?' sneered Chi. As far as he was concerned, the leftover foreign financial community was nothing but a necessary evil – but definitely an evil.

'Was it robbery?'

'We don't think so, Sir. His wife confirmed that he always left his wallet behind and only took his identity card and a few dollars for emergencies. I suppose a robber or mugger could have shot him in disappointment, but it seems unlikely.'

'Drugs? Could he have been meeting a dealer and then quarrelled?'

'Seemed a bit middle-aged and respectable for that, but I suppose we can't rule it out. We'll look into it.'

'What about sex? Could he have been screwing somebody's wife or something?'

'Possibly. But we have no evidence that he was anything other than a respectable, hardworking, if rather boring, banker.'

'What about some kind of quarrel or even a hit? Chinese gangsters from here or the mainland, something involved with loans or financing?'

'We've talked to his superiors and his own staff. He's mostly involved in administration now. Opening new branches round the region, hiring staff, directing policy. Not much scope for dirty business with locals.'

Jimmy paused, and then tentatively made a suggestion.

'Perhaps it goes back further. Maybe we should check out his background in England in case there's anything back there.'

The young Detective Inspector stared at Jimmy Wong with astonishment and scarcely disguised contempt.

'Don't be ridiculous! I don't know the English very well, and I don't like them much. But I *do* know that they don't come halfway across the world to attack people.

Absolutely *don't* pursue that line of enquiry. Understand?'

He turned dismissively to his computer screen.

'Unless I hear anything more useful, I'm going to put this down to a failed attempted robbery and move on. Write up a report to that effect.'

Jimmy Wong nodded and said nothing. He wasn't too keen to retire just yet.

But he thought he might just make a call to London anyway.

* * *

Cameron, he thought, had been older, plumper and going a little bald.

But he still had that same self-satisfied banker's look that had been so infuriating back in Hammersmith.

The big airliner banked up over Macao, heading north-west towards the sunset. A pretty Malaysian flight attendant offered him a glass of champagne.

Accepting one, he smiled, closed up his leather briefcase with its papers and neatly-arranged pens and looked out of the window.

CHAPTER SEVENTEEN

PARK LANE, LONDON

Still recovering from the trauma of her godmother's death, Alice was not really in the mood to attend charity events, and for that matter, just didn't feel she had the cash to keep up even though she earned perfectly well.

The last one she had been to was at The Savoy, and she had watched open-mouthed as tables of City types had bid ridiculous amounts to score off their financial rivals a few feet away. One drunken chap from Lehman Brothers had outbid Goldman Sachs to pay a ridiculous £8,500 for David Niven's old camp bed. *If they behave that recklessly,* she thought, *Lehmans will go bust one day. And it will serve them right.* All in all, it really wasn't her scene.

But she had been rung up by her brother Bryan, a Major in The Parachute Regiment who had had enough of his comrades being blown up or shot by the Taliban to want to do his best for the 'Help for Heroes' charity. She had tried to get John Tibbs to take her and cushion the strain of the evening, but he was away trying to land a client from Germany. She would have to go alone.

So she had gone to the hairdresser, chosen one of the few luxuries in her wardrobe, a black Chanel number, and worn her mother's matching earrings and necklace. She looked pretty good she thought, as she checked in the mirror.

The taxi dropped her in Park Lane, at the ballroom entrance of the Grosvenor House. She found herself reluctantly entering the hotel for what would surely be a hellish evening. In the entrance hall there was a major display about the 'Help for Heroes' charity, with big photographic panels of battle scenes in Iraq and Afghanistan and several proud veterans manoeuvring themselves around in wheelchairs.

The ballroom was vast, with dozens of tables and a crowd of guests in dinner jackets, colourful mess dress and ball gowns. Alice could not spot Bryan yet, so she found her name on one of the table plans and made her way to table 36.

Her brother suddenly appeared. Like many others in the room, he had a cluster of miniature medals and decorations on his dinner-jacket, one of which Alice proudly recognised as the Military Cross. She kissed Bryan, found her place card and shook hands with her fellow guests before sitting down. They then all stood up while the Guests of Honour, Prince Harry, together with the familiar tall figure of Jeremy Clarkson and General Dannatt, filed to the top table.

When she sat down again, Alice remembered the poem she had read, by a woman who had plainly suffered the grisly fate of charity parties once too often.

'The man on my right is a banker,
The chap on my left is in law.
We've been at our table five minutes –
The evening's already a bore.'

The man on her right did indeed turn out to be a banker; plump, self-satisfied and, within a couple of sentences, plainly a potential bore.

However, 'the chap on her left' was very different. He was on his own, about forty, tall, in a well-fitting dinner jacket over his slim frame and with deep blue eyes and brooding, rather sardonic good looks, not unlike Daniel Craig's Bond she thought approvingly. His name was David Hammond and he apparently ran an international security company that he did not discuss at length, preferring to question Alice closely about her line of work.

He seemed to have a slight accent, difficult to define. Scottish? Irish? She was not sure. He seemed to be fiercely intelligent, knowledgeable, amusing and with a taste for things from the past, and above all, with a powerful physical aura. Largely ignoring their fellow guests, they danced to a swing band and he seemed to know rather more about Glenn Miller, Benny Goodman and Artie Shaw than his age would normally warrant.

The evening that she had so dreaded went surprisingly quickly, the speeches were short and in spite of the auction, she had to admit she had had a good time, and said so.

'You know, I nearly didn't come tonight. I had rather shattering news recently. Someone I really adored suddenly died, and I have to admit, I'm not normally mad about this kind of thing. But I'm glad I made it. It's been really good fun.'

David smiled at her, 'I'm glad you did. Too. And I'm sorry about your friend.' Alice decided not to correct him.

People were beginning to drift away and it seemed a good time to go.

'I have my car waiting here. Would you like a lift?'

A slight hesitation.

'Well, yes, that would be kind. But I live in Putney. Is that out of your way?'

'No, that's fine. I go west anyway.'

She paused to tell her brother that she wouldn't need a ride home, to which he responded with a 'thumbs up' and a rather suggestive wink. David did not come over to meet him. They walked through the main hotel past the lobby and emerged into a rain-swept entrance area. There, among some very smart cars indeed, she was surprised to see a dark green, gleaming old Bentley, plainly lovingly restored. David ushered her into its luxurious comfort.

For twenty minutes they drove in silence, with David engrossed by messages through an earphone on his Blackberry, but as they crossed Putney Bridge, he switched it off.

'Forgive me for that. There's always something going on. Now, Alice, do you have a business card?'

'Why? Do you have psychological problems?'

Suddenly she felt she sounded a bit pathetic.

'No. I'd like to ask you out.'

Alice hesitated for a moment, thinking about John. But it wasn't as if she lived with him, or that they'd made any commitments. She'd only had a few dates.

And this man was incredible, with an extraordinary aura. He slipped her card into his top pocket without looking at it.

'I'll call you in about ten days. I have to travel a lot at the moment.'

CHAPTER EIGHTEEN

HONG KONG INTERNATIONAL AIRPORT

Diana Cameron sat with her two daughters either side of her, staring morosely out of the window in the calm of the British Airways Executive Lounge in Hong Kong's vast and crowded new airport.

Probably the last time I'll be here, she thought.

Her youngest daughter looked miserable. Normally the first to plead for a Coke and crisps as soon as she spotted them on display, she now sat silently, slumped in her seat. Diana patted her lap. 'Would you like anything?' she asked, pointing at the bar opposite. The girl shook her head.

To distract herself, Diana picked up a magazine and flicked through it for a few moments, suddenly coming across an advertisement showing a father with an arm around two children, something for an insurance company. She closed the magazine and replaced it on the side table. Everywhere, so many reminders.

When would it ever end? *Did* it ever end?

At least nobody had used that terrible cliché about time being a great healer.

She had to admit that her friends had been wonderful; she would miss them back in England, and it was highly unlikely she would see most of them again. And she also had to admit that the bank had been nice. They had let her stay on in the apartment, use their driver and keep on the *amah*. But of course they couldn't do that forever. Anyway, there was no point living in Hong Kong any more. It was no longer a way of life for her, now more of a foreign, threatening place.

And all because of some wretched thief or drug user up on the Peak. Diana knew that was what the police thought, but she also knew they were no nearer to finding a real clue – and perhaps never would. It could take years, if ever, to bring whoever did it to justice.

Diana thought of life in England as she checked the departures board. With the insurance and bank pension, she'd manage well enough; in fact, she would be reasonably well off. But that would never compensate for a dead husband and three wrecked lives.

She smiled encouragingly at her two daughters. 'Not long now.' Maybe they would recover – maybe the young do, she thought to herself. But it would be hard for all of them to start again. New home. New friends. New schools. A massive upheaval.

Diana looked at her older daughter, now studying the end of a long strand of her auburn hair and twisting it around her finger to the scalp – and pulling. Diana knew what it was; *trichotomania*, the sudden compulsion to pull out hair in times of stress, even to a state of baldness. She had even found clumps of hair on Sophie's pillow in the morning, brushing it up with considerable distress and wondering about how to talk about the problem.

It was easy enough to guess the reason: not only James' death, but the fact that Sophie had just gone to university in Hong Kong and had her first boyfriend – an Australian called Justin – and had no doubt had sex for the first time. Suddenly she was being uprooted from everything she loved, and uprooting her hair was the evidence of her distress. Everything was being uprooted, Diana thought bleakly. Their lives, their house, their friends, their futures. She thought – yet again – of telling her daughter to stop twizzling and twisting her hair, but decided against it. The last time she had tried had been awful. 'Fuck off!' Sophie had retorted. She had never before sworn at her like that.

Diana looked around her. Even the airport was a painfully difficult environment to cope with. Couples enjoying a last glass of champagne. Happy excited families, obviously off on holiday. Older, probably retired couples returning to the U.K. And the sight of all those policemen patrolling the concourse.

At last, the British Airways flight to London was called. 'Is that ours?' asked Ella, the youngest, the first time she'd spoken since arriving in the lounge.

'Yup' said her mother. 'But there's no need to go just yet. Boarding will take ages. In fact, there's still time for a Coke if you want one.'

'It's okay', said Ella, with a blank expression, pulling her jacket collar around her face as if hiding from the world. It was going to be a long, long journey, thought Diana, as she looked at her daughter. And not just the journey back to the UK.

She decided to have a big drink on the plane.

CHAPTER NINETEEN

NEW SCOTLAND YARD, LONDON

Robin Marshal had scarcely been at his desk five minutes when the phone rang.

'Hello, Robin. You may not remember me. Jimmy Wong from Hong Kong?'

'Sure I do. I remember you from the course. It must be years now. How's things?'

'Okay, sort of. There are a lot of changes here, as you can imagine. Not all of them for the better.

In fact, I'm calling you from home, as it's a bit political at work. I'd like to ask a favour. We've just had a British guy, a banker, murdered, jogging in the evening up on the Peak.

The others here think it's just an attempted robbery, but I'm not so sure. Apart from anything else, he wasn't robbed of anything.

So I figure that it could just be something to do with his past in England.'

'Could be, I suppose. What would you like me to do?'

'I'll email you the details of his past employment which I got from his bank here. Try to check if there's anything that would point to any kind of trouble that could have caught up with him. Any grudges, rows, money owed, gambling, women problems. You know the kind of thing.

It's a long shot, I know. But if you do find anything, please email back to my private email address.'

'Sure. I'll put someone on to it. How was he killed, by the way?'

'Well, that's a bit curious too. Single shot at very close range with some kind of little gun. Strange, old-fashioned calibre, too. Very light, 6.35 millimetre, or point two five. They used them decades ago in what were called baby guns. We've got no record of anything like it being used recently out here.'

After a few more minutes talking about wives and families, Jimmy rang off.

Robin sat back.

After a moment, he called in Detective Sergeant Joe Bain and briefed him about the call from Hong Kong.

Joe Bain looked down at the email in his hand.

'That's curious. Kent have just asked us to come as observers to a meeting next week at Bramshill. They and Devon and Cornwall both have strange cases of old people being killed with old weapons. Sounds as if we ought to go.'

CHAPTER TWENTY

BRAMPTON, ENGLAND

It was early evening, getting dark and beginning to rain.

Josef Gierek pulled the big green DAF articulated truck into a BP service station near Brampton. Although he was quite close to the Bedford exit and the distribution depot, he was ahead of time and now desperate for a cigarette. He knew Agnieszska hated him smoking, always wrinkling her nose when he lit up and waving her hand across her face when he exhaled the first puff.

He would have to give up when they were married. With all their money going to the wedding there would be little choice, and it wouldn't be fair to the kids they both wanted.

As he hauled himself back up into the cab, the rain began to tip down. He eased the truck out on to the crowded A1 and shifted up through the gearbox to the eighth gear of the twelve he could use. There was no point changing up further, because he was now staring through the windscreen into a blinding spray that even the big wipers were having real trouble clearing.

'*Holera! Okropna pogoda,*' he cursed the weather.

Josef was one of several Poles recruited recently by the company, and he thoroughly enjoyed the job. It was his last run for a month, because tomorrow he was flying back from Luton to Krakow, and next week he was going to marry his sweetheart.

She called him every night with breathless accounts of the arrangements and the presents. Goodness knows what her parents' phone bill would be. He'd have to work bloody hard to make it up to them.

* * *

Witnesses later testified to a strange and tragic sequence of events. An old blue or black Volvo estate in the middle lane overtook a line of cars, moving slowly because of the poor visibility. One driver later remarked that he was surprised that the Volvo's back window was wide open in that terrible weather. The estate came up behind the DAF truck and pulled out, inexplicably and rather dangerously, into the fast lane, and then slowed down to the speed of the truck. There the Volvo stayed for several seconds before accelerating fast into the murk.

Then, to the consternation of the following drivers, the truck slowly began to drift across the carriageway into the middle lane, and then the fast lane, until it hit the central Armco barrier, reared up, collapsed on to its side and slid some 500 feet down the road in a shower of sparks and smoke.

By some miracle, sliding all over the road, none of the following vehicles hit the truck, although some did hit each other. The wreckage blocked the whole of the southbound A1. Headlights stretched back for miles, reflecting the steadily falling rain, and it took some time for the first police accident team to weave its way through the confused shambles.

They reached the cab, half propped up on the Armco, with one headlight still shining into the sky and one of the wipers still scraping erratically across the shattered glass of the windscreen. By torchlight, they discovered something very strange indeed. Josef was dead in his cab and his cause of death appeared obvious. There was a line of bullet holes marching along the cab and its door. They counted over twenty of them.

Five of the bullets were found in Josef's body.

* * *

It was raining steadily at Bernie Laxton's scrap metal recycling yard. What with the foul weather and the dark, Bernie had sent his two assistants home early and was about to lock up and go home himself.

Suddenly he was surprised to see headlights coming up the narrow access road. A dark Volvo estate splashed through the muddy entrance and pulled up outside the battered old Portacabin that served as his office. Grumbling to himself, Bernie pulled on his yellow waterproof jacket and old hard hat and went out into the rain.

The driver's window went down. Bernie could not make out the man's features too well.

'I'd like you to crush this car for scrap.'

'Sure, I'll have to work out how much to give you.'

There was a pause.

'No need. I'll pay *you* – two hundred quid.' Bernie was a bit astonished. Failed MOT vehicles usually involved him paying out about £80, not the other way round.

'But I need it done now.'

The man reached inside his jacket, and Bernie could see the notes. So there was not going to be any extra money from stripping the car of valuable Volvo spare parts, the normal extra profit that made the scrap business worthwhile. But maybe he could do that when the man had gone.

'Okay, then.'

'And I'd like to watch you do it.'

Suddenly the man was out of the car; tall and looking down at Bernie. At least he seemed to be looking at Bernie, because rather incongruously he was wearing dark glasses under his hat. Wordlessly he handed over a wad of cash, which Bernie stuffed into an inside pocket.

Bernie shrugged. 'Okay, you drive it over there and I'll work

the crane.' This was normally a two-man job. He climbed up
into the crane and fired up its diesel engine

Moments later, a huge magnet clamped itself onto the
Volvo's roof and the car was lifted, swung over the bed of the
yellow crushing machine and dropped with a crash of metal and
breaking glass. Bernie climbed down, went over to a control
panel and started up the machine. He pushed a lever.

Hydraulic rams slowly began to close up the long jaws of
the huge machine. Then there was a groaning of twisting metal,
the sound of breaking glass and the popping as the tyres burst.
First from the sides and then from one end, the rams inexorably
and steadily squashed the vehicle.

In less than a minute, it was a cube little more than a metre
square. Nothing, except a bit of wheel, was recognizable.

The hydraulic rams stopped and retreated and the machine
opened itself up like some huge yellow flower. Bernie glanced
at the man who was still watching in the rain and climbed back
into the cab of the crane, clamped the magnet on to the block
of metal, hauled it into the air and dumped it on to a pile of
similar cubes.

He switched off, got down and walked back. The stranger
was nowhere to be seen. Perhaps he'd gone into the cabin to
keep warm and dry? No, there was nobody in there.

Bernie was used to suspicious characters and to the disposal
of 'hot cars' that needed to disappear, so he didn't trouble
himself further on speculation. Two hundred quid was two
hundred quid.

And even days later when the media talked about the police
looking for a Volvo involved in the dreadful A1 crash, Bernie
was not going to talk about it. He had his own good and selfish
reasons. With prices sky-high, he was deeply involved in the
illegal trade of stolen metal and especially cable theft. It had

become a real hot potato recently, with public anger mounting about power cuts, computers crashing and, of course, the deadly danger to trains caused by signals being disabled.

So, there was no way that Bernie Laxton wanted the police sniffing around anywhere near his scrap yard.

CHAPTER TWENTY- ONE

BEDFORD, ENGLAND

It was nearly midnight, and three men and two women sat in a conference room at Bedford's police HQ, facing a crime situation that was completely unfamiliar and baffling.

Of one thing they were certain. This was not just a murder, but an assassination. But why would anyone want to hunt down a young Polish driver and kill him in such a way? And how was it done?

The usual evidence from CCTV cameras was very skimpy. There were only two cameras on that stretch of road and one was unaccountably not working. In the pouring rain, the other camera had only picked out the shape of the Volvo, and when the pictures were enhanced, the number plate seemed deliberately covered, indicating a knowledge that CCTV footage could be a primary source of evidence.

Then, the only real witnesses.

Two car drivers had noticed the dark Volvo and its strange behaviour. Both were certain that it had only one occupant. Yet the truck's cab had been riddled by an automatic weapon. No cartridge cases or other evidence of the firing had been found in the laborious search in the darkness of the wet road surface that had screwed up the traffic on one of Britain's busiest road for hours.

And forensics had quickly reported that there was also something odd about the bullets found in the body and in the cab. They were not 9 mm, 5.56 mm or 7.62 mm, or any other likely modern calibre. They were old .303 inch like the ones fired from British rifles in World War II.

'I think it might be a Bren,' suddenly muttered Sergeant Jimmy Jones, easily the oldest on the detective team. Grey-haired, he was coming up for retirement.

'What the hell is a Bren?' asked DI Harry Weems. Quite young, he had been one of the new breed of graduate colleagues.

'Britain's light machine-gun for years. Built by the Czechs at Brno and the Brits at Enfield – hence BREN. I used to fire them, you know, *'barrel-locking-nut-retainer-plunger-pin'*, longest word in the army.'

He paused, fondly remembering the Southern Command Cup he'd won at Bisley. His fellow detectives shifted uneasily, fearing more of his old reminiscences coming on.

'Wait. The point is, it used the same ammo as the old rifles, point three-o-three, and it fired a magazine which held 30 rounds. How many holes did we count?'

'Twenty-three.'

'Well, assume they missed with a few both behind and in front of the cab, that would do it. At 600 rounds a minute, as I recall, that would be a three second burst – roughly the time the witnesses saw the Volvo hang around in the fast lane. A Bren's quite bulky, though. The witnesses would have seen the second chap firing it. All they saw was the driver.'

There was silence. But Jimmy was still thinking.

'But suppose that's all there was. Just the driver. Could he have somehow fixed or bolted the gun in the back seat, slanting upwards? Or pulled the trigger with a cord or something?'

Harry suddenly leaned forward. 'German night fighters did that, late in the war.' He was known on the force as a bit of a plane nut.

'They used to sneak up in the dark right up close and invisible under our Lancasters, fly nice and steady and then let go with their guns pointing up at an angle. Our boys never knew what hit 'em. Lost hundreds of bombers. Germans called it *Schrage Musik,* 'jazz music', or something.'

Detective Sergeant Julie Southgate, while easily bored by too much World War II stuff, began to see some logic in all this.

'It all sounds pretty far-fetched, but that might just explain why only one guy was seen. No noise, no smoke. And why he had to pull out into the fast lane – maybe to get the angle just right.'

After a moment's silence, Harry got to his feet. 'We'll meet back in the morning, say seven. Julie and I will go and see the guy who owns the truck.'

* * *

Mick Foley's green trucks were a familiar enough sight on the A1. He had built up the company steadily from small beginnings in the sixties and now had dozens of them with his own Bedford depot. Mick was horrified enough to hear on the phone the sad news about his truck and his dead driver.

But he was really shocked when the detectives came to see him and explained that this was no traffic accident but some kind of murder. However, his visitors did not reveal the true nature of what they had found, confining themselves to 'someone seemed to have shot at your driver from another car.' Mick mentally pictured a pistol pointing out of a car window. Did Josef have enemies? Quarrels with people? Trouble at home? Was this something to do with Eastern European gangs? It all looked pretty unlikely. Josef was popular and likeable.

The police quite quickly turned to Mick himself. Did *he* have enemies? Rivals? Mick couldn't think of any.

'We have competitors, of course, but I hardly feel that Eddie

Stobart or Norbert Dentressangle or Willi Betz or any of the others would do such a thing.'

'Have you had any drivers leave under a cloud? Disgruntled employees?' Julie asked.

'Well, over the years, there could be quite a few of those. I've had to fire a lot of people, I suppose. It's not just bad driving or accidents. Sometimes it's crime or robbery. I've lost whole loads to criminals. Once the driver himself was the 'inside man', pretending to be the victim, tied up and all.' He paused, thinking.

'I've also had to get rid of drivers who've just disappeared in the middle of a delivery. They sometimes fancy some waitress in a caff and go off to bed with her, turning off the mobile. I'm left with customers screaming for their delivery and I've no idea where my truck and driver are, which seems to the customer a pretty rotten excuse.'

'Would you be able to give us a list of all of them who've left under a cloud or in dispute?' Harry Weems asked.

Mick knew that with his less than rudimentary computing skills he would have to wait for his secretary Marjorie to find the list.

'Sure. It'll take time, but we mark them on the list so we'll never hire them again. Other operators also call us to see if they're about to take on a dud. How far do you want to go back?'

'Oh, I suppose five, no ten years. That should be far enough back.'

The police added that they were not ruling out terrorism and that Mick should keep as quiet as possible about the incident. When they had gone, Mick Foley sat slumped with depression. He knew the police were going to have to ask the Polish Embassy to organise breaking the terrible news to

Josef's parents and fiancée. God, weren't they getting married next week? He'd also have to tell Josef's Polish mates clustered outside who had realised he had not clocked in and had seen the police car outside his office.

Much more serious and really frightening was that the police plainly seemed to think someone from Mick's past might kill one of his drivers just to get at him.

* * *

'Dad, we've got to change things, quite a lot of things. And fast.'

Billy Foley suddenly felt sorry for his father. He looked ten years older since that ghastly incident only days ago when that young Polish driver had been shot on the motorway. He remembered that Mick was coming up to seventy-five. He would have to approach this with extraordinary tenderness and tact. His father had spent over forty years building up the company, now a revered and almost loved name as Foley's giant trucks thundered up and down the motorways of Europe with their famous slogan, advertising their excellent delivery performance as 'SAFE AND SOUND'. Everyone knew that the company's founder had come up from humble beginnings and was an international advertisement that anyone could do it if they had the guts, even if they didn't have the education.

'What things?' Mick's voice was distant.

'Look at security for a start – building security, staff security, your security. Mine, for that matter.' Billy suddenly thought of his wife at home, now six months pregnant again after three miscarriages.

'Look, something went seriously wrong.' he continued. 'It was probably someone who knew you, someone who had a grudge, someone who'd worked here. The police don't know, at least, not yet. And if you don't think of yourself, at least think of Mum.'

His father said nothing.

'And there's another thing. I'm afraid we'll have to change the publicity as well. We can't have trucks all over the place driving around with the slogan 'SAFE AND SOUND'. It makes a mockery of us. It was bad enough having the *Daily Mirror* with that headline the other day, what was it, 'M-WAY HORROR FOR THE SAFE AND SOUND COMPANY'. Now, every time people see that slogan they'll remember we're anything but safe and sound, at least, when it comes to our staff. And that would be a disaster for our recruitment.'

Still his father said nothing.

Billy persevered; he had to. The press were all over them, and he was having to answer their questions.

'Look Dad, I repeat. We're going to have to change everything. The trucks' livery, the advertising, our literature, uniforms, the stationery, the annual report, signage at the depot, invoices, letterheads – the lot.'

'And what will *that* cost?' His father had at last spoken.

'I'm not sure.'

'Millions.' His father laughed bitterly.

'More like thousands, but it'll have to be done.'

Billy knew it could take decades to build up a company's name and reputation, and then only days to undo it all with a PR disaster like this. And even a company as successful and as well-loved as Foley's could be brought to its knees almost overnight if it didn't address a crisis like this instantly, however much money it took. He knew that only too well from his degree at Harvard Business School studying cases of disaster strategy: Ratners, Union Carbide, BP, British Airways, Exxon, so many of them had gone through it.

'I'm not sure I'm up to it', his father muttered. He looked exhausted, burned out.

Billy looked at him, remembering the French truckers' union strike about 20 years ago. That had taken its toll on his father, with his drivers becoming desperate, stuck for days out on the autoroutes without food or water in the boiling heat, and with perishable food rotting in their trailers when the refrigeration fuel ran out. And this would be far worse.

'But *I'm* up to it. And something has to be done, and right now. Look Dad, the accident blocked out the whole of the A1 for hours. And it killed a man who was only in his twenties, and about to get married. At least we should put out a public statement. It's not enough to send flowers to his fiancée in Poland.'

'And what do you propose to say? That the Safe and Sound company regrets that it isn't?'

'I don't know. I'll ask the PR company to think of something that works.'

'They'll probably come up with some crappy line about people's possessions still being safe and sound, even if our drivers are blown to pieces.'

'I don't think so, Dad.' He paused.

'Anyway, we have to do *something*. If we don't, we're finished.'

CHAPTER TWENTY-TWO

BRAMSHILL, HAMPSHIRE

Robin Marshal had always liked egg mayonnaise sandwiches, despite what his wife had told him about cholesterol. Now Joe Bain was driving and Robin was free to eat one without criticism, lost in thought.

It was good not to have Pam nagging him and to see Bramshill again. The command courses he'd attended there had been really interesting and he had made friends with several colleagues round the country. But now they were going there for a very different reason. He had been called by one of those friends, DI Brian Young from Kent, who had asked him to come as an observer to a meeting at Bramshill together with Pat Johnson, whom he didn't know, from Devon and Cornwall.

They were both investigating murders with curious similarities involving elderly and respectable people being killed quite expertly and without any apparent motive, and both had sent out detailed reports in advance. Robin was becoming convinced that some information he had was also relevant.

Bramshill House was a magnificent Jacobean mansion in Hampshire, once the residence of the nobility varying from Lord Brocket to King Michael of Romania, and now Britain's Police Staff College. They met in a small conference room and introduced themselves – Marshal and Joe Bain from the Met, Brian Young from Kent and Pat Johnson from Devon and Cornwall.

Brian Young started by describing the killing of the victim in the noisy film show at the old people's home. 'An old pensioner virtually executed in public.'

'Can I ask you about the weapon?' Robin intervened. 'The calibre was small, wasn't it, point two five?'

'Yes. Fired at contact range.'

'Did you get anything from the residue?'

'Nothing special.'

Pat Johnson made some notes.

Brian Young continued. 'He did something strange and very clever too. He had a sort of bag or briefcase and fired the weapon from inside it. The gun was probably a pistol, more easily silenced than a revolver, and that would explain why we found no cartridge case. It may have simply ejected into the bag.'

After some further discussion, Pat Johnson from Devon and Cornwall described his case, a very old lady being shot with a forty-five, probably an old revolver, in her rose garden. Only other clue – maybe – an old motorbike.

'The case sits stubbornly up on my wall. We have our share of murders, but on our patch they're usually domestic, or in a family or community. They almost never involve elderly victims, except in the odd failed robbery. She was an Admiral's widow, who had then done a spot of teaching kids. We've none of the usual stuff to go on.'

They agreed that there was no discernible motive in either case. In two separate incidents, someone had gunned down two people in their dotage and had done it coolly and expertly. And there was something unusual about the bullets. In Helen Mitchell's case, it was bigger than usual, point four five, and with Mark Campbell it was smaller; 6.35 mm, or point two five inch.

Robin Marshal interrupted.

'Well, I've come just come across a couple more peculiar things. Brian, you remember Jimmy Wong from Hong Kong? He called me to ask me to provide some routine UK background stuff on a chap killed out there. A banker. A Brit murdered for no apparent reason and shot with a point two five which he thought unusual, and they certainly have no matches. After what you've told me, I think I'll ask him to send the ballistics report.

And just before we set off to come here, I asked Joe to search the National Ballistics database for anything to do with 6.35mm and old ammunition and also 'HOLMES', and something came up from Belfast. I know things are much quieter there now, but they still have more than their share of backstreet murders, so it hadn't been flagged up as unusual over here. Anyway, another older fellow was shot two months ago in a swimming pool.

And, guess what, with a single 6.35mm again.'

He glanced down at his notes.

'Joseph Patrick Corcoran, 59, ex-British Army Sergeant-Major, once quite a local hero in Northern Ireland for his swimming; Olympics and all that. He was a Catholic, so they initially thought it could have been sectarian, but he was popular enough. It may be nothing at all, but the bullet seemed to be a bit of a link. I'll get the ballistics of that one too.'

He looked up at his colleagues.

'It would be pretty extraordinary if there really *was* a connection between all four incidents.'

Brian Young looked sceptical.

'Four murders. Two in England, one in Northern Ireland and then one halfway across the world. How on earth could they be linked? But I suppose we can't rule it out.'

After some discussion, some of it also sceptical, it was agreed that Marshal would co-ordinate things from the Met and be responsible for keeping everyone informed.

It was getting late and dark outside and beginning to rain, and as they set off for London, the radio was reporting a huge traffic jam on the A1 near Bedford.

* * *

The next morning Robin Marshal walked from Victoria Station and picked up a Cappuccino from the Starbucks halfway down Victoria Street. At his desk, he was just beginning to check his emails for anything new from Hong Kong when the phone rang.

'Robin, it's Alex Wise from Bedford. All well with you, I hope. You know we had an accident that blocked the A1 for miles last night?'

'Sure, saw it on the box.'

'Well, it was actually no bloody accident. Believe it or not, somebody machine-gunned an articulated truck and then drove off in the rain and just disappeared. We've kept the lid on it and luckily the media still think it was an accident. We'll call it suspected terrorism, but we can't figure out what it really was.'

It wasn't as if they were trying to hijack the truck or anything. Whoever it was, or *they* were, just pulled alongside and shot the cab full of holes. Five of them ended up in the poor driver who was just a Polish kid.'

'Anything on the weapon?'

'One of my older chaps thinks it could have been an old Bren gun. We got a rush on ballistics and the rounds were definitely three oh threes. Apparently the army went on using Brens as their light machine-guns for a long time after the war. When Belgian FN assault rifles replaced the old bolt-action .303 Lee-Enfields in about 1960, to avoid muddling up the ammo in battle, they modified the Brens to take the same new 7.62 rounds the FNs used.

So that would put the gun, and maybe even the ammo as well, way
back in the fifties, or early sixties. Strange isn't it?'

'More than strange.' Marshal paused, his mind racing.

'Alex, can I drop in to visit you in Bedford? I'm beginning to think there's something really serious going on.'

CHAPTER TWENTY-THREE

KRAKOW, POLAND

Agnieszska Pasziewicz lived with her parents in the southern part of historic Krakow, once Poland's capital, in an old house across the Vistula river in a little road off Zamoyskiego Street. She could have been a pretty girl if her eyes weren't too close together and her mouth on the small side, features inherited from her father – so unless she was laughing, she was inclined to look pinched. And at twenty, she had long since realized that she needed to compensate by cultivating an attractive personality, a warm winning smile and a good ability to listen.

It had worked – up to a point. Rarely without a boyfriend, they had never been handsome, though considerate and attentive, and Agnieszska had long since settled for the fact that this was unlikely to change. She envisaged a husband, not exactly plain, but like herself, hardly likely to attract the most striking of the species as several of her girlfriends had, and doomed to wonder what life would have been like if inherited genes had been a little kinder. More annoyingly, she was short – barely five feet two – in stark contrast to several of her girlfriends who were astonishingly tall– not to mention the Polish models now gracing the world's catwalks, some of them almost six feet or more.

And then she had met Josef. Josef, with his amazingly soft brown eyes that had looked at her with a real interest, which went way beyond what she interpreted as a sexual interest alone. Not being pretty, she had become well aware of the division between someone interested in her as a personality and their possible interest in her as an easily flattered pushover.

She had been surprised, indeed delighted, by his attention, and by his endearing ability not to appear to notice other more attractive women on the occasions they went to clubs and parties. And one evening, six months after they had met, he had looked into those too close eyes of hers, and asked, 'Agnieszska, will you marry me?'

Still hardly believing it, Agnieszska was finalizing the preparations for the wedding, thinking of Josef in his haulage job in England, helping to earn the much needed money for the wedding that would go on for days, clearing out all of their savings as well as an uncomfortable chunk of both their parents' hard-earned funds.

She winced when she thought about the money that had somehow been set aside: thirty-five thousand zlotis was an awful lot to spend in three days, and she and Josef had only been able to raise a tenth of it. 'Don't worry,' her parents had told her, 'as we see it, it's an investment of a lifetime, in fact two lifetimes – and more when you have children. And we can't have our only daughter getting married without the best possible send off.'

She knew from Josef that weddings in England were usually far less lavish than they were in Poland, and that the celebrations didn't last nearly as long: a service in church perhaps, but very often not even that, followed by a reception and then maybe a dance the same evening. She thought of the three days they would enjoy with about a hundred guests – first the visit to the registry office, then the long church service, and after that a feast and dancing until six o'clock in the morning, followed by lunch the next day, which would last at least until the early evening. She would have to be careful with all that vodka, particularly with Josef twirling her around the dance

floor in her long wedding dress. Thank goodness she had had
the sense to order the dressmaker to create a detachable train so
she could unzip it before the dancing began. How embarrassing
it would be to topple over in front of all those guests, and with
everyone taking photographs of her in a crumpled heap. She'd
seen that happen at her friend Sofia's wedding, and knew Sofia
would never live it down.

She and her parents had long ago ordered the dress and
the bridesmaids' dresses, the marquee and the elaborate floral
archway, and everything for the wedding feast and dance down
to the tiniest detail. And her mother, short like Agnieszska, had
been on a diet for months, determined to get into her chosen
outfit, a silk blue dress that she could ill afford. 'I'll get into
this if it kills me!' she laughed, hanging the dress in the kitchen
in a plastic cover on the door as a constant reminder not to
succumb to a second helping, let alone the calorific puddings
which her husband adored.

Agnieszska, an only child, envisaged children, and certainly
two or more. Maybe, if Josef did well enough in England,
they would settle there, and her children would speak both
perfect Polish and English and could integrate with next to no
problem. And, after all, she had read in the papers that there
were thousands of Polish people in England. If she found it
hard to learn English fluently, there would still be thousands
of people to talk to, opportunities she could find to make
friends, and possibly a local Catholic church where she could
begin that social process. She knew from Josef that there were
many churches around London where Polish people had built
up a real local community and loads of 'pubs' where she could
find amusing Polish company, and in time other mothers with
children the same age as hers.

She suddenly thought of Dariusz, Lucas' friend from Krakow

University, now a carpet fitter in London's Heathrow Airport. Admittedly, not a great job for a chemistry graduate, but he had earned enough to find a relatively decent place until he found something better, and until then, seemed quite content with life.

'We'll get there,' she thought. And weren't there good benefits if they couldn't manage? And she could always be a cleaner. Apparently most of the British needed ironing and light housework; she could manage that. And it would be quite nice to polish silver – there was still little enough of that in most Polish homes since the Germans had raided them, along with valuable pictures, indeed anything of value.

And it wouldn't be like *'Upstairs, Downstairs'* any more. Agnieszska had seen repeats of the famous English TV series, marvelling at the divisions in English society, but realizing that all that was a thing of the past, and that it was even illegal to behave that way now. Poland was part of the EU; she'd have recourse to advice, a right to a decent hourly rate and the respect she deserved. She would miss her parents, certainly. But they could always come and stay, and if she had children she and Josef could have cots in their own bedroom if it was a two bedroom flat. Josef had told her that a two bedroom flat in London was likely to cost more than a thousand euros a month and even then, in a pretty rundown area – but they would pull through somehow, she told herself.

Once again, she found herself imagining them going up the aisle, Josef smiling as he slipped the ring on her finger, the all night dance, and her girlfriends congratulating her on the fabulous occasion, some of them wondering how she could have landed such a great-looking boyfriend and wishing they could do the same thing, perhaps even jealous.

Agnieszska looked around her parents' sitting room. Hers

would be different in England. Despite the fact that her mother kept things spotlessly clean, there was still an amazing clutter, not helped by the numerous photos of her grandfather in wartime uniform.

As she had so often heard, his was a proud and exciting story. After Germany had overwhelmed Poland in 1939, like many pilots her grandfather had escaped to England and had then flown a Hurricane in the RAF's famous Polish 303 squadron, the deadliest in the 'Battle of Britain' whose pilots had taken the greatest pleasure downing 126 'Adolfs', as they had called the German planes. The photographs showed him proudly wearing the *Virtuti Militari*, Poland's highest decoration. Next to it was one of him wearing Britain's Distinguished Flying Cross. A very brave man, and now a very old man, he had thoroughly approved of young Josef, and his decision to go to Britain to earn money.

She was determined that whatever place she and Josef found, it would not be full of such mementos, at the same time realizing that she would be the first to fill it with proud photos of her children – their first smiles, their first steps, their first birthdays. How incredibly lucky she was, she thought.

The doorbell suddenly rang.

Agnieszska smiled in anticipation of another delivery of wedding presents. Not an avaricious girl in any way, it was still lovely to think that her new home in England would have most of the small essentials they needed – the pots and pans, the crockery and cutlery, and the towels and bed linen. There was already quite a pile of unwrapped presents stacked in a corner of the sitting room, which Agnieszska had decided not to open before Josef arrived. Days away now, Josef would already be packing for the plane.

Or maybe it was the wedding dress being delivered – at last?

There had been three fittings to get it absolutely right. And it was exciting to be at home on a Saturday so she could take the deliveries. Agnieszska skipped to the door in a flush of pleasant anticipation.

But it was not the postman. Or a delivery van.

Or the dressmaker.

As Agnieszska opened the door she was startled to see a policeman and policewoman, with their blue and silver POLICJA vehicle parked on the street. She immediately noticed their grave expressions, and that the policeman looked down at his feet after taking in her face, as if giving the woman a cue to speak. Agnieszska's heart raced.

'Agnieszska Pasziewicz?' There was infinite pity on the woman's face.

'Yes,' she replied, in a tiny voice.

'I wonder if we could come inside?'

CHAPTER TWENTY-FOUR

KENSINGTON, LONDON

Sarah Shaw watched the morning news on TV with mounting incredulity; a huge and inexplicable accident on the A1 with the helicopter shots focused on to a vast traffic jam and the truck that had apparently caused it by crashing into the central barrier. The trailer had been separated from the cab unit that was being lifted by a crane, and covered by a giant tarpaulin which Sarah thought extremely odd.

Why bother to cover it up? She could just make out three letters on the trailer, FOL, and immediately knew that it much be one of Mick Foley's famous trucks, as familiar a sight on Britain's motorways as were those of Eddie Stobart.

And why were the police taking so unbelievably long to release the traffic back on to one of Britain's busiest roads, and not appearing to give out any explanation for not moving the truck sooner and the cause of the appalling pile-up?

The accident could have been caused by several things. Driver fatigue or driver error. Wet conditions. A tyre blowout. Or even a heart attack – though very unlikely in any young driver. Or maybe using a mobile or steering failure, or even overloading – though that last one was very unlike Mick Foley. But even so, surely the road would have been cleared faster than that, and some possible reason put out for the crash?

Instinctively, she reached for the phone, checked with directory enquiries and called the Mick Foley company in Bedford, amazed to get through so fast. Perhaps they had extra people on today to cope with enquiries? Or perhaps to fend off the press? Almost certainly both.

'Good morning. I wonder if I could speak to Mr. Mick Foley?'

'I'm sorry, that's not possible. Mr. Foley is extremely busy right now. May I ask who's calling?'

'Sarah Shaw.'

'And may I ask what this is in connection with, Ms Shaw?'

'The terrible accident on the A1. I wondered when the road might be clear, and wished to give my condolences to the poor driver's family.'

'I'm very sorry Miss Shaw, but I'm not allowed to speak about it. All staff have strict instructions from the police not to talk about it until further notice, unless you are an immediate member of the family of the deceased.

If you can assure me that is the case, I could probably put you through.'

'No, thank you' said Sarah, putting the phone down.

So someone *had* died, and the police were heavily involved, certainly enough to silence the staff. This definitely sounded like far more than a routine, albeit tragic, traffic accident.

Or was her febrile imagination working overtime?

She decided to go over to Bruce Bendrey, head of the crime desk and her immediate boss. After the last rocket she had received from him over her interest in the killings of the old people, she was nervous about bringing up any of her hunches.

What was more, Bruce was inclined to be acerbic and chippy in his attitudes in general, and she suspected – as an Australian – had something of the typical old-fashioned Antipodean attitudes towards women, thinking of them as mere 'Sheilas,' particularly in an office environment. Perhaps she should have learned more about cricket and rugby, she told herself.

But this time Bruce was actually surprisingly amenable.

'Alright, look into it. But don't waste too much bloody time if it doesn't look up to much.'

As it happened, Sarah ran into another brick wall. The spokesperson at the Bedford Police headquarters was very unhelpful and said there was nothing to add to what had already been reported.

Sarah suspected that she was lying, but could do nothing but ring off and not 'waste too much bloody time' for the moment, as Bruce had told her.

CHAPTER TWENTY-FIVE

PUTNEY, LONDON

Was all this paperwork really necessary? Alice asked herself the question for the thousandth time as she ploughed through another mountain, furious about the new NHS requirements that demanded all sorts of ludicrous details.

Maggie had just left with her usual well-meant but always irritating parting shot, 'Don't work too hard, love. There's a life out there.' At least she'd avoided that final and even more annoying cliché. 'You're only young once, you should go out and enjoy yourself.'

Some hope, thought Alice, feeling distinctly down. Admin and case report writing was the one part of her job she didn't enjoy, far preferring hands on, face-to-face advice. But it had to be done and now was as good a time as any.

She'd much rather be in the garden planting the geraniums she'd bought last weekend. Probably all wilting or dead by now, sitting forlornly in their trays on the lawn. She hadn't been out there for days. Another load of money wasted at the local nursery.

Ten pm, and she had only a few reports left to finish when the phone rang.

'Hello.'

'Hi, it's me, David.'

Immediately alert, she sat up and tried to sound calm.

'Hi! How are you?'

'Sorry I haven't been in touch. Another business trip. Just got back tonight. Is this a good time to talk?'

'Fine. In fact, a bit of a relief. Endless case reports to finish.'

'I know the score. I'm ready for a break too. Look, I know it's short notice, but I wondered if you were free for lunch this Sunday, somewhere out of town?'

Alice pictured a pleasant country pub.

'Actually, I am. Love to come.'

'Great, see you Sunday then. I'll pick you up at twelve if that's okay, it's about an hour's drive.'

'Where to?'

'I'll tell you when I see you. And if it's nice out, we could go for a bit of a stroll afterwards.' Alice couldn't picture that, but told herself she could probably get out of it.

'Lovely, see you then.'

Alice replaced the phone, flattered that this amazing-looking man was interested in her, although somewhat nervous about a drive and a lunch out of town with someone she barely knew, and with such a powerful and vaguely unsettling aura. Pubs could be jolly and companionable, but this man certainly wasn't. And if it didn't work out there'd be no quick escape route.

Why was she always attracted to men like that? She thought guiltily of John; comfortable, easygoing John. What was wrong with contentment and feeling relaxed with someone? And John certainly wasn't boring. All he was lacking was that slight element of danger that she could well do without. She didn't deserve him.

She thought of David's eyes and the way he had looked at her. She'd met men with that kind of eye contact before. Too long before they looked away, flattering and extremely effective if the man was that attractive, but all too often a technique they'd tried a thousand times before.

And probably successfully.

She'd call his bluff if he tried it again, keeping things chatty and cheery. Or would she?

Feeling vaguely uneasy, Alice went to the kitchen to make a sandwich, but went off the idea after a moment or two. Blast food. She'd take a bottle of wine into the sitting room and have a good natter with Liz. They hadn't talked for ages, ever since that double date.

'Hi, it's me.'

'At last. And where the hell have you been? Must have left scores of messages.'

'Oh Christ, I'm so sorry. The fact is, I've been totally swamped. Seem to be taking on more and more private patients, and trying to fit in anything else is almost impossible.'

'Not from what I've heard.'

Alice laughed.

'So, what have you heard?'

'Well, only that you were seeing a bit of John.'

'True. Really nice guy. But who told you?'

'John, actually. But not in any detail. Just said he'd seen you a few times.' She paused. 'And that he really likes you.'

'I like him too.'

Alice didn't expand, suddenly thinking about her date with David. 'Anyway, how are things with you?'

'Fine. Nothing much. Derek's nice, but... I don't know. Think I've gone off men a bit.'

'I think he's great.'

'Everyone does, and he is in a way. Really kind, and dead honest – that makes a nice change. But it's all rather safe and comfortable, if you know what I mean.'

Alice knew exactly what she meant. Lacking that bite, that edge, that bit of a challenge that kept you on your toes. In many ways, she and her best friend were the same.

'So what else have you been up to?'

Alice wondered if she dared tell her about David. Why not? She decided to risk it.

'Actually, I did meet someone rather interesting the other day. '

'Oh yes?'

'He was sitting next to me at a charity ball at the Grosvenor House.'

Liz laughed. 'Doesn't sound like you. You *hate* charity balls.'

'Usually, but it was for 'Help for Heroes', so I thought I'd go. My brother, the Para officer, asked me, and we were on a table of strangers. The guy next to me was amazingly good-looking, with incredible blue eyes. And he had a fabulous old Bentley and drove me home.'

'And?'

'Nothing. He just dropped me at the door and gave me a quick peck. Very chaste.'

'Probably married.'

'Maybe. Didn't ask him.'

'And you haven't heard from him since?'

'I have, actually. He asked me out and we had a great dinner in Nobu.'

'Nobu? He must be pretty keen.'

'And then he phoned just now and asked me out to lunch this Sunday.'

'And you're going.'

'Why not? It's only a pub lunch.'

Alice was going off this phone call rapidly. She was acutely aware of the shadow of John looming over the conversation.

'Anyway,' she said, changing the subject, 'why don't we meet up for supper next week?'

'I'm surprised you're free with two guys after you.'

Alice was suddenly depressed. If she couldn't talk to Liz, who could she talk to? She was the last friend she wanted to lose.

Maybe she could call the lunch off with David? She suddenly remembered she didn't have his number or address.

CHAPTER TWENTY-SIX

SURREY

Alice awoke to find the sun streaming through her bedroom window.

What a relief. At least it wouldn't be a muddy country stroll, it if had to be a stroll at all. There was something about the idea of a country walk with a stranger that was vaguely unsettling. And David *was* a virtual stranger, she had to admit it. Arm in arm? Too companionable. Hand in hand? Too intimate. Striding out? Too hearty.

What did she really know about him? Almost nothing. Something in security, that was about it. He had said so little that evening at the Grosvenor House, looking at her with those amazing blue eyes, and seemingly content to let her lead all the conversation.

He knew he was handsome, that much was evident. Otherwise, he'd have been forced to put in more effort. What man could get away with being as quiet as that? What woman come to that? Only those who were truly stunning, and even then, most men would surely get bored after a while. Perhaps not.

There had been one date two weeks after the Grosvenor House. And still Alice wouldn't be able to tell anyone anything about him, apart from a vague job in security, and an interest in psychology. He certainly liked hearing about her job, at least what little she was permitted to tell him. Not about precise patients and their case histories – that was off limits – but about the reasons they had come to her in the first place. And certainly nothing about her police work.

She thought back to that dinner at Nobu in Mayfair. She had been excited about it, knowing its reputation as a first-class restaurant, and because it was the first time that she had ever been there. But the food – admittedly incredible – was almost his sole source of conversation as they progressed through the extraordinary ten course taster menu of Japanese delicacies, including a superb sushi of nigri, maki, and oshi with mains of yellowtail fish and black cod, washing it all down with lychee martinis and champagne.

David had explained every dish in detail after Alice had apologized for being an almost total novice, but had given away almost nothing about himself by the end of the long meal – at least two hours or even more – except that he had done business in Osaka and Tokyo, was obviously something of an expert on Japanese cuisine and seemed to have a lot of money.

Alice was certain the bill was astronomical, particularly after spotting several celebrities in the restaurant, and he had firmly declined her offer of a contribution.

She had certainly tried to find out more about him, asking him about the sort of ordinary things one did on a first date, but had got almost nowhere. His job: 'You don't really want to hear about that.' His parents: 'They're fine, better than most.' His childhood: 'Boarding school. Middle class background.' Would she have been bothering now – let alone panicking about a country walk – if it weren't for something about him; something that certainly had women looking at him. How many women had he had? Loads, probably. Silence and stillness were undeniably attractive if you looked as good as he did. Probably she was just another intended notch in his bedpost? But he had made no move in that direction. Nothing.

She'd give it one more go today. And if he didn't open up, that would be it. Finish. She had enough problems with her patients without worrying about an uncommunicative man, however good-looking he happened to be. Flattering to be seen with him, flattering to be asked out, but not enough. But then, Alice reminded herself, she hadn't been forced to come on this date, any more than she had on the one before. She'd agreed to it.

She'd chosen the outfit the night before. Grey trousers and a matching grey polo, with a few gold bangles, and low-heeled shoes, in case they had that dreaded stroll. She'd take a bit of time with her make-up, and that would have to do. It was only a lunch in the country, and probably the last time she would ever see him anyway.

And before that, she would tidy the place up a bit and plant those wretched geraniums still sitting in their trays in the garden. Why not do that now, she asked herself? It wouldn't be the first time that her neighbours had seen her in the garden in her dressing gown at seven in the morning. And who cared if they did?

'Hi.'

He was there at precisely twelve o'clock, in a navy blue jacket and matching shirt. He certainly knew the power of those eyes thought Alice as she opened the door. Particularly when he accompanied them by a smile like that.

'Hi.' No kiss, but a reassuring nod as he stepped back to look at her outfit.

'Perfect.' He looked at his watch. 'Let's get going. It'll take about an hour to get there.'

He opened the passenger door of the Bentley for Alice to get in. Nice manners, she thought. Not many men did that any more.

Soon they were heading up Putney Hill and on to the A3, heading south.

'Where are we going?'

'A surprise. You'll soon see.'

Alice hoped it would be a surprise. Embarrassing if it were somewhere she already knew. But then, she knew it was unlikely. She rarely went out of town at weekends, preferring to potter around at home or go somewhere local.

She looked at his profile, and he turned to her, smiling.

'So, what have you been up to since we last met?'

'Work, mostly' said Alice, suddenly thinking what a boring answer that was, and just as suddenly thinking of John. He'd been over several times.

'You work too hard.'

Not another person saying that. Alice was irritated. What was she supposed to say? Bore him with cosy domestic details? Admit to dating someone else? She reminded herself that this might be their last date. Relax, she told herself.

But her resolve didn't work. Fifteen miles or so later, Alice felt she was prattling, mentioning a book she'd just read, a new restaurant she'd been to, a film she'd seen, and perhaps even worse, chatting about her work in the garden.

'Sorry, I'm sure I'm boring you.'

'Not at all. In fact, I rather like gardens – when I have time to look at them. Restful. One day I wouldn't mind having a look at yours.'

Alice was suddenly pleased. She pictured him sunning himself on her patio while she pottered about planting.

A blast of music suddenly interrupted this pleasant reverie as David turned on the music system. Opera. Something she knew virtually nothing about.

'Sorry.' He turned the volume down. 'Hope you like opera.

Plenty of other stuff there if you don't.'

Obviously, opera interested him more than gardens.

'No, it's fine.'

David laughed.

'Should be. It's Donizetti's *Lucia di Lammermoor*, one of the world's great tragic operas.'

Bit of a put-down, thought Alice. 'I know,' she lied, suddenly alarmed he might ask her questions and catch her out.

'And Callas singing.'

'I know', she replied, this time truthfully.

At least she wouldn't be embarrassed by the protracted silences while Callas was busy filling them in. Plainly he didn't want to talk, and just as plainly he was enjoying the feel of the car, freed from the speed limits of the dreary Kingston bypass as it swept majestically on to the A3, soon passing Guildford on the left.

Alice did notice one thing about his driving. For such a confident man, he seemed very careful, almost obsessive, about speed limits. A little instrument on the dashboard bleeped quietly whenever a speed camera came up and he slowed down until he was out of range, before pushing the big car up to the next one.

Alice tried again, looking out of the window. 'I've never much liked that cathedral.'

'Nor me, except for the stained glass window. John Piper. Fabulous.'

So he'd been inside? Alice never had, let alone seen the Piper window. So not much to talk about there. Another long silence.

Now they were skirting the Devil's Punchbowl and Alice avoided her usual comment that it looked like a vast bomb crater or the result of some catastrophic prehistoric explosion. She suddenly felt truly awkward, and thought guiltily again about John. Comfortable, easy John.

But at last they were nearly there. After a mile or so, David turned off the main road, and entered a narrow country lane. At the end of a no through road lined by rhododendrons, he parked the car outside an enchanting old hotel.

'Thought you might like Sunday lunch in my favourite haunt.'

Alice looked at the building, guessing it was probably sixteenth century with its overhanging storeys, and admiring the mass of overhanging wisteria.

'Wow, it's gorgeous.'

'Thought you'd like it. And it's even better inside. They do an amazing Sunday lunch. Hope you're hungry.'

Alice suddenly felt more cheerful as she got out of the car. Other people around. Not confined in a tight space. And the sun was glorious. Her mood lifted.

As they entered the hotel, Alice noticed that it was heaving with Sunday trade. But the head waiter obviously recognized David, greeting him with evident enthusiasm and quickly ushering them to a corner table overlooking the garden.

She wondered now many times he'd been there before. And who with? A thirty-mile journey, and all she'd been able to find out was that he liked opera, driving fast cars and that John Piper window. Pathetic. She needed a drink.

'What would you like? asked David, passing her the wine list. I'm afraid I'll pass, at least on the alcohol. But have anything you like.'

Alice had noticed that he'd stuck to soft drinks in the Grosvenor House. Why, she wondered? Because he was driving? Surely he could have had one or two? Or maybe he was an ex-alcoholic? She decided not to ask him, although it was always vaguely embarrassing to drink alone.

'House white's fine.'

David smiled. 'But a bit of a waste here. I'm told it's a great wine list. Why not pick something more adventurous?'

Alice felt a fool, suddenly wishing she was back in her garden with a glass of plonk, or in 'The Coat and Badge', her local pub.

'Okay.' She looked at the wine list – and the prices. Even the half bottles cost a bomb. But David must be aware of that; he obviously knew this place. She chose a half bottle in the middle price range, and while they were waiting for it, looked at the surroundings; a pleasant mixture of old and new; crisp white tablecloths, high-backed leather chairs and modern paintings on the walls, probably Topolski prints. With a name like 'The Grouse' she had been expecting old shooting pictures, stuffed game birds in glass cases, or a record trout or salmon with a plaque commemorating some long dead angler.

'This is really lovely.'

'Glad you like it. And the menu's even better.' He handed one over. 'I'm having the classic Sunday lunch, but have anything you like. It's all pretty good.'

This time, Alice bothered to read the menu, and for at least five minutes before she looked up. 'It all looks great, but I think I'll join you. Haven't had a decent Sunday lunch for ages.'

David smiled. 'I think you'll find it more than decent.'

Again, Alice felt a fool. Of course she knew it had to be with those prices. And how bloody condescending. She suddenly thought of John and that spaghetti dinner he'd made her the other night. So relaxing.

She'd already finished the half bottle of wine, embarrassingly fast, and David had noticed, asking the waiter for another one. 'Relax,' he smiled, suddenly touching her hand, 'I'm not going to eat you. You're a funny girl. So confident, and yet not. Strange mixture. Interesting.'

She looked into those blue eyes studying her face.

'I *am* relaxed,' she said, knowing it wasn't true.

David smiled, but said nothing. Unnerving. He knew perfectly well she wasn't.

And it didn't get much better as the meal progressed. Alice liked listeners, but this man was in a class of his own, forcing Alice to make all the running and seemingly utterly content with protracted gaps in the conversation. Used to drawing people out of themselves, and usually good at it, she was failing miserably.

It was a relief that there was a lively wedding party on the long table next to them, filling up the silences in the conversation, and being able to watch the photographer at work, although David seemed to resent the noise and the intrusion, and worse still, being asked to raise a glass to the happy couple. And she suddenly felt awkward, not pleased when he suddenly placed his hand on hers.

'How about some cheese, Alice?'

Alice noticed the trolley had just been wheeled over. 'I don't think I can. Looks marvellous, but...'

David smiled. 'Wasted opportunity.' He studied the array of cheeses, and turned to the waiter. 'I'll have a bit of that Somerset Brie.'

'Good choice, Sir.'

Damn, thought Alice again, suddenly feeling slightly lightheaded. They'd be there for another twenty minutes at least. This was a huge mistake. But at last the meal was over.

'Coffee?' asked David.

'No thanks. Couldn't.'

'I think I'll pass too.' David glanced out of the window and at the sunlight outside.

'Maybe you'd like to see the garden? It's beautiful out there.'

'Love to.' Alice couldn't wait to get outside.

'Why don't you wait for me in the porch while I settle up here?'

* * *

David was right. The garden was lovely, and in fact, there was a series of gardens. Long stretches of well laid out paved paths divided a series of beds, and somebody here was obviously passionate about roses.

Out in the fresh air, she felt more confident, and relieved he didn't try and hold her hand. Somehow she would have been embarrassed after those awkward silences hanging over lunch.

'Wow!' She had suddenly noticed a tree with a vast mass of white roses clambering around it, almost up to its full height.

'That's one of my favourites, a Rambling Rector. I've got one in my garden at home. It drives me mad with all the falling petals, and it's over far too quickly, but I still love it.'

'And that one's a *Rosa mundi*,' she said a few minutes later. 'One of the oldest roses. Incredible. It goes back to medieval times.'

She looked at David, suddenly beginning to relax at last.

'This is an amazing garden. You don't often see old roses like this, or anything like as many of them in one place. It's because they only bloom once, and that's it – the whole show's over. The new ones go on for ever, but they're not nearly as beautiful.'

Alice paused, suddenly feeling she was lecturing, or perhaps boring him.

'I'm sorry, I'm banging on.'

'No, it's interesting.' David was standing by a glorious cluster of pale pink roses. 'And what's this one?'

Alice studied it for a moment.

'I'm not sure.'

She ran her fingers tentatively over a stem. 'But I think I know. It's probably a Fantin Latour – they're not very prickly. And they're always pink, a bit darker on the outside with a sort of shell pink centre. The Dutch painters were mad about them – and of course Fantin Latour. They're in masses of his paintings. He was totally obsessed.'

'Pretty impressive,' smiled David. 'You certainly seem to know your stuff.'

Alice laughed.

'I'm not brilliant, but maybe better than most. At least, most amateurs. I've got an old godmother to thank for that. She used to love growing roses and taught me about them. And I love visiting gardens, particularly when they're laid out like this with borders stretching away from the house. Have you ever seen Monet's garden at Giverny?'

'No. But if you like Giverny, you'll love it through there.'

David pointed to a wrought iron gate at the end of the garden.

'Here' – he held out his hand tentatively. Alice took it, feeling embarrassed. Relax, she told herself, yet again.

They had now arrived at the gate, and both of them peered through it, with David's head next to hers, his hair touching her cheek, too close for comfort. There, just beyond, was a stunning lily pond. So he knew about Claude Monet and his superb garden and pond in Giverny? And at least she knew something more about him.

'Want to go around it?'

'Sure.' Ten minutes later, they were sitting side by side on a bench with David's arm resting casually along the back of it behind her. What should have felt companionable felt awkward thought Alice, suddenly feeling like a shy schoolgirl rather than a professional and normally confident woman of thirty.

She thought of commenting on the lilies, immediately wondering why she had to consider what she was about to say in advance. Still, he had been right. They were certainly beautiful. Thousands of them clustered around the water's edge, with their glorious china white flowers and impossibly polished green leaves lying flat on the surface as the occasional moorhen negotiated around them, bobbing its neck into the water.

She reminded herself that it was rather a relief when people didn't talk all the time, whilst immediately recognizing that it was exactly the opposite right now; to fear sounding foolish was surely the exact opposite of relaxation.

Suddenly she felt his arm lift around her shoulder as he raised it to look at his watch. Pretty insulting, thought Alice. He was obviously bored, or had to get back to London. It must be around four o'clock she realized – that lunch had taken forever. Oh well, she thought, it had been pleasant enough – at least the food and the stroll.

'Time to go?' she asked lightly, forcing a smile.

'Possibly.'

'Possibly?' A strange answer thought Alice. Either it was, or wasn't. She'd expected a vague response about traffic on the way back, business commitments to sort out before the morning, anything but that rather flat one word response.

'Well, tell me when you need to,' she replied flatly, looking out across the pond, and avoiding those searching blue eyes.

'No rush.'

Several seconds passed, and Alice suddenly felt him stroking the back of her hair. Disconcerting.

'You know, you're an extremely attractive woman, Alice.'

A jolt shot through her. Was that a pass, or just an

observation? No, of course it was a pass. Flustered, she narrowly avoided that ghastly cliché. 'Actually, you're not that bad yourself,' instead waiting for him to continue. But David didn't.

Another agonizing silence. Alice didn't think she could bear it any longer. What should have been a pleasant Sunday afternoon was turning into a nightmare.

To her horror, she suddenly fell into another well-worn phrase, immediately regretting it as soon as the words were out of her mouth.

'Penny for your thoughts.'

Why ask it? She knew his thoughts, or thought she did. And it made her sound pathetic.

David turned and studied her face slowly and intently, and then looked out across the pond.

'Actually, I was wondering if you'd like a room.'

'A room?' Alice was stunned.

'Yes, they have rooms here.'

He looked back in the direction of the hotel.

'I can phone for one, if you like.'

He calmly took his mobile out of his shirt pocket. 'Stop me if you want to.'

Alice didn't. Suddenly frozen, she watched him dial in a number, immediately realizing that he knew it by heart. How many times had he done this before? And who with? She heard all the warning signals, but ignored them.

'Done,' said David, clicking off his mobile and replacing it in his pocket. 'We can go when you're ready.'

Alice was physically ready, she recognised that, but suddenly paralyzed mentally by his overpowering presence. What on earth was she doing, not saying anything, meekly getting to her feet when he did in pathetic acquiescence? The tension was almost unbearable as they walked back to the hotel without speaking, and she watched him calmly pick up the keys in reception.

'Thank you, Franco.'

* * *

Three hours later Alice lay back on the pillows watching David, still naked, as he lifted back the curtain at the window. He looked back at her over his shoulder.

'Getting dark already. And it's starting to rain. Damn. Guess we ought to be thinking of going.'

He let the curtain fall back into place.

'Shame we can't stay all night.'

Alice said nothing, suddenly dreading the long journey back. It would be even worse in the rain, and with the Sunday night traffic. But she knew she had to get back, and that he did too. Now she wouldn't know until next time – if there was a next time. She had never in her life had sex as good as that. A one-off experience probably, she thought to herself.

For years she had doubted that she'd ever be capable of it, like a number of her female patients and some of her friends – not to mention the steady stream of women writing to agony columns or buying sex aids. It was a common enough problem: a normal or even a high sex drive coupled with an extreme difficulty achieving orgasm. Alice couldn't count the times she'd given up the struggle, or faked it – advising her patients not to do the same, and feeling a total fraud in the process. If only she could follow her own advice.

She knew it was almost certainly a problem of shyness, being able to tell a man what you liked without being embarrassed or using a vibrator in bed with someone. She'd never been able to.

Why ever not? She had often wondered why.

She was hardly ever shy out of bed. And men could tell women easily enough what they wanted, and show them what to do without any inhibition. It never seemed to change however much she liked – or even loved someone – except on those few occasions she'd tried a line of coke. And she wasn't going there again. Too dangerous. She could lose her job if that got out. Is that why people took coke regularly, even to the extent of serious disfigurement? Alice had often wondered if that explained female addicts. She'd seen a photo of an actress in the papers recently with a hideously ruined septum. What other reason could there be?

Now for the first time she'd met a man who knew exactly what to do, or to be more accurate, coax out of her exactly what *she* would like to do. Supremely unembarrassed himself, and able to overcome her embarrassment, despite the extreme tension.

'Relax Alice – there's no rush – take your time. Tell me what feels good. How am I going to know if you don't tell me? Show me Alice. Talk to me, Alice.'

And Alice *had* talked to him, amazing herself as she did so, and also amazing herself at what she was capable of, too proud to admit it to David although she suspected he may have guessed. But how odd it was that a man who made her feel so supremely awkward out of bed could overcome her inhibitions in such an intimate situation. It didn't make sense.

'You want the shower first?' David was suddenly beside her, picking up his watch from the bedside table.

'No, you go.'

'Okay, won't be long. And there's a fridge over there if you'd like anything. Help yourself.'

Alice flinched. He obviously knew the place rather well. Too well. How often had he been here? And why not ask him? If she could ask him things in bed, why not ask him a simple question like that? For some reason she knew she couldn't. At least, not yet.

* * *

One hour later, they were stuck in a huge queue of cars heading back to London, with the rain sheeting across the windscreen so hard that the wipers could hardly clear it.

'Damn!'

David suddenly shouted over the sound of Callas, slamming his fists down on the wheel in a burst of fury. 'Why does England grind to a fucking halt every time there's a sudden spot of rain?'

Alice looked at him, startled.

Hardly a spot of rain, she thought looking out, though there was no reason for that petulant outburst. She suddenly wished she could turn the opera off, or at least down. Why couldn't she? She glanced at David and decided not to. Not a good moment. He looked livid.

'Might as well get out of the car and walk. We'll be here all bloody night.'

Alice said nothing for a moment or two, placing her hand tentatively on his knee hoping to calm him down. To her shock, David pushed it straight back.

'Sorry, don't do that. And don't talk to me, I'm not in the mood.'

Alice didn't, not until they were back in Putney, two miserable, silent hours later. How to ruin a great afternoon, she thought. If a sudden rainstorm could set him off like that, what else could? It looked as if he needed a psychologist, but it certainly wasn't going to be her.

At last they were outside her house, and her irritation mounted when David didn't even get out of the car. She remembered how he'd opened the door for her so charmingly that morning, flattered at the gesture and thinking how polite he was. Well, she was wrong there.

'I'll call you,' he said, barely looking at her, and that was it. No kiss. No offer to see her safely inside. 'Sorry, got to go.' He didn't even switch off the engine.

'Bye then.'

Alice walked to her front door, listening to the car drive off before she'd even reached it, and slamming it so hard behind her it shook the whole house.

* * *

Several days later Maggie answered the doorbell, bringing back a beautiful bunch of roses.

'Seems you've got a mystery admirer' she smiled, handing them to Alice, 'or maybe it's that nice new chap of yours.'

John? Unlikely. Alice had seen him last night. Nice evening, but no reason to send her flowers. Still, you never knew.

She took the bunch and pulled off the little envelope attached to the wrapping. Just three words on the message inside. 'Thanks for coming.'

So he knew just how hard she normally found it. The pun was embarrassing and surely intended. She dropped the card in the wastepaper basket. For once, Maggie thankfully said nothing.

CHAPTER TWENTY-SEVEN

SURREY

Polly was busy vacuuming the carpet in one of the bedrooms at 'The Grouse' pub hotel in Farnham, when suddenly the machine made an angry clacking noise as it hit something just under the double bed. She leaned down to see what the obstruction was, and found a small watch.

Very pretty; a lady's watch for someone with small wrists like her, but not valuable as far as she could see, though you could never tell these days. She was often amazed when flicking through magazines to see the price of things; ripped jeans for hundreds of pounds, tiny handbags costing a fortune, simple cardigans that would eat through half her monthly wage or even more. But there was no designer name on the watch, and even if there were she would have to hand it in to the Manager, tempting though it might have been not to.

She popped it into her apron pocket. Her employers would be pleased by her honesty on what was only her second day in the job, and that would be a point in her favour.

And indeed it was.

When Polly had finished the rooms and wheeled the trolley out into the laundry room, she took the watch down to reception where the Manager was busy with the accounts.

'Excuse me, Mr Franco.'

He looked up.

'I've found a lady's watch in the Pheasant Suite, just under the bed.' She held it up.

'Oh, thank you, Polly.' He took the watch, and studied it

for a moment.

'I don't think it's very valuable, but it might mean something to someone.' He peered over his glasses. 'And it means a lot to our guests when we return things they've left behind.' He smiled at Polly, 'and a lot to us to have honest staff.'

Polly beamed.

'Thank you,' he said again, taking down the registration book from the shelf behind him and flicking through the last completed pages. Ah, Mr David Hammond. Pretty regular customer over the years. And a pretty cool one, too. Always booking a room in advance if he's coming with a young lady. And he'd stayed in the Pheasant room last weekend. But there was no address to send the watch on to. Strange, that they'd never had it over the years, and that Mr. Hammond had always paid in cash. Still, you couldn't run an establishment like 'The Grouse' without realizing people's oddities. That was part of the job, as was supreme discretion – particularly concerning 'goings on' upstairs.

He snapped the record book shut and went back to the accounts. Mr. Hammond would be back soon enough, but probably with a different young lady. He'd have to find a moment to give him the watch in private, and even then in a sealed envelope when his lady friend wasn't looking.

And the likelihood was that his regular customer wouldn't have a clue who it belonged to.

CHAPTER TWENTY-EIGHT

SCOTLAND YARD

It was very quiet in the office and dark outside. Robin Marshal had decided to go home late because he needed to think carefully. Yesterday, at the Bramshill meeting, two regional police forces had reported strange, apparently motiveless killings, with the victims both elderly and having apparently led blameless lives.

Added to that, there was the Belfast report and then the motorway incident. There seemed to be a curious pattern of old weapons and ammunition being used – whether tiny pistols, heavy revolvers or even an ancient machine-gun for God's sake. The Bedford police had bought time by calling it 'terrorism', but he knew the truth would leak.

The Northern Ireland one could conceivably be linked to terrorism, but none of the others.

Robin knew a lot about terrorism. London had had its fill, with the IRA leaving scarcely an iconic location untouched: Parliament, the Stock Exchange, the City of London, Canary Wharf, Heathrow, the BBC, Earls Court, railway stations, shopping malls, barracks, Harrods and even the Royal Parks, with those dreadful images of dead and wounded cavalry horses.

Then across the Atlantic, the Al Qaeda aircraft horrors of 9/11 had arrived. And, because of his IRA work, Robin had been ordered to fly to Washington with Stella Rimington, the Director General of MI5, and several other specialists. Their RAF plane had been the only aircraft allowed into US airspace and then only by special Presidential permission. After meetings with the CIA and an inspection of the smoking Pentagon, they had reached New York and viewed the terrible wreckage of the World Trade Center. It was truly appalling, and tragic for so many innocent people.

But Robin, with his rather bitter recent IRA experience of British dead and maimed in London, had permitted himself a fleeting mental question as they had gazed at the scene: '*How many of those courageous fire-fighters and policemen who had perished so bravely in the Towers had Irish names. And how many of them had been contributing to NORAID for all those years, funding, perhaps without realizing it, those many bombings and killings in his town?*' He had, of course, kept such dark thoughts very much to himself.

However, there was one prediction he had made at the time that came true. American finance for IRA terrorism had dried up in an instant, and Martin McGuinness and Gerry Adams were suddenly all for peace – and future ministerial posts. Overnight, it was *very* unfashionable in America to be funding bombings in other people's countries.

But leaving terrorism aside, could there possibly be more of these strange killings overseas – like Jimmy Wong's one in Hong Kong, for instance?

He resolved in the morning to enlist Interpol's help to see if the MO could possibly be cropping up anywhere else.

CHAPTER TWENTY-NINE

DUBLIN, IRELAND

Alice was just about to go to bed when the phone rang. She glanced at the clock, almost midnight. Who the hell was phoning at that time of night? She picked up, ready to be vaguely irritated.

'Hi, it's me.'

She was suddenly alert, remembering his eyes as fast as his voice.

'Look, I know it's late, but I've just got back. And I wanted to apologize for rushing off like that. Especially after such a great afternoon.'

Alice said nothing.

'Alice?'

'I'm here.'

'And anyway, I wanted to make it up to you. And I hope you got the flowers.'

'Yes…thanks.'

She was still smarting at the memory of his abrupt and extremely rude departure, let alone that awful journey back from 'The Grouse', yet now – listening to him on the phone, all she could think about was the hours before that.

'Are you still there?'

'Sure,' replied Alice. 'Look, don't worry about it.'

'But I have. I do. And enough to get tickets to Dublin next weekend by way of an apology, just on the off-chance you might be free.'

Alice was stunned. 'Well, that's very nice of you, but

I'm afraid I'm not. Far too short notice. I'm up to my eyes. Anyway...'

'Come on, Alice. Give yourself a break. A beautiful woman like you shouldn't have her nose to the grindstone seven days a week. And anyway, you told me you don't work on weekends or Mondays, not unless you absolutely have to. Look, it's one night Alice, that's all. And if I remember rightly it should be a pretty enjoyable one, without having to rush back to London in the middle of it. Please come.'

Alice dithered, suddenly remembering that John would be tied up all weekend finishing off that big presentation trying to land that chunk of Coca-Cola the day after, and telling herself they weren't a heavy item. A few dates, no more. And what did John get up to on the times she didn't see him? He was a good-looking man. She'd never asked him, and he didn't volunteer the information.

'Look, I'm not sure.'

'For God's sake Alice, it's only one night and a quick look around Dublin, and I'll get you back by Sunday evening, promise.'

'I'm sorry, I don't think I can.'

'Last time I'll ask then. Shame.' The last time he'd call her? Alice suddenly weakened.

'Okay then, just one night.'

'Great. Okay, I'll pick you up on Saturday at mid-day. And you don't need a passport. Just bring hand baggage and a photo ID.'

One more time thought Alice as she replaced the phone. She had to admit she was still intrigued.

* * *

When David turned up, it was in a black cab. Alice was puzzled, but he anticipated her question.

'I have to go on from Dublin on business on Sunday night, so my car would be stuck at the airport.' He made no reference to the fact that he obviously expected Alice to make her own way back. She had a flash of disappointment, and even irritation. This hadn't started well. But at least he was more talkative than usual on the way to Heathrow, discovering that Alice had not been to Dublin since she was in her teens, explaining how it had changed dramatically since joining the European Union and now had a shiny financial centre along the River Liffey.

'Although it's been seriously affected by the banking crisis. That's certainly knocked the stripes off the 'Celtic Tiger'. She was surprised how much he seemed to know.

And when they drew up at Terminal 1, she was again surprised when David hauled a large suitcase from beside the driver.

'I have to go on to a security conference. This is full of samples and brochures.' He didn't volunteer where the conference was being held and Alice was again annoyed he hadn't mentioned it before. She suddenly felt like a perk on a business trip, but decided to hold her tongue.

After checking in the big suitcase and enduring the security system made slower by inexperienced weekend travellers, they set out on the long walk to the gates for Ireland. There, they mingled with a crowd of passengers whom Alice noted were a decidedly mixed lot – Irish families on their way home with their freckle-faced and noisy children, tourists from several countries, big men in rugby blazers, several nuns and priests and a rather rowdy group of young English fellows in green wigs and T-shirts announcing 'Paul's Stag Night', which they had obviously started celebrating back at the airport bar.

Travelling Aer Lingus on Business Class, Alice and David

were the first to board. At least that was nice.

But the flight was delayed by the obvious inexperience of
many of their fellow passengers. Then there was a further delay
when an old Irish farmer in a battered flat cap and tweed suit
loudly refused to sit down in his seat. He had plainly been
drinking his duty-free whiskey in departures and was singing
to himself. Two pretty flight attendants were doing their best
to cope with him, until two of the largest rugby players became
impatient and rose to the occasion, walking back down the aisle
and pressing the old boy down into his seat, with the friendly
advice to 'Fockin' sit down, buckle up and shut up'.

Alice suddenly noticed that while she and the other
passengers were mildly amused, David had completely tensed
up, plainly furious. 'Stupid jerk,' she heard him mutter.
However, the aircraft suddenly pulled back and they were soon
taxiing. Thankfully, David's mood seemed to lift as the aircraft
did, but Alice had once more been reminded of his sudden
mood swings.

As soon as they landed at Dublin Alice noticed the changes
since she was last there. The airport was now huge and really
crowded, obviously due to increased wealth and the low-cost
air flight revolution led by Ireland's Ryanair. It took some time
to extricate David's suitcase and then queue for a taxi, but at
last they were on their way into the city, and Alice noticed how
the roads and streets of Dublin were now jammed with cars,
and smart ones at that. Luckily cabs had their own priority
lane, and they were soon at the legendary Shelbourne Hotel.

Alice was pleased with the room, looking out at its pleasant
view over the trees of St Stephen's Green, but it was disconcerting
to have David pressed right up behind her at the window and
knowing, or rather feeling, exactly what he was thinking.

'Want to go out now or later?'

'Now,' said Alice.

David pulled away. Another awkward moment was over.

'Okay then. I suggest we start at the bar downstairs. Nothing like a Guinness to get in the mood.' Five minutes later they were sitting in the hotel's famous Long Bar while Alice tried some of the 'Black Stuff'. Not bad, she thought. She'd tasted it once before in England, but didn't like it. Maybe it was true that it tasted better in Ireland, 'Liffey water' and all that.

To start their tour, David walked Alice arm in arm through the Georgian streets and squares of the city that had been the elegant heart of Anglo-Irish society, stopping on the corner of Merrion Square to look at the languid statue of Oscar Wilde and read the famous quotations carved into the stonework.

'I never travel without my diary. One should always have something sensational to read in the train.'

'I can resist everything except temptation.'

'Alas, I am dying beyond my means.'

I am so clever that sometimes I don't understand a single word of what I am saying.'

And even the normally taciturn David laughed out loud as he read out Wilde's famous remark to an American customs official:

'I have nothing to declare except my genius.'

As they walked away, Alice had a disturbing thought. Oscar Wilde was a perfect example of someone being brought down by a sexual obsession against their better judgment.

Next came Dawson Street, heaving with shoppers who did not appear to be unduly concerned about minor inconveniences like recessions or national deficits. Alice's father had complained that 'the Irish were visually illiterate', able to spot a split infinitive at a thousand yards while unable to dress smartly or avoid ruining their towns with garish signs and replacing charming old cottages and houses with modern monstrosities. Now, Alice thought, that seemed to be in the past, at least about the dress sense, with the girls, always pretty, now stunning – in clothes not out of place in Knightsbridge, the Champs Elysées or the Via Veneto.

They crossed the Liffey into O'Connell Street and David pointed out the General Post Office, still marked with bullet holes, reminding her that it had been the centre of the abortive but iconic 1916 Easter Rising. Then up the river they visited The Four Courts, smashed up at the beginning of the Irish Civil War.

'Michael Collins even had to borrow guns from the British to shell his old comrades,' said David. In fact, he seemed to know an awful lot about the history of Ireland, and Alice even suspected from his unusual fervour that he might be Irish himself. Why not ask him? she thought. It was typical of the guarded nature of their relationship that she didn't.

Darkness was falling as they crossed over the Halfpenny Bridge, 'named after the toll levied in the old days,' explained David, and began to explore Temple Bar with its myriad bars and pubs. Suddenly they were outside 'The Oliver St John Gogarty', a splendidly colourful pub.

'Ah,' said David, 'Gogarty – great literary hero, let's see what's up in here.'

They found themselves in a huge bar with Irish music playing to an enthusiastic crowd of Irish and foreigners. Some of them kept getting up and leaving, but Alice soon found out that it was only because Ireland had just become one of the first countries to ban smoking in pubs and bars. 'To protect the staff,' explained one of them when they returned, roaring with laughter at the charade, pointing out that most of the bar staff smoked anyway.

The atmosphere was such fun that Alice had been tucking

into wine perhaps over-enthusiastically, and when it became late, David ordered a taxi for the short ride back to the hotel.

Any shyness or anxiety about what would happen next was somewhat offset by Alice's moderate intoxication. Again David was expert and supremely patient. And again she astonished herself, telling him things she'd never told anyone else in bed before, except for that time in 'The Grouse'. And this time it was even better.

He smiled down at her two hours later. 'You're quite a girl, Alice.'

* * *

She awoke to find David in a dressing gown pouring coffee from a trolley which Room Service must have delivered.

'Good morning, Madam,' he said, 'black or white coffee?'

'Black, please. And lots of sugar.' She was aware she had a hangover, thankfully not too bad. She deserved worse. Of course David didn't, because he didn't drink. Again she wondered why.

'I think I'll have a shower,' said David, 'and then go and get the papers.' Alice suddenly remembered reading the papers with John back in bed at home. That had been so companionable, but she somehow knew it wouldn't be, here with David. Once again she wondered what she was doing here, and it was a relief when he disappeared. Not wanting to stay in bed a moment longer, she locked herself in the bathroom, desperate for a shower. Ten minutes later, sitting on the bed and drying her hair, she suddenly noticed the big suitcase in the corner. A hell of a lot of brochures, she thought. It looked as if it weighed a ton.

David was back with the papers, and she was suddenly reminded of John and that ridiculous story he'd told her. He was once staying in a hotel in Ireland and had asked for a newspaper.

'Yesterday's or today's, Sorr?'

'Today's, please.'

'Ah well, Sorr. That doesn't come 'til tomorrow.'

Thinking about John, Alice felt another stab of guilt. What the hell was she doing here? She told herself that she'd feel much better, up and dressed.

And for the most part, she did. The morning started pleasantly enough, and Alice felt more relaxed as they strolled down a street full of antique shops and art galleries. She stopped at one of them.

'Gosh, I'd love to go in here. I know the painter, Thomas Ryan. Well, not personally, just his work. He's amazing.'

They walked inside the gallery, hung everywhere with Ryan's paintings, almost all of them of his own family and crafted with exquisite tenderness. Love poured out of them. His wife, cradling a tiny baby. A family meal. His wife again, arranging roses in a vase. Children playing in a garden. A small boy climbing in an apple tree smiling down. A little girl on a rocking horse. A child's birthday party; seven burning candles lighting the face of a delighted youngster leaning over to blow them out. Alice was entranced, but not for long. She suddenly noticed that David was frowning at them, almost as if he was becoming angry. Whatever was it?

'You okay?' she asked.

'Fine,' said David, flatly. He looked in the direction of the door. 'Just not my sort of thing. I'll wait for you outside.'

She watched him stride off and, after a moment, felt compelled to follow him, baffled and annoyed. They'd only been here five minutes – if that. Damn. What was it about this man? Why did he always have to spoil things? What had set him off? Was he resentful of Ryan's images, somehow afraid of family life?

You'd have to be inhuman not to like these paintings, she thought, or at least very strange. And John would have loved them. She suddenly pictured his reaction with another pang of regret.

Only a very good lunch in a fish restaurant seemed to restore David's equilibrium, and indeed hers, although he did not explain or apologise for stomping out of the gallery.

'This is on me,' said Alice, fishing out her credit card and putting it on the table. 'And to be honest, I'd rather pay you back for the air fare.'

David smiled. 'No need to.' When he smiled he looked gorgeous, thought Alice, but he certainly did not smile enough. So unlike John.

And anyway, that was pretty much his last smile of the day.

At the airport, David was depressingly business-like and brisk, evidently keen to send her off through security before attending to his own flying arrangements. Hardly a high note to end on, thought Alice. Anyone would have thought they were mere corporate colleagues.

David was very strange. Even with her professional background, he was almost impossible to work out, reacting with extraordinary petulance when things did not go his way, even quite small things. God knows what he might be like if he was seriously thwarted.

The short flight back to London seemed to last for ages, and her thoughts turned to John again, finalizing his presentation. She knew it was a big one, and that she ought to phone him tonight to wish him luck. In fact, she should have done that before, and never gone to Dublin in the first place. Checking her mobile, switched off during the trip, she noticed he'd called her three times. She couldn't call back, not now. He'd only ask her what she'd been up to.

And what the hell was she supposed to say?

CHAPTER THIRTY

PUTNEY, LONDON

At mid-day, Alice picked up the phone.

'Hello. Alice Diamond.'

'Thanks for calling to wish me luck.' It was John, sounding distinctly cool.

He must have done the presentation by now. Alice felt terrible for not calling him before. But she couldn't bring herself to do so last night. And at seven am, the time she knew he would be up, she'd lost her nerve, knowing he'd ask her about the weekend.

'How did it go?' She tried to sound bright.

'Brilliantly, actually. I think we may have got it.' But he sounded flat.

'Fantastic! That's great news, you must be really pleased.'

'I am.' John paused. It's just that I thought you'd have been more interested.'

'I am. I was.'

'Funny way of showing it. Anyway, they said they'll be deciding on Friday.'

'The very best of luck,' said Alice, wishing he'd talk about the presentation, and dreading the inevitable question. Of course, it came. It had to.

'And where were *you* over the whole weekend? A call would have been nice.'

Alice panicked. 'Oh John, I'm so sorry. At home, but something really urgent came up.' What else could she say? Her voice tailed off.

'Anyway, as I said, they'll tell us on Friday. And if it's good news we could have a celebration dinner.'

'That would be great,' said Alice, hugely relieved. 'And if it's not good news?'

'Then I guess you could help me drown my sorrows. I'll call you as soon as I know, and we'll fix up something then.'

'Fine. Look forward to it.'

She didn't deserve this nice man. And what a fool she'd been.

CHAPTER THIRTY-ONE

PARIS, FRANCE

Katarina Taliante was staying at the Hotel de Crillon in Paris for the duration of the fashion shows in her role as Beauty Editor of Italian *Vogue* in Milan. She could easily have been a model herself. At 34, she was at the peak of her beauty, with flawless skin, wide apart green eyes, long flaxen hair and a perfectly symmetrical face, and at six feet tall, a perfect model height.

She had little need for make-up with her exceptional skin and features, but knew she could never venture out barefaced, at least whenever she was on duty in her job; it would be an insult to the cosmetics companies who spent a fortune in the pages of *Vogue* each month – 400 pages in the last issue, including dozens and dozens of eye-wateringly expensive full-page advertisements. All the big names were there: Lanvin, Dior, Calvin Klein, Clarins, L'Oréal, Marc Jacobs, Chanel, Givenchy, Yves Saint Laurent, Bobbi Brown, Estée Lauder, Giorgio Armani, Sisley, Mac, Boss, Lagerfeld, Chloe, Clinique and scores of others.

She knew she was lucky to have her job, although it meant frequent travelling, usually on her own, and often when she would have liked to spend more time at home. Furthermore, it was not particularly well paid. Thousands of girls would have done anything to have a position like hers, and that kept the salary artificially low, although it was true that she had considerable expenses – free make-up and skincare from the most luxurious names, free perfume, free membership of a top gym in Milan, free hairdressing and manicures, free health and dental insurance, discounts on clothes, indeed on almost anything remotely connected with health and beauty, as well as free first class tickets to the world's great capitals, and staying for free in their most lavish hotels.

The Crillon was one of her favourites, perfectly situated on the fashionable Place de la Concorde, and with stunning marble mouldings and crystal chandeliers, not to mention huge Louis XV-style apartments with massive beds with ornate draperies. Used to being surrounded with stylish and luxurious things, she still marvelled every time she came here.

She was not married, which often surprised people, though not Katarina. She knew a lot of men were nervous about approaching someone with looks like hers, especially if they were inches shorter, while others would instantly assume she was already married or had a boyfriend. And most of the men she met were gay – the art directors, designers, photographers, hairdressers, parfumiers, stylists and make-up people who surrounded her constantly – several of whom she had met again here at the Crillon. 'Hi darling!' How many times had she heard that since she arrived, as one after another of them had approached her in reception with that typically effusive hug?

But Katarina enjoyed the company of gay men, just as she enjoyed the job. She had never once regretted switching from that position as personal assistant to the Chairman of a large public relations company in Milan, where she had little to do besides pour whiskies and gin and tonics for the clients in a vast penthouse office on the Via Napoleone.

She could have stayed there for years on a ridiculously high salary for what little she did – spending it in the expensive clothes shops in the streets below – but had gone to a careers consultant who had suggested beauty journalism, discovering that Katarina had an unusual talent with words coupled with an interest in beauty, though no wish to be a model herself. And Katarina had been lucky enough to land a junior job at *Vogue*, eventually working up to her coveted position today. Nevertheless, when it came to meeting straight men, there were downsides to it.

But the man she had met in the Crillon bar last night was certainly not gay. Taller than her, dark, but probably not French or Italian, and with startling blue eyes. That is what she'd first noticed as he looked at her, and she had instantly wondered if he was wearing tinted contact lenses as so many models did these days. But somehow she didn't think so; he had enough going for him as it was.

She was sitting with a whole group of models not far from the bar when she had first noticed him watching her, all the more flattering for the fact that the girls around her were, without exception, stunning, and had certainly noticed him. He did not appear to be interested in them at all. One after another, the models had gone to bed knowing that it was going to be a long day ahead, and that it was never a good idea to look bleary-eyed on the catwalk despite the best efforts of the make-up artists. That is when he had asked her if she would like to join him for a last drink.

After an hour of those remarkable blue eyes upon her, and his genuine interest in what she did, she was extremely tempted to take things a little further – as he had suggested when the bar had finally closed and they were going up in the lift. He had studied her face intently with those extraordinary eyes.

'Would you like a nightcap in my room?'

Katarina had declined, with difficulty. She would have to be at her best tomorrow, and it would be thoroughly unprofessional. Moreover, she would need twice the time to look her best tomorrow at the grand finale, especially with Anna Wintour over from American *Vogue* spotting the tiniest flaw through her customary and oversized dark glasses, as critical of those off the catwalk as those sashaying down it.

'Okay,' he had nodded, giving her the lightest of continental kisses on each cheek as the lift swished to a halt at her floor.

'Then maybe we could have breakfast together tomorrow morning.'

'That would be nice,' Katarina had smiled, although immediately realizing what the others would think when they saw them together at breakfast. But what did that matter? She could cope with that. And anyway, she was sure that some of her team were sleeping together – certainly Antonio and Milo – and probably Elena and Greta. Who cared what anyone thought? Anyway, the shows would be over by tomorrow night, and if all went well – and there was no reason to think they wouldn't – she could finally relax and go out to dinner with him as he'd suggested, leaving everyone else in the party to do their own thing. They were all grown-ups, and the girls might even be a bit jealous. Who wouldn't be interested in a man like that? 'Che sparventapasseri! Fantastico!'Katarina could almost hear them saying it.

The following evening was nothing short of fabulous. Dinner in a superb and apparently famous fish restaurant called 'Geneviève', followed by a glass or two of champagne in a bar near the Arc du Triomphe before returning to the hotel.

And there was no doubt that he knew what do in bed. Perhaps not surprisingly thought Katarina, as she lay back contentedly a few minutes after he'd gone back to his room. He had obviously had considerable practice with looks like that.

* * *

Five hours later, Katarina was woken by a sudden shaft of light streaming through the window. She reached her hand up to the bedside table to look at her watch. Seven thirty. She knew he was leaving at one today. He was probably up and packing right now. But there would still be plenty of time to have breakfast with him and a pleasant stroll round the city. She was looking forward to seeing a bit more of Paris, especially with such an attractive man. And he had even mentioned meeting up again in Milan, and maybe coming skiing with her in the Alps.

It would be the second morning they'd shared a table for two in the breakfast room – with the rest of Katarina's party all together on a separate table. She had been mildly embarrassed by their occasional glances yesterday, but today she would shrug them off them again and perhaps even with a hint of triumph.

Katarina had a long hot shower and washed her hair, deciding to wear her Prada jacket and Dolce and Gabbana trousers. Smart but casual. And at 8.30 she went down to breakfast, finding her way to the table they had shared the day before. To her surprise he wasn't there. But no problem. She'd have a coffee and wait for him.

Twenty minutes later he had still not arrived. Where on earth was he? Looking at her watch, 8.45, she decided to go to Reception and call him.

'Excuse me', Katarina said to the concierge, 'I wonder if you could put me through to someone's room. I'm sorry, I don't have the number.'

'Certainly. Can I have the name?'

'Mr David Hammond.'

'Monsieur David Hammond, let's see.'

The concierge checked the records 'Ah, here we are. I'll put you through.'

Katarina watched as he dialled the number, before handing

her the phone. But there was no reply. The concierge suddenly put up his hand.

'I'm sorry Madame, but I've just remembered. He checked out at seven thirty this morning. We booked a taxi for him to the Gare de Lyon.'

* * *

Women. All pretty much the same, even the clever ones. And even they were never as clever as they thought. All programmed from the same computer, even if they think they aren't.

The ugly ones – a pushover, if you were stupid enough to go there. And who would, unless you were ugly yourself? And even the pretty ones were a pushover if you played your cards right.

Hopeless, psychiatrists – all of them, even that Alice woman. Didn't take long to get her in the sack. All the same in the end. All the same in the beginning. It didn't need Freud to see it.

Obsessed with the way you see them. Not as much interested in who you are, but in who they are. And interested in such stupid things. What woman really understands a perfectly made car or a classic gun? What woman's ever really asked about my car? Oh, they all like sitting in it and they say it's nice, 'A nice colour'. But how feeble is that?

Depressing.

And magazines like Katarina's make them even worse. Pathetic eye candy. Layers of make-up but not much underneath. A woman hardly ever buys a magazine without another woman's face on the front.

Compliment them, and they melt. Pay, and they'll play. Flatter, and they'll simper and flutter their feathers. Fuck them, and they think you might end up loving them, or already do.

Look after them for a few evenings and they start thinking you'll look after them for life.

And most men are equally pathetic falling prey to them; their needs, their hormones, their over-weening desire to be cherished, protected, nested.

Birds, the right name for them – bird-brained. Easily caught. Always preening. Twittering when you wanted silence. Grateful to be thrown the odd crumb by way of compliments. And desperate to nest and have fledglings of their own.

Nice on your arm. Burden on your life. Inquisitors, always checking up on you, trying to see what makes you tick so they can tick off the boxes, and they never really make it without making kids.

Or fools of us, if you let them.

Even Alice. Looking me up like that, checking to see if I had 'the right credentials.' Brooding and intruding.

Damn her. Damn them all.

And the last thing I need is another pathetic child. Bad enough, the one I've got.

And it would be even worse if it were a girl.

Screw them all. That's about all they're good for.

CHAPTER THIRTY-TWO

ST-HIPPOLYTE-DU-FORT, FRANCE

Harold Diamond had been first annoyed, and then in turn surprised and amused that the tourist *Green Guide* had once described the nearest town to his home as 'not worth a visit'. He had long since come to realize that whoever wrote that condemning phrase had not even scratched the surface of the town's history.

St-Hippolyte-du-Fort was in fact a 16th century walled settlement with a fort to protect it, and a barracks that had once housed one of France's great cadet schools. Harold always walked through the old drill square on his way to buy his daily *baguette*, admiring the attractive barracks, now converted into doctors' surgeries, offices and low-cost housing, looking on to a leafy central courtyard often used for concerts and arts and crafts shows.

And on Armistice Days, he always joined the locals by the poignant memorial nearby, with a statue of an angel and a small uniformed boy, commemorating the hundreds of former pupils who later, as officers, went on to perish in the First World War. The *Green Guide* writer seemed to have missed all this, as well as the fact that people had once flocked to the town from all over France to watch France's intrepid new *aviateurs* hold flying displays outside the town.

However, Harold had to admit he was relieved that the journalist had been so lazy. It kept the town remarkably free of tourists and everything that inevitably follows in their wake.

Nowadays there were no more flying machines nor bugles in

the streets, not much industry and no railway. But with seven restaurants, five bars, two pharmacies, a wine cooperative selling wine for the equivalent of less than a pound a bottle and a colourful market twice a week on the town's old parade ground, St-Hippolyte undoubtedly provided Harold Diamond with everything he needed. Here, although he lived alone, he was never lonely. There was always a smile in the café, the daily greetings, the odd game of cards and the occasional invitation to someone's home. Harold knew he was luckier than most.

His house was a charming little cottage about two miles outside the town and about 1,000 feet up, on an old mining road winding up into the foothills of the wooded Cévennes. Its altitude made the house pleasantly cooler in summer than the towns on the valley floor like Nîmes and Montpellier, but decidedly colder in winter. The cost of fuel was Harold's only complaint.

Halfway down the hill there were no inhabitants at all except for a tiny hunchbacked old lady who could sometimes be seen bent over her lavender plants, whom Alice on a visit had once irreverently dubbed 'Trolley Dolly'. This was because they had once stopped on a market day after spotting her small bent figure walking up the hill trailing a huge wheeled basket full of potatoes. She had accepted the lift with a toothless smile, but Harold had difficulty even lifting her vastly heavy load into the boot. Cackling away in her obscure accent, the old girl had brushed him aside and effortlessly tossed it into the back.

Retiring from his firm of accountants about ten years before, he had found his move to France much easier than some British people he knew. The key was speaking the language fluently. The fact that he could do so was hardly surprising because his mother was French and he had spent most family holidays in this part of France. He could even drop into the

twangy Languedoc accent if he wanted to. And thank goodness
he could, because nobody in the area seemed to speak a word
of English. This was quite ironic, considering that *The Daily
Telegraph* had recently lauded the Languedoc as 'the thinking
man's Côte d'Azur', conveniently forgetting that if the thinking
man was English, the chances are that he would probably be
quite unable to communicate his thoughts.

Harold's house was a traditional stone one, with an outhouse
which had once been a *magnanerie* – a kind of hothouse for
cultivating silkworms on racks of mulberry leaves until they
had spun their cocoons of miraculous thread, which people,
rich and poor, then delivered in donkey baskets and carts to the
silk factory in town.

Like the mines, the silk industry was sadly long since gone,
but the Cévennes hillsides were still littered with stone buildings
with *magnaneries*, which Harold had always found beautiful
when driving past them, particularly in Autumn when the red
gold leaves of the trees and the almost yellowish light made the
ancient buildings look even more lovely.

About once a week he went to a workshop on the edge
of town where he and other enthusiasts of the 'Club Aero de
Garrigues' were building an exact replica of the monoplane
in which Louis Blériot had flown across the Channel in 1909.
Harold was trying to get them an authentic 3-cylinder Anzani
engine through his British vintage aircraft connections, but so
far without success.

Another member of the club was Jean-Jacques Bertrand, a
big man with brawny arms living in Quissac, who had been
a trade union leader in the trucking industry. Apparently he
had been something of a firebrand, and after several glasses of
Pastis, loved to show his friends his collection of press cuttings
and videos, with Jean-Jacques making defiant speeches while

long lines of his trucks blocked the autoroutes, roundabouts and main roads, bringing France to a standstill.

The other members seemed far too polite to remind Jean-Jacques of how the disruption had ruined many small trucking businesses as food rotted, and for that matter, how many holidaymakers of all nationalities had been stranded miles from anywhere with desperate children without food and water. Several of them remembered being caught up in that fiasco and had wondered why the French Government had not broken up the strike and cleared the roads with their infamous *Compagnies Republicaines de Securité*. The dreaded CRS had certainly scared the hell out of other demonstrators, including the Paris students. Maybe they had been easier targets. Or maybe things had changed.

That morning Harold had been delayed getting to the Club meeting by a long phone call with his daughter Alice, going back over the shocking story of Helen's death some weeks ago. 'Still no progress,' she had told him. He had not known Helen that well, she was more of a friend of his late wife who had chosen her as a godmother. But he fully understood Alice's hurt and need to talk. So it was after eleven before he could set off down the to the Club. There they were sitting around, waiting for Jean-Jacques who was bringing the Blériot's tail assembly.

* * *

Jean-Jacques lived twenty kilometres away, up in the wooded hills near Quissac. The road, very like the one that Harold lived on, had been first built for horse-drawn mining carts and was very narrow, but it was seldom that he had to pull over to let another vehicle pass. Except in summer, the houses buried in the woods were hardly ever occupied, so one usually only met some working people, the odd construction truck and the small yellow Renault van of *La Poste*. France seemed determined to deliver the mail to even the most isolated of her houses.

And it was the postman, Philippe Arnaud, who found Jean-Jacques.

Coming round a tight bend, Philippe was surprised to see a Peugeot blocking the narrow road. He skidded to a halt. The Peugeot's engine was still running, the driver's door hung open and the driver was slumped over the wheel. Philippe couldn't see the face, but he knew the car.

The elderly postman gingerly reached in and turned off the Peugeot's engine, knowing better than to touch Jean-Jacques in case he caused a further medical problem.

A heart attack? A fainting spell? A fit of some kind?

Obviously, he needed help urgently, but now Philippe was in a dilemma. Mobile phones didn't work that far up the mountain, only beeping into life much nearer town. What should he do? He would have to drive down the hill until he got a signal.

He backed off and did an agonizingly laborious ten-point turn before setting off and parking a kilometre further down the hill. Now, at last, the phone worked. Only minutes after his call he heard the siren with a flood of relief, and followed the red ambulance back up to the car.

The burly men of the *Sapeurs Pompiers* gently moved Jean-Jacques and then their Sergeant swore under his breath. The blue-grey gendarmes' police car arrived just afterwards in time to confirm that they were looking at something a lot more complicated than a medical problem.

* * *

He walked quite a long way back to where he'd left the rented car. Up into the wooded hills – not down towards the main

CHAPTER THIRTY-TWO   197

roads, where they might start looking. He took off the painter clothes in favour of a simple white shirt and trousers and his dark glasses.

Then he drove deeper into the Cévennes, up twisting, curving roads with magnificent views across the sunlit, misty mountains.

But his mind was not on the view, but in the past. Back to those days when one very hot summer, the striking French truckers had held their country and Government to ransom, blocking all the autoroutes with their trucks. He had been part of the 'collateral damage', stuck for three miserable days among lines of trapped vehicles – trucks, vans and tourists' cars.

No food, no water, and for company, just an irritating wife and a nuisance son, both whining their complaints.

He'd remembered only too well that triumphant union leader's smirking, odious face on television and it was a real pleasure to see that same face sticking out of that car window – asking 'if he could be of help'. *A bit late, mate.*

He'd drive north and leave the car at a TGV station and then change trains at Lille. Time there to change into a suit and tie and catch the Eurostar under the Channel.

Security for the kind of things he was carrying would never be sophisticated enough.

CHAPTER THIRTY-THREE

PUTNEY, LONDON

Alice was just finishing tidying her desk after a rather long and tedious day when Maggie buzzed through.

'Alice, it's your father on the line'. She cupped her hand over the phone, 'And he sounds a bit upset,'

Alice took the phone. 'Hi Dad, are you all right?'

'Fine, just a bit shaken up. Is it okay to talk?'

'Sure, I'm just finishing up here. What is it?

'A friend of mine, Jean-Jacques, a member of our aeroplane club. He was found dead yesterday.'

Alice remembered him mentioning Jean-Jacques, once a militant firebrand of a trade unionist, and now a gentle and affable old friend.

'Oh, Dad, I'm so sorry. What happened?' She immediately assumed a heart attack.

'The postman found him halfway down the hill to Quissac, slumped over the wheel of his car. The engine was still running and the car was blocking the road, so he thought he must have had a stroke or something. But when the police arrived, they discovered he was shot.'

'Good God,' whispered Alice, suddenly remembering Aunt Helen.

'And then we all thought it must have been a shooting accident – you know, all those rather dangerous wild boar hunters who come up here. But, of course, it's not the season yet. And now I've heard it looks like murder.'

'Murder? But why?'

'God knows. Nobody's got anything much to steal around here. And everyone liked him. Could have been someone with a grudge, something to do with some strikes he led. But that was ages ago.'

There was a long pause.

'I'm sorry, it's just been a bit of a shock. There's never normally any crime around here, or at least nothing like that.'

Alice thought fast. She could probably rearrange her schedule.

'Look Dad, would you like me to come out?'

'No, no, darling. Thanks for the offer, but I'll be okay. It's his wife I'm worried about. She's always been a bit mentally fragile. Been in and out of the local clinic, and this is going to devastate her. We're all rallying around to help.'

Replacing the phone after several minutes, Alice sat deep in thought, trying to remember more about what her father had told her about his friend and whether she had ever met him. Suddenly it came back to her that he had once been famous in France, or rather notorious, with his face on all the French TV channels, exultant that France had been brought to its knees by a haulage strike. She pictured what it must have been like, with lines of his union's trucks blocking the autoroutes for days, so foreign ones couldn't get through and businesses faced ruin, and with desperate holiday-makers stranded in their cars without food or water for their trapped families. And didn't her father once mention that his friend was actually *proud* of his old video collection recording it all?

Certainly enough to have made enemies, she guessed. And a lot more enemies than than a gentle old widow in Cornwall, but as her father had said, it was all years ago. So, two pensioners living in quiet retirement had been killed with no apparent motive. One was mysterious enough. She decided to call Robin Marshal about the strange co-incidence.

'Robin, it's Alice. Sorry to bother you, but something rather weird has come up'.

She then related, in as much detail as she could, the strange events that had occurred in France. Robin had jolted upright and was scribbling notes on his pad. He checked the details.

'How do you spell that Qui, what was it, place? And may I have your father's number? I might want to talk to him, if that's okay. I haven't got round to telling you, but I was called to a meeting which included one of your detectives in Cornwall. Helen was not a one-off. Several provincial forces are reporting really strange, motiveless murders, some of elderly people like your aunt. So this thing from France may just be relevant. Thanks, Alice.'

After a few moments thought, Robin called in Joe Bain and inquired if he spoke French, and then asked him to check with the French police about the trade unionist's murder.

'And don't forget to ask them about the weapon.'

* * *

In fact, Joe Bain did speak French, and well. And after ringing and finding out more from Harold Diamond who was investigating the case, he rang the Gendarmerie in Quissac. Bain also had in front of him emails from both Interpol in Paris and Europol in The Hague referring to the incident in France. He was put through to a friendly investigating officer, Capitaine Blanchet, who explained that an Investigating Magistrate had been appointed, but that they had little to go on so far. However, a couple of the neighbours down the hill had seen a stranger near the old Quissac mine road for a few days running. He appeared to be an artist, with a canvas set up on an easel and sitting on a little portable chair. He had not been seen again since the shooting.

Nobody had spotted a stranger in town, and the hotel had no bookings other than French couples and families. All had checked out as respectable tourists. The many *gîtes* and *chambres d'hôtes* had also been investigated with no result. So if the suspect had been a visitor, he must have based himself further away – Anduze, Nîmes, or further. There was nothing, too, from any of the airports, Nîmes, Montpellier or even Marseilles.

As to the motive, Blanchet revealed they were also at a loss. No domestic situation at Bertrand's home, and attempted robbery seemed most unlikely. Nothing seemed to be missing and Monsieur Bertrand would hardly have been carrying anything of value to go down to St-Hippolyte – except the Blériot aeroplane tail assembly found in the back of his estate car. He had, of course, been a political activist in his trade union leader days, but that went back to the 1980s, and since retiring he had played no role in public life.

'Can I ask you about the gunshot wound, and the weapon?'

'Yes, he was shot once, in the chest and at short range. He was still sitting in the car with the engine running, so it was as if he was talking to someone though the window, like a neighbour, a hitchhiker, or maybe the artist figure. The bullet lodged in his body, no exit wound.'

'What calibre?'

'A bit curious. As we said in our report to Interpol and Europol, quite small and low-powered, 6.35mm. Most people don't use those baby guns now. We haven't seen one for years. Mind you, the area where the murder occurred was a very effective resistance region in the war. The locals gave the Germans a very hard time and the British supplied them with some strange little assassination guns, many using that old Browning calibre. We could send you the ballistics report, including photographs if you like.'

'Thanks, that might be very helpful. We may come back to you.'

CHAPTER THIRTY-FOUR

WANDSWORTH, LONDON

It was Henry Hammond's eighteenth birthday.

Not that Harry, as he preferred to be called, was doing anything to celebrate it. Anyway, it was a weekday and nobody knew at the office – except for the management it seemed. He had found an envelope on his mousemat that this morning and had opened it with some surprise to find a birthday card from the board; a nice gesture. They obviously checked their staff birthdays and sent them greetings. Not expensive for them and likely to promote staff goodwill.

He tucked it into his office desk drawer. There was no need for the rest of his colleagues to know, and he would have been embarrassed if they asked him for a drink in the pub after work, which they would probably feel obliged to.

After all, nobody had ever asked him out for a drink before.

He thought of Auntie Jeni and Uncle Paul. It was kind of them to send him a cheque yesterday, one day early, with a message on the front of the envelope 'Not to be opened until your birthday.' They never forgot, bless them, unlike his father, who was usually abroad anyway. And abroad again right now. It would be typical if he phoned tonight to say when he was coming back without mentioning it, and Harry wouldn't bother to remind him.

He ran an eye over yesterday's work, pleased by what he had done, and knowing that his bosses would be pleased, relieved once again that he had chosen not to go to university like his classmates at Wellington College in Berkshire. With

4 star A levels in Maths, Applied Maths, Engineering and Computer Technology, he could probably have gone to a top one – certainly in the Russell league, or maybe even Oxford or Cambridge. But had never regretted going into business at the first opportunity – in a computer technology job he loved.

Computers had always been his passion, ever since he could remember, and he could understand them far more quickly than he could people or any human relationships. He would have hated sharing digs with other students, and all the team stuff that went on in Uni, far preferring to live within a world of his own. And they would have thought him a nerd for staring into screens all day, and preferring posters of Steve Jobs and Bill Gates to some blonde starlet. He had made the right decision coming here.

He would ring Uncle Paul and Aunt Jeni during the lunch break and thank them for the cheque, and say he was looking forward to staying with them next weekend. They had always been the parents he had never had, understanding his need to be on his own since he was small, ever since his mother had died in a drowning accident.

But right now, he had to get that report done. He knew the presentation was scheduled for tomorrow. It was lucky for him in a way that Paul and Jeni had never been able to have children of their own and had always taken an interest in him and his education, sometimes visiting him or school on open or sports days – although he was useless at all sports. And he had been endlessly relieved that they never asked him why he was always alone when they visited, never in a huddle of friends chatting when the car turned up, and never asking if he wanted to bring a friend to stay in the holidays. He was eternally grateful for that.

Maybe it would all have been so different if his mother

was alive. He knew only the sketchiest details of her death. That they had been on holiday in Spain, that his mother had drowned in a boating accident, and that his father had been unable to save her. Harry also knew he was lucky to be alive himself; that his father had tried to help his mother when she had fallen overboard, and that at four years old he had been rescued from the boat when it had drifted hundreds of yards away from them in the strong current.

But why were Paul and Jeni so reluctant to talk to his father? Why, when he did go and visit them as a small child, was it always the *au pair* girl who would drive him there, or halfway there – with an arrangement to meet in some motorway service area or hotel car park? Somehow he had never been able to ask them, and he knew that the situation was unlikely to change. Once a pattern was set, it tended to stay that way.

* * *

Back in the flat at Barnes that evening, Harry picked up the usual junk mail on the doormat. No more cards as he expected. He went to check the answerphone. No messages, again as he expected. He hoped his father wouldn't turn up that night and ruin what had been a pleasantly quiet fortnight, and with uninterrupted access to his computer in the study – far more advanced than the one Harry had upstairs. He would update his as soon as he could afford to.

He looked around the study as he often did, tempted to flick through his father's files, curious about what he really did and why he was away so often. Had they had a better relationship, he could even have helped him with the computer side of things, but knew that could never be, and that his father would never divulge any details of his business – or indeed any aspects of his private life. He never had, and it was never going to change. It was like living with a stranger.

There was not even a photograph of his mother in the house – even that was a no go area – totally closed off to him – and his father had never talked about her, although his aunt and uncle had – if he asked them. He knew she was stocky and fair like he was, not at all like his father and that she was full of laughter – again utterly unlike his father, and that she had worked in a supermarket before she got married at eighteen.

She probably had to get married, Harry thought. they often did back then. That was something he'd never got out of Paul and Jeni. It certainly didn't seem as if his parents had much, if anything, in common.

At twelve o'clock Harry was on his computer upstairs when he heard the sound of a taxi outside. Blast. His father was back.

He decided not to go downstairs and his father certainly wouldn't bother to come upstairs, even if it was his eighteenth birthday.

Screw him, thought Harry.

CHAPTER THIRTY-FIVE

PUTNEY, LONDON

Alice was feeling in a good mood as she finally got around to throwing away the roses David had sent to her, long since dead in the corner of the sitting room; in fact, so dead that merely lifting the vase sent a huge shower of shrivelled petals over the carpet. Irritating, but she was certainly upbeat enough to clear up the mess instantly and get all evidence of him out of her house, just as she had successfully done to get him out of her mind.

Not a word from him in weeks, not even an email. And she was not going to contact him, although she had Googled his company out of sheer curiosity in those early days after Dublin, tempted to get in touch at a few low moments but realizing that she didn't even have his mobile number.

Now, as she replaced the vase in the cupboard, she pictured him abroad, probably on a date with someone as gullible and foolish as she'd been. But the thought didn't bother her, although the insult of the long silence vaguely did. How long had it been? Must be five or six weeks, she thought. Already it was turning autumnal in the garden and she was starting to dread the endless hours bagging up leaves and taking them to the skip.

John had been brilliant therapy, although of course he knew nothing. sometimes asking her why she was a bit low-spirited in the first weeks after Dublin, but not pressing the point when she put it down to workload and commitments. What was more, sex with John was getting better. David had taught her one thing at least. She'd finally forced herself to open up to John, and he'd welcomed that, also talking to *her* more about what he most liked too. Life was good, the sun was streaming through the kitchen window, and of course he'd won that new account.

That was it, with David. Over. A new beginning thought Alice.

And then the phone rang.

'Hi, it's me.'

Alice tensed instantly, making her response intentionally flat.

'Hello.'

'How are you doing?' asked David, in an upbeat voice.

'Fine.'

'Good.'

'Look, I'm sorry about leaving Dublin like that. I...'

Alice cut him off. 'Forget it, it doesn't matter.'

'No, it does, and I'd like to apologise.'

How dare he, thought Alice. It wasn't the abrupt departure that rankled, although that was bad enough, it was that weeks had passed since, weeks in which he could have said the same thing. Anyway, it was over, the end of that.

'Look, I'm at Heathrow right now and could be with you at around seven if you're free – maybe for a drink, or something.'

'You don't drink.'

'Well, just for a chat then.'

About what, thought Alice. Some trumped up excuse about why he hadn't bothered to call; work commitments, deadlines – she could hear it all. And she wasn't interested any more.

'I don't think so,' she replied.

'Look – half an hour, Alice. That's all I'm asking.'

Alice hesitated. She didn't need David any more, but what she wouldn't mind was some kind of explanation.

'Half an hour, Alice. That's all I'm asking.'

'Okay. But that's all you'll get. I'm pretty busy, and...'

'Seven it is,' said David abruptly, clicking off before she could change her mind.

Alice was dressed in jeans and an old sweater, and thinking about him, decided she wouldn't bother to change. What for? And he'd have to see her without a scrap of make-up. There was no point in tarting herself up.

She had a cigarette while she waited, annoyed with herself for needing one. She had given up months ago, keeping a last pack in a kitchen drawer for a sudden emergency. God, how she still missed them. Could she ever truly give up?

The doorbell rang at exactly seven.

'Hi.' David looked immaculate. Blue shirt, impossibly well tailored suit, obviously expensive shoes – and those amazing eyes. Despite all her intentions to look entirely confident, Alice suddenly felt a mess.

'Hi.She looked down at herself. 'Sorry, I've just been gardening.'

'No problem.'

David stood on the doorstep.

'Well, aren't you going to ask me in?'

'For a bit.'

As he stepped past her into the hall, Alice once again felt a frisson as his body brushed against her.

They were out on the patio at last. Simply walking out there had been tense thought Alice. And the table was hardly welcoming. A lonely can of Coke without so much as a glass, and a small decanter of wine with a glass beside it – and an ashtray and that pack of cigarettes if things got tough.

'I didn't realise you smoked,' said David.

'I don't normally,' said Alice, immediately realising that

made her sound nervous.

'Relax, Alice. I'm not going to eat you.'

Damn him, thought Alice, remembering him saying that last time, and his extraordinary ability to make her – and no doubt lots of other women – feel vulnerable and awkward.

'I'm perfectly relaxed, thanks.'

She pulled up a chair opposite him, folding her arms intentionally across the table, as if defensive and awaiting an explanation. But none came. David simply stared out across the garden.

'It's beautiful.'

'Thanks. But I don't think you've come to admire the garden.'

David turned to her, utterly relaxed, turning on the full force of those eyes. He clearly knew their effect.

'Nice to have a hobby like that, if you have time for one.'

If you have time for one? Alice was immediately rankled. How could she have ever liked this man?

'Everyone has time for one, if they make the time. Even Winston Churchill had time for painting during the war.'

'Yes, but he had a supportive woman.'

So this was a plea for a supportive woman? Alice decided to change the subject.

'I think you said you wanted to apologise?'

David nodded, casually flipping the top off his Coke.

'Sure. You're a great girl Alice, and a very interesting one. And I know I shouldn't have left you like that and not been in touch for weeks.'

'No.'

'No. Anyway, I'm sorry.' He took a sip of Coke. 'So, what have you been up to?'

So that was it? Alice was flabbergasted and furious that he

could imagine it could be that simple, and suddenly emboldened by the fact that she was on her own territory.

'Sorry, but that's just not good enough. Look, up to now this whole affair – if you can call it that – has been pretty strange to say the least. We've had, what is it, three or four dates, made love – if you can call it that too – had the odd meal, and yet I still know next to nothing about you.'

David smiled, and was about to place his hand on hers. Alice withdrew it.

'I'm sorry, I haven't finished yet. What do you really do? No-one goes off for weeks on end without saying where, at least to people they're supposed to care for. Who are your friends? What interests do you have, besides opera? What's your family like? What's your flat like, or your house? For Christ's sake, I don't even know where you live.'

David raised his hand to stop her, but Alice went on, emboldened by the cigarette and determined to be heard out.

'And why do you never talk about yourself, or hardly ever? Oh yes, and fly into a rage at the slightest thing?'

'Well, I...'

'Well, nothing.' Alice took another puff, 'For Christ's sake, I don't even have your mobile number. Virtually all I know about you is what's on Google.'

David suddenly started to crunch up his almost empty Coke can. Alice watched his anger, fascinated.

'Sorry, David, but there's absolutely no question of me carrying on with someone on that basis. It's over.'

Another puff on her cigarette. 'And here's another pretty fundamental question while I'm at it. Are you married? I don't even know that.'

She sat back, finally stubbing the cigarette out, in a way that suggested she demanded an answer.

David glared at her silently, saying nothing. Alice waited, longing to have a slug of wine, but determined to sit there as if not needing one.

'Well?' she challenged him.

David stared at her, crunching up the Coke can again.

'Goodbye, Alice.' He got to his feet and walked out.

Alice heard the door slam and the car drive off.

Relief. Out of her life. But what a fool to have got involved with a married man.

She felt like another cigarette, but avoided the temptation.

* * *

As he drove away, he was furious – but mostly with himself. It wasn't the sudden and unexpected rejection, more the question of why he had allowed himself to be distracted by that girl in the first place.

But it was just a distraction. Surely it could do no harm? She knew next to nothing about him. He'd made sure of that.

He paused, suddenly worried. He'd used his name, his *real* name.

But he shrugged the worry off. Better to get on with things.

* * *

Two hours later Alice was halfway through polishing a tray-full of silver inherited from her mother, tarnished silver plate that her father didn't want and would never find time to clean, and which Alice didn't really want either, but felt she vaguely ought to keep.

Somehow the cleaning and polishing were erasing the thoughts of David, as if she was 'getting her house in order again' and moving on, though why such a dull task was therapeutic was irritating her. Maybe it was she herself who was feeling tarnished, and there was a curious mental link.

What on earth was she thinking about getting involved with a man like that, when at last she'd found someone honest, attractive and decent?

Flattery?

Curiosity?

Because she wasn't quite ready for safety, comfort and acceptance?

Because sex hadn't been too brilliant with John to start with? Well it was now.

Because she was her own worst enemy, as most of her female patients were?

And who was *she* to advise on human relationships, if she herself could be such a mug, as much of a mug as the one she was polishing now?

CHAPTER THIRTY-SIX

WANDSWORTH, LONDON

'Who's this? He's dishy!'

Elaine had picked up a small silver-framed photo of Harry's father from the side table and was obviously admiring it, even though it was black and white, and without the effect of his startling blue eyes.

Harry glanced at it. 'My Dad. When he was about the same age as me.'

'Your Dad?' Elaine studied the photo again, surprised. 'You don't look a bit like him.'

Harry laughed. 'More's the pity.'

Elaine smiled as she replaced the photo frame. 'I don't mind. I like you as you are. And anyway, if you looked like him you probably wouldn't have asked me out.'

So she knew she was no beauty. But that only made Harry feel even more comfortable. After all, he was nothing special to look at himself. Stocky, thick glasses, with an impossible thatch of fair hair. He had long since realized that all that was a handicap, shying away from events like office parties, at the same time recognizing that he was slightly afraid of girls, and even more of their rejection if he ever dared to ask them out. He never had, until now.

And what she did have was a beautiful smile, and a lovely warmth and chattiness. Every time he'd gone to the local supermarket recently he'd chosen to go through her checkout, looking forward to talking to her as she passed through all his items, and realizing that, when he was in a queue, she was just as nice and friendly to the people before him. That was obviously just the way she was.

And one day last week, when there was nobody else but him at the checkout, he had dared to ask her out, checking yet again that there was no engagement ring on the third finger of her left hand.

He had been delighted when she accepted, although she was plainly surprised, and perhaps even a bit shocked that a customer would ask her out.

'When?' she had whispered, looking around her nervously, as if the Manager might appear at any moment.

'Tonight?'

Elaine looked around again. 'Okay, I don't see why not.'

Harry had handed her a card with his father's address, and with his mobile number underneath.

'Do you think you could make it to where I live at about seven thirty? It's only around the corner.'

Elaine had studied the card briefly, before putting it into her overall pocket. 'I know, it's quite near where I live. Okay, I'll be there at seven thirty.' She patted the pocket where the card was, and gave him an endearing little wave.

She had been amazed by the house on that first date, replacing the photo of his father on the side table and looking around the large sitting room with undisguised awe. 'And this is your Dad's place?'

'Yup. Although he's hardly ever here. Works abroad all the time.'

'Lucky you. I'd love to have a place like this all to myself, and without paying the rent.'

Harry was mildly irritated by that assumption. 'Who says I don't?' Though knowing he didn't contribute, he felt mildly guilty. Maybe he should do, now he had a job. It was the first time he had ever thought about it.

'Sorry,' said Elaine.

She looked around the sitting room again. 'And where's a photo of your Mum?'

'There isn't one. She's dead.'

Harry was shocked that he had put it so bluntly. It wasn't fair on her, and Elaine looked horribly embarrassed.

'Don't worry,' he added, 'it was all ages ago. I hardly remember her.'

Elaine didn't know what to say. She looked down at her lap, twiddling her bracelet.

'How about a pizza?' Harry tried to lighten the mood, and was delighted to see Elaine smile, obviously hugely relieved to leave the subject.

'Lovely!'

'We could have one here if you like. There's a great Domino's round the corner. Or we could go out to the High Street.'

'No, I'm happy to eat here. It's not often I've been in a nice place like this.'

It had been a lovely evening, and tonight was their fourth date, always at the house, and so far with his father still away, and with no news about when he was coming back. Always there was that niggling fear of hearing a taxi turn up outside, or the key turning in the lock. But so what, if he was having a girl to supper? There was nothing abnormal about that. Why shouldn't he, thought Harry. Although the smell of pepperoni pizza might irritate his father; there was definitely a faint odour these days in the sitting room that didn't seem to disappear despite the room sprays.

And always there had been the same comfortable routine, or pretty well always the same. A takeaway in front of the television – by now it was clear that neither of them had much money to eat out – then maybe a late night video curled up together on the sofa, and on the last two occasions, a bit more than that. That had been the only worrying part, although he and Elaine had never been in a total state of undress, both afraid of a sudden interruption.

Of course, he could have asked her upstairs. So why didn't he, thought Harry? Maybe it was because his room was on the third floor, and if his father returned suddenly – and worse still, in a bad mood – they would have to pass his room on the way down – and possibly bump into him. He pictured him studying Elaine with those piercing blue eyes: her short body, her plump frame. It would be unbearable. He wouldn't put her or himself through that.

But tonight he would take the risk, even though Elaine was fearful. 'What if he comes back?'

'So what if he does?'

Elaine had eventually relented.

But the rest of the night was a disaster. Harry had never been to bed with a girl before, and the whole thing was over before it had started. And though Elaine had been more than kind, he had felt an utter fool.

'I'm sorry.'

'Don't worry about it.'

But he did. And at 3 a.m. in the morning, unable to relax, and fearful it might happen again, he had walked her home – almost in silence – and not daring to arrange another date. 'I'll see you,' he had said weakly. There wasn't even a parting kiss. She had simply unlocked the door, vaguely looked at him, and walked straight in.

He would have to move out and get his own place. But how? He had almost no friends – no mates he could share with – and even if he had, it would be tough finding a month's deposit. He couldn't bear to be humiliated yet again.

But could he dare to ask his father for a loan?

Suddenly, to his horror, he thought about his mother's life insurance money.

CHAPTER THIRTY-SEVEN

SCOTLAND YARD

'What have we got?'

Robin Marshal was in the ballistics laboratory talking to his principal ballistics expert, D.S. Gordon Burns, who had come up from the ballistics lab in Lambeth. Burns had been tasked to study carefully all the reports sent to Robin relating to the small calibre gunshot homicide.

It had been annoying that they had to wait some time for the Hong Kong report. Apparently, Jimmy Wong had run up against some kind of internal problem about releasing the information.

Burns projected the comparison microscope images of each round.

'It's pretty amazing. All of them were .25 ACP rounds and from the same year of manufacture. Maybe the same batch.

What's more, the rounds from Belfast, Hong Kong, Kent and France were all definitely fired from the same weapon. I can't tell you what it is. A bit unconventional, with curious rifling. But it's the same weapon.'

Robin stared at the screen and sucked in his breath.

Thanking Burns, he hurried from the room. He quickly emailed his British colleagues, thanked Jimmy Wong by email and asked Joe Bain to thank Capitaine Blanchet. But he also told them that their local murders were almost certainly committed by one man – very resourceful and dangerous.

And probably very difficult to find.

Robin Marshal suddenly realised that he should report what

he had been doing to his boss, Commander Bill Jones, and made an appointment to see him on an urgent basis.

An hour later, he faced Jones – a large and rather intimidating man, who had both boxed and played rugby for the Police Service. Robin chose his words carefully.

'I know, Sir, that what I'm going to tell you is not strictly about cases for the Met, but ...'

He then explained being called as an observer to the Bramshill conference by the detectives from Kent and from Devon and Cornwall, and the strange nature of the age of the two victims, with no obvious motive. Then he went on to Corcoran in Belfast and also the bizarre machine-gunning on the A1. Blameless victims, often old. Strange weapons, often old too.

He then described the request for help from Jimmy Wong and the Interpol connection with France. Old people, respectable, no motives, and strange weapons, although he did not feel he needed to reveal the coincidence of Alice Diamond being vaguely connected to two cases.

'Are you telling me, Robin,' interrupted Jones, 'that there's someone going all over the world knocking people off for no good reason. I can't believe it. And I also don't see why we should be involved.'

'Well, Sir, as to the links between them, I asked all the forces to send me ballistic reports, and Gordon Burns had them checked out. All the old-fashioned small calibre bullets that were used match – all the rounds were fired from the same weapon.

So Kent, Belfast, Hong Kong, France. Same weapon, every time. It's almost unbelievable.

I have no idea if Cornwall and Bedford are related. One elderly lady, but one young victim, but old weapons again. But,

I've just got a nasty gut feeling they may be. And, of course, there may be other cases which haven't been reported yet.'

While the Commander was no longer sceptical, he did appear to be getting somewhat irritated.

'While I agree it's fascinating, I come back to the fact that we, and you, have got plenty to worry about and to work on already – not least the Olympic security. All that other stuff is not within the Met's remit – especially France and Hong Kong, for Christ's sake.

I must insist you politely keep a watching brief, but actually let them all get on with it.'

Robin Marshal knew better than to argue and gathered up his material. As he left, he observed, 'Let's hope whoever seems to be doing this doesn't decide to do it on our patch.'

The Commander was already looking at something on his computer screen. Robin would have been even more upset if he'd known that his boss was searching the web for a classy home for his retirement.

CHAPTER THIRTY-EIGHT

LINCOLNWOOD, CHICAGO

Betty-Anne was still there, as Mary-Lou had known she would be. Still driving her mad, and not particularly because of anything she said, but simply because she was there at all, and in a house too small for the six of them. *And* a dog! It was everything that Mary-Lou had predicted three months ago – only worse.

Not an impossible mother-in-law; in many ways she was charming, and always ready to help, but nevertheless a constant presence. She was no longer obviously depressed, having ceased to wonder aloud and often about why the police had not caught the killer. She never once mentioned when she might be leaving, and always parked in the same chair every evening in the sitting room when Mary-Lou would have liked the chance to watch TV without the volume turned up, and without Sean, the dog, trying to take up the last space on the couch.

And it was even worse having her in the kitchen from nine every morning, asking if she could do anything to help. There always was, but Mary-Lou preferred doing it alone.

The kitchen was very much Mary-Lou's territory. She loved cooking and people coming over, but hated this space so constantly invaded and was increasingly frustrated by the fact that no two women ever did things quite the same way. 'Shall I help you chop the beans?' 'Do the sprouts?' 'Make the salad?' 'Roll the pastry?' It was never quite like how Mary-Lou wanted it done, and she felt petty being so privately irritated, often remembering some old Chinese proverb about how it was easier for two women to share a man than a kitchen. Now, when she thought about it, she was doing both.

She simply couldn't stand this permanent hovering, still less her husband's infuriating inference that somehow they made a pretty good team. 'Congratulations, you two – this pie is real good!' And she loathed the fact that her husband had almost become like a small boy, luxuriating in the attentions of two women, and as a result she had become increasingly switched off in bed, resenting him to the point of thoroughly unfamiliar anger which was becoming less and less suppressed.

She couldn't even have her friends over for a coffee without Betty-Anne popping her head around the kitchen door. 'Mind if I join you?' And why should she always have to go out to *their* houses to have a private conversation? That was something she realized she was doing more and more, and the conversation always got around to Betty-Anne in the end, and the inevitable advice.

'You've got to do something. This can't go on.'

And you couldn't ask friends for advice all the time – if you didn't take it. In the end, that would just annoy or bore them, and it was probably starting to already. 'The longer you leave it, the harder it will be.' Her friend Roseanne's advice rang in her head all day. And so did that of her old college pal, Suzanne. 'Sometimes, you have to be cruel to be kind.'

'Maybe you should get a job,' Sandy had suggested. 'At least that would get you out of the house.'

But why should she? Mary-Lou had never worked since her marriage, perfectly content to look after Patrick, the children, the house and garden, and not fussed by the endless debates between stay-at-home mothers and professional mothers dominating the media. That had never worried her. And what would she do, if she did get a job? And, come to think of it, what would her mother-in-law do, then stuck in the house all day alone? After all, even if she did get a job, she'd need a car to get to work, and Patrick would need the other one. She had awful visions of Betty-Anne rearranging the furniture in sheer boredom or clocking up endless phone bills to her friends back home.

It wouldn't work, and neither would she.

What was more, her rare evenings out alone with Patrick hadn't been much fun. All too soon he would start fretting and looking at his watch. 'I wonder if we ought to get back?' On the few occasions she had been out, there had always been that mental shadow hovering over them. And it wasn't even as if his mother were in her dotage, barely sixty, young these days, perfectly able to cope.

'I'd rather like another glass of wine. There's no need to rush back.'

She had been irritated by Patrick's frown on the last occasion.

'Do you really *need* one?'

'Quite frankly, yes.'

So the evening had already been ruined, as she knew he wouldn't have another glass with her, and would be making strenuous efforts to avoid discussing his mother as he watched her sip at her glass, eking out the occasion for as long as she could before she returned to the nightmare.

'Look Patrick, I need to say something.'

'Not now.'

'Not ever,' was what he meant.

'You've got to get rid of her,' said Mary-Lou bluntly one night in mid-December, as she brushed her hair at the dressing table with unusual vigour, her back to Chris who was already in bed. She was ready for battle after a particularly irritating day. Betty-Anne was becoming far too comfortable, taking over.

That morning her mother-in-law had suggested that they go to the woods together with the dog and find pine cones to paint for Christmas, or perhaps hazel branches on which to hang tiny baubles for the hall table, and think of making the Christmas pudding and hanging the cards on red ribbons.

It was all too much. As if Thanksgiving hadn't been bad enough. Her mother-in-law had virtually taken over that too. But this was a nightmare. Did one person's recovery always have to mean another person's downfall? She wondered how psychiatrists managed to keep things compartmentalised, while realizing that her mother-in-law never moaned and groaned, which made her feel guilty.

It was evident that Patrick couldn't or wouldn't see the problem – after all, he was mostly at work– and the children were blissfully oblivious to it, far more interested in their own lives as teenagers were. The two youngest had got used to sharing a bedroom, rubbish tip though it now was, and both of them had accepted Betty-Anne being there – no doubt encouraged by their father behind her back. And they liked having the dog around – although of course they never had to take it off for walks.

'What?' asked Patrick. Mary-Lou turned her head. He was reading a book. 'You've got to get rid of your mother,' said Mary-Lou again. 'I can't stand it any longer.'

'Don't be ridiculous. It's almost Christmas. We can't possibly ask her to go now.' He looked up from his book. 'Especially as she's just done all the decorations.'

That was it. Mary-Lou was about to explode. She took a deep breath.

She suddenly remembered that John, her eldest, would be staying out tonight – some party and sleepover at the basketball club.

In twenty years of marriage she and Patrick had never slept apart, except when he was away on his rare business trips to another city.

Patrick made no attempt to stop her as she went to John's room.

CHAPTER THIRTY-NINE

QUISSAC, FRANCE

Viviane Bertrand sat at the writing desk by the window looking out over the beautiful lawns and borders around the Clinique de Quissac. In late summer, the flowers were now in full bloom, and on the occasions she was permitted outside she found strolling around them restful and noticeably restorative.

Only three people were on Viviane's chosen rota of visitors, all of them extremely close women friends, and she had not even seen her son and daughter in law and little grandson Louis for the past six weeks, alarmed that the child would be upset about why she was here, with other patients being escorted around the grounds with uniformed carers, and not in the familiar and pretty gardens of her own home and with his grandfather Jean-Jacques.

He had been told that his grandfather had gone to heaven suddenly. That was enough for him to cope with for now. It would be years before he would be told what exactly happened.

'Are you having any visitors today?' asked a voice behind her – Julianne, her room-mate, who had lost her only son in an accident two months ago. All the women at the Clinique shared a bedroom with someone of their own age, and over the past few weeks Viviane had come to understand why. Being on one's own for long periods was mentally frightening after a severe nervous breakdown.

'Yes, my friend Annelise.'

'That's nice.'

'Are you going out?'

'Probably. We may go to the flea market in Quissac and have a coffee.'

Viviane was looking forward to looking around the local flea market, with wonderful second-hand clothes for next to nothing. Maybe she would buy something nice for Louis; he was growing out of his clothes all the time. And it would also be nice to stroll around the town in the sunshine, as long as strangers didn't speak to her. That still filled her with fear of another panic attack.

But Annelise could be trusted to intervene and tactfully handle any purchase with the stallholders. How long before she would get over that fear? The psychiatrist had been optimistic, reminding her that such attacks were not uncommon after a major trauma.

'Our prognosis is good. We believe you'll be ready to leave here in about a month. But first we have to be absolutely confident about your medication programme, as you of course need to be. But you're doing well.'

But would she be able to cope with the nights, Viviane wondered? They were the worst, and she had often woken Julianne when she was no longer able to cope in the dark, or when she had woken from a dream – or rather a nightmare – about Jean-Jacques, in which she relived the terrible moment she had heard about his death.

She had seen too much of death in her thirty years as a hospice nurse in the big hospital in Alès. Recently retired at fifty after comforting hundreds of patients in their last days, she had longed for the years ahead, quietly living with Jean-Jacques, going off on their annual walking holidays and visiting the regular exhibitions in the little towns around Quissac where Viviane's paintings would be displayed. She was no great painter, Viviane knew that, but she loved painting and the company of the regular art classes, and even more than that, the fact that Jean-Jacques was so flattering and encouraging.

'You're really good, you know!' he had smiled delightedly over her latest work; a still life. She knew she wasn't. The napkin was wrong, the jug was crooked, the fruit bowl wasn't quite right – cut glass didn't reflect light like that, not in shafts and beams. But she was always touched by his praise.

Suddenly there was a knock at the door.

Viviane opened it. 'Madame Bertrand, your friend is here.'

'Thanks, I'll be out in a minute.'

'I'll be in reception to sign you out,' smiled the charge nurse.

CHAPTER FORTY

PARKGATE, CHESHIRE, ENGLAND

Harry was reading a computer magazine on the Friday evening train to Chester, where Uncle Paul and Aunt Jeni would pick him up before the drive to their house in Parkgate. But even though the article was interesting, he was finding it hard to concentrate. Maybe certain days – like birthdays – made one think more about life he thought, as Christmas and New Year usually did. At times like that, he had always looked backwards not forwards. And since his birthday, his thoughts had been turning more and more to the past, and to so many still unanswered questions.

On this visit he was determined to dig deeper, find out more, and why so much of his life had been cloaked in embarrassed secrecy, or in the case of his father, almost total silence.

Had his father had some terrible row with Paul and Jeni, as he now called them, feeling old enough to drop the prefix Aunt and Uncle? He must have done, or why did he never see them, or even ask about them when he returned? That would have at least been polite, considering all his aunt and uncle had done for him over the years, and still did.

Or was it a row about money? That was often the cause of family arguments, and it was true that Paul and Jeni didn't seem to have much, with a tiny house that was hardly enough for the two of them, let alone the countless times he had stayed there.

His father certainly had an appalling temper. He had seen enough evidence of that. This weekend he would try – at long last – to find out why, and why they weren't on speaking terms, and if his aunt and uncle weren't forthcoming, he would have to give up. There was nobody else he could ask, although there might be some family papers and correspondence in his father's study – he had often been tempted to have a look. He was eighteen now. It was high time he knew more, much more, about his past – and his mother. Did he even look like his mother? He didn't even know that.

They were there on time as he knew they would be, waiting with their usual smiles and waves as he walked up to the ticket barrier. They were that kind of people, utterly trustworthy and reliable, and not the type to wait in the car park and wait for him to find them, and never once late when he came by train.

'Hi!' He gave each of them a big hug; roly-poly, warm-hearted Jeni, as always in crazy boho clothes and costume jewellery – even on a station concourse on a Friday night, and affable, comfortable Paul. They were the parents he had never had, and the only people with whom he could really relax. It was always a glorious escape coming up here, away from the tensions of getting on with his own age group back in London, let alone coping with his moody father.

'Hope you're hungry,' said Jeni as they set off for Parkgate. 'I've made you a special birthday supper.' She glanced over at him in the back of the car. 'I can't believe you're eighteen. Did you do anything nice?'

'Not particularly,' said Harry, thinking of his birthday night alone at home, eating fish and chips and watching a video. 'We're a bit busy at work, with a big presentation coming up. And I thought Dad might come back, so I couldn't ask anyone over.' A sudden silence fell over the car, as it always did when he mentioned his father.

He knew Jeni well enough to know she was wondering if his

father had bought him a present, but had decided not to ask.

'And the job's going well?' She predictably changed the subject.

'Fine. I love it. And the pay's not bad. Which reminds me, thanks again for that cheque. It'll help me get a new computer. Mine's about to give up the ghost, and there'll be hell to pay if Dad ever finds out I've used his.'

'I'm sorry it couldn't be more,' said Jeni, 'but....'

'No, it was very generous. I'm really grateful.'

At last they were there, in the cosy surroundings he had always loved as a child; ornaments and little mementos everywhere, so many there was scarcely a place to put a glass down. Jenny could never resist anything or putting it on display: seashells, interesting pebbles, even glass vases full of strange buttons to sew on her boho outfits.

And she was right about it being a special birthday supper – well, not what most people would call special these days, but one that he had always asked for on his Sundays out from Mostyn House, his prep school just down the road from their house: a simple roast chicken with all the trimmings, and lashings of Jeni's own home-made bread sauce.

She had even been kind enough to make a birthday cake, complete with eighteen candles. However, could he manage it after that baguette on the train and then that gargantuan main course? Harry decided he would have to give it his best shot. He owed it to her.

Jeni handed him a knife as soon as the last candle was lit.

'Go on, you've got to make a wish!'

Harry already had, days ago. Once again, as he sliced the cake, he wished he would be getting answers at last, starting tomorrow.

* * *

The next morning, Harry accompanied Jeni on her usual daily walk along the marshland and estuary opposite their house, while Paul went to the garden centre where he worked six days a week, and always on Saturdays and Sundays – the busiest time.

It was freezing cold, and the sun was struggling to emerge from the mist, but thankfully Harry was wearing Paul's huge duffel coat, though he doubted if his aunt would want to stay out there for long. He mustn't waste this precious time. He would have to start asking questions. With Paul around, she might not be so forthcoming.

'So tell me more about what's been happening in your life,' said Jeni.

Harry laughed. 'There's not much to tell. No girlfriends, if that's what you're asking.' He didn't want to mention Elaine, at least not yet.

'I wouldn't dream of it!' She knew Harry wouldn't find it easy to get a girlfriend – stocky, awkward with strangers, and with thick old-fashioned glasses and badly cut hair. Why couldn't his bloody father at least get him contact lenses and send the boy for a realy good haircut? For God's sake, he had enough money.

They walked along the shoreline for a minute or two.

'Actually, talking about my life, there's something I want to know. Quite a lot of things, actually.'

Jeni had waited for this moment for years, knowing it would have to come sometime. He was eighteen now, she reminded herself. He'd waited too long already; it was high time he knew more and he deserved truthful answers. But she would have to be careful.

Anticipating his questions, she steeled herself. 'Okay. Fire away.'

'I want you to tell me more about Mum and Dad. And why you never meet Dad, or talk about him.' Jeni noticed his voice was less diffident than usual. 'And about what really happened. I hardly know anything, and I really need to know.'

'But I've told you most things.'

'Not nearly enough.'

Suddenly, he felt her arm around him. 'Shall we sit over there?' They were coming up to a bench on the shoreline.

They sat companionably, side by side. 'Well, I don't know what to tell you that I haven't already. It was just a terrible accident when you were four years old. What you *do* need to know – and I've probably never told you – is that your mother adored you. She was a brilliant mother, absolutely wonderful. It was lovely to see her with you; she was an absolute natural. I'm sure your father loves you too – deep down – although he has a funny way of showing it. Maybe it was the shock that changed him.'

Harry stared out over the estuary. 'Tell me more about the accident. What *really* happened?'

Jeni was immediately guarded.

'It was a long time ago.'

'Not that long. Only fourteen years. You can't have forgotten.' Harry waited for an answer.

'I haven't. I never will'.

'So, please tell me.'

There was a long silence as Jeni composed herself, wondering what, and how much, to tell him. Again. she reminded herself that she would have to be careful, whatever she and Paul happened to think.

'Well, it was very complicated.'

'In what way?'

'Well, it wasn't a straightforward accident – although it may have been. There was quite a long case about it in Spain. All kinds of questions about how it happened.' Harry flinched. A court case? Why? And what kind of questions?

'They wondered why none of you were wearing lifejackets. And especially you. You were only four. And exactly how your mother died. And how. She was a reasonable swimmer. In fact, she was teaching you at the local pool at the time. I think I've got a photo of you both there.'

Jeni paused. 'It was probably cramp; even good swimmers can get that. And there was a strong tide, they knew that. She probably drifted out before he could reach her, just as you did in the boat. You were several hundred yards away when they rescued you.'

'And Dad managed to get back to the beach.'

'Yes.'

'Anyway, it was a long time before the court case was over. And then it was ages more before your father got the life insurance money.'

Life insurance money? It hit Harry like a bolt. The thought had never once crossed his mind. So that was why his father had been able to afford expensive boarding schools, a string of au pairs and highly-paid nannies and buy a three storey house in Wandsworth. Or had his business paid for that? He couldn't help wondering how much his father had received. It must have been a lot. After all, how old was his mother? Barely into her twenties.

'I never knew about that.'

'What?'

'That he got life insurance on her.'

'Oh yes, a lot. Maybe I shouldn't have told you.'

'No, I'm glad you did.'

'Your mother was only twenty-two, with her whole life ahead of her. It would have been a fortune.'

Harry detected a touch of bitterness in her voice. He suddenly thought the unthinkable.

'You surely don't think that Dad was somehow involved?'

'No, of course not. It's...well, it's that I can't stop wondering why he couldn't have saved her. And why none of you had lifejackets.'

'But surely that would be Mum's fault, too.'

'Probably, but it's so unlike her. She wasn't a fool, far from it. If anything, she was over-protective of you. She hardly ever let you out of her sight. It makes no sense.'

There was a long silence as Harry pictured his mother with him as a child, and then falling off the boat. It was too much. He decided to change the subject.

'And were they ever happy? Did Mum and Dad *have* to get married?'

Jeni laughed. 'Nobody ever *has* to get married these days, not if they don't want to.'

'You know what I mean.'

She smiled at him. 'If you mean was she pregnant with you at the time, yes.'

'I thought so.'

'Why do you never see Dad?'

'Because he never wants to see us. No great mystery there. Although *why* he doesn't want to is a mystery. Maybe it's because he can't face Paul. He and your mother were very, very close. He was much older than her, about thirteen years older. And he always felt like her protector. And in the end Paul probably couldn't face seeing *him*.'

She paused for a while, gazing out over the water. 'But then,

your father had a tough childhood. That's probably why he's
so distant now.'

Jeni wondered whether she had already said too much. But
maybe he could manage a little bit more. It might help him to
understand.

'You know he was adopted?'

'Yes, you've told me that before.'

'And that he spent some time in a children's home?'

'No, I didn't know that.' Harry was startled. He pictured
a miserable orphanage where a small boy was waiting to be
adopted.

'And that his real mother died in a car smash and his father
killed himself?'

Again Jeni wondered whether she had gone too far.

'No, I didn't know that either.'

Harry was having trouble taking it all in. Just as he had
bottled up the questions all these years, Jeni had obviously
bottled up the answers. But why if his father had lost his own
parents, would he not try and be a better father himself? It
didn't make sense.

He suddenly wondered if Jeni had been out to that court
case.

'Did you two go out to Spain after the accident?'

'No. We don't speak Spanish. We wouldn't have understood
anything. Anyway, it was all in the papers here.'

Another shock.

'What, all about the accident?'

'Yes.'

'With pictures of Dad?'

'Yes, and you and your Mum.'

'And did you keep them? The papers, I mean?'

'No. Paul destroyed them all.'

Jeni shivered, as much at the recollections as at the cold. She cleared her throat and looked at her watch. 'Look, I think it's time we got back, but if you want to talk more tomorrow we can come down here again.'

'I'd like that,' said Harry.' 'Thanks.' He had enough answers for now. His mind was already reeling.

'By the way, there's no need to go on about how my father really loves me, and all that. I actually think he hates me for some reason. And I *definitely* hate him. He treats me like dirt. Always has. Really, actively, unpleasantly. So nothing much you've said would have changed my view, which is that he's a bastard.'

Jeni looked at him, shocked but not surprised.

'Well, okay.' She tried to recover. 'One last thing for now. You can always talk to me, but I'd rather you didn't talk to Paul about your mother. As I said, they were incredibly close. It's still raw. That's why we don't have any photos of her in the house – at least any put out that you can see. Paul can't bear having them around. He hid them away years ago.

So there were photos of his mother? Maybe he could ask Jeni if he could see them, or give him some to take away?

* * *

'So, tell me more about Mum...or Dad, anything.' They were back on the bench on the riverside overlooking the estuary, and Harry noticed that his aunt was visibly more relaxed this time, perhaps because he had kept his promise to say nothing to Paul about yesterday's talk, and that she knew she could trust him, not just now but in the future. And he loved his uncle; he would never let Jeni down.

'Well, what can I say? Your father was a very attractive man. It's not hard to see why your mother fell for him. I could have done too, at least in the looks department.'

Harry knew his father was attractive, very attractive, even now in his mid-forties. On the very rare occasions they'd been out together he had noticed women looking at him, sometimes vaguely annoyed that he didn't return their glances, which he was vain enough to be aware of, or return them more than a fleeting one. He suddenly wondered why his father had never had any girlfriends, or if he did – which he surely must have done looking like that – why he had never brought any of them home. Perhaps because he was embarrassed by having such a lump of a son around.

'And was he in love when he got married to Mum?'

Jeni laughed. 'Well, as I said yesterday, they didn't have to get married. And they certainly looked happy enough at the wedding.'

'And christening?'

'You weren't christened, but then loads of people aren't.'

'But I think he was probably always, well, a kind of distant person. Didn't give much of himself away.'

'And what happened when he came back to England, you know, after the court case?'

'He got in touch with us, and asked if we could help. Said he couldn't cope and had to be away all the time. And of course, we did.'

She looked at him, with intimate gentleness. 'And we've always been thrilled we did. You're family; the son we could never have.'

Harry suddenly felt tears, but he had to go on. It might be weeks before he could afford to come up here again. The train tickets cost a bomb, and he had to buy that new computer soon. He needed as many answers as he could get now.

'And where's Mum buried?'

Jeni could hardly bare to look at him. 'She wasn't, she was cremated. Out in Spain.' She wished she didn't have to tell him that.

'So he didn't even bother to bring her home.'

There was a long silence, only broken by the sound of geese flying overhead.

Jeni placed a hand on his knee. 'Look, I know he's not the best father, but I'm sure he cares deep down. He probably didn't know how to cope with it. Or a family funeral. Especially after all that stuff in the papers. And he probably didn't know how to cope with you either. You were only a baby, Harry.'

She looked at him tenderly. 'Did you know that her second name was Harriet? That's why you're called Harry.'

Harry was suddenly lost in thought. Jeni looked at him. Maybe she had said enough.

'Incidentally, did you know that Mostyn House – your old prep school – is closing down?'

Harry glanced behind him towards where his old prep school was. It hadn't exactly been the scene of thousands of treasured childhood memories, but it had been lovely to go to school so near to Jeni and Paul and they had taken him out often – or as often as he was allowed – treating him to ice creams at the renowned shop called Nicholls on the waterfront, and buying him bags of the famous local shrimps, as well as giving him that favourite Sunday roast and coming to the end-of-term art exhibitions.

He had always painted a picture of Jeni and Paul. He suddenly remembered his words when they came to see them. 'Sorry, it's not very good. They don't look at all like you.'

'Thank God for that,' Paul had always said, 'and thanks for giving me all that hair. Though I think you probably need better glasses!'

'And thanks for taking stones off me!' Jeni had added, delighted that her boho dress didn't make her look like a tent.

* * *

Harry arrived back in Wandsworth at last, after midnight, and after an exhausting train and tube journey. But he still decided to unpack his suitcase before turning in.

Zipped into the back pocket, he was thrilled to find an old photo album and a small wrapped present. Unwrapping the present first, he found a miniature silver frame with a photo of his mother which he looked at for several minutes before putting it on the bedside table. Fair, like him, and with a lovely smile. It would be safe up here. His father never came to his bedroom.

He then spent three hours studying the album, photographs he thought he would never see, poring over every tiny detail. Him and his mother, lots of them. She was not conventionally pretty, but she had a wonderfully warm face, and yes, she was like him, as Jeni had told him. Maybe if he smiled more, had a decent haircut and didn't wear thick glasses, he would look even more like her. Perhaps he should make more of an effort, he told himself.

There was one of his mother with him in a swimming pool, with him in armbands. He remembered Jeni saying she was teaching him to swim. And several of a toddler's birthday party. Three candles on the cake. And was that him blowing them out? It must be. And there were a few of his father, but only a few, and mostly in the wedding pictures where he seemed happy enough. Maybe he didn't like being photographed, as Harry didn't, although it was strange when one was as handsome as that.

At 4.a.m. the album slid to the floor as Harry suddenly fell

asleep, exhausted by all the weekend's revelations and the long
journey back. The bedside light was still on.

CHAPTER FORTY-ONE

PUTNEY, LONDON

Alice pottered around her kitchen, truly looking forward to the evening ahead. One month after David had stormed out she was feeling relaxed and happy, conjecturing that she was possibly happier than at any other time in her life. When she thought of David at all, sometimes when sitting on the patio and looking at the empty chair opposite, it was mostly with a professional curiosity, a conviction that there was a wife and perhaps children somewhere, and a feeling of irritation and utter amazement that she had never had the guts to ask questions earlier.

Now, laying the table for five people, she felt a pleasant wave of contentment. Several of her cases were going well, and though that was a mixed blessing in her profession – because patients who were starting to cope with their demons were less likely to see her – it was deeply satisfying to hear of their steady progress, particularly in the case of the Down's syndrome child, whose mother had phoned that morning to say she was making good progress and that her stealing habit seemed, at last, to be under control.

And things were going well with John as she gradually learned to open up to him, telling him things she'd never – or only once – been able to say before. Maybe David had done her a favour after all.

She thought of the people coming and knew it would be a great evening – John, Liz, Derek and Jimmy Mason – an old mate from training days whom she hadn't seen for ages, now involved in psychology with the military – and who had phoned out of the blue the other day.

John had phoned earlier, after two nights in Paris. 'Look, I'm running a bit late, I'll try and be there by 8.30 – but if I'm not, start without me. I'm really sorry.'

'Fine, no problem. See you whenever.'

Trust was great thought Alice as she replaced the phone. If he was later than 8.30, there'd be a good reason, and moreover, a truthful one. He wouldn't be sitting in a bar with some strange woman, and even if he *had* been these past few nights, she knew she needn't worry. Suddenly, it was supremely pleasant to potter about, forget about her patients and simply look forward to guaranteed good company – and at last a man in whom she could truly confide and open up to.

The doorbell rang. Liz, with that same wonderful hug and smile, and coming early enough to have a good natter before the others arrived. Twenty minutes later, Jimmy turned up with a huge bunch of flowers tied in a bag of water, which Alice promptly placed in the middle of the table, thanking him with a warm hug. Orange; not exactly her favourite colour, but it was a lovely gesture. Thanks, they're gorgeous.'

An hour later, Alice was relieved to hear the sound of a taxi pulling up outside. John looked flustered, apologizing for the delay, but was pleased to see Alice so relaxed.

'It's fine, don't worry,' she assured him as she let him in. 'And stay for the night if you want to. You must be knackered.'

John smiled. 'I am.'

Alice enjoyed dinner all the more for knowing that John would be staying, and for noticing that despite being exhausted he was still thoroughly entertaining, telling his usual hilarious stories and anecdotes, and obviously hitting it off with Jimmy, normally fairly withdrawn.

And suddenly it was well past midnight, and the others had to go. John suddenly looked totally drained. 'Want me to help you clear up?' he asked, looking at the huge stack in the sink.

'No, leave it. I'll do it tomorrow.'

'Thanks.' He smiled at her, looking relieved. 'Incidentally, I've got you a little something. Want to see it before we go to bed?'

A present? Alice was delighted.

'It's out there in my case – zipped up in the top pocket.'

Alice returned clutching a small and beautifully wrapped box. 'What is it?'

'Open it and see.'

She sat beside him and carefully undid the bow and the paper.

'Oh John, it's beautiful!' She held up a sapphire brooch in the shape of a flower, the tiny jewels dancing in the glow of the candles.

'I knew you'd like it. I saw it in a little antiques market on the way back to the hotel yesterday, and … well, I thought of you.'

'I don't just like it … I *love* it!'

She smiled at John, suddenly wondering if she was starting to love him too.

CHAPTER FORTY-TWO

WELLINGTON BARRACKS, LONDON

Colonel Sir William O'Farrell looked out from his office window over the expanse of Wellington Barracks. Built on the site of King James the First's aviary, which gave the road in front of it the name 'Birdcage Walk', he knew that they had been named after the great Duke, and created back in 1833 to provide a military presence very close to the Royal Family's residence at Buckingham Palace.

It had a magnificent long neo-classical façade, looking out over a huge parade ground – 'The Square' – and there was always one battalion of the Brigade of Guards stationed there, with the Queen's Guard taking up daily duties both at the Palace and also down the Mall at St James's Palace.

Bill O'Farrell was descended from an ancient Irish family and liked to muse about tradition. His regiment was just back from Afghanistan, where it had lost several officers and men to snipers and roadside bombs and had won several decorations for bravery, and was now providing 'Public Duties'. This meant the far less dangerous, but less exciting tasks of the ceremonial guarding of Buckingham Palace and St James's Palace, the Tower of London and Windsor Castle and providing at least one Guard at the annual 'Trooping the Colour' on the Queen's birthday.

Bill's regiment, the Irish Guards, had been formed over a century ago in 1900 on Queen Victoria's orders, because after a rather stumbling and humbling Boer War, she considered 'the bravery and performance of my Irish soldiers' to be one of its few positive highlights. Bill knew Irish soldiers had always provided a disproportionately high proportion of the British Army. Never mind all that sentimental 'Men of Harlech' Welsh singing in *Zulu*, he thought, there were actually more Irishmen at Rorke's Drift than Welshmen.

'Colonel Bill' had spent a lifetime in the Irish Guards, serving in hotspots like Bosnia and commanding the battalion in Iraq. He was rather tall, still slim and elegant, and was now, at 56, the Regimental Adjutant, a retired officer re-employed as a civil servant. His main duties were to recruit about five young officers each year (not much of a problem since Prince William had married Kate in his uniform of the Irish Guards Colonel of the Regiment), to run the Regiment's 'old boys' club', look after the benevolence side and organise their veterans' annual march to the Guards Memorial the week before St Patrick's Day.

He watched as the Queen's Guard marched back in through the Birdcage Walk gate led by 'Sean', the regiment's mascot, a huge but gentle Irish Wolfhound, and then on to the Square, smiling to think that 'Changing Guard at Buckingham Palace' had not changed much since A.A. Milne had sent off his son Robin, the real 'Christopher Robin', to watch it with his real nanny, 'Alice', in 1930.

The ceremony must bring in billions he thought, judging by the thousands of tourists who milled about every day to watch it. And one of the reasons they liked it, he figured, was tradition – and that the Guardsmen were literally dressed as for the Crimean War – in grey greatcoats in winter and in scarlet uniforms, 'bearskin caps' and white leather belts in summer. Only the modern SA- 80 assault rifles would remind spectators that this was the 21st century.

Of the five Regiments of Foot Guards, Bill was convinced that the Irish Guards were easily the friendliest, and frankly, the most amusing. There had been many formal occasions when it had been difficult for him to keep a straight face after some quirky reply from a guardsman or NCO, often in the most exotic of accents from all over the island.

'Sar'nt Shannon, I'm going over to the Mess to catch the Commanding Officer and then I'm out to lunch. So we'll look over the Paddy's Day parade plans about three.' O'Farrell never stayed in the office at lunchtime, preferring a change of scene whether he had a lunchtime companion or not. 'Right you are, Sorr,' replied his Regimental Clerk, who had been with him for years.

As he walked over to the Officers' Mess past the Guard being dismissed, O'Farrell thought how ironic it was that if those tourists had been invited inside the Mess, what a very different sartorial picture they would have seen. Except for the Picquet Officer in Service Dress, everyone there looked like guardsmen dressed for 'fatigues' in mottled camouflage, with only tiny stars or crowns denoting their ranks. The army had learned, at last, that in battle anyone clearly dressed as an officer and 'waving his arms about and shouting' was the first to be knocked off by any self-respecting sniper.

'The two young chaps you're getting from Sandhurst at the end of the month should be excellent, Mick,' he said as he took a quick drink with the Battalion's Commanding Officer, whose tanned face reminded him that it was only three weeks since they had been fighting daily in Afghanistan. 'With them now all coming on from university, it's amazing how much more mature and, frankly, cleverer they are than my generation was. I sometimes shudder to remember us not very bright boys just out of school being asked to command men who were mostly older than them.'

After chatting to several other officers, he put down his

glass. 'Well Mick, better be off. I'm meeting Deirdre and the girls for lunch.'

'See you, Bill,' said Lieutenant Colonel Mick Mullen, finishing his gin and tonic and getting up to go into the dining room with the others.

As he strolled back across the square, the Colonel reflected that all in all, it was a good thing that some things had changed, like not having to wear bowler hats any more. It seemed very sensible compared with back in the fifties and sixties when the curious rules for officers in the Brigade of Guards were much stricter. Then you were not even allowed to travel on a bus, carry a parcel or hold hands with a girl in public. And there were all sorts of places you were not allowed to visit, including jazz clubs for some curious reason. And on top of that, there was also a very strict dress code even when you were out of uniform.

He smiled remembering the 'Swinging Sixties' when Carnaby Street was the apex of trendy fashion and there had been that memorable and amusing order issued by the Adjutant of the Coldstream Guards, which he knew by heart and often recounted to an amazed younger audience:

'Officers are reminded that the correct dress for walking out in London is a bowler hat, dark suit, furled umbrella, stiff white collar and highly polished lace-up shoes.

This order of dress does not include the so-called 'loafers' of Mr Gucci, and the wearing of them is therefore strictly forbidden.'

By the late seventies, when nobody else in Britain wore bowler hats (or rarely any kind of hat, for that matter) let alone stiff white collars, that dress code had become more than slightly old-fashioned, even ridiculous. Now, thank goodness, you were allowed just to wear a dark suit.

Bill was now running a bit late for his lunch date with his wife and daughters at 'The Tapster' off Caxton Street. So he was hurrying when he went out through the barrack's back entrance in Petty France, a street whose curious name he knew recalled the Huguenots who settled there in the 15th century.

On the gate, Lance-Sergeant Rory Sheehy, a familiar face from their last stint together in the desert, greeted him with a cheery 'Arfnoon, Sorr', and he and the armed Guardsman sentry on the gate both saluted him as he went out into the sunlight of the street.

It was very bright and it dazzled him as he began to cross the road.

Even if the weapon itself is silenced, the supersonic sound of a high-velocity bullet near the target is a loud, distinctive and frightening crack.

'Fockin' hell!' grunted Sheehy.

After a year of being shot at by the Taliban, instinct made him and the Guardsman throw themselves flat on the pavement.

But Sir William never heard what hit him.

CHAPTER FORTY-THREE

NEW SCOTLAND YARD, LONDON

Considering the hours he put in, Detective Inspector Robin Marshal felt himself fully entitled to one smoke break in the morning and one in the afternoon. After all, his mobile phone would keep him in touch.

He was standing outside the huge New Scotland Yard office block off London's Victoria Street, reflecting that 'Scotland Yard' was as much a nickname for the Metropolitan Police as 'Harley Street' was for medicine, 'Fleet Street' for the press or 'Broadway' for musicals. He knew the origins of the name Scotland Yard went right back to Sir Robert Peel whose decision it was to create a proper police force in London and its location in Whitehall Place, whose back entrance was an alley, Great Scotland Yard. We still keep horses there, he thought to himself.

More important, he was mulling over what to do about the extraordinary ballistics results. It really *did* seem that someone was going round the world killing off quite old people, usually with some little gun.

Robin had scarcely started to smoke the cigarette he had been looking forward to all morning when he muttered a curse. His phone was ringing. It was his assistant Joe Bain upstairs.

'Robin, CCC says there's been a shooting, right around the corner in Petty France outside Wellington Barracks. One dead, Trojan's already alerted.'

From that brief message Marshal realised that Central Command and Control were in the picture and that BMWs

with their three man crews from Trojan Central Operations
were on their way, maybe with one of the helicopters, 'India
98' or 'India 99'.

'Bloody terrorists!' he blurted. 'Right, Joe. It's no more than
two hundred yards. I'll leg it there. Join me ASAP.'

Half running and half walking, he made it in a couple of
minutes. *Please don't let it be another Mumbai* was the main
thought that raced through his mind.

There was absolute chaos at the scene. With the body right
in the middle of the road, the traffic was stalled back down
Petty France. Pedestrians had mostly scattered, but now, with
no further shooting, a crowd had gathered; passers-by, office
workers, tourists and people from the 'Buckingham Arms' pub
opposite the gate. Half a dozen soldiers from the Guardroom
were trying to hold people back.

No police had arrived, so Marshal waved his Warrant Card
and loudly took charge. He could hear sirens a couple of streets
away, but they weren't getting any closer.

Suddenly, and at last, two uniformed sweating policemen
fought their way through the crowd. They were from one of
the Trojan BMWs.

'Sorry, guv. Stuck in the bloody traffic round the corner, it's
solid.'

'Don't worry. Help me to push these people back. And try
and find someone who actually *saw* anything.'

He was tapped on the back by a young Irish Guards
Lieutenant in smart Service Dress uniform, complete with a Sam
Browne belt. Breathing heavily, he had plainly been running.

'Hello Sir. I'm the Picquet Officer. Our Commanding
Officer's on his way. Let me know what we can do.'

'Thanks. Well, to start with, you might know who *he* is,'
said Marshal, looking at the body.

The young man bent down until he could see the face.

'Oh God. It's 'Colonel Bill'. I mean, William O'Farrell, our Regimental Adjutant. He's not even a serving officer, he's retired.'

'Well, I'm afraid we'll have to leave him there for forensics.'

Some London Transport Police turned up from their nearby building and Robin Marshal put them to work sorting out the traffic in Petty France. Gradually the 'civilian' cars and vans were backed off out of the street, allowing the first police vehicles to arrive, including the white forensics van.

Marshal knew that a wide cordon would have now been set up and that the Whitehall Government Security Zone would be in lockdown. He could hear the clatter of an approaching helicopter.

Mick Mullen, the Commanding Officer in mottled camouflage uniform, emerged from the barracks and was visibly distraught at the death of his friend. 'God, I was having a drink with him twenty minutes ago.'

'Is there anywhere in there we can meet, rather than out here in the street?' Robin asked him.

'Sure. Just inside the gate we have an ICP, an Incident Control Point, a sort of briefing conference room.'

'Right, we'll go in there if we may.'

He turned to find his assistant Joe Bain there, who had also run from Scotland Yard.

'Joe, get all the witness statements you can, including any of the military. Start the CCTV trawl going. There are dozens of cameras around this area. They must have seen something.

And say nothing to the media. They'll be along in a minute and we don't know what the hell we've got here.'

CHAPTER FORTY-FOUR

'THE TAPSTER', WESTMINSTER, LONDON

'Can't we start? I'm starving.'

Lady Deirdre O'Farrell looked at her younger daughter, Fiona, 11, slumped back against her seat. They had already been in 'The Tapster' for twenty minutes, a comfortable basement bar-restaurant in Caxton Street, just round the corner from where her husband worked.

'Please Fiona, let's wait for your father. He'll be here in a minute. Have a bit of bread.' She pushed the basket towards her daughter.

'I don't like it with oil,' said her daughter grumpily, looking with distaste at the selection that was a speciality of the place. 'Why don't they have any butter?'

Her older daughter Lucinda was looking at her mobile again. 'Still no answer,' she looked up. 'Where *is* he? Don't we have to be at the London Eye at 2.30?'

Deirdre herself was getting worried. It was so very unlike Bill to be late, probably because of his military background – thirty years in the army. And it was even more unlike him not to answer his mobile, or at least answer his messages as soon as possible. And his office wasn't even answering, neither that nice Sergeant Shannon or the lady civilian clerk; that was surely most unusual she thought, and even unprofessional in a military establishment.

She might tell him about that when he arrived.

And it would be hard not to be irritated by his late arrival unless there was a bloody good excuse. It was rare enough that they'd been out as a family recently; her husband was always so busy at Wellington Barracks, and they had all been looking forward to the visit to the London Eye; at least, three of them had. At sixteen, Lucinda had needed some persuading, and had barely spoken since arriving at 'The Tapster', a place she used to love when she was a little girl when they had always given her a chocolate before leaving. But that was teenagers, Deirdre thought, looking at her watch again.

Looking up, she decided to relent. 'Okay, we'll order a starter and Dad can just have a main course when he arrives.'

'Prawn cocktail!' piped up Fiona, suddenly perky again.

'Nothing for me,' said Lucinda, dialling her mobile again. 'I'll have a steak when he gets here.'

Deirdre suddenly wished they weren't in a basement restaurant two floors down, although she loved it, one of her favourite haunts for years. Slightly dark, but with lots of character, with lovely old-fashioned wood panelling and nicely muted jazz music in the background, and of course good food. But right now she'd have liked to have been able to look out at the street to see the familiar figure of Bill striding down it. He'd surely be here soon.

Suddenly, she heard a loud siren coming from right outside, extremely loud considering they were sitting in a deep basement. 'What's that?' asked Fiona looking up. The noise was so deafening Deirdre could barely hear her.

'Wait here!' she shouted above the racket, suddenly alarmed. 'I'll go and find out.'

Everywhere in the restaurant people were getting up from their tables and starting to pour up the stairs to see what was happening, and it was a struggle to get up to the street where the noise was even louder. And when she finally managed it, there were crowds of people walking hurriedly or even running down Caxton Street, and not just on the pavements, but even negotiating themselves around a line of stationary, hooting cars.

It was an ambulance stuck in the jam that was making all the noise, and there was a police car halfway up on to the pavement. A helicopter clattered overhead, adding to the din.

'What's happening?' she shouted at the first person she could grab hold of before he pulled away and rushed past. 'I dunno.'

Deirdre panicked. Was it a bomb? Terrorism?' And if it was, would they be safer in a basement? Probably not, she thought, her heart pounding. If the police were telling people to get out of the area, she would do exactly that, and she would have to get her daughters out of the restaurant right now.

Customers were still coming up the stairs, and it was an even greater struggle to get back down two flights and to the table where her daughters looked terrified and where she noticed an untouched prawn cocktail in front of Fiona. Even in her panic as she slapped £20 on the table, Deirdre marvelled how one could notice such an incongruous detail.

At last they were out on the street, where everyone was running to the left away from the direction of the barracks. Suddenly, she realized with horror that something might have happened there. Against all her maternal instincts she decided to go against the direction of the crowd and to her husband's workplace.

It took an eternity to get there as she clung on to the hands of her daughters. With a line of three people hand in hand, everyone was bumping and shoving into them hard and swearing as they did so, or shouting 'Other way!', astonished that she was defying their advice and with two children with her. At every second, Deirdre was terrified her daughters would be wrenched away, lost in the milling throng and pandemonium.

At last she was nearly there, but there was suddenly a long red ribbon stretched across the road. Twenty yards ahead she spotted what was obviously a body under a black sheet on the ground surrounded by policemen and figures in uniform.

Looking on with horror, she felt someone touch her shoulder, and spinning around saw the familiar uniformed figure of Colonel Mick Mullen.

'Deirdre, don't look.' He put an arm around her shoulder, looking at her daughters, 'I think you'd better come with me.'

* * *

Alice had just said goodbye to Maggie when the phone rang.

'Alice, it's Bryan.'

'Hi, how are you?' She was always happy to talk to her brother.

'Very busy. The whole camp is on full alert. I just phoned to check you weren't in central London'

'Why?'

'Haven't you been looking at the news?'

'No, I've been stuck with patients.'

'It's been chaos. An officer called Bill O'Farrell just got shot dead outside the back of Wellington Barracks. He's actually retired now, but he was my instructor at Staff College. A good guy.'

'Christ. What happened?'

'They think he was shot by a sniper, with a rifle. So we're on full alert in case it's an anti-army thing, even though we're miles away. But it may be terrorism. We simply don't know.

Anyway, I've got to go. Just wanted to make sure you were okay. See you.'

Click, he was gone.

She put the phone back in its cradle. What was the world coming to?

CHAPTER FORTY-FIVE

WELLINGTON BARRACKS, LONDON

Forensics reported that the bullet had hit O'Farrell in the back just to the left of his spinal column, destroyed the left auricle of his heart, exited at the bottom of his thorax, hit the road surface twenty feet further on, ricocheted and lodged, by real good fortune for the police at least, in the back door of a FedEx delivery van. It was flattened and deformed, but the base was nearly intact and of .303 calibre.

Calculating the trajectory backwards led them to a first floor window in an apartment block in Buckingham Gate, overlooking Petty France and 105 yards from where the body had fallen. The apartment was furnished but not yet let out, and there was significant gunshot residue on the furnishings. No cartridge case, no fingerprints and no DNA evidence so far.

Armed with this latest information, Robin Marshal arranged to visit the Irish Guards Regimental Headquarters in Wellington Barracks. He reported to the gate and was checked by the Sergeant of the Guard, who assigned a Guardsman to take him through the Barracks and up to the office. He was greeted by Shane Mahon, a young Captain who was the Assistant Regimental Adjutant. No replacement had yet been appointed for the position that poor 'Colonel Bill' O'Farrell had occupied only a couple of days ago.

Marshal was ushered into O'Farrell's old office. The room was very comfortable with paintings, glass cases of medals and regimental memorabilia. Sergeant Shannon came in and handed round cups of coffee made by the civilian secretary and then joined them. His knowledge of the regiment went back many years, and he hoped that something in that knowledge might be useful.

Marshal explained his latest thinking.

'We've found where he fired from. From the first floor of a block of flats, unoccupied, with the window looking straight down Petty France. It was a long shot, about 100 yards, but clearly not impossible. Virtually no wind, so no deflection. But it does point to a marksman of some skill. Maybe, or maybe not, a former soldier, perhaps one trained as a sniper.

Then there's the victim. Colonel O'Farrell was not in uniform, but in civilian clothes, an overcoat. So this was not a random hit on just anyone in the army coming out of a barracks, but on a specific middle-aged semi-civilian. So, we think the shooter may have known the victim.'

He paused to drink some coffee.

'Now, if he *did* know him, it may have been some time ago and he may have had a serious grudge. And I have to tell you that we've got some other unsolved murders on the go and they may also be the result of strange and long-term grudges. It may not be the same man, but it's a possibility.'

Marshal looked down at his notes.

'Whatever happened, it may go back to when Colonel O'Farrell was *directly* commanding men. Iraq and Bosnia were a bit too recent. Where was he about fifteen or twenty years ago?'

Sergeant Shannon studied a chart in front of him.

'Apart from Public Duties here in London, the Battalion was in Germany for three years. Part of Fourth Guards Brigade and stationed in Germany, in Hübbelrath near Düsseldorf.'

'And what would O'Farrell have been doing then?'

A pause. 'He was a Major, commanding Number One Company. I was serving under him as a Lance-Sergeant.'

'Timing sounds about right. And can you remember anything special happening, anything difficult, unpleasant, involving the men under his command?'

'Well, yes, Sorr, there was the problem with one of our NCOs, Let's think. Yes, Sergeant Walsh.'

'What was that?'

'One Saturday night Lance-Sergeant Walsh went into the Altstadt, the old town of Düsseldorf, and into a bar, and then got into a fight.

Not with a German, which sometimes happened, but with another British soldier – a Grenadier Sergeant. And he nearly killed him, beat the bejasus out of him, half to death. It was no normal fight. Really unpleasant

There was no covering it up. Too serious. So he had to be court-martialled.'

'Do we know why he got into such a vicious fight?'

'Apparently it started over a woman, and then with the Grenadier calling him a bastard.'

'That's not much of a reason.'

'Ah,' intervened the Captain, 'but it *could* be. I remember, when I was a very young officer, calling one of my chaps 'a silly bastard'. Thought no more about it. But two days later I was marched into the Adjutant and forced to apologise, in front of him, to the Guardsman. Apparently, he really *was* a bastard, well, illegitimate, and he thought I knew it and had really taken offence and formally reported me.'

There was a long silence.

'So what happened at Walsh's court-martial?'

'Major O'Farrell, as his Company Commander, tried to put in a good word, but he was a bit stymied because the Prosecuting Officer brought up the fact that Walsh had got into fights before.

I knew him; he was a bit weird, very touchy. Not exactly good Sergeants' Mess drinking company, if you know what I mean, Sorr. So they threw him out, dishonourable discharge.'

'My man,' said Marshal, 'the person we're interested in, may have used other names. Could Walsh have been a false one?'

The Assistant Adjutant leaned forward, 'Perhaps. It's not impossible for people to get into the regiment under a false name. In fact, one of our most famous ones who did that actually won the Victoria Cross. He won it in the desert, single-handedly attacking whole German companies – not once but twice in 48 hours. Everyone knew this 'Fighting Mick' as Patrick Kenneally. It turned out years later that he was really called Leslie Jackson, and not Irish at all. He was on a building site in Glasgow and Patrick Kenneally was going back to Ireland and gave him his identity card. So he joined up using that name.

Although we're not quite like the Foreign Legion, the army can be a bit casual about names. I suppose with computers and so on it might be different now, but not when Kenneally got in – or perhaps Walsh.'

Captain Mahon paused, then smiled remembering something.

'Here's another example. Twenty years ago the Regimental Adjutant was suddenly rung up by the Mayor of Rio de Janeiro, and asked to send the Pipes and Drums to their Carnival the next week, all expenses paid. Trouble was, none of them had passports. So he had to march into the old Passport Office across the road in full scarlet uniform and bully them into making out thirty passports.

But some of our pipers and drummers from really rural Ireland had no idea of their real place or date of birth, so the Regimental Adjutant just made them up. Some of their names may have been made up too.'

Marshal felt time was slipping and raised his hand. 'It would be very helpful if I can have any records of your Sergeant Walsh's service. A photograph would be good too, although he'd look older now.'

His mobile phone suddenly rang, and with some irritation he answered it, and with visible shock before he clicked off.

'Good God!'

He got to his feet.

'I have to go. Something's just happened in St James's. This time, it's a General!'

CHAPTER FORTY-SIX

ST JAMES'S STREET, LONDON

Major-General Sir John Hewitt had felt his years as he climbed the steps up to White's, his club near Piccadilly.

He had decided to walk across the park, and the aches and pains were really getting to him as he passed the sentries outside St James's Palace. Once they would have recognized and saluted him, even in civilian clothes, but none of them would know who he was now. The thought saddened him a little.

But he knew he had a lot to be thankful about. His successful career had even surprised him, and it was only by luck, he mused, that he'd even been in the military at all. Neither of his parents had military connections, they were both doctors, and he had only found himself in the army by being one of the last drafted to do National Service. He looked back to those good old days, when had liked it so much that he had signed on as a regular officer – and never looked back. Even to winning the Military Cross for bravery while saving the life of a wounded rifleman in a desert ambush in Aden, and going on to command his regiment, the 1st Rifles, then commanding a Brigade in Germany and playing a key role as a General in the first Gulf War.

His thoughts turned to his son, as they often did. It was sad that the boy, now a man of course, had been hoping to follow in his footsteps, but had been struck down by that frightful illness, multiple sclerosis, while still at school. At least that had prompted him, on retirement from the army, to devote himself to the M.S. charity. He hoped that some good would come out of his son's affliction., and it was a comfort to know that he was now recognised as one of the best fund-raisers in the country, recently creating a new centre for those with MS and their families, which the Queen had opened.

Arriving at the steps of his club, he was relieved that such places still existed in this bustling modern world. Yes, the 'gentlemen's clubs' of London were probably something of an anachronism, but many seemed to be thriving, including several he had passed: the Carlton Club – traditional home to the Conservative Party; Boodle's – named curiously after Lord Shelburne's butler, and across the road, Brooks's.

But he was glad to be a member of White's, he thought, as he entered the door for the umpteenth time. Surely the pinnacle of all London clubs, and with an amusing quirky history.

It tickled him to know its name came from an even stranger source than that of Boodle's, having heard that in 1693, an Italian emigrant Frances Bianco, or Francis White, had set up his wife in what they called 'Mrs White's Chocolate House'. Of course he knew that being able to drink hot chocolate was sufficiently rare and expensive to represent one of the ultimate signs of privilege and wealth.

But even so, it was a fun anecdote, and one of many that had probably bored his godson, Archie, on their visits here. How many times had he told the poor boy that the most valued seat in the club, in its bay window, became 'the throne', which the Court's arbiter of fashion – the flamboyant 'Beau' Brummell – occupied every day, only relinquishing it to his friend Lord Alvanley when 'Beau' was disgraced and banished from Court by one of the stupidest flip remarks in history. As he had always told Archie, Brummell had commented loudly – and fatally – about his furious mentor and protector, the Prince of Wales, by asking him, 'Alvanley, who is your fat friend?' Hewitt reminded himself not to tell his poor godson that yarn *again*.

Living on his rather skimpy army pension, and not taking any more than meagre expenses for his MS work, the General was glad to see that the clubs were no longer famous for their gambling, in the past so ruinous to the wealth and health of members. He'd even heard that Lord Alvanley himself was famous for betting £3,000 – £180,000 today – on which raindrop would reach the bottom of the bay window first. Incredible what went on in those days.

Anyway, here he was, a White's loyalist for forty years, ever since his father and uncle had put him up for membership in the fifties. In retirement, it was still a convivial and convenient place for him to drop into on Thursdays every month. But this Thursday it was very crowded, though that was to be expected because it was the 'Christmas Lunch', an event he hadn't missed for a good twenty years.

And though some things had changed, a lot hadn't. The club still had its fair share of splendid eccentrics. Only last week he'd been told about one of them. Apparently, some old codger, a peer, came up to White's from the country every few months.

'Hello, m'lord. Haven't seen you in a long while,' had said the doorman. 'There's been some changes. You may not have seen what we've done to the lavatories. They're all done up, redecorated, and with brand new tiles.' Later, the doorman had asked him what he thought of this makeover.

'Very nice. Very smart. But, it certainly makes one's tackle look shabby!'

Carrying his drink, John Hewitt carefully worked his way through the crowd to the notice board with the table plan, and was delighted to see he was on the same table as several old military pals. Most were guardsmen, including two who had been the 'Major-Generals in charge of London District' years ago. But as a Rifle Brigade officer, Hewitt did not feel excluded; they had always got on well with the Brigade of Guards and he had served with two of their regiments out in Germany.

Soon they settled down to the traditional turkey and Christmas pudding feast and the equally traditional moan with his friends about the cuts in military spending and how it was affecting the modern army.

After a splendid meal and a second glass of port, the old General decided it was time to go. If he took a cab, he'd have a comfortable half hour to catch his train to Haslemere.

Outside, he stood on the steps for a moment in the afternoon sunlight – but suddenly collapsed back into the doorway.

At first the porter thought he had suffered some kind of heart attack.

Until he saw the blood.

CHAPTER FORTY-SEVEN

PICCADILLY, LONDON

With her boss flying safely at 35,000 feet somewhere above Dubai on his way to his long annual Christmas holiday in Sydney, Sarah Shaw had taken a rare afternoon off from the *Daily Mail* offices on December 15th, determined to meet her all-time crime heroine, Ruth Rendell, at her latest and possibly last book-signing, at the famous Hatchard's bookstore in Piccadilly.

Now, standing in the crowded lift to the top floor, she knew it would be a long queue before she would get to meet and shake hands with the legendary and fabled Baroness and receive her personally-signed copy of *The Vault* which would join the forty or so other Rendell books she owned. Sarah had devoured them all, marvelling at the writer's extraordinary insights into the criminal mind and her almost unbelievable string of crime-writing awards, including no less than four 'Gold Daggers', and even a Crime Writer's Association 'Dagger of Daggers', the most coveted of all.

Thirty minutes later, and still with around twenty-five people ahead of her, Sarah suddenly heard the sound of sirens outside, but was determined not to go across to the panoramic windows looking down on Piccadilly and find out what the din was all about – a certain way to lose her place in the queue. Once she had her signed copy she would soon discover, and then if it was just a traffic incident, she would go to the Food Department in Fortnum & Mason next door and pick up a few small Christmas presents until it all died down and she could take a bus or a tube back.

At last she was on the street again, *The Vault* safely in her bag, thrilled and flattered that the great doyenne of crime novels had talked to her for several minutes, but astonished to see the pandemonium all around her. Hooting stationary cars, buses and taxis stretched in both directions as far as she could see, with thousands of stranded shoppers crowding the pavements, and a whirring helicopter overhead adding to the din.

What on earth was going on? A bomb scare? Terrorism? Rather than feeling fearful, Sarah's journalistic instincts immediately kicked in, and she was suddenly pleased that she had her iPad with her in case she could find out something on the spot and report it back to the office.

She noticed that the police didn't seem to be evacuating the general area, so it was unlikely to be a bomb scare. However, there was a POLICE, DO NOT ENTER cordon stretched across Piccadilly, east and west of St. James's Street, which also had a cordon two hundred yards away down beyond Jermyn Street. Whatever had happened had obviously taken place behind there.

Sarah struggled over the pedestrian crossing with considerable difficulty, against the heavy surge of pedestrians coming the other way, most of them loaded with Christmas shopping. A group of three smartly dressed and distinguished-looking men had just been escorted out under the cordon by a policeman and one of them had just lit a cigar.

'What's happening,' she asked them casually.

The one with the cigar looked at her. 'Someone dropped down dead. And right on the doorstep of our club.'

Sarah thought quickly. Someone dropping dead outside a club couldn't be the reason for all this pandemonium. At least, not unless the person was pretty important. And even then it was odd. Gentlemen's clubs were full of old people. It wouldn't be the first one to drop down dead.

The man glanced behind him, down St. James's Street. 'Happened at White's, just back there. We had to be evacuated through the loo and out of the basement.'

'Alastair,' frowned one of the others, 'you know you're not supposed to talk. The police told us not to.'

'Can't see why not' said the first man, taking a heavy puff on his cigar. 'It'll all be in the news soon enough. And anyway, this charming young lady hardly looks like a policewoman.' He looked approvingly at Sarah through a haze of smoke.

'And you know the person who died?' asked Sarah, with as much charm as she could muster.

'Certainly do. Or should I say, did. A good friend of ours, General John Hewitt, retired. Coming out of our Christmas lunch. Collapsed on the doorstep.

We had to stay behind for ages, until a senior police chap arrived and let us out. They're crawling all over the place now, so they obviously suspect something strange.'

'Troughton, that's *enough*,' said the third man, pulling him away.

'Bye' said Sarah, 'and I'm very sorry about your friend.' The cigar man weaved away and turned to wave.

So the person she'd been talking to was called Troughton, and the victim – if he was a victim – was a General John Hewitt. She looked around again carefully, noticing that the cordon had blocked off Piccadilly from Green Park as well as from St James's. It was obviously a crime scene, and judging from the number of police, a major one at that. Moreover, she now spotted the unmistakable white suits of a forensics team. It looked far more than someone just dropping down dead.

She had to get this back to the office fast. The breaking news, of course, was not too late for the evening press and television, but it was highly unlikely that the name of the deceased would be released. So, by lucky chance, she might be the only one with it and could get it into the *Daily Mail* tomorrow.

Only the north side of Piccadilly had been left open for pedestrians and as she hurried past Caffè Nero on the corner of Dover Street, Sarah noticed that every table was crammed, so she immediately decided to walk further on and cross over through the vehicles in the stalled traffic to go to the Rivoli Bar at the Ritz. It would almost certainly be less crowded with the kind of prices they charged, and she could quietly get an article back to the *Mail* on her iPad, complete with Googled information about that General.

It could be just a natural, sudden death. But if not, it could be a scoop. What's more, Sarah smiled, she would get the credit and the by-line. And stroppy old Bruce couldn't block her this time. He must be over the Indian Ocean about now.

PICCADILLY MURDER: TOP BRASS GENERAL; she had her headline already.

CHAPTER FORTY-EIGHT

ST. JAMES'S STREET, LONDON

Robin Marshal was just down the road from Sarah Shaw. Even in a police car with flashing lights and wailing siren, he had struggled to get there though the traffic jam that stretched right back though the park. Indeed, he had been forced to get out and walk the last two hundred yards up from St James's Palace. Just before he reached White's, he spotted the ironic name of the fashion store next door, BERETTA, once also the makers of small-calibre pistols, the kind that James Bond had been ordered to abandon in favour of a Walther PPK. More relevant, it was exactly the type of weapon that had been recently coming to his attention in the real world.

He was now interviewing the doorman of White's, a silver-haired Irish retainer from County Sligo who had been there for years, and who usually sat in a rather grand wood and glass cubicle in the hall.

'Right, we have the full list of members, and more importantly the names of everyone who came to lunch today, and for both sittings. And you say you know all of them.'

'Yes, Sir. Certainly by sight, and almost all of them by name and correct title.'

'And you say there were no strangers?'

'Absolutely not. Our Christmas lunch is strictly for members only. No guests.'

'And you checked them all in personally?'

'Well, I didn't exactly check them in. That's not, shall we say, how we do it. Let's say, I greeted every face who came in, and wished them a Happy Christmas.'

'And you never moved from your place here?'

'No. Never moved from my Porter's Lodge.'

'Or went off to relieve yourself?'

'No, not when all the members were arriving.'

'Or went to look out on the street, perhaps for latecomers?'

'No.'

'And you have absolutely nothing unusual to report?'

'Only that one of our members tried to take a briefcase upstairs. That's most unusual. All business items must be left downstairs.'

Marshal smiled briefly at the splendidly antiquated club rule.

'Think back over the past week or so. Has any stranger come in? Has anything occurred, anything at all that seemed unusual?'

The doorman paused. 'Well, now I come to think of it, there was something a little odd a few days ago, Sir. Someone rang and asked if Sir John would be at the Christmas lunch, and if so, at which of the two sittings. I assumed it might be a friend of his, another member who wanted to join him, and we still had a couple of places left on the second sitting. But the gentleman rang off as soon as I confirmed that Sir John would be there, and without so much as a thank you.

Not exactly the behaviour of a White's member. And nor, may I say, was the voice. A bit of an accent. Maybe Liverpool Irish.'

Robin smiled inwardly at the out-dated snobbishness.

'And do you have a record of that phone call?'

'No. I'm afraid I don't.'

'But would you recognize that voice if you heard it again?'

'Almost certainly, Sir.'

'Then if he *does* call, please inform the police immediately, and also log all calls from now on until further notice.'

The doorman groaned inwardly. Another thing to arrange before Christmas.

'And I repeat, you never moved from your place here?'

'Absolutely not. At least not until I saw the General come crashing back through the door.'

'And did you go outside at that moment and see anyone?'

'No, I stayed with the General. And then I saw the blood, and immediately phoned 999.'

'And when you'd phoned, did you check the street?'

'No, Sir. I felt my place was with the General. He'd been a member for many years.'

Marshal looked at him kindly. 'I'm sorry, it must have been a terrible shock for you.'

The doorman nodded. He had been fond of the old boy. A member for a very long time, and always with a courteous greeting when he came.

Marshal allowed him a moment to recover.

'And have any members ever been asked to leave? Members who might have had a grudge against the club, or Sir John Hewitt?'

'Well, the Secretary would know about that, Sir. But it's very rare we get any trouble. All our members are proposed by other members and very strictly vetted.'

'Thank you. I'll be seeing the Secretary next.'

At last Marshal and his team had left, and the doorman breathed a sigh of relief. Apart from the poor man's family, it was going to be difficult for everyone, never mind the appalling publicity for the club, and now there was all that mess still to clear upstairs: a hundred places for a three course lunch that would now have to be done on catering staff overtime, as well as half drunk decanters of port and brandy, their stoppers probably left off, and an avalanche of dirty wine and port glasses and soiled cloths and napkins.

This was exactly the kind of tragic incident White's didn't need, especially in a recession, and with membership now costing almost two thousand pounds a year. For the first time in thirty years, he regretted his job.

* * *

When he emerged from his helpful interview with the Secretary of White's, Robin Marshal felt a real sense of foreboding. Something really unpleasant and terrible was going on, and it was also something difficult to understand. And the immediate repercussions were hard to anticipate, too.

The media, national and international, would have a field day. The Colonel's death in Petty France was high-profile enough, but it would be dwarfed by this event. Television audiences would have watched as the whole of the West End of London had been paralyzed for hours, ten shopping days before Christmas. The retail losses would have been enormous and the Government would be dragged into grandstanding about law and order in the capital.

Thank goodness at least nobody knew the victim's name yet, he consoled himself.

Then his mobile buzzed.

It was a friend in the public relations department at Scotland Yard. 'We have the news desk of the *Daily Mail* on the line, going to press on the first edition. God knows how they got it, but they're asking whether we'd like to confirm the St James's victim's name. General Hewitt?'

Robin swore under his breath. 'Tell them that we have no comment at this stage, none whatever. But it won't stop them. Damn!'

What else, he wondered, could possibly happen?

* * *

Alice poured herself a glass of wine and switched on the Channel Four evening news to catch up with the latest situation in central London. John had phoned her from Langan's restaurant in Piccadilly two or three times that afternoon, telling her that there had been a major incident down the road, and that the whole place had come to a total standstill. Apparently somebody had been killed coming out of a club down in St James's, although he didn't know who, and the Manager at Langan's had obviously been asked by the police to advise guests to stay put rather than brave the milling throngs outside, or even think about public transport.

'It looks like being a long haul. But at least we're getting drinks on the house.'

* * *

'Good evening.' The familiar face of Jon Snow on the television news.

'This afternoon, the centre of London was hit by unprecedented chaos for the second time in four days when a man was killed, probably shot, outside one of London's oldest and most exclusive gentlemen's clubs, White's, off Piccadilly. The name of the deceased has been withheld, but the club has a prestigious list of members, headed by the Prince of Wales. The Prime Minister, David Cameron, was a member for fifteen years, only recently resigning over its men-only rule.'

The screen was filled with an aerial shot of the congestion.

'Throughout Piccadilly and the surrounding areas, traffic rapidly came to a complete standstill, with buses, taxis and cars gridlocked and thousands of shoppers unable to get in or out on the busiest shopping day of the year, and with whole streets cut off and tube stations barricaded to avoid dangerous crowding.

Restaurants and bars throughout the West End report that people have been coming in all evening to use their cloakroom facilities and ask for water, or simply for somewhere to sit down with their young families.

Let's join our reporter on the scene, Stephen Owen.'

'Thanks, Jon. I'm standing at the Piccadilly end of St James's Street where the incident occurred this afternoon at around 4 o'clock, about a hundred yards behind me at White's, a well-known member's only gentlemen's club. We're having to use a handheld camera because there's no chance of getting a vehicle near here. There are still long traffic jams stretching all round the Piccadilly area, back to Knightsbridge and up as far as Oxford Street, with shoppers stranded and with tube travel severely congested at Green Park and Piccadilly. An estimated two hundred thousand people are in the area today, and I talked to several families about the chaos.'

On the screen appeared an exhausted-looking couple, with a father holding two young toddlers fast asleep in his arms.

'It was absolutely horrific. Me and the wife brought the kids up to see the lights in Regent's Street and do a bit of shopping, and when we tried to get back by tube, hundreds of people were crammed up behind us and we were terrified the kids would get crushed.'

The camera pulled back to reveal that they were sitting in what looked like a crowded hotel reception area, and then back to a close-up of the family.

'We've been here for hours in the Regent Palace. They allowed us to stay here with the kids until we can get away.'

The next person to be interviewed was the Regent Palace's General Manager.

'We've had people coming in all afternoon asking for water and to use our cloakrooms, or simply for somewhere to sit down until they can get home, and we've already had lots of cancellations for our Christmas bookings. It's incredible to think someone can be killed around here in broad daylight, terrible for his family coming just before Christmas, and disastrous for the hotel trade and tourism in London. This is the very *last* thing we need.'

Next on, in Piccadilly, was the normally upbeat Boris Johnson, the Mayor of London, now looking anything but his ebullient self. The only thing familiar about his appearance was his blonde hair flying about in the wind.

'This proves what I've always said. What London needs is more police on the streets. It's appalling that this can happen in the centre of London, and right before Christmas, and I hate to think what it might do to our Olympic Games bookings. My deepest condolences go out to the poor man's family, and to everyone caught up in the chaos. I've asked the Metropolitan Police to strain every nerve to solve this.'

'So there you have it Jon, absolute chaos in our capital city. Back to you.'

'Thanks, Steve.

Well, this is obviously a new crisis for the Met. It's only a few days since just a mile away a retired Guards officer was gunned down by a sniper. We asked Scotland Yard to comment a few minutes before we came on air. This is what their spokesman, Commander Elliot Wilson, told us.'

'Well, first of all we're trying to clear the congestion. We've funnelled the traffic away, often down normally one-way streets and...'

'But surely Commander, that's not the real question. This is not a traffic problem, it's a *murder* problem. We've got respectable people being shot on the streets of our capital just as we enter Olympic year. What are you doing about it? The public will want to know.'

'Well, Jon, I can tell you that a full-scale investigation has been launched, including any possible connection with the death of Colonel O'Farrell. So far no link has been established. We have a large team working on this, and terrorism can't be ruled out. But at this stage we can't comment further.'

Alice's phone suddenly rang. John was at last back in his office in Soho, having been stuck in Langan's for hours, and then having to struggle through the still heavy crowds in Piccadilly.

'Look, it's pretty pointless trying to get to you tonight.'

'I know,' said Alice, 'I've been watching the news.'

CHAPTER FORTY-NINE

CHELSEA, LONDON

It was three days before the Parliamentary Recess, when Members of Parliament went off for their Christmas break. Martin Lonsdale, M.P. sat and listened intently. David Cameron was doing a pretty good job of putting forward the case for the new Government's progress in such difficult times.

Because they had the Prime Minister as their speaker, the Burke Club had attracted many of its members that night – even those who lived far away. So they were sitting in Room A, the biggest of the dining rooms in the basement of the House of Commons.

'The Burke Club' had been formed in the 1950's to form a bridge between the Conservative Party and the media, so there was a fair number of newspaper editors present – mainly, of course, from those right of centre ones like *The Daily Telegraph* and *The Times*, as well as their provincial equivalents like *The Yorkshire Post*.

As Cameron was answering the last of the questions, the ten o'clock Division Bell started ringing all over Parliament, with dozens of television screens to remind Members what they were voting for. *That's the good thing about this club*, Martin mused. *You know that most people have to go off to vote. It ends the evening neatly, so you can set off for home just after ten. Thank God it's not like that other bloody Conservative club, where most of the members and their guests are young aspiring political wannabees who waste the long tedious evening toadying up to the guest Minister with footling questions –*

which are merely designed to get them noticed.

Having duly voted as he had been ordered, Martin set off down the ornate Gothic gallery lined with the busts of past Prime Ministers, through the Central Lobby and down past the elaborate security booths in the 'Saint Stephen's Entrance'.

'Goodnight, sir,' said a policeman at the door whom he'd known for years. A taxi pulled up at the other side of the unsightly concrete blocks placed to deter car bombers. At least there were some taxis, he thought, unlike the other evening when the whole of London had come to a standstill after that poor old General's murder in St James's. He'd had to walk to the tube and that had been jammed with desperate people who'd been stuck in the West End. A bloody nightmare.

Martin Lonsdale was a jovial bachelor, soon to celebrate his seventieth birthday. It was not that he was actively gay, especially nowadays. It was more that he had never had any sexual desire for women. Nor was he a misogynist. In fact, he had a great many women friends. When he first considered politics, he had of course been worried that not having a wife might prove a disadvantage when facing a Selection Committee – up against lots of nice young men with supportive and attractive wives. But he had made such a well-received speech on well-researched local issues that his Conservative Association had decided to choose him to be their candidate.

And when he was elected to Parliament, it actually proved quite an advantage not to have the distraction and commitment of a wife and children. He found he could spend more time with his constituents (who duly rewarded him with re-election three times) and was better off financially, especially during the early years when MPs were not paid that well.

He had opted to live on his pride and joy, *Evening Haze*, a forty-foot yacht, which he moored in the marina of the shiny development of apartments called 'Chelsea Harbour'. Occasionally, he sailed it down the Thames and off round the coast with friends – or even to France, although most of the time the yacht sat in the marina.

The taxi dropped him off at Chelsea Harbour's Conrad Hotel and he went to the bar for a last drink.

'Usual, Mr Lonsdale?' said the barman.

'Yes please, Carlos.'

'The usual' was not what most people would order. It was simply a pint of tomato juice with ice and lemon. Martin did not drink alcohol. Indeed, he had not touched a drop since that terrible night when his car had killed that poor young woman. After all these years, over thirty now, it was still sharp in his memory and he knew he had been fortunate, due to a faulty breathalyzer, not to be sentenced – and ruined.

Time and again he'd thought about it.

So while that terrible evening had never affected his career, it had certainly put him off the booze for ever.

As he nursed his tomato juice and looked out over the dark water towards Battersea, he mused that this was to be his last stint as an MP. In the last twenty years of political life he had never been a high flyer, nor had he been given a ministerial post – and with this new young team in charge, he was now certainly always destined to stay on the Back Benches. Fair enough. He'd enjoyed it, but his imminent retirement and his boat looked more welcoming every day.

'Goodnight, sir', said Carlos as Martin Lonsdale got up to leave. Martin waved, and went out on to the terrace and down on to the marina. His boat was about thirty yards away. He climbed aboard, unlocked the cabin door, slid it open and went in.

* * *

It was a pump engineer, Jim Haskins, who found him next morning. He had beaten the traffic up from Lymington so successfully that he'd decided to see if he could do the contracted servicing job on *Evening Haze* a bit early and then be able to pack in more appointments.

He had knocked on the cabin door. No response. Bit strange, he thought. Mr Lonsdale would normally be up early. As he slid open the door, the whole cabin reeked of whisky and Haskins found the portly MP slumped in a chair, with an empty one litre bottle of 'The Balvenie' 12 year-old whisky on the floor, gently rolling about with the slight swell.

The shaken engineer ran to The Conrad to raise the alarm. A guest who was a doctor ran back with him and pronounced the MP dead before the first police car arrived.

Once the word was out that a Member of Parliament was involved, Counter Terrorism Command, the result of a recent merger with Special Branch, pitched up. Although strictly trained not to jump to conclusions, they could be forgiven if, at first glance, they thought things might be quite simple.

However, it didn't take many minutes of questioning both the hotel staff and the neighbouring boat owners to establish that something was very wrong with any 'old drunk overdoing it' theory. The first person to blow that was the Conrad's barman.

'No. I'm telling you he never, ever touched the stuff', insisted Carlos. 'I saw him nearly every night and most weekends. It was always tomato juice, a pint with ice and lemon. Never changed his order. At least in all the time I've known him, and that's *got* to be fifteen years.'

Other guests and staff agreed, and a call to the House of

Commons' catering and bar staff confirmed that Mr Lonsdale was indeed completely teetotal.

The senior detective was then called back to the yacht. The forensics team had discovered something suspicious.

'Look, there are distinct marks and bruising on his wrists. I think he may have been restrained. He may have been forced to drink that whisky. When the body reaches the lab, we can look at those marks more carefully and look out for anything else.'

'This boat is now a crime scene,' the investigating officer announced. 'Dust everything for prints and check for anything else – especially anything that gives us some DNA'.

'Now, do we have CCTV here?'

'Certainly', said the marina manager, 'we have to watch for pilfering from the boats. Most of the owners are pretty well off. If you come to my office, you can see it there.'

On the way up, the detective decided that with everything else going on, he had better talk to Robin Marshal, and fast.

CHAPTER FIFTY

PUTNEY, LONDON

'Hi.' It was John, obviously on a tube train.

'You okay?'

'Fine', said Alice, though she knew she sounded weary. A long day of back-to-back patient sessions, and then the inevitable notes to write up.

'Thought you might like to go out tonight.'

'Couldn't think of anything nicer. I could do with a break.'

'Okay, We'll have to go local, near you in Putney. I'll stay on the tube. The car would be impossible. First it was the West End, now it's all over Chelsea and Fulham.'

'What is?'

'You must have heard about it.'

'No. What?'

'The whole place is jammed up again. *And* there are police checks on the bridge slowing everything down. Haven't you seen the news?'

'No, been locked in with patients all day.'

'There's been *another* murder, or at least it looks like one. An M.P. on his boat in Chelsea Harbour. I first saw it flashed up on a screen in the City.

I've just read the *Evening Standard* and they say he was found dead of a drink overdose, although everyone says he was completely teetotal. It may be nothing to do with those other shootings, but the police seem to be taking it pretty seriously, so the papers may not be far off.'

'Jesus. What the hell's happening?'

'That's exactly what the *Standard's* saying. How London's no longer safe. Anyway, I'll be at least an hour, so you catch it on the news before I get to you. I'll see you as soon as I can. Bye.'

Alice duly switched on the television and Martin Lonsdale's death was the top news item. After aerial views of his boat and the marina and interviews with neighbours and the staff of the local hotel, there was a review of his parliamentary career and interviews with his colleagues.

He seemed to be very popular with Members of Parliament on all sides of the House. The Home Secretary came on and was obviously under pressure over the law and order issue, but was also quite emotional about the loss of an old friend, vowing with more than usual feeling to 'bring the perpetrator to justice'.

After a while, Alice switched the set off and went up to change. Her looking forward to seeing John was somewhat spoiled by the depressing news.

This wasn't the London she used to love.

CHAPTER FIFTY-ONE

WANDSWORTH, ENGLAND.

Harry hadn't phoned or contacted Elaine for days, still embarrassed about that night, and avoiding the local supermarket, while gradually accepting that it was a common enough problem when you were as young and totally inexperienced as he was. Still, it would help if he got out of his father's house, or at least knew when he might be coming back. Then he might dare ask her out again.

But would he dare phone Ingrid, his father's secretary? He had strict instructions not to do so, unless the call was of the utmost urgency. And Harry doubted that could be anything much less than a fire or a burglary at his father's home, not something like a broken ankle over the icy doorstep that winter, let alone the need to know he would have an uninterrupted evening with a plain checkout assistant from Waitrose.

But he wanted to see Elaine again. He was missing her. And he would risk it. And he would also risk going to bed with her again, if she would let him, and if he were absolutely sure his father would be away. Whilst now not exactly blaming him, he knew it didn't help, suddenly hearing or fearing that key in the lock, and possibly being in a partial state of undress downstairs with a girl who wasn't exactly glamorous.

But he was frightened of Ingrid, his father's German secretary, and knew she would almost certainly still be working for him. Who would want to marry someone as fearsome as that, or want to whisk her away to another life and children?

He couldn't imagine it. He was convinced she would still be there.

It was nine a.m. She would have arrived by now. He looked at the scrap of paper on which he'd jotted down the number. It was so long ago since he'd phoned it, he had even had to look up the website.

'Hammond Security'.

'Hello, may I speak to Ingrid Meyer?'

'Speaking'. The same brisk voice.

'It's Harry Hammond.'

'Is there a problem?' No friendly greeting of course.

'No, not exactly.'

'I thought your father had given you strict instructions never to phone here unless there was. We're extremely busy.'

'Yes, I am too.' Harry suddenly felt good. They weren't the only people who were busy.

Ingrid was obviously taken aback, clearly still picturing a gawky, bespectacled eleven-year old all those years ago, cowering under her withering gaze.

'I need to know when my father's coming back.'

There was a pause.

'Next Friday.'

'Fine. Thank you.'

He rang off. Two could play at this game. If she could be brusque, so could he. Good, he now had almost a week to ask Elaine out again.

Waitrose would be packed tomorrow – a Saturday – but he could always slip her a note, hoping she'd answer it. And remembering how kind she was, she probably would. So different from bloody Ingrid. Tall, terse, Teutonic, terrifying. He remembered only too well when his nanny was ill, and his father had asked her to look after him for the day in the office. All day long he had sat miserably in reception reading computer magazines, which in those days he didn't understand, and without so much as a Coke from the drinks dispenser, let alone a visit to McDonald's at lunchtime.

Harry almost felt like going out for a beer to celebrate.

* * *

It was Tuesday morning at the office in Richmond, and Harry was finding it hard to concentrate, thinking ahead to what he was planning that evening. Elaine was involved in some late staff meeting after work, and he had the whole evening and indeed night if he needed it to check his father's study for anything that could throw further light on his past.

Jeni had filled in a great many gaps, but not enough, and anyway, she probably knew no more than she had told him. He reminded himself that he should send her an email to thank her for the weekend; and ought to do that before he went through his father's desk.

For a moment, he wondered whether he should phone Ingrid again to make doubly sure that his father wasn't back until Friday, but instantly thought better of it. Ingrid, if he remembered correctly, was the model of efficiency, and would suspect something strange if he phoned again, probably thinking he was planning some all-night rave at the house, though thinking back to when she had looked at him so witheringly on his last visit to the office, that was unlikely. She'd probably picture him in exactly the same way now; stocky, gawky, hopelessly ill at ease with strangers, not the typical teenager.

At last he was home, and at his father's desk, looking through the computer, and deciding to delay supper until later, or indeed forego food altogether depending on what he could or couldn't find. And so far his searches had been fruitless; only endless records about Hammond Security, absolutely nothing about family affairs.

He had certainly built up a far clearer picture of his father's international activities, and the type of products and systems he was involved in promoting and selling, but whatever name or title he logged in there was nothing personal.

At eleven o'clock, a pang of hunger told him to take a break, but Harry ignored it, deciding to go through the drawers. But it turned out to be the same fruitless search. There was file after file on Hammond Security again, but no records of his mother, no family photographs or records, absolutely nothing about his past.

By midnight, having gone through all six drawers, and carefully replacing everything in exactly the same order that he had found them, he was about to give up when he came to two envelopes in the bottom of the last one. Harry opened them, fascinated by what he was reading.

The first had a British Airways letterhead. He almost discarded it, thinking it would be some dreary confirmation of a flight or something about his father's obviously extensive air miles. But something made him read on. And what he read amazed him.

Dear Mr. Hammond,

On behalf of British Airways, I would like to send my deepest condolences on the death of Mr. William and Mrs. Mildred Picken in the tragic recent events at Phuket in Thailand.

In response to your correspondence, we would like to confirm that there will be no charge for repatriating the body of Mr. Picken back to the UK, and also that of his wife, as and when it is discovered. In addition, we enclose a cheque covering the full cost of their return air fares back to Manchester Airport, for £3,700.

The body of Mr. Picken will arrive at Manchester Airport on February 1st 2010, and will be taken to the Chapel of Rest in the British Airways Cargo building for an identification by a family member as required by British law, before it can be released for burial or cremation.

Please make your way to the Chapel of Rest the next day – using the enclosed map of its vicinity in the airport – or inform us if that date is not convenient to you, or if you wish another member of your family to make the identification for you.

Up to three individuals of the deceased's family will be permitted to attend the Chapel, and you can rest assured of a dignified and respectful reception and environment, in keeping with our strict policy on such matters, and especially in such unforeseen and sad circumstances.

I must ask you – or any other family member with you – to bring this letter, or a copy of it, with you, and a passport or other means of legal identification.

If there is any further information you would like, please do not hesitate to contact me, using the reference number on the top of this letter.

Once again, our sincere condolences for your bereavement,
Yours faithfully,
William Ewbank

Harry read and re-read the letter.

Who were William and Mildred Picken? They surely had to be very close relations, or else why had he spent so much money on them? More than £7,000, if just two return air fares cost £3,700. One hardly forked out that kind of money for people one didn't know, and anyway, the letter quoted him as a family member. Were they his father's adoptive parents? The letter said something about identification by a family member.

Maybe he was getting somewhere at last.

The second letter was equally fascinating, from an estate agent called Bristow's in Richmond.

Dear Mr. Hammond,

Thank you for your cheque for £1,500 for the rental deposit on the property at 37, Pagoda Avenue, Kew. We understand that, Mr. James McMahon will be paying the rental from now on, and will be responsible for all further rent payments as the legal tenant.

We confirm that he has already been in touch with us.

Yours sincerely,

Timothy Skipper

So his father had, or used to have, a property he didn't know anything about. And if he still had it, it was very close to where Harry worked in Richmond. Did he ever go to it? Or was this McMahon chap still living there? Was that where his father took women? He obviously took them somewhere, knowing him. But *did* he know him? Not really. The evening had finally thrown up more questions than answers.

He decided to take both letters to the office and photocopy them.

Suddenly starving, he went to the kitchen to make a sandwich before going up to bed.

CHAPTER FIFTY-TWO

HASLEMERE, ENGLAND

Winter had arrived. Alice looked out of her bedroom window at the huge horse chestnut tree, now stripped of its leaves, dreading the hours or even days it would take her to clear them up, an annual penance for having such a giant of the species so close to the house. But winter certainly had its pleasures she thought to herself, not least the glorious strolls in Richmond Park with John over the last few weeks, watching the deer.

Life seemed good, and also comfortable, and the best thing was that comfort didn't mean lack of excitement, as it so often had in Alice's life. She reflected that utter relaxation with a partner had, up to now, always led to lack of physical interest, and that maybe, just maybe, she had broken that vicious cycle. Although she had hesitated when John had suggested that she move into his flat. If there was to be a move at all, it would have to be a totally new place for them both she told him, and John had immediately understood. And Alice had to admit to herself, she loved her house, so full of memories of her parents; it would be a tough parting.

The only shadow was the continuing mysteries swirling around the recent murders involving her friend Robin Marshal. She had tried to call often. He had texted her once, but only with the cryptic words, 'Up to my eyes, I may need you soon,'

The previous Sunday she had met John's parents for Sunday lunch at their house in Haslemere, as relaxing an event as that Sunday lunch with David Hammond near Farnham had been conversational agony. It was immediately obvious where John's energy and vitality had come from, not to mention his ready laughter. She knew a certain amount about them beforehand from John who was obviously proud of them both.

He had told her that his mother was Norwegian, a former actress, and that his father was a botanist – 'or to be more precise, a bryologist – someone who studies mosses and liverworts. It's a pretty rare form of biology – I think there are only about twenty in the country.'

'It must be,' Alice had laughed, 'I've never even heard of the word.'

'I wouldn't have done either, if not for Dad.'

Alice found it hard to imagine anyone studying mosses all day, let alone spend a lifetime peering at green clumps. Did they even have any flowers? If so, they must be microscopic.

'It all has to be done with a microscope, and a pretty powerful one at that,' said John as if reading her thoughts.

Alice immediately pictured a classic professorial type with a shock of snowy white hair like Albert Schweitzer.

'And he's still working?'

'Yup, at home. Incidentally, he'll probably ask if you want to see his specimens in the study.'

'I'd be fascinated' said Alice, intrigued.

John laughed. 'Don't count on it!'

'And your mum was on the stage?'

'Yup, and in films. She was even in one of the early Bond ones.'

'Gosh, she must have been pretty.'

'She *was*. Still is, actually.'

'Which Bond film? I've probably seen it.'

'Goldfinger. But it was only a bit part, not exactly like Shirley Eaton. She was one of the cast of exotic females. But she did bigger things after that. Even took the starring part in

'Separate Tables' in the West End once, you know, the Terence Rattigan play.'

'Wow, pretty impressive. What was her stage name?'

'Astri Elholm, but you wouldn't know it. It was all ages ago. She gave it all up when she had me. Couldn't stand long runs being away every night, or being on location. And she hated the thought of a nanny.'

'She sounds lovely.'

'She is.'

Alice smiled. It was nice to hear a son talk about his mother like that. And his parents seemed to be a great pair. She pictured the unlikely combination of a studious young botanist and a glamorous Norwegian starlet all those years ago. She'd never really believed that opposites attract, or at least attract successfully, but it was obviously true in this case. John was thirty-five after all, and they were still happily together, rare enough these days. She was looking forward to meeting them. And she reminded herself she shouldn't assume anything. They were probably far more similar to each other than different.

John interrupted her thoughts. 'She loves plants like you. And painting them. You'll see her stuff all over the kitchen. Pretty good, actually. I always tell her she should sell them, but she never does.'

Alice chuckled. 'Don't tell me she paints mosses!'

John laughed. 'Nope. They're both totally mad, but not as mad as that.'

Alice had wondered what to wear for the lunch, but not being someone to agonise on dress code, had quickly decided on a simple blue woollen dress, with John's sapphire brooch. Too dressy? No, the brooch was discreet, and John would like it. A kind of communication between them if things were heavygoing. But why would they? They sounded great fun.

Alice pictured their house in her mind: a study crammed with books and specimens of mosses, a kitchen with flower paintings everywhere and probably a gorgeous garden outside.

John read her mind. 'And you'll love the house. It's as mad as they are. So many books you can't move, and dozens of extraordinary things everywhere. Rather like a cross between a junk shop and a museum. Neither of them can throw anything away, even if it's falling to pieces. A total madhouse.'

He turned to her. 'In fact, when I come to think about it, it's a psychologist's dream.'

'I'm looking forward to seeing it. And them.'

* * *

It was easy to see that John's mother had once been an actress and Bond starlet; she was still extremely striking with natural Scandinavian blonde hair, obviously where John had got his from. And Alice immediately warmed to her and her husband, not at all the academic professor she had envisaged – tall, with brown eyes and actually quite handsome.

'So you're a psychologist?'

They were obviously surprised and flatteringly impressed, asking various questions about where she'd trained and what kind of cases she handled. But Alice had changed the subject as soon and as politely as she could, asking his parents about their careers, and commenting on the plant pictures in the kitchen with genuine praise: all of them were extremely good, and painted in exquisite detail. She agreed with John – she ought to sell them – and told Astri, who was obviously pleased, but immediately self-deprecating. 'Oh, I only do it for a hobby.'

Alice longed to tell her about Aunt Helen and her love of plants, and how she'd inherited that same passion, but chose not to go there – the memory of her godmother was too painful

– instead chatting about her own modest garden and accepting an invitation to look outside after lunch.

'Not at its best, I'm afraid', laughed Astri.

'Nor mine,' agreed Alice. 'Just a vast pile of leaves to clear up. And masses of moss to scrape off the steps' she added, smiling at John's father. 'Maybe you should tell me the best way to do that.'

By four o'clock, there had hardly been a silence in the conversation, such was their enthusiasm for what they did and their wide-ranging interests, opera being perhaps the only one she didn't share, with the very mention of it reminding her uncomfortably of David, the only moment of the lunch that made her feel uneasy.

The table was now a glorious mess. Astri was not the sort to clear much up in front of guests, quite content to leave empty bottles on the table or sling them in the bin with gay abandon, and happy to leave jars of horseradish and mustard on the table when it was time for dessert, utterly relaxed with herself, as was her husband and John.

This was obviously a great marriage, and the response between them – and of theirs with John – was a delight to experience. No wonder he was so easy to be with, so well balanced. If only more of her patients had parents like that, Alice thought.

'I suppose we ought to get going' said John, suddenly looking at his watch, and then at Alice. 'If you want to have a look around the garden, it had better be now.'

His mother got up from the table. 'Leave all this, I'll do it later. It's getting a bit dark outside, but if you'd like to see it …'

'I certainly would,' smiled Alice.

It was past six and dark when they finally left.

'Lovely to meet you, Alice' said John's father in the drive, giving her a hug. 'I don't think we've ever had a psychologist here.'

John smiled at him. 'It's high time you did!'

His father beamed at Alice. 'I rather agree.'

* * *

What a fabulous couple thought Alice as they drove back to London, with John filling in more about them: how they had met in a bar in Soho in the seventies, how his father had asked her out on a trip on the Orient Express only days later, and how they'd been gloriously suited and happy ever since.

Suddenly, there was a huge crack of thunder, and rain pelted on to the windscreen. Alice suddenly remembered that Sunday night drive weeks ago.

'God, this is going to take ages.'

'What if it does?' said John, patting her lap. 'It's only a spot of rain. Stick on some jazz,' he added, tapping the box between them, 'which reminds me, it's time we went to the 100 Club again.'

Again she'd been reminded about David Hammond. Alice tried not to think about him, feeling a sharp stab of guilt.

What if John ever found out?

* * *

After a huge Sunday lunch, John's parents usually had a nap – leaving all the clutter in the kitchen until later – then spent the evening browsing the Sunday papers over a simple boiled egg snack, and distractedly watching anything remotely decent on TV.

But this time they stayed up as Astri cleared away the detritus into the sink and dishwasher while Arthur, as was his usual custom, made only half-hearted attempts to help. Astri had long since given up on this aspect of him, preferring to remember all his good points – which were considerable, she often reminded herself. After all, he did virtually all of the driving, was unfailingly loyal, delighted to hear about those interests he didn't share, and at those odd times she became depressed, could – and indeed did – jolt her out of it like nobody else. It was a good marriage. She hoped for the same for John.

'Lovely girl,' said Arthur as she scoured the pans. 'Wouldn't mind her for a daughter in law.'

'Nor me. But don't count on it,' Astri laughed. 'How many girlfriends have we seen down here? God, must be about twenty. But if it lasts 'til Christmas, it would be great to have her here. A real asset.'

'I wonder what her parents do? She didn't mention them much.'

'She did to me. You were probably boring her about your mosses. Anyway, her father lives somewhere in France – a retired accountant, and her mother died some years ago. Her house in Putney used to belong to them. Apparently her father wanted to get away from it all, start a completely new life, go somewhere completely different.'

'I think I'd want to do the same.' Arthur looked around the large kitchen, their favourite part of a spacious nineteenth century home, almost every bit of it crammed with memories. 'I can't see either of us carrying on here alone.'

'Nor me. Incidentally, did I tell you John's been able to give himself a large rise after winning that account?'

'No, but I'm not surprised. Intelligent, like his father.'

'*And* mother, thank you! Anyway, you ought to send him an email to say congratulations. I can't remember the client they won, but I wrote it down somewhere, something in software.'

'I will. Remind me tomorrow.'

Arthur riffled through *The Sunday Times*.

'Incidentally, isn't this *all* very weird? Three people killed and no-one has any idea why. A Colonel, a General, and now an MP. Incredible. Must be some kind of class or anti-political thing.'

Astri glanced at the paper. If he wouldn't help clear up, she'd have to read it later. But it was certainly more than odd.

* * *

The next day John arrived in his office at eight am to find his father's short but warming message:

Dear son,
Lovely to see you, and what a great girl. Bring her down again! And your Mum reminds me to say congratulations on winning the Permacon account – great news.
Our best to you, as ever, Dad.
P.S. Maybe you'd both like to come for Christmas? I promise not to bore her about mosses!

John smiled, thinking of all the various girlfriends he'd taken to meet them over the years – all of them welcomed, because if his parents' reactions were ever negative, at least they'd had the decency to keep it to themselves – or to be more accurate, until the whole thing was over, at which point they'd always approached any advice or criticism with caution.

Although, come to think of it, John remembered, they had been rather rude about that actress with the Gothic makeup who told them lurid jokes after far too much wine, another girlfriend who couldn't walk round the garden in her Louboutin stilettos and who'd refused to get into a pair of boots, and the Indian girl who'd told them she was completely unable to admit to her parents that she was going out with a white English boy.

John thought of the lunch. There had certainly been an instant affinity between Alice and them. Not one moment of awkwardness or any niggling worry that he needed to fill in for her or give her a bit of encouragement or support. And he knew that Alice would send that wonderful old-fashioned thing: a 'thank you' letter. It was the kind of girl she was.

He thought of her, probably in the shower now, her notes and her office all ready to see her patients. And for the first time he pictured her as his wife.

CHAPTER FIFTY-THREE

NEW SCOTLAND YARD, LONDON

The telephone woke him with a start. Robin Marshal realised with shame that he was so tired he'd dozed off at his desk. But then he hadn't been home for three days.

It was an internal call. 'Robin, can you come up to my office please, and right now.' It was an order, not a question, from Commander Bill Jones, who sounded extremely tense.

Marshal ran up the stairs two floors rather than wait for a lift, and went into his boss, who motioned for him to sit down while he continued to watch a television screen intently. It showed a crowded and noisy House of Commons with a plainly beleaguered David Cameron at the Despatch Box during the traditional Wednesday 'Prime Minister's Questions'.

'Can the Prime Minister explain why the streets of our capital have become like those of Kabul, and no longer safe for even the most respected of our citizens?' intoned the Leader of the Opposition, rather smugly. The Prime Minister rose to his feet, frowning.

'Of course, we're deeply shocked and saddened that brave former officers have been cut down in central London, and that even one of our own, an admired and well-liked Member, also appears to have been a victim of an apparently motiveless killing. I can only repeat that I have asked the Home Secretary to ensure that the most rigorous effort is made to find the perpetrator or perpetrators and bring them to justice.'

The Commander switched off the volume and turned to

Marshal. He was at first sympathetic. 'Christ, Robin, you look exhausted.'

Then he got down to business. 'Well, you don't often get into the firing line over this kind of thing, but I can tell you this is all getting bloody dodgy – real pressure. I've just been watching as the MPs all stood up for a minute's silence for Lonsdale, and then the place went into uproar.

Before that, I had the Home Secretary on the phone, almost shouting at me. Apparently Lonsdale was a really good friend of his, and had been his mentor since he first went into Parliament. So he's taking it pretty personally. The Mayor was also putting his oar in earlier – and none too politely.

I know it's my job to take the flak and let you get on with yours, but I need to know how you're getting on so I can at least field some of the questions. So what's happening?'

In his haste to rush upstairs, Robin had not brought any notes with him, but quickly launched into a report from memory.

'Both victims were former army officers, both shot from quite a distance with the same .303 rifle and using old-style Mark 7 ammunition, not modern sporting rounds. The two victims may also be linked in some way through the military, and the army records that we've asked for may provide a breakthrough.

As for the M.P. James Lonsdale, he was definitely murdered. Made to look as if he'd died of a whisky overdose. But he had, in fact, been a teetotaller for as long as anyone could remember. And our evidence shows he'd actually been restrained and *forced* to drink the stuff.'

'Christ, this is all getting out of control. When will you have anything concrete – anything at all?'

'I really can't say, sir. We think we've got everything we can out of the forensics. This man, and the rifle shooting indicates that it *is* a man, not a woman, is very competent and very careful. No CCTV, no cartridge cases, no fingerprints, no DNA so far. But, we're still expecting a lot of background stuff from various people. I've asked them to move fast.'

Robin paused. He had to be careful how he brought up his next point.

'You remember, sir, those strange murders I mentioned a few days ago?'

Bill Jones nodded, suddenly wary.

'Well, you'll recall the similarities. No obvious motives, use of old-fashioned or out of date weapons and ammunition. Nearly all the victims middle-aged or really old. We know from ballistics that four of them were linked by the small-calibre rounds.

And the old lady in Cornwall and the young Polish driver were killed, virtually executed, with old weapons.

I can't think of a linkage, let alone prove one, but I feel instinctively there might be.

Anyway, we're putting together a conference tomorrow to review everything and try and establish a profile. You're very welcome to attend sir, we need all the help and support we can get.'

'I'll be there', said the Commander, somewhat relieved that Marshal had chosen not to mention his previous dismissive comments about the theory of linked murders.

CHAPTER FIFTY-FOUR

LAVENDER HILL, LONDON

How difficult it must be for people to send her Christmas cards this year thought Diana Cameron, as she opened the post. What on earth to say to a recently bereaved woman, and not even one whose husband had died of natural causes, but been murdered? When was it? Only three months ago.

Just a name under the printed greeting would have appeared thoughtless, uncaring; they had to say something, and would resent having to think of a message with other cards to get through, possibly dozens of them. They would either leave her off their list altogether hoping she wouldn't notice, or struggle with some message, possibly writing and rewriting it on a piece of scrap paper and asking their friends and spouses if it sounded anything like alright in the circumstances.

Nothing would sound right; she knew that. 'Hope you're over the worst of it'. Too blunt. 'Thinking of you.' Just about right, but the brevity would suggest a dilemma. 'Our best to you and the girls'. Okay, but they would be uncomfortable with the word 'best', knowing that Diana would be at her worst. 'Our thoughts this Christmas' – okay, but so bleak, terse and funereal.

Maybe the only thing they could do was suggest that she come and stay, but if the cards were from Hong Kong they must have known that was unlikely.

Opening the cards – far fewer this year – she felt sorry for the senders, and was initially having as much a problem as they were thinking what to say in the few she was sending out. She decided that she could get away with a simple message – as they couldn't – 'With much love from me and the girls', and leave it at that. And even then, she wondered if it was a good idea to send any cards at all, in case people who hadn't yet sent one descended into a 'however to reply' nightmare. It was grim, but fascinating in a way to have this kind of insight into tiny things one had to think about in such circumstances.

And she was agonizing about accepting the one or two invitations they'd had this Christmas from old friends and family, at the same time worrying about what she and her daughters would do at home. Strangers around the table in other people's houses would have been strictly briefed to keep off the subject of her husband, and terrified that they might descend into some *faux pas* after too much port or paralysed into not making toasts 'for the dear departed'. Murder threw everything in life askew, and even the few decorations around the flat in Lavender Hill looked somehow too festive, although she had decided it was right to put some up for the children, as well as a small tree.

Central London had proved far too expensive, indeed anything until at least seven miles away. Diana couldn't believe how much prices had leapt, despite reading the English papers regularly in Hong Kong, and being married to a banker who was perfectly well informed of property inflation in the UK. It was only when you saw what you really got for those prices that reality had struck, and she was quickly aware that if she were to buy an even reasonable three bedroom flat, it would have to be some way out of the centre.

It was her children that had liked Lavender Hill, or rather, a street just off it; not a sprig of lavender anywhere in this built-up area south west of the city, but enough green spaces like Clapham Common a short stroll away, lively cafes, bars and restaurants, and a health centre where she could take up Pilates again if she ever got round to it. And it was a pleasantly mixed community, not too rough, at least the area they were living in. Plus, the flat was nice enough, although a far cry from their spacious and luxurious Hong Kong apartment.

She looked at the tree at the end of the sitting room, with her two Hong Kong sofas leading up to it on either side. It was all a bit of a squash, but at least her daughters' friends had somewhere to sit, or even to sleep on if they wanted to stay overnight. And each of them had their own bedroom upstairs. For that, she was thankful. At least she had the money to give them a bit of their own space, and send her younger daughter to a good local school where she seemed to be settling in.

She was much less sure about her elder child, now at Thames University nearby as a day girl. Her hair had been recently cut into a short crop only inches long. At least, it suited her gamine face and tiny frame, although Diana was sad to think of that former mass of unruly auburn curls. More important things in life than hair she told herself as she threw the envelopes into the wastepaper basket, and arranged the day's cards on the tiny mantelpiece.

They would get through Christmas somehow, and then the years ahead. But so much had changed, and not just for the girls. It was hard enough to accept that she no longer had the status of being married to a rich, respected and well-known Hong Kong banker, recognized and even fawned upon wherever they went – at the Banker's Club and golf club, when they went to the races in Happy Valley or to Hong Kong's finest restaurants. Even at the Pilates group she'd enjoyed a special social standing among her friends and was the first to be asked to their numerous dinner parties with her husband. All that was gone forever, as were things like drivers and maids. She had never had to lift a finger in Hong Kong. Here in London she was just another anonymous face in a population of eleven million people.

And it wouldn't be easy to make new friends here, not as a single woman of fifty who had spent the last fifteen years abroad. Although still slim and attractive with her thick auburn hair and green eyes, she knew she wouldn't be invited to many dinner parties as a middle-aged singleton, particularly if people knew about how her husband had died. Most people would feel embarrassed for her, and would have to warn their other guests about it.

Mind you, the spate of murders in London was putting her husband's killing during a botched robbery in the shade. Really shocking. A Colonel. a General and now an MP.

Going to the Chinese drinks cabinet, an extremely valuable piece with beautifully carved golden dragons, Diana poured herself a stiff whisky, guiltily looking at the clock. Five p.m. Too early, she scolded herself.

And it was getting earlier every day.

This would have to stop.

* * *

'I think we ought to ask her over sometime.'

Tricia Grimlord had noticed the auburn-haired woman and her two daughters moving into the flat next door three months ago. Her new neighbour, the mother, seemed to be about the same age as she was, and maybe she thought, they might become friends. She and Mike loved entertaining, and it might be nice to have a new face at the table. There didn't seem to be a man about; she was probably divorced and moving to a new area, and might appreciate an invitation from the people next door. And she was certainly quite glamorous with that striking auburn hair, and possibly quite an asset at a dinner party if she turned out to be nice. And it must be tough bringing up her two daughters on her own. It had been hard enough with Caroline, her own daughter by her first husband; she might need some support. And she was probably lonely as so many people in London were. The vast majority scarcely bothered with their neighbours, not even knowing their names for years, if ever, and sometimes never knowing about them until they were dead. Tricia had read loads of stories in the papers like that.

'Okay,' Mike had agreed. 'But not for too long. Just a drink or two. I'm getting pretty knackered finishing off the last paintings, and the exhibition is only a week away.' He had glanced at the kitchen diary hanging up behind him. 'I hope you haven't forgotten the date.'

'Of course not. And I hope you haven't forgotten to invite Caroline and Nick to the Chelsea Arts Club for dinner afterwards and book a table.'

Michael looked sheepish. 'As a matter of fact, I have.'

'Oh Michael,' she groaned, 'you can't have done! You know how the Arts Club gets filled up after exhibitions, and now they probably won't have a table left.'

'Sorry, I'll phone in a minute.'

'No,' said Tricia, '*I* will. And then at least I'll know it's done. And I'll ask our new neighbour over for a drink tomorrow night at seven. Do you think you can make it back by then?'

'I'll try.'

The next morning Tricia rang on the top bell next door, remembering that it was the top flat that had been for sale on the estate agent's billboard. In fact, the board had only just been taken down. Estate agents always kept their signage up for ages after the sale to keep their names advertised for as long as possible, and Tricia had become increasingly irritated by the

Foxton's sign that had been there for months, long after the new owner had finally moved in.

'Hello.' A nice voice came on the intercom.

'Hi, I'm Tricia Grimlord, your next door neighbour. I wondered if you'd like to meet me and my husband, maybe for a drink together in our flat tomorrow evening?'

There was a slight pause. The woman was obviously surprised. 'That would be very kind. Hang on, I'll come down and say hello.'

Tricia waited at the front door where they shook hands as her new neighbour introduced herself. 'I'm Diana Cameron. I've just come back to England from Hong Kong where I've lived for fifteen years. And I don't know many people in London, so I'd love to come over. It's really kind of you to ask me.'

'Seven o'clock then?' smiled Tricia.

'Fine, I'll pop over then.'

The doorbell rang just after seven ten the next evening, and Tricia immediately realized that Diana had that pleasantly upper middle class habit of arriving slightly after she had been invited: time to let the hostess get it together. She approached the door with pleasure, looking forward to meeting her properly.

But she was slightly dismayed looking at Diana's outfit. While Tricia was in jeans – albeit good ones – with a polo-neck sweater, Diana was in a long velvet skirt with a glittery top.

'I'm sorry, I should have mentioned it was just us.'

'You did,' Diana smiled. 'But I thought it would be a nice excuse to get my glad rags on for once. I hardly ever go out these days. In fact, it's a rare treat to meet anyone new.'

Tricia ushered her into the hall, and Diana was immediately entranced by the paintings that lined the walls, as people always were when visiting the flat for the first time. There were dozens of them, with scarcely an inch between them, and although obviously done by the same painter, there was an astonishing variety of themes: mostly horses – racing and polo events – but also jazz trumpeters, football matches, landscapes, dogs, cats, nudes – and even a delicate pencil portrait of Marilyn Monroe.

'Wow! It's just like an art gallery!'

'It is, in a way. My husband Mike is an artist.'

'And certainly a prolific one. He did all these?'

'Yes. And there are dozens more at his studio.'

'Amazing!' She studied the walls again, taking her time.

'I adore the ones of the races. Back in Hong Kong my husband and I used to go racing all the time. They're mad about it out there. But then, the Chinese are mad about all kinds of gambling.'

Tricia suddenly realized that she could be a customer for Mike if she liked horse racing pictures. Maybe suggesting a drink together was going to be as fortuitous as it was pleasant and neighbourly. She reminded herself to tell Diana that he was a member of the Equestrian Artists Society.

Suddenly Mike was at the door, shivering with cold as he wiped his shoes on the mat. 'God, it's bloody freezing out there.'

He smiled at Diana. 'Hi, I'm Mike.'

'And I'm Diana Cameron,' she replied, shaking his hand. 'I've just been admiring your paintings. They're amazing.'

'Thanks.'

'And there are loads more in the sitting room,' said Tricia, wanting to get the occasion started and knowing that Mike wanted to make it short. 'Shall we go in? I've put the drinks in front of the fire.'

An hour and a half later, Diana was on at least her fifth glass of wine, and not a small glass at that, and was making no signs of leaving. Tricia was getting mildly irritated, wishing that Michael would say something to help her, perhaps about him being busy and his exhibition coming up. She didn't want to turn this into a late night any more than he did after what he had said about being tired, and she still hadn't cooked dinner. But it would be embarrassing to throw her out. There was no easy way to do that when people outstayed their welcome, and certainly not if they were strangers. But it surely couldn't be long now.

Diana took the last sip of her wine. At last, Tricia thought, looking forward to a quiet evening with Michael – at least what was left of it, and wondering how he had done that day. But to her dismay and utter astonishment, Diana held her empty glass up. 'I wonder if I could have just one more for the road. This wine is delicious, and it's so nice to meet new friends. As I said, it's difficult in London.' She turned to Mike. 'And it's so nice to sit in an art gallery.'

Tricia groaned inwardly. She would give Diana one more glass she decided, and that would be it. She went to the kitchen to fetch another bottle, noticing that it was the last one on the rack. Damn Diana; now they wouldn't have anything to drink over dinner, if she ever got around to cooking it at all. She glanced at the kitchen clock. It was already 8.45.

At long last Diana had finished the glass after mumbling incoherently about her two daughters and was finally heaving herself out of the armchair, her words slurring badly. She could barely stand, Tricia noticed with alarm.

All at once, and to Tricia's horror, Diana stumbled over the glass coffee table sending the remains of the red wine – at least three quarters of the bottle – all over the carpet, worse still, a cream carpet that had only just been fitted; the present she and Mike had decided to give themselves for Christmas. Tricia grabbed for the still rolling bottle before it did even worse damage, but there was already a huge red pool spreading everywhere. Christ, she thought, it'll take ages to get out, even if that stain would come out at all.

She was suddenly livid.

'Mike, could you take her home? I'd better see to this.'

'I'm sho shorry.'

Mike took Diana's arm as she stumbled to the front door, knocking one of the pictures sideways. However, was he going to get her up to her flat? She was blind drunk. He couldn't possibly just leave her at the front door; she wouldn't even be able to get the key in the lock. And he'd have to help her upstairs, and with his bad back. And whatever would her daughters think seeing their mother coming home like that, and wondering if she'd been out on a binge with him?

It was all too much.

Twenty minutes later he reappeared, exhausted.

'Well, I got her up to the sitting room at least. I could hardly take her into her bedroom. And anyway, from what I could see, it was another floor up. And one of the daughters was there watching TV, only about ten years old, poor kid. Still, she didn't seem too worried, didn't even talk to me or turn the TV off.'

'She's probably seen it all before. Still, I've got other things to worry about right now.' Tricia looked dismally at the carpet, now pale pink and covered with salt. Perhaps she ought to cancel that trip to Kew Gardens with Linda tomorrow and spend all morning scrubbing it, or else the stain would never come out. She certainly didn't have the energy to do it tonight. What if it didn't come out? Adding to her fury, she suddenly realized their insurance was out of date.

She looked at Michael, stooped over, rubbing his back. 'Well, she's certainly not coming back here in a hurry – if ever. She's got a real problem.'

Mike looked at the bottle that Diana had knocked over, now sitting upright on the table with only dregs left. 'Is that the last of our wine?'

'Yes. And probably the last of her as well.'

CHAPTER FIFTY-FIVE

PUTNEY LEISURE CENTRE, LONDON

Harry had painful memories of anything to do with gym or games.

It was bad enough puffing around the football pitch at Mostyn House Prep School, obviously never to be selected by the school team for matches, or by a sportier member of his class if they were asked to select a side in the meantime, and even worse when he had to bare his tubby white body in the swimming pool in the Summer term. His friend, a Lebanese boy called Emile, made him feel hopelessly inadequate, diving into the water like an arrow leaving scarcely a splash behind him. And the Townend twins were even worse with their athletic wiry frames. Even at eleven years old, they were able to swim at least a length underwater, and emerge without even a puff – whereas Alec could barely manage a few yards or so without spluttering and coming up for air.

And though on parents' days Paul and Jeni had always egged him on and been pleased if his relay team had ever won anything – rare if he was even a member of one – it had always been an agony, especially if the headmaster was present – the fearsome K.T. Leighton, often called Katy, whom Harry had always feared since that first interview when he had studied seven-year old Harry with obvious distaste, realizing that he would never be a physical or perhaps even scholastic asset to the school.

But why was he stocky? Harry had never understood that at the time, knowing that his father was slim, though nothing about his mother's frame. It wasn't that he ate more than any of his school friends, or not that he could see, and he had no pocket money to spend on sweets in the school tuck shop as his schoolmates did. Maybe he was just born to be overweight, however little he ate. It was hard not to be jealous of his classmates who seemed to stay wiry thin, despite gorging on Mars bars and crisps at every opportunity, and rarely offering him a bite of anything. It was horrible to be fat, at least fatter than anybody in his class, and so pastily white as well; whiter and pastier than all the boys in his class, usually the sons of rich Northern industrialists or bankers who could easily afford the Mostyn House school fees which he knew were considerable. He was supposed to be lucky to be there. His only comfort was sausages and visits from Jeni and Paul, or going to their house down the road.

Deciding to join a gym with Elaine has been a big decision. At eighteen, he was still far tubbier than he would have liked, probably one of the reasons he was going out with a distinctly overweight girl, and afraid to bare himself on a foreign beach if he ever dared to ask her to one, and if he could afford it. Like every other teenager, he was bombarded with images of slim young people in the media apparently completely relaxed with their own bodies, and unlike Harry, not depressed every time they went to bed. Every time he rolled over, his stomach followed.

Much worse, he sweated badly. The office in Richmond had good air conditioning, but not enough to stop patches appearing on his shirt underarms before lunchtime, and to stop him buying a new mini pack of Kleenex every day at the station along with his paper. It had to stop.

Now he was busy scouring the net for the nearest gym he could afford, preferably with a swimming pool, hoping that

Elaine would not be offended by his suggestion to join him.

It would be good to look his father in the eye, slim at last, not cowering under that critical and cold blue-eyed gaze.

He had looked up LA Fitness and Virgin Actives, both horribly expensive and possibly far too chic for either of them, eventually discovering that Putney Leisure Centre had everything he, or they, needed: good and free machine and weight equipment, wide swimming lanes, great diving boards, a sauna, a hot tub and steam rooms – and at a fraction of the price.

Harry had weighed himself that morning. Twelve stone, and just five feet nine. Far too heavy. He had to do something. And maybe Elaine might want to as well. And he might just persuade her to join him, if he was tactful enough.

Her birthday was coming up. Perhaps it would be a nice present, a year's membership. Or would it be an insult? Harry knew so very little about women. Maybe he could ask Jeni? But then Jeni would ask him all sorts of questions, and comment on how coincidental it was that he'd found a girlfriend who was a supermarket checkout assistant like his mother had been.

He wasn't ready for all that yet.

CHAPTER FIFTY-SIX

HASLEMERE, ENGLAND

Alice was flattered and pleased that she'd been asked to spend Christmas with John's parents, and had pictured it all, fascinated if when she arrived, she'd got it all wrong. A tree, possibly in the hall, and a large one. A few decorations around the house, maybe a bit of holly from the garden, but not much, and definitely no looped paper chains underneath the ceilings. Perhaps the odd glass vase or two with white painted branches, hung with tiny baubles, and the inevitable poinsettia, that horrible red plant which everyone felt they had to have at Christmas but would never consider at any other time of year. Did it grow at any other time of year? Alice didn't know, and disliked it enough not to care.

Should she take a present for them both, or individually? Maybe for them both, Alice thought. A giant box of chocolates, perhaps? Or was that too boring? But a book on mosses would be impossible, and anyway, John's father would probably own anything worth having. And something personal for his mother would be just as difficult, while a cookery book might suggest that was all she did; cooking. A silver photo frame? A beautiful salad bowl? A vase or maybe something else to eat, perhaps a basket of dried fruits, even if they didn't much like them? Christ, why did Christmas have to be so difficult? For the umpteenth time, she thought of Christ's humble birth in the stable and the millions of needless traumas that had erupted since, not to mention the crowds in central London and even Putney High Street now panicking about getting it right, or even getting it at all before tomorrow.

And should she get something for Joanna and Josie, John's sister and her long-term gay partner who were coming over from Australia? She knew almost nothing about them to guide her choice, only that Joanna was a TV producer in Sydney and her girlfriend worked on the foreign desk at the BBC.

And what would she give John? He had never hinted about anything he wanted. Maybe a glossy tome on advertising? She had seen in the papers that some US copywriter had written a well-respected one about advertising in the sixties, but that was a long time ago. And who was it by? Jerry Della Femina? John had probably never heard of him; too far back, although he might know he was one of the muses behind the TV smash hit *Mad Men*. She'd think about it later, perhaps even ask him if there was something he'd particularly like.

In the end, she'd bought him a stylish, but discreet pair of cufflinks from Asprey, frustrated that he'd never suggested anything, packing the tiny box in her suitcase before setting off with him to his parents' house.

'Perhaps we ought to phone them' said Alice, suddenly realizing that they were going to be at least an hour late. The traffic was horrendous on Christmas Eve with everyone trying to get away.

'No, it's fine,' said John. 'They won't expect us on time, and anyway, nothing much happens on Christmas Eve. Relax, it'll be okay.' He patted her hand.

And Alice *had* relaxed, looking forward to a couple of days with lovely people who seemed to like her, and maybe even pictured her as a potential daughter-in-law, hoping they'd like their present in the back of the car – a hamper full of delicacies from Fortnum & Mason.

This was going to be a lovely Christmas. And she didn't

need to worry about her father being alone. He had phoned to tell her that he'd been invited out, and not only for the evening, but to stay for a couple of nights with friends.

Life was good, and Christmas was going to be even better.

* * *

'*Dear Arthur and Astri.*' Or should it be Astri and Arthur? Perhaps that was better; Astri had obviously done most of the hard work. Alice was writing a thankyou letter three days after Christmas, deciding that she would take care over it, and not send an email: much too hasty and businesslike, however well she composed it.

It had been wonderful, and the occasion deserved a proper letter. And now, sitting at her kitchen table, Alice was taking care with her words, picturing how they would be received the other end, and how her letter might be read out by Astri to Arthur. And of course, she would thank them warmly for that lovely cashmere pashmina, which she was wearing now. The house was freezing, and it was a relief that her central heating had clicked on a few minutes ago, at last. There were serious downsides to owning a house too big for her, even if she loved it.

'*What a wonderful Christmas! Thank you so much, and it was lovely meeting Joanna and Josie, and all your lovely neighbours. Also thank you for the beautiful – and wonderfully warm pashmina which I'm wearing right now. The house is freezing, and it's a real godsend. Love the colour, too! The drive back wasn't too bad, as John probably told you. I was dreading an anticlimax to such a lovely occasion, but the roads were surprisingly empty, and apart from the house being a total icebox on arrival, it was all fine, and at least the pipes hadn't frozen up as they did last year.*

I also enjoyed going to your lovely church. I have to admit, it's a long time since I've been to one – the vicar here in Putney seems to be into amateur dramatics and it completely put me off – but I really enjoyed the service, and the drinks party afterwards. And as for that dinner, it was superb. Congratulations!

I'd love to return your hospitality here one day, and you must tell me if you like curry which I always enjoy doing. And if you don't, I feel rather guilty about some of the sauces in your hamper!

Thank you again for making the weekend so very special, and I very much look forward to meeting you again. Your house was a real home away from home, and I loved every minute of your amusing and interesting company.

With love,

Alice.'

Would that do? Alice re-read the letter, wondering if it all sounded too effusively schoolgirl. It would do for now. She'd have another look at it tomorrow before sending it off.

The phone rang.

'Oh, hi. I'm just writing a letter to your parents; good timing. Could you remind me of their address and postcode?'

'Sure. Incidentally, they loved having you. They're already talking about when you can come down again. And you obviously hit it off with Joanna and Josie. I've just heard from them too. And they want you to be at their civil ceremony in March. Maybe we could go out to Australia together.'

'I'd love to! First time I've ever been to a civil ceremony. And to Oz, for that matter.'

'Me, too. Anyway, I can't be long. See you tomorrow.'

Alice wrapped her pashmina around her, enjoying its

warmth which reminded her of the warmth of John's family. Replacing the top on the Mont Blanc pen which John had given her, she smiled in pleasure. She was a lucky girl.

CHAPTER FIFTY-SEVEN

NEW SCOTLAND YARD, LONDON

Why on earth hadn't she done it before?

When Alice had returned from the Christmas lunch at John's parents, she decided that once too often she had been forced to squeeze past Helen's old and heavy trunk on the landing where she and Tom had dumped it all those months ago. Three days into the New Year she decided to look through it once and for all – and to throw away any old junk. She had only glanced through it in Cornwall, but there might be stuff worth keeping for sentimental reasons, and of course, her wretched cousin Oliver had rung more than once to ask her to see if there was anything inside of value. Typical. No thought, as usual, about Aunt Helen.

Placing her mug of coffee carefully on the stairs, she opened the trunk. As she had guessed from the weight, it was crammed full. And as she began to extract things, she realized it was all personal and family mementos. Helen must have kept paperwork like accounts and tax returns somewhere else, or maybe the police had taken it. And they must have gone through everything before allowing her to take it away.

Some bulky photo albums caught her eye, and she leafed though them. Mostly family scenes, starting years ago in black and white and then progressing in colour to the more recent past, where she was delighted to see quite a few pictures of herself with her aunt. And there were several pages of pictures of the Admiral with his various ships. Alice didn't know the difference between any of the ships with guns, but she knew what a big aircraft carrier looked like.

There were also several group photographs in black and white of little children labelled 'St Bede's Primary School', with her aunt sitting with other teachers in a sea of smiling young faces. Alice remembered, with John Mitchell so often at sea, that Helen had started to fill her time by teaching art at a primary school near Plymouth.

Suddenly there was a noise downstairs. Maggie had obviously come in to work.

Alice put down the photographs and noticed a roll of paper. The ancient elastic band snapped as she unrolled it and then unfurled what turned out to be a series of paintings. Needing to weigh them down and have a better look at them, she took the roll down to the kitchen table. Each was signed 'David, 7 years old'. They were excellent for a child so young – extraordinary – almost the work of a prodigy. But they were also profoundly disturbing. Alice studied them very carefully, her psychologist's analytical mind homing in on what she saw.

'A day at the sea.' With two people obviously drowning, and a small boy watching them from the beach, with his hands over his ears.

'My parents', with a picture of two graves.

'My Mum', with a woman's face painted with a big question mark forming the back of her head. Alice was fascinated and horrified at the same time.

Rolled in with the drawings was a rather faded carbon copy of a letter, signed by 'Heather Ewbank, Headmistress, St Bede's' and drawing attention to a Mr and Mrs Campbell that *'David appears to be disturbed and probably needs some kind of psychiatric help'*.

The phone suddenly rang, interrupting her thoughts. 'Alice, it's Marshal again. He says it's urgent.'

Alice put down the old letter, dusted off her clothes and walked down to where Maggie was proffering the phone.

'Hi, Robin.'

'Alice. I need you at the Yard, and as soon as you can get here, if you don't mind. All hell's breaking loose about these London murders, and I need all the brainpower I can get.'

Alice thought quickly. 'Okay, I can be there in an hour. Luckily, I've got no appointments this morning.'

'Great. Call me on my mobile when you're five minutes away and I'll send Joe down for you.'

In the minicab, Alice looked through the two newspapers she'd asked Maggie to bring in. Both had the London murders splashed on the front page, with the *Daily Mail* castigating the police about lack of progress. She read the headlines with dismay, LONDON KILLINGS – POLICE BAFFLED and ANOTHER TOP BRASS MURDER.

Poor Robin Marshal had even been identified by name, so he must be having real problems. How on earth was she going to be able to help?

* * *

As instructed, she phoned in when she reached Victoria Street, and DS Joe Bain was already waiting for her when she arrived to usher her through security and quickly up to a conference room.

There were eight people already there; Joe Bain, of course, and Dr Eric Syme, a senior psychologist with whom she had worked before. He smiled at her, and indicated the chair alongside his. There were several detectives she recognised and a big, older man she figured was Robin's boss, a Commander, who was looking fairly tense. The media pressure probably wasn't helping. A big white screen was at one end of the table

together with a laptop and projector, with an analyst helping
to work it.

'Thanks for coming, Alice,' said Marshal, who was standing
at the end of the table, looking distinctly harassed and very
tired.

'To anyone who doesn't know her, I'd like to introduce Dr.
Alice Diamond, who has been very helpful with several cases
in the past. Alice, I'm afraid you'll have to catch up as we go
along. Everything's very urgent here.

Now, let's look at what we've got. We're not just talking
about the two recent shootings in Westminster and the murder
of the MP. We now think we're looking at multiple homicides,
committed over several months, and probably by the same
individual, in various parts of the UK, and almost certainly
abroad – culminating in the three in the Met area in the past
two weeks.

We've got evidence, including definitive ballistics reports,
which point to one person, almost certainly a man, killing four
victims in Kent, Belfast, Hong Kong and France. Other murders
are linked by patterns we'll be examining.'

He pressed a button on the laptop.

PSYCHOPATH appeared on the screen. 'He may well be a
psychopath – and we're assuming it's a 'he' for various pretty
good reasons – and involved in some strange pattern of revenge.
The advanced age of most of the victims implies this could go
back a long way, even into childhood.'

Dr Syme raised his hand.

'Robin, I'd like to comment on that later.'

Marshal nodded. 'Sure'. He turned back to the screen. OLD
appeared.

'He seems for some reason to like, or even to be obsessed
with old objects. Rather rooted in the past. There's a definite

pattern of what we would consider out-of-date weapons – little 6.35mm pocket pistols, an old heavy revolver, .303 rifles, and even perhaps, a Bren light machine-gun last used back in the sixties. It's conceivable that he may like other old things, like vintage cars or motorbikes, antiques and old music like classical rather than modern stuff.

Next, GEOGRAPHIC SPREAD came up on the screen, and then a chart.

'Now here's the list of the possible linked victims that we've identified so far, thanks to HOLMES, various UK forces, the Irish Gardai and Interpol. Names, locations and dates.'

Alice studied the list, quickly amazed to see her aunt's name 'Lady Helen Mitchell' at the top. So there *was* something really unusual about her murder? But it was the next one on the list that made her start. Campbell? When had she last seen that name? Christ! Two hours ago. On a copy of that letter she'd just found in Helen's old chest – talking about a boy called 'David'. But it was a common enough name. She looked down the list further. She had no thoughts on Hong Kong, Belfast, Bedford or any of the London locations, but the unmistakable French name of St-Hippolyte jumped right out at her, and so did the name 'J-J Bertrand', her father's friend.

She looked down at her iPhone scrolling through dates, her hands now shaking slightly.

Marshal had turned back to the computer. Click. TRAVEL.

'If any of the foreign killings are *really* connected to the UK ones, we can deduce that he travels a lot, knows how to get around internationally and to get himself in and out of countries undetected, especially...'

Click. SECURITY SYSTEMS.

'...because he seems more than familiar with security and its technology, and how to get around it. He's been very careful to avoid CCTV, and somehow he's getting weapons through airports.'

FIREARMS went up on the screen.

'Talking of weapons, he looks as if he's very good with firearms. The Petty France and St James's rifle shots were pretty competent by any standards. So he could well have been in the military.'

He paused for a sip of coffee.

'Now, from the Irish Guards, we do have one potential lead, and one with a possible grudge motive. In the eighties they had a Lance-Sergeant Walsh, though that may not be his real name. He was, for the most part, an excellent soldier. He was an expert shot, Bisley champion standard, and a Weapon Training Instructor, but, apparently, rather difficult and belligerent and not popular, and was court-martialled and then thrown out for fighting with another Sergeant, what's more, brutal and unpleasant fighting, not just a barracks scuffle.

It transpires the retired Colonel killed outside the barracks was his Company Commander at the time.

And the old General killed last week in St James's *may* have been the President of the Court Martial in Germany that found him guilty, though we've yet to confirm that.

We've now been provided with a photograph of Walsh, not very clear, and his cap and moustache don't make it any easier, plus it's nearly twenty years old. But it's all we've got.'

A rather fuzzy picture came up on the screen, distorted by being blown up from an old photograph.

Under the peak of the cap were eyes that Alice would recognize anywhere.

She was totally stunned. Her adrenaline soaring, her professionalism nevertheless took over. She had to tell them, even if what she was about to say was shocking.

'Robin, I'm sorry to interrupt, but I believe I actually know this guy.'

There was a sudden hush in the room, as everyone turned from the image of 'Sergeant Walsh' to stare at her. She felt herself redden, but persevered.

'Yes, I think I even went out with him.' She could see the shock on the faces round her. 'And broke it off because he was so moody and difficult.'

She paused. 'And, maybe, potentially violent. I tried to Google him to check him out and question him about things, and he went completely ballistic. That was the end of it.'

Robin Marshal was astonished. 'Are you absolutely sure, Alice? It's a very old photograph.'

'I'm afraid I think I am. Can we have the dates back on the screen, please?'

The picture of 'Sergeant Walsh' was replaced by the victim list and the dates and times of their murders. Alice consulted her iPhone.

'At least two of the dates match those when he said he was going abroad, or had just come back. Hong Kong and France. I only had about three dates with him, so it's difficult to talk about any of the other connections, but the French one must be, literally, a million-to-one coincidence.

Believe it or not, the victim, an old trade unionist, was a vague friend of my father.'

'Can we have a name of the man you're talking about?' asked Marshal. The man you went out with, not Bertrand.'

'Hammond, David Hammond. Or at least that's what he called himself. But I think it may be real, because I Googled a security company under that name.' Pause. 'Security. Tick the box. You see why I'm getting sure about him. He drove me in an old, restored vintage Bentley, tick – and he always seemed to be travelling – tick. Military, firearms – two more ticks.

And then Robin, there's something I was about to tell you this morning. I went through my aunt's things and found some very disturbing drawings by some kid called David aged seven and a copy of a sort of complaint letter to the child's foster parents. They were called Campbell, the same as that chap in Kent. Another tick.'

Marshal interjected, 'We could look him up now.'

She went over to one of the computers and brought up Hammond Security. There, under 'Contact us', was an address in an industrial zone off the King's Road in Fulham, built on an old reclaimed gasworks site.

'Well, there's an office address for you. He never gave me a home address, as if he had something to hide. Come to think of it, he always called me on my landline so I never even knew any of his phone numbers. You can see now why I was trying to check up on him.'

Robin Marshal stared at Alice. 'Good God! Well, we may *just* have found our man – and almost by complete chance.'

He didn't waste a moment. He ordered immediate discreet surveillance on the Fulham office building, while he made Joe Bain sit down with Alice and start detailed questions about everything she knew; Hammond's movements, habits, clothes, cars, the lot. They agreed to take a break and meet up again in half an hour.

* * *

Even sitting in the corner with friendly Joe Bain, Alice was immediately embarrassed about how little she knew, and that was bad enough. Hammond's house was probably 'somewhere in Wandsworth', but exactly where she had no idea.

The old Bentley was green. She had no idea about its age or

model number and you certainly didn't start a relationship with a new man by walking round and noting the number plate. Even concerning his movements, she was skimpy, although she did call her father in France and knew the exact date of the death of his friend. Bain had scarcely been able to fill a page of his notebook by the time the others came back in.

He was called out of the room by a message, as Marshal re-started the meeting.

'So to catch up, it looks as if Alice's aunt Helen Mitchell might have been killed because of something she did when teaching a boy called David, aged seven, and then it caused trouble with the Campbells, one of whom now *may* have been killed for something *they* did.'

A Detective Sergeant cut in, 'You'd have to be extremely strange to do something like that, and after all those years. Okay, there have been lots of revenge killings, especially in America. Boys being turned down by girls, kids hating their school – Columbine, for instance. Anti-socials like Bundy, Gacy and Berkowitz. Or one chap I read about in a small town who kept writing down '*retal*' in a notebook any time anyone offended him – serviced his car poorly, sold him rotten fruit and so on. Then one day he loaded two pistols and walked up and down the street shooting any of his neighbours with '*retal*', or retaliate, against their names. Died in a hail of police bullets after he went home to re-load.'

'To be fair, it's not just America,' said Marshal. 'After all, we had Thomas Hamilton kill all those poor Dunblane five-year-olds just because he'd been turned down by their school. And after that, they meant to get rid of handguns. Fat chance.'

The Commander was looking thoughtful, if not sceptical.

'But all those killings were fairly local and caused by something recent that happened. I've never heard of anyone going all over the place – indeed, the world – to avenge something from literally years ago. Frankly, Robin, it really does sound a bit far-fetched.'

'I know Sir, but bear with me. It gets a bit less far-fetched if we jump a few years to something, or rather someone, we're now getting fairly sure about. Lance-Sergeant Walsh. He got in a fight in Germany with another NCO over some trivial insult in a bar and was then violent enough to nearly kill him. So he gets court-martialled, and drummed out.

And lo and behold, our Colonel O'Farrell at Wellington Barracks turns out to have been his Company Commander, and that old General may have been the President of the Court – both killed years later. Definite links. Here's a man who really *does* seem to have decided to take revenge years after the event. Although at the moment, we don't know why.

Let's go back to childhood. Alice tells us that Helen Mitchell, or rather the headmistress she worked with, seemed to have written a letter to a couple called the Campbells – perhaps one of the people killed at the old people's home. What happened after the letter? What triggered such hatred towards them?'

'Maybe they rejected him in some way,' suggested Alice. 'From the tone of the letter, it sounded as if they weren't his real parents, but foster ones, in which case, what happened to his *real* parents?'

'The sister of Mr Campbell up in Rochdale has now been interviewed,' Marshal intervened. 'Seems they *did* foster a child, but something went very wrong. He was very difficult, and something at school was the final straw. He had to go back to a home.'

'But what kind of person, or nut, would do that kind of thing to old people?' asked one of the younger detectives.

Dr Syme intervened. He got up and walked to the computer.

'Let me try to answer that. Earlier, Robin, you wrote 'Psychopath'. Perhaps 'nut' as a general term *would* have been more appropriate, if not exactly professional. I know I've bored some of you before about this, but I'll remind you again anyway. Mental health problems can be much more complex than physical ones. We know when it's mumps or measles, but with the mind it can often be in the form of curious, interlocking combinations.

Round this table we've already started to talk about revenge killings. You may be surprised to hear it, but the word 'revenge' actually doesn't appear in any psychology manual. In fact, this man may be feeling all kinds of emotions that we, here, would have trouble understanding. Guilt, shame, envy, fear, lack of self-worth – all of which he may be trying to cover up. He may be, for instance...'

He turned to type in the word SCHIZOID.

'Schizoid personality type was in fact a concept introduced by a Scottish psychoanalyst, Fairbairn, to denote a personality who may be *outwardly* successful, but who is in fact solitary, withdrawn and unable to relate to people. Even when they *are,* apparently, reacting with others, the schizoid gives nothing away. In fact, they have a detachment from social relationships and a restricted range of emotional expression.

And they can either be idle or catatonic – not our man. Or else hyperactive creative geniuses – perhaps more like our suspect. Individuals who have no struggle with shame or guilt about their actions. That might fit.'

The psychologist added in NARCISSISTIC RAGE.

'In this category we have so-called *narcissists*, often driven by grandiose ideas to protect themselves from unconscious feelings of low self-esteem. This personality can develop in early adulthood, indicated by signs of self-importance and boastfulness. There's often a pre-occupation with fantasies of unlimited success, power, beauty or other desirable attributes.

Our suspect – very good-looking, tidy, well-dressed and with a beautiful old car, could be what we call a pseudo-perfectionist and have suffered what are often referred to as 'narcissistic wounds' or 'injuries' in childhood and later. Any threat to the fragile 'infantile self' as it's known, can lead to fury that the sense of omnipotence has been challenged.

Therefore, it may be possible that such narcissistic rage can be directed *outwardly* towards people whom they feel have slighted or thwarted them, however incoherent and unjust it might seem to us. And that, in rare cases, *could* lead to the desire for some kind of revenge.'

Tap. Tap. PARANOID appeared.

'Paranoid personalities can be different again. Suspicious, rather humourless and again given to grandiosity. They tend to suffer from fear, anger, vindictiveness. They feel that everyone is out to get them, and such irrational fear can wreck their lives – remember how suspicious President Nixon became, and it certainly ruined him.

Until we catch him, we'll be guessing. We may *never* know what makes the fellow act in the way he's doing, if indeed he's our man at all. It certainly won't fit in a neat pigeon-hole. No, there are all kinds of nuances. I think we may be dealing with a combination of several of the problems you see here. Alice has probably only seen some of them in the man she met, if indeed it's the same man.'

Alice nodded.

'But I do have *one* observation based on past experiences. He may not be killing for revenge, as we might simplistically imagine. No. He may be killing, in his strange warped mind, to cover things up, to avoid, as it were, his inadequacies being found out. He is, so to speak, killing the *witnesses* to his failings.'

The roomful of people stared at him as he moved to sit down. Many of them now didn't care much about possible complex motivations or were utterly confused, and simply wanted to get on with the job and nail the possible perpetrator.

The silence was broken when Joe Bain came back into the room with a piece of paper in his hand. He leaned over and gave it to Robin Marshal, who put on his glasses and read it carefully. He looked up.

'It seems Martin Lonsdale, our Member of Parliament, also had something in his past he wanted to hide. We know that he never took a drink, which made his whisky overdose more than suspicious, and that he never drove a car. I think we now know why. Apparently, when he was very young and a bit of a tearaway, he drove a sports car under the influence and crashed, killing a pedestrian, a young mother, who had a son of about five who survived. Her husband killed himself shortly afterwards, and,' he paused looking up, 'the kid was put in a foster home. And do you want to know the woman's name?

It was Hammond, Deirdre Hammond. And her husband was called Dermot.

And the kid, guess what, was called David.'

CHAPTER FIFTY-EIGHT

FULHAM, LONDON

He knew something was up.

His office security cameras had picked up two strange cars hanging about, and cars didn't hang about the industrial estate. They parked and their drivers came and went – salesmen, delivery people, some collecting work from the printers next door. He went up to his first floor office and looked carefully out through the louvered blinds with his Zeiss binoculars.

He was right. With their superior magnification, he could see that each car had two occupants, not doing much, just hanging about.

He moved quickly and decisively, gathering some things together and then went down and walked into the store room.

He called over the store-man, Jimmy McMahon, an Irishman of about his own age who had been with him for years, and handed him an envelope. After a few minutes of urgent and quiet discussion, he patted Jimmy on the shoulder and went to the back of the store room. He looked out through the blinds covering the barred window, staying there for several minutes looking through the Zeiss glasses. After a while, he became sure there was nobody watching from that direction. A bit surprising, but the layout at the back was rather confusing and it was not entirely clear which brick wall *was* the back of his building.

He put on a flat cap and dark glasses. *Anything to disguise the blue eyes. Such a boon with women, but a real curse if trying not to be noticed.* He released several locks on the back door and carefully opened it. Still nobody in sight. Jimmy closed and locked the armoured door behind him. He walked though the mass of parked vans and other vehicles and then strolled away into one of the streets that surrounded the old gasworks site, full of little 19th century working men's houses – incredibly now worth half a million each.

After a brisk few minutes' walk, he pulled out his mobile and called his secretary, Ingrid.

'Hammond Security.'

'Ingrid, I've been called away on an urgent sales trip. Got to go abroad again, to France. Look after things, would you, it may be a few days.'

'Fine, Mr. Hammond.' *What's new?* She was now resigned to his frequent trips abroad, although she was surprised that the recent ones had been so sudden and had resulted in so few concrete orders, either for consultancy work or sales of security equipment. She didn't even know exactly where he'd been. Lately, he'd made all his own travel bookings on the net, himself. She wondered idly if her boss was embroiled with some woman. Probably. Not her business, of course, and she didn't care either, as long as her salary was paid.

* * *

Jimmy McMahon had never driven such a magnificent car, and there weren't many other vehicles he *hadn't* driven – from armoured personnel carriers and ten-ton construction lorries right down to minicabs. So he had found it rather fun driving the green Bentley to the coast, especially imagining people thinking he was the owner of such a splendid vehicle. Of course, what Mr Hammond had asked him to do was both illegal and risky, crossing borders on a passport forged and with his face replacing that of his boss, but he comforted himself that they'd be far more interested in the car.

He had dressed as well as he guessed a Bentley owner would, and left smart luggage on the back seat in full view.

It was now 7.15pm and quite dark. At the Portsmouth ferry terminal, he pulled the car into the short line marked CAEN – OUISTREHAM. The Brittany Ferries girl checked his last minute booking, glanced at the passport and took an appreciative look at the gleaming car – as did the UK immigration officer. If they had bothered to scan the passport, it would have recorded that David Hammond had left the country at 7.25pm.

Jimmy nearly had a worrying setback at the security shed. Two officers decided that the Bentley was a good choice for a random check. They noted down the number, looked under the car with a parabolic mirror on a long handle, asked Jimmy to open the boot, looked in the glove compartment and checked the registration documents. Jimmy said nothing, slightly anxious that his Irish accent might arouse curiosity. He needn't have worried. At least one of the security men was Polish and probably just wanted to examine the vintage car. He was waved through.

On the ship, Jimmy McMahon had a quick drink and a baguette before retiring to a sleeping cabin, where he stayed for five hours.

At Ouistreham, the French policeman was even more interested in the gleaming car and far less interested in the passport that Jimmy proffered.

'Bonne route, Monsieur.'

Appearances can still be crucial, thought Jimmy. He'd always been amused flying back from Ireland in the past, at the very height of the IRA troubles, watching the police at Heathrow, for some reason only pulling over and questioning people from the Belfast or Dublin flights who had beards or wore jeans. Any sensible IRA man would have shaved, worn a smart suit and carried the *Financial Times*.

He skirted Caen, pulverized during the 1944 invasion battles, using its crowded *Peripherique Est*, and turning south after about six exits on to the N158, signposted 'ARGENTAN, FALAISE'. About seven miles inland, he pulled over and consulted his map and instructions.

A mile later he turned off towards Falaise, and, on the nondescript fringes of the town duly found a row of lock-up garages. He unlocked number 12, the end one, and lifted up the door. It was completely empty. Very gingerly he eased the Bentley in, worried about chipping the paintwork on the door edge. Then he saw a large panel of thick foam rubber glued on the wall in exactly the place where it was needed. He took the dust-cover from the car's boot and carefully draped it over the gleaming bodywork. *Jesus! Mr Hammond really does think of everything*, he marvelled as he closed the door and pocketed the key.

After a five minute walk into Falaise town centre, he had a rather pleasant meal of mussels and frites. Only 12 euros and paid in cash. He asked the waiter to call for a taxi. It arrived in minutes, and once inside, he directed it not to Ouistreham, but further up the peninsular to Cherbourg, where Jimmy McMahon boarded a ferry for Rosslare.

Ten hours later, an Irish passport officer noted that a foot passenger called James McMahon had proffered an Irish passport and entered the Republic.

It was about eight hours after Robin Marshal's office had alerted all UK borders that David Hammond was to be apprehended at all costs – apparently twelve hours too late.

* * *

The trouble is, it takes time to mount an armed raid, thought Marshal. First you had to conduct a 'Dynamic Risk Assessment', especially in a built-up area with plenty of innocent bystanders likely to get hurt.

Lines of fire, hostage-taking – it all had to be justified and approved. So it had taken all night to prepare and get a green light.

He had decided to lead the raid on the Hammond Security building personally, and it went in at 09.15. Unlike the 'middle of the night' raids of suspects' homes, this one was designed to catch anyone working and with their computers on.

Using the cover of darkness, two sniper teams had moved into position. The day before, the surveillance cars had reported the presence of someone who looked like Hammond, but had not seen him emerge again. Another unknown male had left at 3pm, and then a tall Teutonic female had locked up and left at 5.30.

In the event, all they got was Miss Ingrid Meyer, who promptly went into a lather of Germanic fury rather than shock when masked men, dressed in black and wielding sub-machine-guns came bursting and shouting into her office, quickly followed by other quieter men and women who started removing things.

With no sign of Hammond, Marshal quickly ordered a check on all borders and turned to question Ingrid. Once he had calmed her down and treated her to a cup of her own tea, he began to realize that she knew very little, although she was co-operative enough. He remembered his uncle who had been in the war and who had said that there were some Germans who were either 'at your throat or at your feet', and had watched, at the liberated Belsen concentration camp, the very same guards who had been exterminating the inmates days before, now nursing them diligently back to health because they had been ordered to by 'a higher authority'.

Like many similar companies, Ingrid explained, Hammond Security had gradually changed –from providing companies with watchmen and guards – to creating hi-tech solutions including sophisticated alarms and remote cameras and CCTV. It had also graduated from thwarting the theft of money, valuables and equipment to that of information, data and fraud.

She also confirmed that Mr. Hammond seemed to be a resourceful and effective businessman, for whom she had worked for about ten years. Yes, he travelled a lot, all over the world in fact. However, she admitted to some surprise that his recent spate of travelling, even to America and to the Far East, did not seem to have produced the successful results and firm orders that she would normally expect from Mr. Hammond's sales trips.

Mr. Hammond seemed to have kept his private life very private – although she knew he had once been married and had a teenage son. The business of Hammond Security was split in two, she told them – consultancy and equipment. Jimmy McMahon, the storeman, could help them about the equipment sales – except that he wasn't there. He had been called away very suddenly yesterday. Some medical problem with his sister in Canterbury, apparently. He'd probably be back tomorrow.

Mr. Hammond himself? Well, he'd been in yesterday in the morning but then called in to say he was off on a sales trip. Something in France. He might still be at home in Wandsworth. They dialled the number she gave them. No reply. Uniformed and armed officers were quietly sent off to the address that she helpfully provided.

'Mind you, Mr. Hammond hasn't been quite himself for a while, ever since just after last Christmas. Something seemed to have upset him, and since then he's been even less forthcoming than before.'

The team that had broken into the Wandsworth house reported in to Marshal's mobile. No Mr Hammond, but plenty of evidence of him living there and definite signs of occupancy by a teenage boy.

Two computers, very few pictures of anyone, no weapons, nothing very helpful at all for the moment, but a photo album kept by the boy upstairs, with somewhat dated but still usable colour photographs of what may be his father.

Second call. The boy, about eighteen, called Henry or Harry Hammond, had just arrived at home, but had no idea where his father was. They would bring him in.

It was soon afterwards, at about noon, when Marshal was called by his office. It was Joe Bain.

'I hate to tell you this, Robin, but the port people in Portsmouth have just got around to telling us that a Bentley L715AGT boarded the Caen/Ouistreham ferry at 7.25 last night. I checked. It's registered in the name of Hammond Security.'

'Christ, Joe, we've lost him. Call and email the French police first. That car would surely stand out.'

But he could have been driving now for four or five hours, reckoned Marshal, so he by now he could have left France and be in Belgium, Holland or even Germany. And, of course, there are no proper bloody borders in Europe any more.

'Better get Hammond's face to the media, and fast. At least, we've got a colour one.'

CHAPTER FIFTY-NINE

WANDSWORTH, LONDON

Harry had returned home to Wandsworth after work on Wednesday evening, shocked to find a POLICE. DO NOT ENTER ribbon outside his father's house and a policeman stationed outside the front door. The policeman had asked him for his identity, and proof of that identity which he provided with his Oyster card, before being allowed into the house. Escorted into the sitting room, there were several more police sifting through everything, and someone in plain clothes at his father's computer.

He had not been allowed to stay there that night, and after an extensive interview they had suggested a local hotel nearby, asking him to return the bill to them and handing him two cards, one of them with the address of a police station and the other with the address of a local Travelodge and a small map of its location.

He was told that he may not be able to return for several days, and that they would immediately inform him when it was permissible to do so. Furthermore, he would have to be contactable at all times on his mobile.

He had been given half an hour to collect what belongings he needed under the strict gaze of a woman police officer, who did not allow him to take the photo album Jeni had given him.

'I'm sorry Sir, we may need that.'

On the way to the Travelodge hotel, still in deep shock, Harry had decided he would go and stay with Jeni and Paul in Parkgate that weekend and escape what he was terrified would suddenly escalate into a storm of horrifying publicity about his father, possibly encircling him as well. Wanted in an international murder scandal? The thought was horrifying.

Now, at Euston station, he felt strange, even unworldly, as he waited for the train on the crowded concourse. He had been right about the sudden onslaught of publicity. His father's face stared out of the news stands at WH Smith, just as it had on the newspapers in the reception area of the office that morning. His employers always had several newspapers laid out on the glass table, as a courtesy if clients were ever kept waiting and as a perk for the staff, each one stamped NOT TO BE REMOVED. At least there had been no mention or a picture of him.

Here at the station he was just another face in the milling Friday night throng, and with luck, might remain one. He suddenly remembered that hardly any photos of him existed, if indeed any since he was four years old. Only his mother had ever photographed him – his father certainly never had – and being a shy and overweight boy he had always kept well away from the camera, even when Paul or Jeni had brandished one.

But did the press hound you out in the end? Harry didn't know how they operated and what was legal and permissible and what was not, at the same time realizing that at eighteen years old he was no longer protected as a minor would be from unwanted and unwelcome press intrusion.

At last he was on the crowded train, surrounded by people reading papers and looking at his father's face every time the passengers opposite turned the front page of the *Evening Standard*, directing the headline and lead article towards him.

He would have to spend three hours staring out of the window.

This was going to be the worst journey of his life. And by

the time he got to Parkgate, Jeni and Paul would have watched the seven o'clock news. They always did.

CHAPTER SIXTY

NEW SCOTLAND YARD, LONDON

'Joan's been shot!'

It was Joe Bain on the phone, conducting the search of Hammond's safe house.

'What?' Robin Marshal gasped. 'Is she alright?'

'Yes, she sort of shot herself. She's okay, thank God, bandaged up and gone to hospital. We were searching the house and she came across a briefcase and one of the pens inside it seemed unusually heavy, so she tried to unscrew the top.

And it suddenly just went off, and a bullet went through the bottom of her left hand. The doc says no bones or ligaments were broken, so it won't do real damage. It was a heck of a shock, but she's pretty much okay.'

'Thank God for that,' said Marshal. He had always liked DC Joan Palin. She was young, keen, but a bit too hasty. She'd probably be a bit less hasty in future.

'Well, it looks as if this clears up the mystery of how Hammond travelled with firearms,' Joe Bain continued.

'I've got the pen gun in a plastic bag ready to go to forensics. It's really very realistic – looks just like a normal pen. Airport X-ray would be very hard-pushed to pick it up with lots of other pens in a briefcase. I checked it on the web. It's a commercial product – amazing. Called a Stinger Pen gun – perfectly legal in the US. You can't silence it, but then he didn't need to. All those shootings were in remote areas, and in the film club the briefcase would have deadened the sound.

By the way, the website also tells you how to avoid shooting yourself,' Joe chuckled before collecting himself.

'We puzzled about how he hid the distinctive shape of the bullets, though. In the US he could have just bought them locally, but not in Europe. We then checked his carry-on wheelie suitcase, which again seemed a little heavy. We examined it and it turns out he'd modified the sliding handle and replaced the two aluminium tubes with heavy gauge steel. With an extra catch he'd installed, you can slide the handles right out and we found the little bullets at the bottom of each tube. They must have been perfectly shielded from X-ray by the thick steel.

That's off to forensics as well. But I bet we've found the weapon in most of the murders.'

Marshal was not entirely surprised that Hammond had been so ingenious and methodical. With a security company's facilities behind him, he could have fabricated something like the suitcase bullet holder and then even carefully checked out its detectability on his own X-ray machine, or other security equipment.

'Keep looking, Joe. We were very lucky he had no time to get to his briefcase and make the pencil gun disappear. I doubt if you'll find the big revolver, or the rifle and Bren gun. He probably got rid of them.'

CHAPTER SIXTY-ONE

FARNHAM, ENGLAND

The frost had settled outside the pub hotel and it was freezing cold, especially before the central heating turned on at 8 a.m. The guests wouldn't be stirring out of their beds at any time soon thought Polly, as she took the delivery of the Sunday papers, a tied batch of only about four editions of papers, although with all the extra sections remarkably heavy.

How did people have the time to read all that, she wondered? In the same breath, she realized they didn't. Every Sunday, she had to clear the rooms of virtually untouched sections lying on the floor or side tables, and throw three quarters of the news into the black rubbish sacks when clearing the rooms.

She had been pleased by her small rise recently, possibly because of her honesty about the watch. And she knew that such jobs weren't easy to come by; too many of her friends were struggling these days, not exactly envious of her still meagre salary, but some of them envious that she had a job at all. And her earnings weren't much less than those of her friend Janice, a junior in X-ray at the local hospital, who had done all that training only to be rewarded by a piffling weekly wage, and a meagre flat shared by other nurses until they could afford something better, maybe years away.

It wasn't fair that doctors were now earning so much, while people on the front line were struggling so hard – she had read about all that recently and had realized how desperately unbalanced it all was with most of the money going on bureaucracy and advisors who never did anything with patients directly, being disproportionally reimbursed for their efforts.

She remembered how her mother, who had fractured her leg last year, was stuck in a ward with loads of people who were having their stomachs stapled on the NHS. There was certainly money for that, she thought, with everyone getting so fat, and enough for the surgeons who looked after them, but not for the nurses who were having a hideous time.

No, her job would do for now, until she found something better, and even then, she would leave with good references. It was easy enough to be dishonest; people leaving valuables in rooms, accepting tips in the bedrooms which she knew should be returned to reception; occasionally being offered the odd gift – she wouldn't succumb to any of that, and she hadn't.

Better still, she knew that Mr. Franco trusted her, ever since she had returned that ladies' watch, and that he liked her and smiled at her every time she was on duty. Now, at seven a.m. in the morning, she lugged the surprisingly heavy stack of bound Sunday papers into reception, thumping them on to the desk in front of him.

'The papers, Sir.'

'Thanks, Polly.'

'I'll do the names, if you like.'

'Thanks, I'd be grateful.'

Polly took a pen out of the holder and carefully wrote out the names of the guests on a sticky label for each packet, taking care to get the spellings right. Her boss might notice that, another point in her favour. So many foreign names these days; it wasn't always easy to get it right, and even Irish and Scottish names could be difficult – she almost always had to refer to the bookings to make sure she got it right.

And her last job would be to take off all the polythene wrappings – something that the establishment insisted on – so

that the main news would always be unobstructed and on top
of the pile, without an irritating plastic cover. There – on the
front page of *The Sunday Times* – was a handsome gentleman
of about forty with surprisingly dark blue eyes. Not bad, she
thought, although he was at least twenty years too old for her.
Something about him being wanted for murder: she could read
it later, if she had the time. But handing the pile of papers over
to Mr. Franco, she immediately noticed his interest.

'Thank you, Polly. You can go now.'

Polly was surprised to be dismissed before taking the papers
upstairs. That wasn't like Mr Franco at all.

Franco studied the picture on the front cover. That *had* to
be Mr. Hammond. Caught up in a murder inquiry? It couldn't
be. His heart raced. Maybe he should call Scotland Yard? And
how did one phone Scotland Yard? Through an ordinary 999
number?

But what if he was making some mistake? He studied the
picture closely again. No, it had to be him. It *was* him. A regular
customer over the years. Unmistakable.

Maybe he'd talk to the Press as well. There might be money
in it.

Franco decided to wait another half hour before trying to
phone, not sure Scotland Yard – if he could get through at that
hour – would be open at all, and determined to get his facts
right, going back through the record books beforehand and
making sure of the dates that he had been at 'The Grouse'. It
couldn't be him surely? But looking at the picture again, he
knew it was. Those unmistakable blue eyes.

And who was the lady with him? He remembered her well
enough. Short, very pretty, petite, with dark hair. Slightly
nervous. If he was asked to describe her, he would have little
enough information, but would do his best.

And what would it do for publicity for 'The Grouse' if they had a murderer as a regular customer? Probably increase it, thought Franco cynically in the same breath, suddenly despairing of human beings and their avid and increasing interest in grisly crime.

He remembered pubs in the East End where gangsters had positively put up the revenue, like the Kray brothers had at 'The Blind Beggar', and the extraordinary interest in detective programmes like *CSI*. Maybe it would be no bad thing for 'The Grouse' to have a bit of lurid and sensational publicity. But in the same breath, he scolded himself for thinking that way. Nevertheless, there was a recession on. Maybe any publicity was better than none?

He looked at his watch. He would try and get through to Scotland Yard in thirty minutes. And Giussepina would be fascinated when he got home tonight.

'A murderer? Staying in the hotel? You can't be serious!' Looking at the face on the front cover on *The Sunday Times* for the umpteenth time, Franco was certain he was right. Nobody else he'd ever seen had eyes like that.

CHAPTER SIXTY-TWO

COURMAYEUR, AOSTA VALLEY, ITALY

Katarina's face was now getting lightly tanned on her skiing break with Alessandro in the Italian Alps, despite her pages and pages of editorial in *Vogue Italia* over the years warning readers of the dangers of sun damage to the skin. In Courmayeur, in March it could easily reach 40 degrees in the mid-day sun, although a skier would never feel it whizzing down the slopes at the speed Katarina was capable of, though she found it hard to keep up with Alessandro.

She had certainly brought loads of sun protection, and in the highest factor, but for once she didn't care if she ended up with a tan. Suddenly the office seemed a million miles away, and for the very first time she thought how vain and superficial the world of fashion and beauty was. Maybe it was because she was 34 she thought to herself, and 35 tomorrow. Perhaps it was time to move on.

Alessandro was a brilliant skier; she was well behind him on the slopes, and behind his standards. And he definitely looked at his best on skis, and not bad she thought, at any other time, although certainly not as striking as that man in Paris. It still rankled, the way he had left the Crillon like that, even though it was months ago now.

It had been lovely driving up from Milan on the Val d'Aosta motorway in Alessandro's Ferrari to this delightful little town, with its cobbled streets full of chic fashion shops, bars and restaurants, and with its attractive centre where all cars were banned. And better still, they had even managed to book a room at the last minute at the appropriately named Romantik Villa Novecento thanks to a last minute cancellation, a beautifully restored 19th century building with stunning views, and a terrace in front from which to admire them.

Katarina loved these annual excursions to Italy's North West, with all its staggering peaks including Mont Blanc and some of the most breathtaking vistas of alpine scenery in the world. It offered just as much if not more than any other European destinations she'd been to she thought, as well as the North American ski resorts she knew.

And it was good to be back here with Alessandro again, a friend since childhood, and still, she realized, just as besotted with her as he was when they were both sixteen.

It had been an on-off relationship ever since, with Katarina never thinking she was exactly in love with him, but loving him certainly, trusting him totally, and feeling completely comfortable, and now for the first time inclined to accept his endless proposals of marriage. Again she reminded herself she was almost 35, and that she had been jealous last time they had split up, spotting him out with another girl on his arm.

He would make a good faithful husband and a great father, although he would probably never loosen up much in bed. It was a constant mystery to her why he was mildly prudish, so unlike that man in Paris. But nevertheless, she would be a fool to lose him, and as one of the girls in the office had said, though somewhat crudely, women were often their own best lovers anyway, freed from the restraints of teaching men what to do or not do, and then putting up with their often unsatisfying efforts whilst pretending they were perfect, afraid of frightening them away. Dear old Monica, she thought. Never afraid to put things bluntly.

She thought of tomorrow when they could do the off-piste

SERIAL DAMAGE

run down to Chamonix, the Valle Blanche. They had decided to put off celebrating until the evening, booking the best table by the window. He would almost certainly buy her a lovely present, he always did every year, and was able to afford it so she didn't feel guilty. He was doing well in Banco Italiano, and was naturally generous.

* * *

It had been a superb day's skiing, and they had wisely avoided a bottle of champagne at mid-day, reserving that pleasure for dinner. Alessandro was already dressed for it, in an immaculate Gucci dinner suit, and had gone to the bar downstairs to wait for her.

Katarina slipped on a fabulous Valentino cocktail dress that she had been given by a grateful client after the last Milan fashion show, and pinned on her favourite Bulgari ear-rings, deciding to wear her long blonde hair down. Alessandro had always preferred it like that.

And when she went downstairs past reception she felt all eyes looking at her, not an unusual experience, but tonight it felt particularly good. She wanted Alessandro to see her at her very best. Maybe he would propose again.

Suddenly, as she walked past the news stand, she saw a face staring out from the front cover of that day's edition of *Corriera della Sera*; a dark man with extraordinary blue eyes.

It had to be him. No-one else had eyes like that.

And there he was again, on the front page of *La Stampa*. What had he done? She picked up a copy of *Corriera della Sera* and scanned the story in utter disbelief. There was his name, David Hammond. Wanted for murders across four continents.

Her heart raced. It *couldn't* be the same man.

Katarina looked through the doors of the bar and spotted

Alessandro. She would have to read it later. But how could she possibly get through dinner without telling him? He would almost certainly want to make love to her later, and she couldn't face it, not thinking about that face in the papers. And should she tell the police that she had met him in Paris? No, she thought quickly. They would ask awkward questions and she would have to tell them everything, and Alessandro too.

Her birthday had been ruined.

* * *

The next morning on the snow was beautifully clear, but Katarina was not enjoying her skiing, any more than she had enjoyed her birthday dinner. Alessandro had constantly asked her if she was feeling alright and she had found it almost impossible to relax. And as she had guessed, he had been disappointed by the chaste night afterwards.

And she was constantly thinking about David Hammond, especially after reading more about him in the papers again that morning. She had managed to lock herself in the bathroom for half an hour after breakfast, until Alessandro had knocked on the door. 'Are you alright?'

'Fine,' she had answered, 'I'll be out in a minute.'

Those blue eyes were constantly in her head as she sped down the slopes, and the appalling things she had read about him. An old lady murdered in England. A Polish boy, killed days before his wedding. Some banker murdered in Hong Kong. Perhaps even, years before, his wife. It couldn't be him. But those blue eyes told her it was. And hadn't he even suggested coming to Milan, or even skiing with her? My God, and he even had her card with her address.

Halfway down the fabulous Valle Blanche run to Chamonix, Katarina was too distracted to notice the tree stump sticking out of the snow as she rounded a bend at speed, falling with her left leg twisted underneath her. For thirty seconds the pain was excruciating until a blessed rush of adrenalin enveloped her. She tried to move her lower limb, but couldn't. Immediately she knew she had done something serious.

All at once a wave of nausea overpowered her, and she was violently sick on the snow.

* * *

Katarina looked at her Piaget watch for the umpteenth time since arriving in the ambulance at the clinic, her birthday present from Alessandro last night. How much longer would they have to wait before the X-rays had been examined? They had already been here three hours, and she couldn't face looking at the papers, not with those blue eyes staring out of them all. She slumped back in her wheelchair, suddenly feeling Alessandro stroke her hand. 'It can't be long now.'

And it wasn't.

'Signorina Taliante?' Katarina looked up at the nurse standing above her. 'The consultant is ready to see you.'

'Grazie.'

At last she was wheeled along the corridor to the consultant's office, where a kindly-faced man was waiting behind his desk. He got up to his feet to greet her. 'I'm sorry to have kept you waiting, but it's been a desperately busy day.'

He studied Katarina briefly, thinking what a striking woman she was, with wonderfully high cheekbones and clear green eyes. They had a number of celebrities skiing in this part of the Alps every season. She was probably one of them, though a face he didn't recognize. Probably a top model. But it would be a long, long time before she returned to the catwalk if she was. He would have to choose his words carefully.

'I'm afraid to tell you it's a very serious fracture. A lower left fracture of the tibia and fibula.' He looked at her gently. 'It must have been very painful.'

Katarina nodded. 'It was. So how long will I be in plaster?'

The consultant hesitated.

'Well, you start off in plaster … for the first few days. But then, you'll have to wear a frame for some time. As I said, it's not a straightforward break.'

'A frame?' What kind of frame?'

'I'll show you a picture. It's what we call a Taylor frame.' He reached up to a shelf behind his desk and brought down a book, flicking through the pages until he had found a photograph and turning the book round to face Katarina.

She recoiled with shock. There on the page was a photo of someone's leg surrounded by bulky circular steel braces with various screws and crossbars, and about a dozen metal spokes going right into the flesh.

Katarina gasped. 'It looks agony.' She studied the photo again. 'And it's totally hideous.'

'No, it's not agony, but I agree, it's not pretty. But you'll soon get used to it, and you won't be in it for ever.'

'How long then?'

'About four months.' There was no easy way to tell her. It was always a shock when people knew; particularly young professional people whose lives would suddenly be turned upside down.

'Four months?' Katarina was stunned. How could she do her job with that hideous brace, let alone have it stuck around her leg for four months? How could she even get to work on a crowded train or bus? Or even walk at all with a heavy contraption like that? It looked as if it weighed at least five kilos.

'And how long will it be before I can walk?'

'Well, most people of your age can walk at once with crutches after the operation, although it's difficult because of the weight of the frame. And you absolutely mustn't put any weight on your leg. And with this type of accident, many people feel safer in a wheelchair. The problem with crutches is that your hands aren't free, so things like cooking and cleaning can be very difficult. Do you have any help at home? Someone living with you?

'No.'

'Then you may need social services for a while. Or a friend to stay with you. It's extremely important not to fall again. Often one accident like this can be quickly followed by another.'

Katarina's brain was spinning.

She would have to give up her job. You couldn't be a beauty editor of Milan *Vogue* looking like that. And how could she even get dressed with that hideous frame around her leg? You couldn't even get trousers over it. And could she ever ski again? She may be the love of Alessandro's life, but skiing wasn't far behind.

Suddenly, she dissolved into tears.

CHAPTER SIXTY-THREE

NEW SCOTLAND YARD, LONDON

By the summer, the dramatic London murders were no longer leading news, but Robin Marshal had certainly seen no let-up in his workload. Indeed, the Hammond case was still very much open.

Personally he was not entirely convinced that Hammond had left the country, and had not ruled out the possibility that, even if he had fled Britain, he might have returned.

After all, it was far too easy to get into the U.K. nowadays, and it would pose little problem for a competent operator like Hammond. All sorts of border checks had been relaxed to reduce queues; furthermore, entering England or Scotland from Northern Ireland or the Republic had always been easy, and on top of that, there was the 'Brussels-Lille loophole', with Belgian police even hassling the British officials trying to exert some control over suspects who merely stayed on the Eurostar trains and went on into Britain.

A lot of useful material had come in. The Interpol posting had unearthed a curious incident in the United States; a retired police chief killed in his garden, in the woods of Washington State. The bullet had been a .25 ACP. While there were plenty of little guns and lots of such ammunition floating around America, the coincidence had been enough to prompt Marshal to ask for the ballistics report. At least there was only one American source, now that the FBI's 'Drugfire' system and the ATF's 'Ceasefire' had thankfully been merged into NIBIN, which while sounding like a name out of *Lord of the Rings*, actually stood for 'National Integrated Ballistic Information Network'.

NIBIN's report turned out to be crucial. The electronic image comparison of the .25 round's ballistic signature exactly matched not only the French report but also the one sent over by Jimmy Wong in Hong Kong – and moreover, the Hollingbourne and Belfast bullets.

The pencil gun found in the Wandsworth house was test fired by Gordon Burns. The bullets it fired, and the one that had accidentally gone through Joan Palin's hand – all matched and all had been fired from the same weapon.

So it looked as if, for his overseas forays and for two of the British ones, Hammond had used the pencil gun – easily-disguised, and looking like something ordinary and innocent. It also fitted the evidence that only one shot had been used. No spent cases had been found from which one could normally compare the tell-tale marks from the firing pin, extractor or ejector, or deduce the unusual type of weapon. Indeed, in all the small-calibre shootings, the pattern of gun shot residue had indicated firing at very short range – almost contact range.

Whatever Hammond's motives or psychological shortcomings, Marshal had to admit that he was highly ingenious. He had put a lot of thought into how he was going to deal with those who had 'slighted' him.

But for the extraordinary coincidences thrown up by meeting Alice Diamond, he could have merely stopped when his 'task' was complete, confident that the geographic spread of his killings would ensure that no co-ordinated investigation would be successful.

While any possible motive for the American killing was still obscure, the Hong Kong one had at last become a little clearer. The NatWest bank in Hammersmith had now dug through their archived records and the former Branch Manager, long since retired, had been interviewed.

Apparently a small local company called Hammond Security Ltd. had been a customer of the branch for several years, but had then suddenly closed its account after a row with the bank. Its proprietor, a Mr. David Hammond, had heard that the branch needed a new security system and had bid for the contract.

But in a letter on the file, it turned out that the Assistant Manager, Mr James Cameron, while acknowledging that Hammond Security was a valued customer, had refused the tender on the grounds that *'Hammond Security is still too small and too new a company for the bank to be able to entrust its security to it, as opposed to one of the more established companies like Reliance or Banham'*.

According to the records, Mr. Hammond had then not only written a very abusive letter to the bank with copies to headquarters, but had actually burst into the branch, and in a very embarrassing incident had confronted and even threatened James Cameron in person – and in public.

It had all been covered up, Hammond Security had closed its account and James Cameron had soon afterwards been promoted and posted to Hong Kong.

Robin Marshal was growing increasingly worried. It was emerging that Hammond was a serial killer, but a very unusual one. Something had sent this strange and unstable man down a path of revenge or retribution that few could contemplate – let alone carry out.

Then something arrived from the other side of the world which might just begin to explain things.

Robin Marshal stared at the email in front of him. It was from a friend in the Communications and Criminal Investigations

Division of the Melbourne Police Department at their Babcock Street HQ, which Robin had once visited.

He had asked the Thai police if they had any information about the tsunami death of Mr and Mrs Picken mentioned in the British Airways letter that Hammond's son had found and eventually remembered to turn in. *What else had he forgotten?*

Marshal's recent searches had revealed that the Pickens had rescued the young boy called David Hammond from a foster home and had then looked after him for years. This might be a vital clue to his personality.

The Thai police had unearthed the only witness to the tragedy, an Australian, and after some time the Melbourne Police had found him and obtained a statement.

STATEMENT

Dr Rob Bennett, Melbourne

When we went to the pool that morning, it was about 11, sunny and already warm. Very calm sea. No wind to speak of. Most of the tourists had gone to the beach. By the pool the only other people were an elderly couple.

We soon got to know them. They were very nice, called Millie and Bill. I think from Manchester in the UK, in their seventies, white haired. He was pretty deaf. I later heard they were called Picken.

We'd been to the Christmas party the night before, with lovely giant dragons with guys inside them, which the kids loved. We shared a table with them and they said something about a man who had given them the holiday, something they said they could never normally have afforded. I thought that was pretty generous.

We'd just reached the pool and I'd put on my daughter's arm-bands and helped her into the shallow end when there was a sudden commotion. Several people were walking, even running past us towards the beach. I asked a porter what was going on. He clasped his hands together in the usual Thai greeting, and said something like;

'Funny thing. Sir. Sea go away. People find fish on beach.'

I work on oceanography at Melbourne University, so I suspected something at once. It was typical of what we call 'drawback', when the sea recedes just before a tsunami strikes. So I shouted to my kids, Lachlan and Hannah, to get out of the pool and run up to their Mum in our room on the first floor. I remember they argued, so I had to scream at them.

Then suddenly people appeared, running away from the beach and there was a roaring noise coming from beyond the trees. I heard shouts of alarm and a siren started wailing in the distance, then another one – closer.

I shouted really loudly for the old couple to get out of there, and started running to catch up with the kids.

The old lady, Millie, was trying to shake Jim awake and get him out of his deckchair. At that moment, a sandy wave about three foot high came through the trees and slopped brown water into the pool. I remember that it was loaded with beach junk, hats, umbrellas and sun-beds. I reached the bottom of the stairs.

I'm afraid my priority was my kids and family. I really couldn't stop to help the couple. The last time I looked back, unfortunately, she'd stopped to fiddle with her Kindle. Then a huge new wave burst through the trees, I'd say ten feet high this time. It raced across the pool in an instant. It swept the old couple off their feet and engulfed them. There was nothing I could do. I just reached the first floor and saw them pinned helplessly for a few moments against the shower booth by the surge of water, and then a large red piece of shattered beach hut slammed into them and swept them away.

I heard that a helicopter found Bill's body, a mile out to sea floating among the debris that had washed back out of the town. They never found her, as far as I know.

When we left three days later, the hotel manager, a German, had been able to find the couple's passports and had also looked up the records of their booking. I suppose he would have found the next of kin.

Signed,
Rob Bennett

Robin Marshal suddenly remembered something. He looked through his calendar. Hadn't that German secretary said something about Hammond 'becoming upset and changing behaviour after Christmas'?

He thought with real concentration. Suppose the Pickens were the only people who had shown any love to the young David Hammond? And the only people he'd loved back – in what he felt was a unfair world? And what if he had rewarded them with the holiday of a lifetime, only to have them snatched away by an act of God?

Would that be enough to be the tipping point? To send him on a grotesque killing spree against those who he felt did not love him and had done him harm?

Just possible, he supposed – if you already had a warped, strange mind. And it just might explain the otherwise inexplicable.

This man seemed to be prepared to kill people who, often years ago, had thwarted or threatened him, and in sometimes quite minor ways. There might be some possible logic in revenge on a drunk driver who was responsible for the death of one's mother, or being rejected by foster parents.

But being fired from a job? Dismissed from the army? Or turned down for a security contract? What on earth kind of person would kill for that, and especially years, or even decades, later?

Someone who could wait to kill.

All at once, a truly chilling thought.

So what about a girlfriend who had rejected him, played a role in his downfall and had ruined his careful, if maniacal, plans?

Budgets might be tight and personnel difficult to find, but Robin Marshal was suddenly determined that Alice must be protected.

He reached for the phone.

CHAPTER SIXTY-FOUR

PUTNEY, LONDON

PC Sydney Sykes was bored. It was pleasant enough in the kitchen of the house on Putney Common South, but still bloody dull stuck there all day or outside the front door. Thank God his eight-hour shift was about to end.

It wasn't even somebody terribly interesting he was guarding; just a rather pretty young woman called Alice Diamond who worked occasionally for the Metropolitan Police and was vaguely involved in some enquiry about a certain David Hammond, who was on the run. She had popped in occasionally to ask him if he wanted a cup of coffee, as had her nice secretary during the day, but that did little to allay the tedium.

He thought about his colleagues up the road, equally bored, stuck outside the house of the Deputy Prime Minister, Nick Clegg. How dull to have to stand there all day at the end of the street.

And wasn't the fact that they were there at all a perfect advertisement that somebody important must be there in residence? Surely nobody would ever know unless there was a policeman in constant attendance. That just gave the game away. None of it made sense to him.

And it made no sense to his twins either, Olly and Ona, both of whom had been furious that he was unable to attend their birthday party last week. Unusual for teenagers, they had actually *wanted* him there. At least he was glad of that, not being thought of as an old fogey.

Maybe the sight of a gun strapped to his hip had made him seem a bit less boring than the average Dad, and they had been nurtured on a constant diet of *NCIS*.

It was almost time for the switchover, and he hoped that Tony Hannaford would not be late as he usually was, and would be armed with another good Irish joke for him when he arrived.

Anything to break up the endless tedium.

No misogynist, he was still annoyed that he had been seconded to look after a woman's house all day.

But thank God, this wouldn't last forever. They'd told him he'd only be there for about a week longer. He was lucky. His poor old mates up the road like Mark and Billy, guarding Clegg, might be there for years. Or at least until there was another election and the politician they were guarding was kicked out.

He longed for a cigarette.

CHAPTER SIXTY-FIVE

PUTNEY, LONDON, ENGLAND

That autumn, Harry was pleased about certain things, but still traumatized about his father. The police were still looking for him, and had talked to him numerous times, although he had repeatedly assured them that he hardly knew anything about him, giving them the full run of the house in Wandsworth together with the keys as he had been asked to, and moving in with Elaine until the authorities had completed their searches and enquiries.

They were still astonished by how little he seemed to know, and how little they had ever done together.

He had only taken a small suitcase with him, and as he had been asked by the police, taken nothing that belonged to his father.

Except, that is, for those strange letters he had found in the bottom drawer of his father's desk; the curious one from British Airways about that couple who had been killed in the tsunami in Thailand, and the other one about the rented property in Kew.

He was still puzzling about them, feeling slightly guilty that he hadn't left them behind.

It had been nice of Elaine to take him in, sharing a cramped flat as she did with two other girls in Putney, and with only one bathroom, and kind of her flatmates to agree to it, especially with his father's face all over the news. Elaine had told them they had taken some persuading, only agreeing when she told them he would contribute generously towards the rent, and that he wouldn't be staying for very long.

The one thing that really pleased him was his sudden and dramatic loss of weight, almost a stone and a half less already after joining Putney Leisure Centre, and Elaine had done almost as well, and both of them were enjoying their early morning sessions, and the late night results of them as their physical confidence grew and they were able to expose themselves with far less embarrassment and restraint.

Though lifting weights was a bore, thought Harry, especially when you did that three or four times a week, they were certainly working, as were his lengths ploughing up and down the pool; thirty-six at the last count. And even his hair had been looking better since Elaine had persuaded him to go to The Cutting Room in Putney, as well as get contact lenses at last.

It was lucky that he had had a rise after that successful presentation; getting into shape and sprucing oneself up was an expensive process and now he would have to pay rental on a flat for the first time.

But it was certainly worth it. Some girl had even made a pass at him on the tube yesterday, or at least had looked at him with more than a passing interest as she sat next to him on the way back from work, even giving him a clue for the crossword he was doing in the *Evening Standard*.

'Cow parsley!' she had suddenly said, looking at his last unsolved ten letter word, with the clue 'A common British wild-flower.' Things were definitely looking up.

In the next week, Harry decided, he would check out that address in Kew that he had found searching through his father's desk. Perhaps he should have told the police about it, but something had stopped him. And surely, as they seemed to think, his father had fled abroad. Harry hoped he had.

After all, he had travelled continually throughout Harry's

lifetime and had probably had thousands of bolt-holes he could disappear to, and it was extraordinarily unlikely that he would stay in England with the continued police search and media publicity.

It was a huge relief to Harry that he looked nothing like his father, and most of all, that he had not inherited those striking blue eyes. Had he done so, Harry knew his life would have been unbearable, especially with the same surname.

And these days, looking in the mirror, he was at last happy with the face he'd got.

CHAPTER SIXTY-SIX

KEW, LONDON

In the middle of December, it began to snow – unexpectedly early.

As usual, snow brought Britain to a virtual standstill. It delayed, (with the usual lame excuse the 'wrong kind of snow') the commuter trains into Victoria Station and made Robin Marshal late for work. It quickly turned to grey slush in Victoria Street and outside Scotland Yard, but over in Putney it made Alice's garden look really pretty.

Down in Cornwall, the snow covered Helen Mitchell's grave and the fresh flowers that Jessica Coade had left there.

And it was really thick in Hollingbourne in Kent, and over in Belfast.

In Krakow it not only carpeted Josef Gierek's grave, half paid for by Agnieszska's family, but with Poland's harsh winter it would not be gone for months.

Nor would it up in the Cascades.

In Scotland, General Hewitt's grave soon disappeared under a blanket of white, as did those of James Lonsdale and Mick Foley, a recent one in Bedford. But outside Dublin, where Bill O'Farrell rested in the family plot, the snow soon turned to rain.

Even the Catholic cemetery in Quissac had a light dusting, while in the north, the snow blanketed the garage in Falaise.

In Hong Kong, of course, they didn't really know what snow was.

* * *

In Kew, a tall figure stared out at the weather. The cold suited him just fine. Everyone was bundled up in hats and scarves. He lived quietly and frugally, seldom shopping or eating in the same place more than once in a month. He made sure the radio and television were turned down low, and especially his opera CDs. And, of course, there were no women.

Anything to avoid drawing attention to himself, while he waited patiently to let his beard grow and his appearance to alter, with tinted glasses to hide those memorable blue eyes, and his hair grey – achieved with actor's dye bought off the internet. Luckily, the police had so far only been able to issue that very old Irish Guards group photograph, plus one taken at his wedding years ago and a rather misleading photofit.

He bought several newspapers a day, each one in a different shop to avoid being noticed. These he looked through very carefully, following the spectacular case of the 'POSH MURDERS', and the suspect who had apparently slipped away so easily to the Continent, to the embarrassment of the police, the Mayor and the Government – and to the cynical delight of the Opposition.

The criticism of Robin Marshal had died down in most of the media, but the *Daily Mail* was not letting the matter drop. And it was in the *Daily Mail* that something caught his eye. The newspaper was running a four-page review of the murders and on the last page was a photograph taken several weeks ago of Robin Marshal emerging from Scotland Yard. And just behind him was a rather pretty girl, with short dark hair and a briefcase. Hammond reached over for a magnifying glass. It was Alice Diamond; he was sure of it.

So she was something to do with the police, and must have

played a role in his downfall. A bolt of anger shot through him.

* * *

Weeks passed. The political and media importance of 'THE POSH MURDERS' and the suspect's disappearance was slowly fading. Every three days or so, an old bearded man with a brown hat, muffled up against the cold and using a stick, came slowly walking across Putney Common.

Sure enough, he noted, the policeman outside Alice Diamond's house had long since disappeared. And the patrol car that used to come past regularly every hour or so had now stopped coming.

It was nearly time.

* * *

It was dark as Harry arrived in Pagoda Avenue in Kew. He had spent the earlier part of the evening with a new friend from the office in The Orange Tree, a pleasantly old-fashioned pub opposite the station in Richmond, conveniently close to where he was now, sitting on a low wall opposite number 37.

He looked at the house, guessing it was probably split into two flats, and relieved to see that the lights were on in both of them. But his adrenalin was racing at the thought that his father might be sitting in one of them right now. He could hardly knock at the door to find out, even if anybody answered. And anyway, people often didn't at this time of night.

And should he phone the police with his suspicions that his father had never gone abroad? Maybe he should call them, having established someone was in residence. But reaching his hand in his pocket, he suddenly realized that he'd left his mobile at the office. Damn. Probably he should go home and stop playing detective.

He began to feel as stupid as he felt cold.

But then, the lights suddenly went off on the bottom floor. Whoever it was in there was coming out, or were they going to bed? No, thought Harry, not at eight thirty p.m., a bit early. He had noticed it was eight twenty when he left the 'Orange Tree', and this street was only about a ten-minute walk away.

Pulling the hood of his jacket over his head, he slipped behind a bush in the garden just behind him, relieved to notice that when turning into their leafy pathway, the curtains opposite were firmly closed. And seconds later, a man came out of the front door of number 37. But it wasn't his father. Even in the dimmest of lighting, he could easily see that. The person he was looking at was an old man, heavily stooped and with a stick, and muffled up in a broad-brimmed hat and a heavy overcoat as he locked the front door and looked cautiously around him, and then set off slowly down the street in the direction of the station. Perhaps it could be the McMahon person?

All the same, Harry decided to follow him for a few moments, and at some distance, aware that if he was too close he might frighten an old man, and especially a frail one who needed a stick.

Then suddenly he noticed something extraordinary.

The man he was following suddenly stopped on the pavement, leaned down – seemingly with no difficulty – and picked some litter off the pavement, looking around for where to discard it, eventually carrying it into someone's drive, presumably to drop it into a dustbin. A slight clang of a dustbin lid confirmed exactly that.

Who would ever do that if he needed a stick to steady himself, and even then unless he was fanatically tidy? And the one person Harry knew was fanatically tidy was his father, always obsessing about the flat on his returns from abroad and noticing the slightest things out of place. He had even seen him pick up a cigarette butt once from the pavement in Wandsworth and toss it into a litter-bin with disgust.

He hung back until the figure reappeared and set off down the street again. And wasn't he now walking a good deal faster? Instead of tapping the stick along the pavement, he even appeared to be holding it above the ground. And what was more, he was walking on the outside, not the inside of the pavement as elderly people tended to do, when they needed the assurance of walls and fences.

And there was something else strange, he noticed. His pace, having speeded up with no-one else around, was slowing down dramatically as they neared the crowded area around Richmond Station. Now he was almost hunched over again like a shambling octogenarian, pausing to wrap his scarf around his face. It couldn't be his father, or could it? How could he discover, short of bumping into him? And if he was wrong, he would feel such a ridiculous fool, or even cruel, bumping into someone crippled, and of that apparent age.

Harry held his distance until the man had bought a ticket. Using his Oyster card, he followed him through the barriers and down to the platform, and then into the train about three minutes later, noticing the person he was following alighted easily enough without the help of his stick.

Harry had still not seen his face, and couldn't now, while he stood at the doors and the man had his back to him staring out of the window, muffling himself from the cold – or the gaze of the passengers opposite.

And at Barnes, noticing the man get up, he followed him out, now more and more certain that it might be his father and wondering where on earth he was heading and why. By now he had also noticed the highly polished shoes, not comfy old brogues, but expensive leather ones, totally incongruous on such a shambling old man. He remembered the gleaming rows of shoes in his father's bedroom wardrobe on the one occasion he'd ever looked in there, hoping to borrow a pair for a date with Elaine in his father's absence, but then discovering they wouldn't fit.

Half an hour's walk later they were at Putney Common, half an hour of Harry realising that the figure in front of him had been progressing faster and faster, again with the stick well off the pavement and occasionally whisking the litter on the walkway into the undergrowth.

Harry was now hiding behind a bush, heart thudding, watching the man standing under a large tree and looking up at a big house with its lights on, and with a Volkswagen parked in its large driveway. The figure was now standing perfectly easily without his stick, even stretching to his full height, a height that would match that of his father, about six feet three.

What the hell was he doing here?

Who was in that house?

And why on earth had he come out at this time of night and in the freezing cold?

A full hour later, Harry was turning into ice still watching the man, who seemed to be able to remain quite still in the cold. What was he doing? But Harry reminded himself, since he had come this far, he had to keep waiting and see it out. And then suddenly, the ground floor lights went off in the house. And ten minutes later, the first floor ones followed.

After about twenty more minutes, the man suddenly moved – and with lightning speed – towards the house. His heart pounding, Harry watched in horror and disbelief as he fiddled with something beside the front door and then the door itself before slipping inside. It was at that precise moment that he finally knew he was right. His father was in security. Of course he would know how to get through a door, disarm a security system and get into a house in seconds.

He ran towards the open door before it blew shut. Whoever it was in there needed help and fast.

* * *

Alice was not asleep.

Indeed, the last two nights she had slept very badly. There was no doubt that those policemen in the house had been a comfort, and now that they had been withdrawn she felt alone and vulnerable. Robin Marshal had been anxious too, but with everything gone quiet, he could not justify the expense to his superiors. Even the occasional police car drive-by had been stopped. Hammond really did seem to be long gone, perhaps still somewhere on the continent.

She turned over and stared at the ceiling in the dark. She really hadn't wanted to switch off the light, but knew she'd never sleep if she didn't.

A big old and isolated house like hers was not a place to be when feeling nervous. Every sound seemed to echo round it. Like the clicks and groans of the cooling radiators and pipes when the heating switched itself off, let alone the sudden squalling of cats, and the foxes outside defending their territory. They often sounded horrible, like dying children.

Then she suddenly heard a noise. Downstairs, a slight but unmistakable click. Her front door had been opened. No doubt about it.

Alice felt a flush of adrenaline, raw fear. Where was her phone? By the bed? She didn't dare turn the light on.

She lay in bed, paralyzed, trying to think what to do. Another sound. A creak from the stairs. But they often creaked.

She couldn't be sure.

But the next moment she was. A louder noise. Someone had knocked into that big trunk. Terrified, she reached out towards her bedside light.

The door opened very slowly.

She switched on the light.

A bearded man in a hat. With a gun and a silencer. He looked different – but she knew who it was at once.

The light dazzled him, but only for a moment, and he lunged towards her. Horrified, she suddenly twisted sideways out of the bed, and wide-eyed, grabbing the lamp, instinctively smashed it into his face with all her strength, plunging them into darkness.

He gasped as the pain of the shattered bulb glass in his face forced him to drop the gun.

But as they both collapsed untidily on to the floor, he was easily able to use his weight to roll and smother her much lighter body. Now, with mounting fury, he pinned her down on her back, bunched his fist and slugged her brutally in the face – twice. Her head lolled to one side.

He looked around, spotting the glint of the gun on the floor. Limping over, he bent down to retrieve it, pausing to wipe away the blood streaming into his eyes.

When he turned, he stared, astonished, at a figure standing in the gloom. He tried to raise the gun, but was bowled over, his bulky clothing making him clumsy, and with the silencer caught in his coat. The two wrestled with the weapon in the dark.

'Pffft'.

The little bullet went through his clothing, and slowed down a little, but still punctured the femoral artery in his left leg and smashed the heavy bone.

At 120 beats a minute, he began to lose blood fast.

Hammond slowly slumped back, the pain spreading. Before his eyes closed, he dimly noticed that the figure standing over him was much taller than Alice.

* * *

Harry didn't know what had happened, except that his father didn't move again. He stumbled back to the door in the darkness and turned on the light.

There were two bodies on the floor and Harry's first instinct was to run. But the other figure suddenly moaned.

He gingerly approached. It was a girl, obviously injured but alive. There was a phone on the bedside table and he dialled. Then he noticed his father stir slightly, but Harry made no move towards him.

The police arrived at the same time as the ambulances – after all, they knew the house well enough.

Alice, her face covered by an oxygen mask was carefully taken down the stairs on a stretcher, as was Hammond, but his unconscious figure was accompanied by an armed policeman.

Detectives sat Harry down and started to question him.

It didn't take them long to call Robin Marshal.

CHAPTER SIXTY-SEVEN

CHARING CROSS HOSPITAL, LONDON

Alice was lying in her bed in the orthopaedics ward at Charing Cross, still unable to speak on her third day there. Perhaps that was a good thing she reminded herself, and not for the first time since arriving at the hospital. John would be coming to see her at any minute, desperate to ask her all kinds of hideously awkward questions after seeing her face all over the news.

She fervently hoped that he would believe the widely held theory that she had been attacked because of her connections with the police, but even that would have come as a shock.

But there was no reason he'd suspect anything else she kept telling herself, though she remained terrified that further details would leak out.

Her upper jaw had been badly fractured, and it had been wired to the teeth in her lower one to stabilize it, making it almost impossible to form words. She had been told by the surgeon that the wires would have to stay in place for six to eight weeks, that her speech would gradually return, and that she must only drink liquids or very soft foods until the wires were removed.

She was already struggling to keep down the slop that arrived three times a day on the hospital trolley, and knew that it would be dangerous to be sick. The surgeon had also told her if she ever felt she was going to vomit, the elastics around the wires in the mouth must be cut at once, and that she must press the alarm bell if the nursing staff weren't immediately on hand.

She picked up the mirror to check her appearance before

John's arrival. It was still a shock. Her eyes were heavily bloodshot, her face was badly bruised, and it didn't help to have bandaging all the way around her head to keep her jaw in place.

No wonder John had not been able to hide his shock the first time he'd seen her.

And Maggie had looked as if she was about to faint. She had arrived at the hospital with a huge bouquet of lilies which Alice knew would have to be thrown away as soon as she left, or given to one of the nurses to take home. These days, hospitals didn't have the time to change the water that putrefied so quickly in the stifling heat of a hospital ward, let alone allow lilies near white hospital sheets with their habit of scattering pollen everywhere.

Alice had tried to smile when taking the bouquet, but the wires in her mouth had made it impossible, let alone say a thank you. And there was little that Maggie could do except sit beside her and wait patiently for Alice to finish a rather scrawled list of written instructions about people to call and things to do at the office with a thank you for the flowers at the end – a laborious task with her left hand. She had always been firmly right-handed.

At last Maggie was about to go. Alice was extremely fond of her, but it was hugely embarrassing not to be able to communicate in an intelligible way or even show emotions such as gratitude for bringing in flowers and magazines.

'Would you like me to come in again in a couple of days?' Maggie had asked her before leaving. Alice had nodded as best as she could. Even that was difficult.

And now John was there, sitting beside her bed, and naturally finding it awkward to talk with no response. All those questions that must be buzzing around in his head. But what could she say, even if she *could* speak? In many ways, it was a blessing she couldn't, but she'd have to tell him one day. And what then?

And tomorrow her father and brother would be coming to see her. And the next day, Liz, and Maggie again. No more than two visitors a day she'd been told. And even that was physically and mentally exhausting.

John's briefcase was on the end of her bed, with a newspaper sticking out of it. Alice flinched. Her face was probably on the front of it. At least nobody on the ward would ever recognise her looking like that.

But that was scant comfort.

CHAPTER SIXTY-EIGHT

KENSINGTON, LONDON

It had taken ages for Franco to get through, and he had almost given up.

'Crime Desk.'

'Good morning. Can I possibly speak to Sarah Shaw?'

'Speaking.'

Sarah noticed a strong accent, maybe Italian.

'My name's Franco Bertelli, and I have some information that may interest you. About Alice Diamond, the woman in connection with the David Hammond case. I read your article today. In fact, it's in front of me right now.

'Go on.' Sarah was immediately interested. But it was probably just another of Alice's patients ringing in with hopes of a quick buck. She would have to be extremely careful whom she spoke to from now on. She had already been warned about that.

'I'm the Manager of a hotel called 'The Grouse' near Farnham, and Mr Hammond has often stayed with us. In fact, he came to lunch quite recently.'

Sarah was only mildly interested. So what if Hammond had eaten out in, or stayed in a hotel near Farnham? That was hardly earth-shattering news, although it might fill in a picture of his habits in later editions; readers were often hungry for those tiny titbits that nobody else had got hold of.

'And he brought a lady with him, the same woman I'm looking at in your paper right now, the psychologist lady who works with the police.'

'Excuse me,' said Sarah, suddenly sitting bolt upright in her chair. 'Are you absolutely sure?'

'One hundred per cent sure. Like him, the young lady has a very memorable face. Italians don't forget a beautiful woman.' Franco waited for a laugh that didn't come.

'And I also know for certain that he shared a bedroom with her upstairs after lunch. I gave Mr Hammond the keys personally to him in reception as I always do. We have, what shall we say, rather an unusual arrangement.'

Sarah was stunned, hardly able to believe what she was hearing.

'Mr Bertelli, are you absolutely sure of that?'

'Absolutely, one hundred per cent sure. As sure I as I am about my children's names. A hotel manager is trained to remember people. And I can prove I'm right. 'The Grouse' has a very sophisticated CCTV system, in fact, I've been assured that it's state of the art.'

Sarah was on full alert.

'There are several clear pictures of them coming through reception. And there was a wedding party on that day. Our own photographer has a photo of them on the next table raising a glass to the happy couple.

And in the photo, Mr. Hammond's hand is on hers.'

Sarah felt a surge of excitement, but knew exactly what was coming next. It always did.

'I'm happy to talk to you, but if I *do* give you the story and the photos, and shall we say, more intimate information, would there perhaps be some agreement we can come to?'

Sarah knew it would be a huge story, a scoop, if it were true. 'I'll have to ask my superiors. Can you hang on a moment?' Franco heard muttering at her end of the line.

'It's not as easy as that. Mr Hammond is in custody, and

there will be a trial. We can't report on anything to do with him until the trial is over. It's called sub judice.

We might be able to offer you something later, but only if the timing is right and your story holds up. And even then, we'd have to check everything out to make sure that anything you tell us would stand up in court.'

'It will.'

'And we can talk about that later when I see you. And I'd like to make that as soon as possible, in fact later on today if you could suggest a good time.'

Franco suggested mid-afternoon when 'The Grouse' was at its quietest, with only a few stragglers in the dining room, and gave Sarah the address, hoping that a sizeable chunk of his mortgage would soon be wiped out.

* * *

Kieran Donovan was reading the *Irish Independent* with the story about the capture of David Hammond, with the photograph issued by Scotland Yard months ago. He remembered the face from the Shelbourne last Summer.

As the bar manager there, he recalled the couple well. A man with unusually blue eyes and his rather pretty girlfriend. What would he get for handing this story on to the newspapers? He would be a fool not to. After all, there was a recession on in Ireland and money was short.

He decided to get all his facts together before he phoned anyone, checking the date they had stayed, the precise room number, anything else he could remember, and asking Fionn, the front desk manager, whether he could recall anything. But it was certainly the same pair. He was sure of that.

The man had extraordinary blue eyes. He'd noticed that when they had stopped for a Guinness in the bar. They were a memorable couple, unlike the scores of forgettable people who trooped through the hotel and his bar each day. Tourists, mostly American these days. Not many stylish English people, let along a pair as striking as that.

* * *

Ria Shigamatsu was also reading a paper at Nobu, in the Knightsbridge area of London, and suddenly noticed a picture of the extraordinarily blue-eyed man she had served recently. She remembered how knowledgeable he had been about Japanese food, and how little explaining she had had to do, bringing course after course to the couple's table.

Normally, it took her ages to explain every delicacy, but the man she was serving seemed to be an expert. Maybe he had spent time in Japan; many people had these days, even greeting her and talking to her in Japanese.

She earned good money; Nobu could afford to be generous to its staff. Eating there cost an astronomical amount, and she had often seen bills for hundreds of pounds when celebrities came in, and even non- celebrities; people who seemed quite happy to pay that sort of money for a meal, and give her a good tip on top.

However generous her salary, and that of Shiku – her fiancé working at Nomura Bank – rented flats were horribly expensive anywhere near the West End of London, and she wasn't prepared to commute any more than Shiku was.

She was sure she could make some money out of this, but less sure how to proceed. There must be a way, she told herself.

CHAPTER SIXTY-NINE

CHARING CROSS HOSPITAL, LONDON

Alice had now been in hospital for ten days, and was at last beginning to be able to speak properly again, although she knew that was a mixed blessing, particularly where John was concerned.

Robin Marshal was suddenly at her bedside.

'Are you okay?'

'Much better, thanks.'

'You certainly look it.'

Alice couldn't remember that he'd visited three times before. The last week or so had all been a bit of a blur.

'And how are you?' she asked.

'If you mean work, it's better, or dying down a bit, at least the focus on me and letting Hammond get away. Some of the newspaper articles were pretty damning, and there was certainly a lot of stick from on high. But I'll survive, hopefully.'

'But', he paused, 'I'm afraid it's not over yet. It would be better if he'd died, but now he'll have to go to trial. It'll be big, and I'm sorry, but you'll be involved and asked to give evidence.'

Alice nodded miserably. 'I know. It's going to be terrible.'

'He's saying nothing, incidentally. We don't even know how he'll plead. Although it won't really matter of course. The evidence from everywhere is getting overwhelming.

We've even had some Americans in touch because of the publicity. They had a chap shot there, an ex-police chief, and they think it fits the pattern.

Certainly seems to. The ballistics fit. And it's that same little pencil gun. They're trawling back through the past to try and find a link, a motive.'

Alice turned to look out of the window. Right now she couldn't bring herself to think about America. All she could think of was the horror of having to go to court and suffer even more public humiliation.

Noticing that, Marshal sought to change the mood.

He looked around the sunny private room, far better than the public ward. 'And are they treating you well in here?'

'Fine. Thanks for arranging it. I'm really grateful. And I'll be out soon, probably in a couple of days. Though God knows what I'll get back to. I don't expect many patients will want to see me like this, let alone someone who's been out with a serial killer. It hardly says a lot for my judgment.'

Robin looked at her kindly. 'They will. Give it time. And there may still be police work you can do on the quiet at home, certainly if I can arrange it.

After all, if it hadn't been for you, we may never have got him. I'll certainly be saying that.'

She looked at Robin; kind, steady, always supportive, who had brought in another bunch of flowers destined for the hospital trash.

He was a great friend.

Would there ever be an end to the nightmare? A life in dark glasses seemed the only answer. 'People will eventually forget your face', her father had told her. Would they?

For once, Alice wished she had a face that never attracted a second glance.

CHAPTER SEVENTY

THE OLD BAILEY

The trial had been a nightmare for Alice.

To start with, the whole process had been highly intimidating. The sheer history and solemnity of Number One Court, with its wood panelling and with everyone dressed in wigs and robes, was bound to inspire awe, if not fear, even for someone used to courtrooms.

To be at centre stage was even more unsettling. In this grave, historic and exalted atmosphere, it was hard to realise that most of the players in the room had known each other for years and were jovial friends for most of the time – except when they were required to be legal adversaries.

Robin Marshal had privately intimated to Alice that he considered that Hammond was one of the strangest and cleverest serial killers that he had ever come across – apparently avenging perceived slights of decades before – and, moreover, going all over the world to achieve his revenge. But there had been no point in including murders outside British jurisdiction or where the evidence was too flimsy.

Alice, as was normal, had only been allowed into court after several hours until she was called as a witness, in case previous evidence might colour her own. As she understood it, Prosecuting Counsel had asked for her to testify as to Hammond's movements and behaviour, and her short relationship with him, as well as giving her own detailed account of his break-in and her attempted murder.

This, she felt, she had handled relatively well – avoiding, after a first glance, looking at Hammond at all, because she knew he would try to intimidate her with that extremely disconcerting sardonic half-smile. While somewhat paler than before, he no longer had the beard and was as handsome as ever. For a moment Alice wondered if that might sway the female jurors.

Hammond had pleaded 'not guilty' to the two murders that the prosecution had decided to settle on – Mark Campbell in the old people's home and Joe Corcoran in the Belfast swimming pool. As for his attack on Alice, he had pleaded guilty to 'assault, occasioning actual bodily harm'.

It was now that the strategy of the Defence became clear, because it was to imply that the events in her home were no more than a pre-arranged date that had gone wrong and that Alice had provoked Hammond into such a fury that he had attacked her.

Defence Counsel had kept suggesting that Alice's version of events was at best mistaken or at worst a lie, until Alice became frustrated and forced to intervene against her better judgement; 'You can say that as much as you like, Sir, but it simply isn't the case.'

Her firm response was, however, not enough to reduce her underlying fear that some very embarrassing facts were going to be served up to the Jury – and, of course, to the media crowding the gallery. It would have been scant comfort to realise that Defence Counsel was, in fact, clutching at straws in the face of an overwhelming tide of forensic, ballistic and other evidence.

She, after all, was one of the straws.

However, she soon realised that her evidence, and indeed her reputation, were going to be tarnished by the evidence given by two people brought to Court by the Defence and whom she had certainly not expected to see – the Manager of 'The Grouse' and the barman from the Shelbourne. Their evidence plainly reinforced the image of a torrid affair.

David Hammond went into the witness box and gave quite a polished performance, as Alice knew he would. His contention was that he and Alice had continued their affair in secret and that on the night of the attack she had let him in. He had lost his temper when she had refused to have sex with him, and also criticised his amorous abilities. He professed to have been amazed by the intervention of his own son, who had then assaulted him.

However, Harry's description of his suspicions about his father and the dramatic events of that evening were to make his father appear even more of an unpleasant villain and himself into something of a hero. He had, in effect, rescued a damsel in distress.

Prosecuting Counsel, in his cross-examination, did much to shred Hammond's version of events, particularly the obvious question as to why Hammond had needed an unlicensed, silenced handgun to go on his 'date'.

After giving her evidence, and enduring her own cross-examination, the Judge had announced that Alice was free to stay, but she had absolutely no intention of sitting there any longer with a crowd of people speculating about her sex life with the defendant, and worse, while they were in the same room. Such indignity would have been unbearable.

Her worst fears had been confirmed as her father helped her to leave the building surrounded by a barrage of photographers and a chorus of shouted questions. But even in her wildest imagination she had not prepared herself for the avalanche of media attention in the next few days.

'Come to France', begged her father, and it took little persuading for her to agree, pack and leave.

The wait at Gatwick airport and the flight were not much

SERIAL DAMAGE

less of a nightmare, with Alice now imagining that everyone
was staring at her.

* * *

She might have been right the next day. Fortunately, or
unfortunately for Alice, most of the English newspapers are
reproduced in Marseille, and are not even a day late. And her
father had an English television package too. Typically, the
media soon moved on from Harry's moment of heroism, far
preferring anything that smacked of sexual scandal.

Her ashen-faced father brought in the papers every day at
Alice's request with the appalling revelations about her sleeping
with David Hammond at 'The Grouse' hotel near Farnham,
and much, much worse, going for a weekend to Ireland with
him.

Now that they were legally allowed to, the journalists had
had a field day and the managers of both establishments – 'The
Grouse' and the Shelbourne Hotel – had plainly been richly
rewarded for their information. They had gone on to give
interviews, and in the case of 'The Grouse', to provide the
media with CCTV footage of Alice and David as well as quite a
clear photo of them together.

Her face – her former face – was now staring out of the
papers, and everyone knew the juicy details of her affair with
David Hammond. Not exactly an affair, just three dates, but
nobody would ever believe that. It was, of course, made to
sound so much worse because she was involved with the police
and judicial system.

And it was even more distressing that the papers had
mentioned John, and were almost certainly now pestering him
and his parents for other juicy nuggets to make the story even
more sensational than it was already.

The headlines were horrifying.

PSYCHO LOVER had screamed the *Daily Mirror* headline, SEX ROMPS WITH SUSPECT had been emblazoned on the *Sun*, and ALICE IN MURDERLAND on the *News of the World*, and other appalling circulation boosters included COP DOC IN SEXFEST in the *Daily Star*, A DIAMOND IS ACCUSED'S BEST FRIEND in the *Daily Express*, and SHRINK WITH SUSPECT in the *Daily Mail*, complete with a photo of them lunching at the Grouse taken by that wedding photographer, with a smaller blown-up shot of David's hand on hers.

Even the normally more sedate *Times* and *Telegraph* had gone for unusually salacious front cover headlines, almost certainly afraid of losing readers to their rivals. And it surely wouldn't be long before Nobu, the Japanese restaurant she'd been to with David, would jump on the bandwagon and dig out CCTV footage if they remembered her and David going there. Somebody there would recall him, certainly the attentive girl who served them through all those endless courses. Plenty of time for her to be able to remember his face.

In the safety of the farmhouse Alice was able to watch English television and to read the papers about the continuing court case. She saw that the Prosecution, while going over the links between the various murders, had not tried to include them all formally.

They had not even used the murder of her godmother. No physical evidence had been found: no gun, no motorcycle. Only the evidence of an old letter pointing to a motive.

Although the motive trail *did* seem to link the A1 machine-gunning, the murders of the Irish Guards Colonel, old General Hewitt and Martin Lonsdale, once again insufficient physical evidence had been found because the Volvo, the Bren gun and the rifle had all disappeared. Nor were the forensic links between Hong Kong, Washington state and France more than scantily noted. Indeed, any mention of them immediately produced vigorous objections from the Defence.

The Prosecution had instead confined the accusations to Hollingbourne and Belfast, where the forensic evidence and the motive were very strong, together with the attempted murder of Alice, where her evidence was backed up by the solid testimony of Harry.

After his own evidence about the attack on Alice, David Hammond had apparently remained silent; his face impassive except for that slight sardonic smile, as if he was pointing scorn on the whole proceedings.

Psychiatric studies were produced by the Defence, including one based on the 'trauma' that Hammond had suffered over the death of the Picken couple, but the prosecution painstakingly pointed out their weaknesses to the Jury compared with the strength of other evidence. This the Judge echoed in his summing up, and after a relatively short deliberation, the Jury found the defendant guilty of the murders of both Mark Campbell and Joe Corcoran and the attempted murder of Alice.

For three weeks, Alice had hardly left the farmhouse, too terrified that she would be recognized and pointed out by the locals, not only mortifying her but ruining the respect that her father had earned in the vicinity, especially as the French papers had her photograph too. Not only was it an international 'serial killer' story, but, of course, Hammond was also suspected of killing that French trade unionist, her father's friend near Quissac. Indeed, *Midi Libre*, the regional paper, had devoted pages to the local aspects of the story.

So there was absolutely no question of taking the normal pleasures, a coffee and croissant in the café or going to a restaurant, or strolling about buying vegetables in the market on Fridays. She did not even feel like going up the path through the woods, in case she came across a curious hiker. So she felt trapped in the house with *Sky News*, rarely even wandering out to the garden, and on the rare occasions when she did, barely noticing the profusion of wild flowers, always so glorious in the late springtime, let alone the staggering mountain vista. It was one of the main reasons her father had bought the farmhouse, and why he often called it 'Mon petit coin du paradis'.

Drifting from room to room when not watching television, she often thought of the irony of the old expression, 'Physician, heal thyself' as she made daily efforts to stave off mounting despair and depression. There was too much to work through, and without friends to lean on, it was becoming impossible despite her psychiatric training.

Alice's main connection with her normal world had been some near-tearful calls with Liz, to whom she had texted her father's landline number. From John, whom she had also texted, there was silence.

Alice did call her secretary, Maggie, every few days and she seemed fairly cheerful.

'Lots of media, of course. I just tell them you've gone away. And a lot of letters and emails of sympathy – your friends, people in your profession. And your patients, too. They're really missing you.'

'And how are *you*,' Alice interrupted.

'Oh, I'm okay. I come in here just for the mornings to log the messages and look after things. I've got a temporary afternoon job as a receptionist at the dental clinic in Putney High Street, but I can leave that when you come back.

Oh, and I nearly forgot to tell you. A Chinese fellow called Wong, a friend of Robin Marshal's called. Apparently he used to be a detective in Hong Kong, but he's just retired and gone to live in Singapore. He said he's writing an article and then a book about how he suspected that it was Hammond who killed some local banker, but he wasn't allowed to pursue it by his superior. But now he's out of Hong Kong and away from the Chinese, he can tell the story.

It may cause quite a row, because he's going to say that if they'd listened to him, those killings in London might not have happened, and you might not have been attacked. Anyway, he thought you'd like to know.'

As the days passed, Alice began to feel she was as much a prisoner as David Hammond, wondering if she could ever hold her head up again.

Two weeks later, when she felt she could bear it no longer, the media finally reported that David Hammond had been sentenced to life imprisonment. But the notoriety still felt like a life sentence that she doubted she would ever be able to escape, any more than Hammond could. How many lives had he wrecked? How much damage had his obsession caused?

And what about her professional life? In spite of what Maggie had said, would any patient ever trust a psychiatrist who had shown such appalling judgement, and whose face had been splashed over the media for weeks? On the personal *and* the professional front, there seemed to be no way out, or not one she could envisage.

Her father's kindness, welcome though it was, added guilt to the daily turmoil. His life, too, would never be the same again. The damage had been done – serial damage – from which she could see little escape.

Thunderstorms were common around St Hippolyte-du-Fort. And they were certainly coming now, sometimes ripping whole pines out of the ground so the landscape looked like timber territory, with bare hillsides and piles of logs.

After the storms, there was always peace, and Alice found that consoling. What little peace she now found was in that analogy. But it was not enough, especially as there was also a deep reservoir of guilt for how she had let down John, his parents, Liz, her father, indeed everyone she'd ever loved, albeit unwittingly.

CHAPTER SEVENTY-ONE

ST-HIPPOLYTE

Her biggest problem, Alice now realized, was how to handle John. He hadn't returned any of her calls from England or from France.

The only thing she could possibly do was to send him a long letter of apology, but what good would that do? She pictured him tossing it in the nearest wastepaper basket.

He'd been made to look an utter fool, and had probably even worked out that the weekend she and David had gone to Ireland was when he was finalizing that huge presentation, and she hadn't even called to wish him good luck.

And how could he ever share a bed with her again, imagining her double-dating with a vicious serial killer?

She had been utterly and publicly humiliated. As had John. And even if *that* wasn't bad enough, the press were now hounding Maggie, and both Maggie's and her own job were threatened. Who'd ever want a psychologist with such appalling judgment about people? And journalists might even come to her surgery pretending to be patients.

She thought of John on his last visit to the hospital, obviously relieved to see her face returning to normal and to hear her first words. He'd asked her a lot of questions as she knew he would, but they'd all been about the police work that she'd never really revealed to him, notably nothing to do with anything personal.

She pictured him in his office, probably finding it hard to concentrate on whatever he was doing, and with the other staff sniggering behind his back.

A picture had even appeared of him in one of the papers in an article titled KILLER'S TWO-TIMING GIRLFRIEND.

She thought of phoning John again, but snapped her mobile shut before finishing dialling. She knew he wouldn't answer. And he probably wouldn't ever speak to her again.

* * *

Astri Tibbs was getting livid. They were having their next door neighbours, the Paices – Sue and Peter – around to lunch, and the doorbell had already rung at least five times, not to mention her and Arthur's mobiles and the landline. It was never ending; this had gone on for days.

It was impossible even to get a simple lunch together without being disturbed every five minutes by some journalist from the nationals, or even the locals – the *Surrey Herald*, the *Woking News* and the *Surrey Comet* just that morning – asking her questions about Alice and about her own film and stage career decades ago.

And she dreaded the press digging out the news about her daughter's imminent civil ceremony to Josie; that would only add to the spice of the story. The papers had even dug out a picture of her in *Goldfinger*, and one of Arthur at a lecture at the Linnean Society.

And it was all very well for Arthur to lock himself up in his study and refuse to answer any calls. Life had to go on. And it might be John on the phone, wanting to escape down to Haslemere, if escape were possible from the media frenzy. Even the Amateur Dramatic Society in Haslemere, Arthur's Bryology Society and the old James Bond fans' society had called up. The whole thing was getting intolerable.

She slammed the basted chicken into the oven at mid-day, deciding not to answer the doorbell– and to tell the Paices to let themselves in with their spare set of keys. It would be good to see them, although they'd be hugely embarrassed having met Alice when she came for Christmas, and almost certainly having read the last few days' headlines, especially the one KILLER'S TWO-TIMING GIRLFRIEND.

She had to admit she'd liked Alice, and even gone to bed after Christmas thinking that she might be the right girl for John, just as she had after that curry dinner in Putney. It was still inconceivable to her that she could ever have got involved with that terrifying man in the papers, who had probably killed, what was it, five people? Maybe more.

And poor John must be suffering unbearably at the office with all that publicity swirling around him. Both on a personal and business level it hardly put his judgment in a good light. Astri paused from her cooking to pour herself a stiff gin when the doorbell rang again, suddenly remembering it might be Lucas, the Polish gardener, coming around to bag up the leaves. She left it ringing. The garden would have to remain a sodden mess.

And then the phone rang again. Astri waited for the answerphone to come on and realised it was John. As soon as she heard his voice, she picked up.

'Hi Mum, you okay?'

'Just about, but more to the point, how are you?'

'Pretty rough. Probably the same for you down there.'

'I'm afraid it is.'

'I'm really, really sorry, but it can't be worse than it is up here. Even before the trial, we were bombarded with calls from the media. And we can't *not* answer the phones – we're running a business. And it's been even worse since the conviction. All sorts of foreign calls, too. The High Court may have focussed on the British murders, but there are lots of journalists who think Hammond killed people in their countries.

So I've had calls from people in Seattle and Everett – even someone from Wenatchee –wherever the hell *that* is. And French people and even a Pole with an unpronounceable name.'

John paused. 'Incidentally, I've seen her.'

'You mean Alice? What, in the hospital?'

'Yes, she looks pretty bad. Broken jaw, broken arm, bruising everywhere. But they say she'll mend.'

Astri was suddenly stuck for what to say. She had been looking forward to a possible daughter-in-law. John was almost thirty-five, and she had liked the prospect of grandchildren. Her daughter was unlikely to have any, unless it was by artificial insemination.

Suddenly the doorbell rang again.

Astri swore with a word she hadn't used in years.

CHAPTER SEVENTY-TWO

WANDSWORTH HOSPITAL

'Is that an Irish accent?' the young surgeon asked the blonde anaesthetist as he started to brief her in the anaesthetics room.

'Irish-American', she replied. 'Moira, Moira O'Hare – like the airport.'

He looked at her a bit blankly, never having been to Chicago – or even the United States. 'I'm James. Glad to have you aboard.'

'Thanks, but it won't be for long. I'm over here on an exchange. Nearly finished now. Back to Chicago next week.'

James looked up from a file.

'You know who we've got coming in, don't you?'

'No. Just rushed over here. But I heard we got the call from a prison doctor.'

'Well you're not going to believe it. It's that murderer, Hammond. You know, the chap who killed all those poor people for no apparent reason. Even old people, unbelievably. A thoroughly nasty piece of work. A real bastard.

Anyway, I've seen him in A and E, and he's quite a mess. God knows how it could have happened in prison. You'd think they'd guard him properly, although he doesn't deserve it. Anyway, he's somehow been stabbed in the same leg as the one he was shot in when he tried to kill that girl. We'll have to patch him up, but frankly it might have been better all round if he hadn't made it.'

Moira eyed him carefully. 'Yeah, I remember. Saw it on TV and in all the papers when I first arrived. Not a very nice guy.

As you said, a real bastard.'

She suddenly thought the unthinkable.

She couldn't.

Or *could* she?

An avalanche of confused feelings gave her a massive adrenaline rush.

'Anyway,' said James, 'they'll be up in a moment. Better get ready.'

Moira nodded, and turned to Lyn, her operating department practitioner, or 'opd', to brief her on what would be needed.

* * *

Pushed by a theatre porter, Hammond was guarded by two police officers and chained to one of them.

Moira pulled up her mask and attached the monitoring ECG blood pressure cuff and oxygen saturation probe. An intravenous cannula was then attached to Hammond's left wrist, and to this she then connected the tubes that were to deliver the initial liquid anaesthetic, Propofol, and the pain-relieving opiate, Fentanyl.

Now, just as Hammond started slipping into unconsciousness, she leaned over and whispered one word into his ear.

'Skykomish.'

For a fraction of a second, she saw his eyes widen with sudden fear before closing. The last time she had seen that instant horrifying realisation with such dilated pupils was when the vet put down her beloved spaniel 'Bran'.

Still barely believing what she was doing, and with her own heart-rate now going through the roof, she gave the patient a massive dose of the paralysing agent, Rocuronium.

Now with Hammond unconscious, he was unchained from the police officer and wheeled into the operating theatre where

James began to examine the wounded leg, while Moira, near the head of the patient, adjusted the equipment to deliver the anaesthetics, with screens on stands monitoring blood pressure, heart rate, and other bodily functions. She turned these towards her as if to view them more easily, taking them from the surgeon's line of sight.

'Shattered femur and an awful lot of muscle damage,' announced James through his mask. 'Let's start.'

He began to operate on the shattered leg, steadily cutting away the damaged tissue.

'This'll take some time'.

Moira was relieved her face was masked, as she turned to her 'opd', Lyn, asking her to go and get some bags of iv fluid, and telling her to take a break after that if she wanted to.

She knew that after about fifteen minutes the effect of the first liquid anaesthetic and the Fentanyl would wear off as they were meant to – normally to be topped up by more Fentanyl and morphine.

But she had decided not to do any such topping up. And nor would she deliver enough oxygen and nitrous oxide either.

Hammond would soon wake up, but nobody else in the theatre would know – because the huge dose of paralysing agent would take much longer to wear off.

For the rest of the operation he would feel the agonising pain in the normal way.

Moira watched the body – completely still. However, her screens soon told her something else. The blood pressure had rocketed, as had the heart rate – to over 160 beats per minute. She now knew exactly what Hammond was going through, and that she was breaking every oath in the book. But fate had delivered this man into her hands, this monster who had damaged so many lives.

He deserved to suffer like everyone else.

It did not last long.

The pain, the helplessness and horror overwhelmed Hammond's system and suddenly the heart rate line went flat. A stroke? Heart failure? Or both?

Moira waited for as long as she dared, and then turned up the volume on the monitor.

'I'm afraid we've lost him.' she said, turning the monitor so that James could see it.

There was a frantic attempt at defibrillation, but Hammond was gone.

'Couldn't have happened to a nicer fellow', said James as they peeled off their gloves.

Moira knew that her beloved aunt Betty-Anne would agree. And also that she herself would safely be back in Chicago before the coroner got involved.

CHAPTER SEVENTY-THREE

PUTNEY, LONDON

Alice had never much liked coffee bars, let alone her local Starbucks. The first time she'd been there had been her last. Nice enough staff and coffee, but it had been overcrowded – and with a sea of babies in oversized buggies.

Places like this now dominated Putney High Street in the south west of London, along with the usual charity shops and mini supermarkets. There were hardly any independents left these days. The change over the years depressed her, and it depressed her even more that it was here in Starbucks that John had suggested they should meet. The last place you could talk – especially at nine on a Monday morning – which she guessed was precisely why John had chosen it.

He obviously knew the score. At this time, it would be crammed with commuters – all bright lights and briskness before the 'buggy brigade' descended later. She sat at a table by the window, deciding not to order until he arrived, and wishing he'd suggested meeting up somewhere quieter, and in the evening, not now.

At least, in dimmer lighting, she would have looked less of a wreck. The cuts and bruises to her face were nearly healed, her jaw was far better, but there were still marks which stubbornly refused to disappear, and the once black eye had now decided to go a pale yellow and green, which make-up struggled to hide. She knew she'd look ridiculous in sunglasses at nine o'clock on a rainy day. Time would mend all that. But her and John?

It was *her* that had phoned him, a week after returning from

France, and after a long and difficult conversation with Liz, who'd come to see her.

She had seemed pessimistic. 'Well, I don't know Alice. You can try phoning him. Nothing ventured, nothing gained, I suppose. But, well, just don't build up your hopes too much. He's been pretty shattered. He had absolutely no idea what was going on. None of us did. And all that ghastly stuff in the papers, that didn't help. Made him look a total fool.

You probably don't know that he was bombarded by the press, even calling him in the office. And of course, everyone there knew about it with his face splashed all over the papers. Pretty embarrassing to say the least. And Alice, what made it worse is that it wasn't just the odd dinner date with that man. You even went abroad with him for a weekend, and to some hotel in Surrey. That must have been a hell of a smack in the face.'

Liz had shaken her head in disbelief. 'I mean, what if John had done the same to you?'

Alice had lit a cigarette, hating herself for needing one, and already up to five a day after a year of virtual abstinence.

'I'm sorry,' Liz had continued, 'it's been front-page news and all over the telly. I can't pretend I don't know the facts.

But why did you *do* it, Alice? I thought you and John were so good together.'

'We were. We still could be. And I only saw him three times.'

'Three times too many,' Liz had said. '*I* believe you, but millions wouldn't. And John probably doesn't either.'

'So you don't think there's any hope.'

'I didn't say that,' Liz had replied cautiously. 'I just don't know. At least you might find out if you phone him. Just don't be too optimistic.'

Alice had rung John, and soon after Liz had left, before she lost the courage, and was relieved when he picked up. She knew she wouldn't have left a message.

'Hi, it's me.'

A long pause.

'Hi. How are you?' His voice sounded flat.

'Well, at least I'm back at home. I guess I'll mend.'

'Good. I knew you would.'

An uncomfortable silence fell as Alice struggled for what to say.

'Well, I haven't exactly mended. Not in some ways.'

John said nothing.

Alice persevered, feeling horribly foolish and awkward.

'Look, I wonder if we could meet up some time? Nothing heavy. Just a drink.'

Another silence.

'John? Are you there?'

'Yeah. It's just I'm not sure it's a good idea.'

'Please.' How hateful it was to plead.

He'd finally relented, just.

'Well, I've got a meeting next week down in Kingston. Ten thirty on Monday. I guess I could stop off in Putney and have a coffee with you. I could meet you in that Starbucks opposite the station, say at nine. But it'll have to be quick.'

* * *

Alice had been forced to agree. It was better than nothing. But not much. And here she was in Starbuck's, as the tables filled up around her and the queues at the counter lengthened. She felt bleak, embarrassed sitting there with her face all bruised like that, and with her arm in plaster. And what if he didn't come? She looked at her watch. It was already 9.15.

And then she saw him outside the window, smartly dressed in a navy overcoat. Even the businesslike way he looked accentuated her vulnerability, which was now about as low as it could get. And he was carrying a briefcase, a reminder of his meeting, literally a signal to keep things brief. Alice struggled to smile and get out a sufficiently muted 'Hi.'

His return 'Hi' was warm, but there was no kiss of greeting. Only his hand on her shoulder before he pulled up a chair and sat down. He studied her face briefly and then her left arm – in plaster.

'How's your arm?'

'Fine.' Alice looked at him, remembering his tight timetable, and suddenly decided to take a risk. Twenty-five minutes max. Nothing to lose, or everything to lose.

'It's not the arm that hurts.'

John looked down, avoiding eye contact, and Alice knew at once she'd ventured on to unwanted territory. He sighed before answering.

'Look Alice, it's too soon to go there. You've been through a lot, a hell of a lot, but you have to understand, so have I. Nothing like you of course, but not easy. The last few weeks have been hell for me too.'

He paused for a moment, shifting in his chair, obviously trying to find the right words.

'Look, I thought we had something going. Something really good. Amazing really.' He shook his head, but smiled. 'Obviously, I was wrong.'

'You weren't.' I...'

John put up his hand to stop her.

'Listen Alice, I haven't got long. I'm really sorry for all

you've been through, I really am. But the Hammond thing –
that was a bit too much. Got my pride, I suppose.' He took a
deep breath, exhaling it slowly as if considering his next words.

'I don't think you really realise what it's been like – and still
is. Reporters turning up at the agency, television crews talking
to the staff, my face in the papers, me and my parents hounded.
Oh yes, and all my clients knowing about it.' He laughed, but
without warmth. 'And with me made to look a total idiot.'

'I'm really sorry', whispered Alice, finding it hard to look
at him.

A ghastly silence, only broken by John's sudden awareness
of noise and clattering behind the counter.

'Anyway, guess I'd better get some coffee.' He looked at his
watch. 'What do you fancy?'

Alice didn't fancy anything. And queuing for coffee would
be a hideous waste of precious time. But she felt forced to have
one.

'Anything. A latte's fine.'

'Small or large?'

'Large' answered Alice, hoping he'd follow suit.

'I'm sorry, but it has to be a small one for me. A bit pressed,
I'm afraid.'

Alice watched him join the queue, with at least four people
in front of him. Damn. Why had she ever agreed to this, and not
insisted on meeting somewhere after work?' For the next five
minutes she thought of all their happy times together in a series
of flashbacks. So easy, so companionable. Chatting, dancing,
slumped in front of the telly, reading the Sundays in bed, that
surprise glass of champagne and beautiful sapphire brooch.

All ending up with a miserable *latte* at Starbucks.

At last John was back.

'Look, the real reason I'm here is to see how you were.

We've all been really worried about you.'

Not enough to call, thought Alice. And '*were?*' She noticed the past tense. And did he mean worried about her physically or emotionally? Alice felt tears coming and struggled to stop them. What the hell did she expect? All sweetness and light? A swift agreement to 'start again'? She'd been mad to come. This wasn't someone who'd forgive easily, if at all. And why should he? Would *she*, if it were the other way around? Alice suddenly remembered Liz asking her that.

'You need time Alice, and so do I. I hate to see you like this, I really do, but you're a tough cookie.' He patted her hand lightly. Alice immediately noticed its familiar warmth, but also the emotional distance in the gesture – almost a 'There, there, you'll be alright', as if comforting a child who'd just fallen down in the playground and was about to burst into tears. 'You'll pull through. And you've got a great job to help you.'

Alice almost laughed. Psychology? A great job to help her? Listening to other people's miseries all day? And she'd probably lost the police part of her job anyway, as well as most of her clients. She said nothing. At least he hadn't said 'We can still be friends.' She'd been spared that humiliation.

John tipped his head back drinking the last of his coffee.

Quite suddenly Alice's mood changed, furious that he'd only really been thinking about himself.'

'Look, John, I've got something to say. I know it's been awful for you, but I've nearly been *KILLED.*'

She didn't care that the people around them were suddenly agog.

'I have three dates with a guy over a year ago, and then drop him. He goes on to kill a whole lot of people, and if it wasn't for *me*, it would have been more.'

Alice knew the people around them were now engrossed,

but didn't give a damn.

'I know you're embarrassed, and I'm really sorry about that. But, I repeat, I was nearly *killed*, in hospital for weeks, and then there was that terrible trial – and with my face in the papers a hundred times more than yours was. And now my reputation's in shreds, while all you seem to think about is your clients and yourself.'

John looked at her, shocked, and wishing they were somewhere private.

'I'm very sorry, I have to go. I'll call you.'

* * *

Would he? Alice wondered.

She watched him picking up his briefcase and disappearing into the street. He didn't even wave at the window as he hurried back to the station.

But then, why had he come at all?

Alice got up from the table, her coffee untouched. Suddenly, her iPhone buzzed. She looked down, pleased to see the familiar number.

'Hi, Robin.'

'Morning, Alice. Hope you're better. Well, I just about managed to keep *my* job. And I think I may have another one for you ...'

LIZ AND DONOUGH – WIFE AND HUSBAND
WRITING TEAM

Liz Cowley has had a long career as an advertising copywriter and Creative Director, working in several of the world's leading agencies. A long-time fan of poetry, she enjoyed success with her first collection, *A Red Dress*, published in 2008 and her second, *What am I Doing Here?* (2010), which were then made into a theatrical show – first staged in Dublin, then chosen as the finale of the West Cork Literary Festival and later touring the UK. Her next book *'And guess who he was with?'* was out in February 2013. Two poetry books for gardeners, *Outside in my Dressing Gown*, and *Gardening in Slippers* are selling very well, not only in the book trade but also in garden centres.

A further humorous poetry book, *Pass the Prosecco, Darling*, all about cooking disasters and other kitchen dramas, will be her next publication.